PASSION REVISITED

"I want tonight to be special," Diana said. Her face looked earnest and very young.

Gervase laid one hand on her waist, feeling her slim warmth through the layered silk. "It will be. I promise that."

She smiled briefly, but her smile didn't reach her eyes. "Tonight, let's pretend to be young lovers. I will play the maiden, and you the man who teaches me the wonders of first love and the awakening of passion."

He bent forward, closing the distance between them. This time his kiss was not hungry and demanding, as when he had first arrived, but leisurely and probing, bent on exploring every surface and texture of her yielding mouth.

And Diana had her first taste of the passion of this night that would be an endless lesson in love. . . .

October 10, 1989

Dear Reader,

DEARLY BELOVED is a special book for me, and I hope it will be for you as well. Much as I've loved writing Regencies, I wanted to do a story with greater depth and intensity, a book about emotional devastation and the healing power of love.

DEARLY BELOVED is the result. On the surface, the plot is a simple one: a wealthy lord chooses a beautiful mistress and they fall in love. But what seems like chance is really the working of a strange and challenging fate.

A bitter past had turned Gervase Brandelin into a man without dreams. Then he meets Diana Lindsay, and her warmth and compassion soon melt his icy defenses. But a dark secret lies between them, a secret will shatter Gervase's hard-won trust once it is revealed.

Diana Lindsay's dangerous beauty had cost her dearly in the past, and it seemed only fair that she use that beauty to earn security for herself and her child. But the moment she met Gervase Brandelin, calm calculation crumbled. She knew that destiny had brought them together—and that that destiny was love.

The characters are part of me, their tears and laughter and striving rooted in my own emotions. I hope Gervase and Diana will be as real to you as they are to me, and that when you read DEARLY BELOVED you will laugh, and cry and end up feeling happy and satisfied. If you do, I will feel happy and satisfied as well.

Happy reading!

Mary Jo Putney

DEARLY
BELOVED
by
Mary Jo Putney

AN ONYX BOOK

NEW AMERICAN LIBRARY

A DIVISION OF PENGUIN BOOKS USA INC.

Copyright © 1990 by Mary Jo Putney

ONYX TRADEMARK REG. U.S. PAT. OFF. AND FOREIGN COUNTRIES
REGISTERED TRADEMARK—MARCA REGISTRADA
HECHO EN DRESDEN, TN, USA

SIGNET, SIGNET CLASSIC, MENTOR, ONYX, PLUME, MERIDIAN and
NAL BOOKS are published by New American Library, a division of Penguin
Books USA Inc., 1633 Broadway, New York, New York 10019

First Printing, March, 1990

1 2 3 4 5 6 7 8 9

PRINTED IN THE UNITED STATES OF AMERICA

To my fishy friend John,
who was the first one to notice
that I could tell stories

Prologue

Isle of Mull, Scotland, 1799

THE young man in the corner of the smoky taproom drank alone. It was not just that he was solitary: a nearly palpable wall separated him from the islanders. It had been over fifty years since Bonnie Prince Charlie had led the clans to destruction on Culloden Moor, but Scots have long memories. Though their hospitality was legendary, none felt compelled to seek out a man who was obviously rich and English, particularly not a man whose cool gray-eyed glance conveyed no welcome.

Being alone bothered the Honorable Gervase Brandelin not at all; he preferred it. He swallowed the last of his raw Scotch whiskey, feeling it burn even though it followed numerous earlier drafts. There was nothing subtle about either the spirit or the effect it produced, but after a month in the Highlands and Islands he'd begun to develop a taste for it.

The tavern was replete with the signature scents of farmers and fishermen, the acrid, eye-stinging bite of burning peat predominant. Glancing across the low-ceilinged taproom, Gervase caught the eye of the barmaid and signaled for another whiskey. He was drinking too much, but after a day of riding through Mull's relentless rain he was in the mood for warmth and comfort. This inn was an unexpected find, its English owners having created an un-Scottish air of conviviality.

The barmaid sauntered over to him. She could have left a bottle at the beginning of the evening, but then

7

she wouldn't have had an excuse to parade her wares.
Every time she poured a new drink, her bodice was
pulled lower and the swing of her hips was more de-
liberate. "Will yer lordship be wanting something
more?" she asked, her tone suggesting a wealth of
possibilities.

Gervase responded with a half-smile, enjoying the
warmth spreading through his loins. Their courtship,
if it could be termed such, had been progressing for
the last two hours, and clearly she had heard that he
was a rich English aristocrat. Gervase was not a lord
yet, but his man Bonner would have mentioned that
the master was heir to Viscount St. Aubyn. The remark ensured the maximum in deference and service
for both man and master; it would also add a few
crowns to the price of bed and board, but both were
still cheap by London standards.

"What more do you have to offer?" he asked lazily,
brushing his dark hair back, grateful that it had finally
dried. He had begun to wonder if anything in the Hebrides was ever dry.

Taking her time, she leaned across him as she
poured more of the dark amber whiskey into his glass.
Her full breast brushed his cheek and shoulder, and
he could smell the musky, not overclean scent of her
body. Gervase preferred a more refined kind of doxy,
but he hadn't had a woman in weeks and this one was
clearly available and willing. The girl was roundly attractive and he ran an appreciative hand down the curve
of her hip.

Confident of her allure, she smiled provocatively.
"We have anything you might want."

His gaze fell to her low-cut bodice, where half-
exposed breasts were ripe for the plucking. "Anything?"

"Anything." The barmaid clearly had experience
and enthusiasm for this sort of private business, which
should make for a rewarding night.

Under the clatter of tankards and conversation, Gervase asked softly, "Do you know which room I'm in?"

"Aye."

only by blood and duty; affection played no part on either side. It would have been pleasant if the older man had expressed a more personal interest in his son's continued existence, but that question had never arisen.

Gervase leaned over to scoop up more pebbles and almost lost his balance. Straightening, he swore softly as he resolved not to underestimate the power of the local whiskey again. The benefits of self-discipline had appealed to him from an early age and he disliked the loss of control induced by too much alcohol. Not that this remote corner of the Hebrides presented many threats, but he preferred keeping his weaknesses at bay.

How long had he been outside . . . perhaps three-quarters of an hour? It was late and the taproom was silent behind him. Time to return to his room; perhaps the buxom barmaid was waiting.

The inn was claustrophobic after the fresh night air, and he felt another wave of dizziness as he climbed the stairs and tried to find his way back to his room. *Damn* the whiskey! The stone building had been built at random over several centuries, and was a rabbit warren of haphazard corners and uneven floors. The landlord had left him an oil lamp in the entry hall, and odd shadows swayed as Gervase carried the lamp upstairs.

When the upper hall split, he had to stop and think which direction to take; his tour of Scotland had encompassed other rambling inns much like this one, and they ran together in his mind. After a moment's thought he turned right, fumbling the iron key into the lock when he reached the room at the end of the hall. Either the crudeness of the hardware or his own jug-bitten state made the lock difficult, and the key required considerable jiggling before the door would open.

Any worry that the whiskey had inhibited his ability to function disappeared at the sight of the rounded form waiting in the bed. With a surge of anticipation, Gervase set the lamp on the small bedside table and quickly stripped off his outer clothes. The barmaid was

dozing when he slipped under the blanket; he must
have been outside longer than he had thought. She wore
only a thin lawn shift, and as he ran his hand down
her body, Gervase was dimly aware that the girl
seemed less voluptuous than he had expected. But she
was also cleaner, and her fresh female scent increased
his arousal.

The reasoning part of his mind was almost totally
disabled by lust and whiskey, and he hoped she would
waken quickly since he was in a hurry. Surely the down
payment he'd given the doxy entitled him to her conscious participation; she'd seemed warm and willing
enough downstairs. This first time wouldn't last long,
but there was a whole night before them and he would
rather she didn't lie there like a poleaxed steer.

As he pulled the shift above her waist, he was glad
to see her eyes opening. He leaned over for a kiss, and
her soft lips parted easily under his, though her reaction was drowsy and without expertise. As his hand
slid between her thighs, the slight body stiffened under
him and began moving, inflaming him to the point
where he no longer thought at all. He began kissing
his way down her neck, and as he did, she twisted
violently and screamed.

Her first cry was a breathless gasp, but she gained
her wind and let loose with a high-pitched, mindless
shriek so close to his ear that he thought the drum
would shatter. Cursing himself for not taking the time
to waken her properly, Gervase lifted his head and said
soothingly, "Relax, sweetheart, it's just me. Quiet
down before you wake everyone in the inn."

He tried to kiss her again as the one guaranteed way
of quieting her, but the girl twisted her head away for
another scream. The body under his was thin, not at
all like the ripely curving barmaid, and he was just
beginning to realize that something was horribly wrong
when the door burst open and a harsh, angry voice
filled the room. *"Ye filthy, rutting beasts!"*

Gervase whipped sideways away from the girl, turning to face the intruder. The entrance to the room was
blocked by a tall rawboned man dressed all in black.

As Gervase stared in shock, the whiskey slowing his reflexes, the innkeeper and his plump wife appeared in the hallway behind the intruder, both of them wearing hastily donned robes and appalled expressions.

The black-clad man's hoarse breathing filled the room. In one hand he held a candle and in the other was a cocked double-barreled pistol. The weapon alone would have commanded caution, but what transfixed Gervase was the man's eyes. The whites were visible all around the dark irises and the gaunt middle-aged face shone with the unhealthy glow of a furious fanatic.

For an endless moment the mad eyes raked the scene, finding some obscure satisfaction in it. Beside Gervase, the girl's screams subsided to gulping sobs as she gripped the blankets tight around her, her dark hair obscuring her face.

"So ye succumbed to her whorish lures. She's been my punishment, Mary has." The man in black stalked toward the bed, his Scottish accent adding rolling power to his denunciation. "My name is Hamilton and I'm an anointed minister of the Lord. I've done my best to keep my daughter pure, but even my prayers can't save a female who was damned before she was born. I've seen how she looks at men, how they sniff around her. She's a bitch in heat, sent to tempt men to their doom. God knows I've tried to save her from her own vile nature, but no more. Now she's yours."

The voice dropped to a harsh whisper and the dark figure repeated, "Aye, she's yours," with vicious satisfaction. He stopped by the bed, looming so near that a hot spatter of candle wax scalded Gervase's chest. Oddly, Hamilton's clothing was that of a gentleman, in spite of the severe cut and color.

For the first time in his life, Gervase was frozen to immobility, his mind a jumble of sexual frustration and whiskey-sodden confusion. For the last ten years nightmares had haunted him, and for a moment he wondered if this was another. But then the self-proclaimed cleric prodded him with the pistol, and the steel barrels were too cold and hard to be a dream.

"Oh, yes, she's yours, my pretty lord." The words were almost caressing. Then he exploded, *"You whoreson aristocrat!* You couldn't control your lust and now she's yours for life, in all her corruption." The vicar was so close that Gervase could see spittle on his lips as he gloated. "You deserve each other, you do, and I'll be free to live a godly life again."

Fear began to clear Gervase's mind, closely followed by fury. "For God's sake, man, I don't know how this female got into my bed, but it was none of my doing. Your little trollop is as intact as when I found her. If she's your daughter, get her the hell out of here."

The man's eyes shone and the cocked pistol stayed centered on Gervase's heart. "Oh, no, you whoreson," he said, his voice harsh and uncanny. "You'll marry her. She may have the soul of a slut, but in the eyes of the world she's an innocent."

The madman paused to draw a breath, then continued with heavy sarcasm, "Even *gentlemen* such as you are not permitted to despoil gently bred girls. It's no' my fault you succumbed to her sly, insinuating ways. You'll marry her and you'll do it now, this very hour. And then I'll be free of her."

The words snapped the scene into nightmare focus and Gervase realized two inescapable facts. First, Hamilton was quite insane, a fanatic obsessed by sex and sin. And secondly, with the cunning of his madness, he had very cleverly trapped the Englishman in a compromising situation.

Gervase cursed himself for his own stupidity. The only worldly caution his father had ever given was to beware of entrapment: rich young men with more randiness than sense were vulnerable to the schemes of those who wanted to share their wealth. It was one reason Gervase limited his roving to round-heeled sluts like the barmaid; wellborn girls were dangerous.

The barmaid must have cooperated in the plot. She had been very bold with her lures; once he had taken the bait, she had only to step aside, doubtless for more money than she would have received for a routine carnal transaction. Since he expected his bed to be occupied, he hadn't thrown this other girl out when he'd found her. Something similar had happened once at a country house, but he'd been sober, not expecting company, and had gotten rid of the bitch before her mother could ''happen'' upon them.

Gervase glanced across the bed at the girl whose screams had triggered the trap. She was playing the role of outraged virgin to the hilt, her face invisible behind a dark tangle of hair from which artistic little sobs still emerged. Her father had surely planned the whole business, and the sight of the man's obscene pleasure in his handiwork destroyed the last shreds of Gervase's control. Attempts at domination had always infuriated him; damning the consequences, he leaned forward to grab the pistol with both hands and twist it from Hamilton's grasp.

In his arrogance the vicar was caught off-guard and Gervase was able to wrench the pistol away. The triggers were spring-operated and both barrels fired, jerking the weapon violently under Gervase's hands and sending the balls into the bed by his side. If the angle had been slightly different, half his chest would have been blown away; as it was, one ball grazed his right forearm, scorching without drawing blood.

Continuing his forward velocity, Gervase rolled off the bed and onto his feet, glad that he hadn't removed his drawers; he was at enough of a disadvantage without being stark naked as well. The pistol in his hand was an expensive weapon, elegant and deadly, the sort carried by a gentleman in London's meaner streets. An odd choice for a Hebridean madman. Now that the gun was discharged and harmless, Gervase hurled it across the bedchamber to a corner where it would threaten no more.

Hamilton had lost none of his self-possession, even now that he was disarmed and his victim upright and able to look him in the eye. In his harsh, panting voice he said, ''Ye'll not get away from me that easily.

You've compromised my daughter and there are witnesses to prove it. She's yours.''

Gervase would have given half his inheritance to have a clear head. Glancing at the landlord in the doorway, he said tightly, "For God's sake, get this madman away from me. I don't know what kind of rig he's running, but I'll have none of it."

Hamilton said with mad cheer, "Aye, Hayes, come in. You and your wife can be witnesses to the marriage."

The landlord and his wife had been out in the hall, but they stepped in now, their faces stiff and wretched over the disaster befalling their inn. More figures hovered back in the passage, prudently keeping their distance.

Gervase drew a deep breath, then said in his most aristocratic voice, "We can talk about this in the morning. I can't marry the girl in the middle of the night."

"Oh, no, my pretty lad, it will be now." The wild eyes were implacable, and carried a mesmerizing air of conviction. Money may have been the motive behind this charade, but the cleric had convinced himself of the virtue of his cause. Perhaps he thought persecuting the ungodly was his duty, or that this was a profitable way to dispose of a daughter he clearly despised.

"If it's money you want for the injury to your darling daughter's nerves, I'll pay it," Gervase snapped. Much as he loathed being compelled, giving in to blackmail might be the better part of wisdom.

"Keep your filthy money." Hamilton sneered. "Nothing less than your name will redeem your wickedness." The gaunt face grimaced with vicious satisfaction. "Ye couldn't marry her so soon in England, where the established church is just another name for the Whore of Rome, but this is Scotland. No banns, no archbishop's license required. These God-fearing people know me, and they'll stand witness. They know how hard I've tried to keep her pure. They know it's not my fault I've failed.''

The nightmare was worsening. The ease of getting married in Scotland had made Gretna Green, the southernmost corner of the country, the destination of eloping couples for years. By ancient tradition, a man and woman could wed with a simple declaration in the presence of witnesses, so a ceremony performed by a legitimate clergyman would surely be valid.

But beyond the legal questions was a devastating realization that tightened the sick knot in Gervase's stomach. A clergyman was by definition a gentleman, and the nubile daughters of the upper classes were sacrosanct. No matter that it was entrapment, Gervase had been caught in bed with the girl, and by the code of his class, there could be only one honorable solution.

In the struggle between confusion, fury, and his own inflexible sense of duty, duty won.

The details of the ceremony were never clear in Gervase's mind. Holding a candle, Hamilton recited the words of the marriage rite from memory, pausing only long enough to ascertain the groom's name before beginning. The bride stayed in the bed, held fast by modesty or hysteria, while Gervase stood a dozen feet away, taut and bare-chested, his back to the wall.

Mary Hamilton mumbled the responses in a halting, almost inaudible voice as the landlord and his wife shifted uneasily in the background, wanting the sordid business done and forgotten before it ruined the good name of their house. After the ceremony Hamilton produced pen, ink, and wedding lines so speedily that it confirmed Gervase's furious conviction that he had been entrapped, a rich pigeon for the plucking.

As he withdrew, the vicar's eyes glittered with triumph. "I wish you joy of the slut, Brandelin." He licked his lips with his pointed tongue; then, with a last satisfied chuckle, he was gone.

Before the door closed, Gervase snapped to Hayes, "Get my man up and tell him to prepare the horses and baggage. We're leaving within the hour."

The landlord stared as if the order confirmed that Gervase was the madman, but nodded obediently before he scuttled away. Then the door closed and Gervase was alone with his bride.

With angry deliberation he turned the key in the lock, as he should have done when he first came in. If he'd had enough sense to do that before ripping his pantaloons off, perhaps this whole bloody-minded farce could have been avoided. The only light was from the lamp he had brought up earlier, the guttering flame testifying that it was almost out of oil.

He stood over his bride and studied her with cold-blooded contempt. The nondescript figure was turned away, the blanket pulled armor-tight against him. Grabbing her shoulder, he pulled the girl around to face him, exposing a pinched face swollen and blotched with tears. Hardly surprising that her father had married her off the way he had; no one else would ever want her. And only a man as obsessed with sex and sin as Hamilton could imagine that this unappealing waif would attract men's admiration.

Gervase had been played for a fool, and this little bitch had been a party to it or she wouldn't have been in his room. How many other beds had she slithered into during her career in extortion? How many times had she screamed with outraged virtue? Her act was well-polished, and her father's was downright inspired. Gervase was doubtless the richest prey to come their way, so he had been awarded the dubious honor of marrying her. Unless this scene had been played identically before, and little Mary Hamilton was a bigamist?

The line between anger and passion can be very thin. As he gazed at the girl, Gervase's fury rekindled the appetite that had been suppressed during the bizarre wedding, and the whiskey he had drunk blurred any inconsistencies in his logic as it hardened his desire. He said harshly, "Well, Mary Hamilton, you wanted a rich husband and you've got one. Unless you're a bigamist, someday you'll be the Viscountess St. Aubyn. Was it worth this sordid little game? Or were you just doing your father's bidding?"

The dark eyes watched him warily from behind the

veiled hair but she said nothing. Her silence infuriated him as much as anything else this ghastly night, and Gervase ripped the blanket away, exposing the thin, shift-clad body. She gasped and reached vainly for the bedclothes, and he grabbed her wrist, feeling his wife's sparrow-delicate bones under his fingers.

It was hard to believe that a girl so young could behave with such duplicity, but she made no attempt to deny the charges, and the flickering light revealed a smirk behind her tangled hair. Her smugness fanned his outrage and contempt, and in a soft menacing voice he said, "Oh, no, my lady, it's too late to play the innocent. You've gotten what you wanted, and a good deal more. You already know how to be a whore. Now I'll show you what it means to be a wife."

The girl shrank back, her eyes wide and dark, but made no real effort to escape as he joined her on the high bed. Releasing her wrist, Gervase rolled over and covered her slight body with his own hard, muscular frame, pinning her against the mattress while he pulled up her shift. Her figure was scarcely more than a child's, quite unlike the lushly feminine type he preferred, but in his present mood of mindless fury Gervase didn't care. She was female, and he was in the mood to take the traditional revenge for a woman's treachery; the bitch would pay for what she and her father had done. She was, after all, his wife, and just this once he would claim a husband's rights.

At first she was passive, her legs separating easily, the thin body shifting beneath him as she gasped words too muffled for him to understand. Perhaps she was excited. Gervase neither knew nor cared; he had never had less interest in pleasing a partner. All his anger was concentrated into vengeful lust, and with one hard thrust he forced his way inside her.

Her dry, tight passage resisted, and penetration hurt him, but his pain was minor compared to hers. Mary Hamilton jerked violently and screamed, her shrill anguish assaulting his ears from mere inches away. He automatically clamped one hand over her mouth to stop the outcry, his rage pierced by a horrified realization

of what was happening. Her teeth tore at his hand, but
it was too late to cease what he had begun. His body
was out of control and in a dozen furious strokes he
was finished.

As his seed spilled into her, his anger splintered and
dissolved. Gervase had never before had sex with a
virgin, but he knew enough to recognize what he had
done. There was blood on him as he withdrew, and he
was sickened by the knowledge that whatever Mary
Hamilton's other crimes might be, she had never before lain with a man.

His wife's blank apathy had been shattered, and she
shook with racking sobs as she wrenched herself away
from her tormentor, her body convulsing into a tight
knot of slender limbs.

His head whirling with sick vertigo, Gervase rolled
onto his back and threw one arm over his eyes as he
gasped for breath. In the ashes of fury lay guilt and
disgust as reason reasserted itself. He had behaved no
better than an animal, abusing a helpless female. The
girl had conspired to entrap him and was doubtless a
slut at heart, but she did not deserve this kind of revenge.

When his dizziness subsided he sat up, swinging his
legs over the side of the bed and burying his face in
his hands as he struggled with self-contempt. Finally,
feeling unutterably tired, he raised his head and contemplated the girl he had married.

Though inexperienced with virgins, he saw that action was necessary, so he stood and picked up a linen
towel from the washstand. After folding it, he handed
it to her and said curtly, ''Put this between your legs
and press your thighs together.'' She stared through
her tangled hair, then took the towel in a trembling
hand and did as he bade her.

Drawing the blankets over the girl, he realized how
very young she was, perhaps only fourteen. When her
father put her to this scheme, had she known what
marriage meant? Or did she think this just a game that
would get her jewels and fine clothes?

''Look at me.'' Though Gervase's voice was neutral

and free of inflection, she cringed away. He reached down for her chin, turning her face toward him. The girl was completely broken, without even the spirit to close her eyes against him.

Wearily he said, "Stop crying, I'm not going to do anything more to you. Listen carefully, because I will say it only once. I don't ever want to see you again. My lawyer is John Barnstable and you can write to him at the Inner Temple in London. I will inform him of this hell-born 'marriage' and he will arrange for you to receive an allowance. It will be a generous one, and you and your father can live in comfort on my money for the rest of your life. But there is a condition."

The girl's dark eyes were still dull. Exasperated, he asked, "Do you understand what I am saying? Surely you speak English." Many of the island Scots spoke only Gaelic, though he would expect the daughter of a clergyman to have some education.

When her head nodded, he continued with icy precision. "I never want to see or hear from you again in my life. If you ever come near London or any of the St. Aubyn properties, I will cut off your allowance. Am I making myself clear?"

Again she nodded faintly, but as Gervase studied her with suddenly narrowed eyes, he realized with shock just how strange her face was. The girl wasn't normal; there was a slackness in her expression, and something indefinably wrong about the eyes. The child he had raped was simple, too crippled in mind to understand what her father had arranged for her.

Releasing her chin as if it were a hot coal, he stood up, fighting down nausea as he grasped the extent of the crime he had committed. To force a scheming young virgin was despicable, even though she was legally his wife; to rape a creature too afflicted to know why she had been abused was a sin as unforgivable as the one he had committed when he was thirteen.

With cold, shaking hands he dragged his clothes on, wanting only to escape this hellish place. The girl had curled into a tight little ball on the bed, the only sign of life her strange, unfocused eyes. Since an incompetent was hardly likely to remember his words, Gervase reached for the ink and pen that had been used for the marriage lines. On the back of one of his cards he printed his lawyer's name and address, then wrote, *Hamilton: Don't ever bring her near me again. She may not use my name.* After a moment's pause he added, *Take care of her well; when she is dead, you will receive nothing more from me.*

That should ensure the girl decent treatment from her father, since it would be in the man's best interest to keep her safe and healthy. She had smelled clean; perhaps her father already had some kind of keeper for her. A full-time nursemaid must cost almost nothing in this godforsaken part of the world.

Gervase stood, placing the card on the table. The girl was shivering, and he took a moment to rummage in the wardrobe for a blanket. She cowered fearfully away as he spread the blanket over her, and his mouth tightened at the sight; it was no more than he deserved.

Her dark unfocused gaze followed him to the doorway, where he paused. His legal wife was like a frightened woodland creature frozen in panic as a predator waited. His throat tight with guilt, he whispered, "I'm sorry."

The words were more for his benefit than hers, since she seemed to have no idea what was happening. Though he had never had grounds to believe in a benevolent Deity, Gervase prayed she would soon forget what had happened. He knew better than to hope that he would do the same.

Five hours later Gervase and his servant Bonner were in a fishing boat carrying them toward the mainland. Bonner was a tight-lipped former military batman who nodded without comment when ordered to discuss the events of the night with no one, ever, and he had efficiently taken charge of packing his master's gear. Gervase had waited outside, unwilling to be in the same room with his bride a moment longer than necessary.

As the boat threaded its way between the islands, Gervase's face was set in granite lines, his attention focused on rebuilding the mental walls that prevented his self-hatred from overwhelming him. Logically he knew that the events of the previous night were of no real importance. The thousand pounds a year he would settle on the girl would keep her and her appalling father in luxury without making a significant dent in his own fortune. Though most men would curse the loss of their freedom to marry whom they chose, it made no difference to him. He had known for the last ten years that he could never marry.

But no logic could dispel his implacable guilt when he thought of the hapless child he had abused. No amount of legitimate anger or whiskey was great enough to justify those moments of violence, and the incident was one more cross he must learn to bear. His remorse taunted him, mocking the resolution he had made to become his own man in India, to free himself from the past by building a new life. Perhaps Hamilton was right, and men were damned before they were even born.

Gervase had always distrusted intuition, but as he watched the dark shore of Mull fall away behind him in the misty dawn, he could not escape a heavy sense of doom. Somewhere, sometime in the future, he would pay a price for last night's disastrous stupidity, and for his own unforgivable loss of control.

1

THE wind blows without ceasing on the high Yorkshire moors, in the spring bright with promise, in the
summer soft as a lover's caress, in the autumn haunted
with regret. Now, in the depths of winter, the wind
was ice-edged and bleak, teasing the shutters, threatening the doors, taunting the impermanence of all
manmade structures. But High Tor Cottage had held
firm against the wind for hundreds of seasons, and its
thick stone walls were a warm haven for those sheltered within.

As her son's lashes fluttered over his dazed lapis-
blue eyes, Diana Lindsay gently touched his dark hair,
feeling the spun-silk texture before settling in the bedside chair to wait until he was soundly asleep. Most
days, as she dealt with the demands and occasional
irritations of an active five-year-old, her love for Geoffrey was not on the surface of her mind, but at times
like this, when he had suffered a bad seizure, she was
so filled with tenderness that she ached with knowing
how precious life was, and how fragile. For all the
worry and occasional despair it occasioned, her son's
disorder gave Diana a greater appreciation of the wonder that was a child.

When Geoffrey's breathing was steady, Diana rose
to leave the room. She could have spent all night quietly watching him, yet to do so would be mere indul-
gence on her part. Even now, years before he would
leave her to make his own way in the world, Diana
knew how hard it would be to release him when the

time came. Walking out this night was just one more of a thousand small disciplines she performed in preparation for the day when Geoffrey would belong to himself more than to her.

As she walked from her son's small bedchamber into the hall, she heard the wind beginning to gust, the windows rattling to protest the oncoming storm. Though it was only four in the afternoon, the light was almost gone and she could not see the small farm shed across the yard when she looked out.

Usually Diana enjoyed the winter storms, loving the solitude and peace of the high moors when the weather was too harsh for trips to the village. It made her feel safe, for if the inhabitants of the cottage could not get out, surely no dangers could get in. Security was a fair compensation for the lonely simplicity of life in this remote corner of Yorkshire. But tonight the cottage was too quiet, in spite of the wind, and she felt anxious for reasons she couldn't explain.

In the kitchen Diana brewed herself a cup of tea and sat down to savor the solitude. The third member of the household, Edith Brown, was suffering from a heavy winter cold and Diana had packed her off to bed for a rest before supper. Edith was officially housekeeper, but she was equally friend and teacher, and the two women shared all the tasks of the household, from cooking and milking to child-rearing.

There was no need for Diana to rush to the milking; apart from that and a little mending, there were no other chores and she would be free to spend the evening reading or quietly playing the piano. The prospect should have pleased her, but tonight she felt restless without understanding why. The solid gray stone walls had stood firm against the wind for over two hundred years, and there were food and fuel enough for weeks if need be.

Yet still she found herself crossing to the window to gaze out, seeing only whirling snowflakes. Absently brushing strands of dark chestnut hair from her face, she tried to analyze her deep sense of unease. Over the years she had learned that such feelings could be

ignored only at her peril. The last time she had felt a
warning this strong, Geoffrey had been two years old.
Diana had thought he was napping, and then blind
panic had driven her frantically from the house barely
in time to pull her son from the stream where he had
crept out to play, and where he had slipped into a
drowning pool.

Just remembering the incident made her heart beat
more quickly, and she made herself sit down again in
her Windsor chair by the fire. Closing her eyes and
relaxing, she tried to analyze what she felt, patiently
sorting out the threads of concern for Edith and Geoffrey and the other minor worries of daily life. What
was left was a hazy, unfamiliar perception that she was
hard-pressed to name. It wasn't danger that approached; she was sure nothing threatened her small
household.

But she felt in her bones that something, or someone, was coming with the storm. Diana's fingers tightened around each other, and she forced herself once
more to relax. In a flash of intuition she realized that
what approached was something she both feared and
welcomed: change.

Madeline Gainford had been born and bred here on
the rooftop of England, but she'd forgotten how bitterly the wind blew. She had been only seventeen when
she left, and her blood had pulsed with the fires of
youth. Now she was past forty, and when the carter
had set her down on the small village common of
Cleveden, her home village looked strange to her. Yet
Cleveden itself had changed very little; the differences
were all in her.

The cart had been nearly full and the driver allowed
her to bring only the small soft bag now slung over
her shoulder. She had left her trunk at an inn in Ley-
burn, not wanting to wait for different transport because the coming storm might have trapped her for
days among strangers. And more than anything else
on earth, Madeline had wanted to die among friends.

She pulled her fur-lined cloak tightly around her as

if she could blot out the aching unpleasantness of the interview she had just had with her widowed sister. They had been friends once, until Madeline had left home in disgrace. The occasional letters the two women exchanged had been terse and to the point, but Madeline thought she had sent back enough money over the years to buy a welcome back into her family home. Isabel had been widowed early, and had it not been for the funds Madeline sent, it would have been hard times for her and her four children.

When Isabel opened the door, her body had stiffened at the sight of her younger sister, her expression of surprise quickly followed by anger and disgust. Then, in a few vicious sentences, Isabel Wolfe had made it clear that while she had graciously accepted her sister's conscience money, she would not let her children be corrupted by having a whore under her own roof. Her last bitter words still rang in Madeline's ears: *You made your own bed, and a whole legion of men have lain with you in it.*

Madeline would not have thought words could hurt so much, but then, she had never been called a whore by her own sister. Only now that the hope was gone did she realize how much she had counted on finding refuge here, and her despair and pain were so great that she might have crumpled to the ground where she stood if the impulse to escape had not been stronger. Shelter could be bought in one of the other cottages, but there was no point to it, no point at all. Why buy a few more months of increasingly painful life surrounded by disapproving strangers?

Slinging the strap of her bag across her shoulder, Madeline continued walking uphill along the rough track that followed the stream to the top of the dale. As a child she had followed this path when she could escape her chores, finding empty dells where she could dream of a world beyond Cleveden. It was only fitting that she escape along this track for the last time.

The wind sharpened outside the shelter of the cottages, and icy snowflakes bit her face before whirling down to whiten the ground. Though it was almost dark,

the meager available light diffused through the snow
to lend a soft glow to her progress. In spite of the years
that had passed, Madeline recognized the moist heav-
iness of air that heralded a major blizzard, the kind
that could cut off the high country for days or weeks.

Madeline had heard that freezing was a painless way
to die, though she wondered who had come back from
the grave to recommend it. The thought produced a
faint smile and she was glad that a ghost of humor was
left to her. It had been foolish to hope Isabel would
be different than she was, and Madeline had no strength
left for recriminations.

It was surprising how far she was able to walk before fatigue finally stopped her in the protection of one
of the few stubby trees, her tired body slowly sinking
to the ground. She could have chosen a tree nearer the
village, but she had always preferred action to waiting,
and even now that was true.

The snow was beginning to drift, and its silence was
as pure as she remembered from childhood; Madeline
could have been as physically alone in the world as she
was emotionally. The warm, heavy folds of her cloak
cushioned the hard earth. She had missed the snow;
there was little in London, and it never stayed clean
for long. And of course London was never quiet.

Resting her back against the tree trunk, Madeline
closed her eyes against the night and wondered how
long it would be until she fell into the final sleep. One
was supposed to see scenes from one's life when dying, but mostly she thought of Nicholas. In her mind
she could see the hurt and the anger that would have
been etched on his thin face when he discovered that
she was gone. Even now he would be attempting to
find her, but apart from her lawyer, no one knew where
she had gone, or even where she had come from in the
beginning. A courtesan never burdened her protector
with the mundane details of childhood.

For the first time she felt tears on her face, icy in
the bitter wind. There had been more than business
between her and Nicholas or she would not have gone
away. But if she had stayed in London, he would never

let her dismiss him, and she had her pride; the thought
of him watching her waste away, losing what remnants
of beauty she had, was unbearable. Nicholas might
have abandoned her, which would have hurt dread-
fully. Much more likely, he would have remained with
her to the end. The agony on his face would have mul-
tiplied her own hurt. Far worse would be knowing the
intolerably high price he would be paying to watch his
mistress die. Loving him, she could not ask that he
pay it.

Her breath escaped in a sob and Madeline pressed
a hand to her breast, uncertain whether the pain there
was physical or emotional. The lump was hard under
her fingers and she quickly dropped her hand, unwilling to feel the alien growth that was eating her life
away; soon it would no longer matter whether the pain
was in her body or in her spirit.

Only the soughing wind broke the silence, and there
was all the peace one could wish for. Her dark blue
cloak was now frosted with white and she wondered
absently if anyone would find the pouch of jewels and
gold slung under her dress, or whether animals would
scatter her bones first. Better that a needy person find
her treasure trove and use it than have it go to Isabel.
After all, Madeline thought with dry amusement, she
didn't want to corrupt her sister any more than she
already had.

There was a certain poetry in the image of the rav-
aged beauty dying peacefully alone in the snow. It was
one of life's anticlimaxes that as the long minutes
passed and strength returned, Madeline found she
wasn't ready to die just yet. Had she been the sort to
give up easily, she would have died in a workhouse
before she was twenty. Waiting for death turned out to
be a bloody boring business, and she had never welcomed boredom.

There was a little breath available for laughing at
herself as Madeline grasped the lowest tree branch to
pull her chilled body upright. Her feet were entirely
numb and she had doubtless left her change of heart
too late; she would never make it back to the village

and there were few houses out this way. Still, she would try. Vaguely she remembered a cottage that had been inhabited by an old lady when she herself was a child. After the old woman died, High Tor Cottage had been left vacant. Perhaps it was still empty, although surely even it was too far.

But there was no other possible shelter and Madeline continued along the track, now nearly invisible under the snow. Only vague memory and an occasional stunted tree marked the trail, and she doubted that she would find shelter, did not even really care. But at least the Reaper would have to work to cut her down; she'd be damned if she would do the job for him.

Of course, Isabel would say she was damned already.

It was full dark when Diana stepped outside to go to the shed and the vicious wind shoved her back against the door, snatching the warm breath from her mouth. She clung to the doorknob as she peered into the swirling snow, where visibility was no more than an arm's length. Thank heaven Edith insisted that during the winter they tie a guide rope between house and shed. The rope was essential tonight and Diana followed it slowly, sliding her left hand along as she carried a lantern in her right. The snow was more than ankle-deep and had drifted against the shed door, making it difficult to pull open.

In the shed, the animals' bodies produced an agreeable warmth and there were soft clucks from the chickens as Diana entered, hung the lantern on a ceiling hook, and stripped off her gloves to begin milking. While she rubbed her hands together to warm them, she glanced around the rough stone walls, checking that everything was in its proper place. Even this small amount of farming had been alien, and Edith had educated her as if she were a child, introducing Diana to the cows with the assurance that the beasts meant no harm, for all they were so large. Now Diana could enjoy the pungent smell of healthy livestock that blended with the fragrant sweetness of summer hay.

The wind worsened while she was milking, and it grabbed her as she stepped outside, nearly spilling the pail of milk. Diana edged her way carefully along the rope with the pail in one hand and the lantern in the other. She had reached the back door when she heard the voice above the wind. She almost dismissed it as just another sound of the wild night, but it came again as she opened the door.

Diana looked doubtfully into the darkness, seeing nothing but swirling flurries of snow. Surely it was only the wind, crying around the buildings. As she stepped into the house, the cry came again, this time hauntingly human, and she stopped. She would be lost in minutes if she ventured into the snow, yet she could not leave any creature to die in the storm.

After a moment's thought Diana put the milk pail inside the back door, then returned to the shed. Like most smallholders, she kept a good supply of rope, and she was able to knot together a line perhaps a hundred yards in length. She went outside again, the rope in her left hand, the lantern held high. Pitching her voice against the wind, she called, "Is anyone there?"

Once more the cry came twisting along the wind, so Diana felt her way down the track toward the voice. The lantern was useless to illuminate the formless drifts beneath her feet, so she held it high above her head, hoping it might be visible to anyone approaching. Even on her own land, it was nearly impossible to find her way through the blinding whiteness, and once she stumbled to her knees, barely saving the lantern from smashing to the ground.

At the end of the rope, she waved the lantern and called until her voice hoarsened. Just when she was ready to give up, a dark shape reeled out of the night, a woman swathed in a hooded cloak. Diana put an arm around the frail exhausted body and pitched her voice to carry over the piercing wind. "Can you keep walking? It's not far."

The woman nodded, then with obvious effort
straightened herself and took hold of her rescuer's arm.
The journey seemed endless in the bitter cold and Diana was numb to the bone by the time they reached
the shed. God only knew how the other woman kept
moving. How far could she have come on such a night?

The last hundred feet was accomplished at a snail's
pace, and Diana was near collapse as she dragged the
two of them into the kitchen. Alerted by the unusual
sounds, Edith was entering the kitchen, hastily tying
her robe. "Diana, what on earth . . . ?"

"I heard her calling when I finished milking. She
must have seen the lantern," Diana gasped, lowering
the woman onto a chair by the fire. Even frosted with
snow, the richness of the velvet cloak was obvious.
What was a lady doing out on such a night?

Diana pushed her hood back and leaned against the
wall by the wide stone fireplace, working to catch her
breath. She had never been so grateful for the welcoming warmth of her spacious kitchen, gleaming with
copper pans and scented with braids of onions and
bunched herbs that hung from the ceiling.

Faced with an emergency, Edith was swift and sure
as she set water to boil, peeled off the snow-encrusted
cloak, and gently began chafing the visitor's white
hands. When the water was boiling, Edith brewed tea,
adding sugar and a generous dollop of brandy. The
housekeeper was near fifty, her grayed hair falling in
a braid over the shoulder of her dark green dressing
gown, her austere features marred by a livid scar
across the left cheek. She was a woman of few words,
but those held wisdom, and there was kindness behind
her fierce visage.

Diana wrapped cold fingers around the hot mug
Edith gave her, grateful for the internal and external
warmth it provided. Then the housekeeper spooned
some of the mixture down the woman from the storm.
The stranger choked at first, but soon was sipping from
the mug Edith held to her lips.

Diana studied her visitor curiously as tendrils of
steam curled from the saturated cloak. The woman was

too thin, but she must have been a great beauty in her youth. The oval face was still lovely in early middle age and her dark brown hair showed only a little silver. She was nearly unconscious and her large brown eyes showed dazed incomprehension.

"Put her in my bed," Diana said, her voice faint even in her own ears. "I'll lie down with Geoffrey." She finished her tea and made her way upstairs, knowing Edith would do what was needful. Shivering, she stripped to her shift and crawled into Geoffrey's bed. His warm, almost-six-year-old body snuggled against her, and soon she was adrift in dreams.

If Madeline hadn't seen her past life when sitting under the tree waiting to die, she made up for it in her feverish dreams. She alternated between raging, helpless nightmares and occasional periods of semiconsciousness when she was vaguely aware of female voices. Gentle hands fed her and gave her medicine, sponging her when she was drenched with sweat, wrapping her with blankets when she shook with chills.

Then she was lucid, so weak she could barely raise her hand from the bed, but free of the racking chest pains. She was in a small room with whitewashed stone walls. It was night, and the only light came from a candle on the bedside table. First she fixed her eyes on the flame, then gradually extended her focus to the woman sewing beyond the light.

Madeline's first thought was that she was still dreaming, or perhaps she had died. After death, did one wake up in heaven with an angelic guide? It must be so, because the woman by the bed was surely the most beautiful being Madeline had ever seen. But one wouldn't expect an angel to be so ripely erotic; more likely Madeline had gone in the other direction.

Hearing her patient's movement, the young woman looked up, revealing eyes the intense, mesmerizing blue of lapis lazuli. Flawless, exquisitely sculpted features were set in a heart-shaped face, and her rich hair shone with the burnished red-brown of true chestnut. The plain, practical blue wool dress could not disguise

a small-boned figure that combined slimness with a
lavishness of curves that would command a fortune in
London. Madeline chided herself for her vulgar
thoughts; while the woman had a beauty and sensuality that could match or surpass any demirep in England, the perfect face glowed with the unstudied
sweetness and innocence of a Madonna.

Seeing her patient's eyes open, the young woman
smiled and set her sewing aside, placing a cool hand
on Madeline's forehead. "You're back now, aren't you?
We were very worried."

Her low voice was as lovely as the rest of her; though
her dark, high-necked dress had a Quaker's simplicity, her manner and speech would not have been out
of place in a London drawing room. "Would you like
something to drink?"

Madeline nodded, conscious of the dryness of her
throat. The woman raised her and held a glass of
lemon-scented tea to her lips. Its honey-sweetened
taste was soothing, and after several sips Madeline
whispered, "Thank you, that is much better."

The young woman laid her back on the pillows and
set the glass down. Anticipating Madeline's questions,
she said, "My name is Diana Lindsay and you're at
High Tor Cottage, near Cleveden. You've been feverish for three days."

"The last thing I remember was seeing a light
through the snow and trying to find it. Was that you?"

Diana nodded. "Yes, I had been milking. When I
left the barn, I heard you call out and went to investigate."

It was hard to imagine such a lovely creature milking cows, but the hand on Madeline's forehead did not
have the silky softness of a woman unused to manual
labor. "Surely you don't live alone here?"

"No, my son and housekeeper live here also."

Unusual to find a household in this remote place
without a man, but Madeline was too tired even for
curiosity. She whispered, "My name is Madeline Gainford and I grew up in Cleveden. I had come back . . ."

Her voice trailed off, lacking the strength to explain why she had been out in the storm.

Diana's lovely face was shadowed with concern. "Hush now, and rest. There will be time to talk later."

Obediently Madeline closed her eyes and drifted off again. This time there were no troubling dreams.

It was morning before the patient woke again. Diana entered the room to find Madeline Gainford just opening her eyes. At this time of day sunshine flooded the room with warmth and the whitewashed walls glowed. The older woman's gaze scanned the oak chest and wardrobe, the oval hooked rug and pretty watercolors of flowers. Though it must seem humble after what she was accustomed to, her face showed no disdain.

Diana said, "Would you like something to eat?" At her visitor's nod, she went to the kitchen and returned with a steaming bowl of richly flavored cream soup, thick with small pieces of chicken and leek. After propping her patient up on the pillows, Diana spoon-fed her like an infant.

When the bowl was empty, Madeline said, "Thank you, Mrs. Lindsay. You are very kind." Her voice was stronger now and there was healthy color in her face. Edith had braided the dark hair and dressed her in a white flannel nightgown. Her large brown eyes were calm, though there was sadness in their depths. "I don't know how to thank you. I would have died in the storm."

"Much better this way," Diana said with a smile. "It would have been unnerving to find your body during the spring thaw."

That drew a smile in response. Diana had been right that the visitor had been a beauty in her youth; when she smiled, she was still beautiful. Madeline's dark eyes met her hostess's gaze squarely. "If you can get a wagon from the village, I will leave. I shouldn't be here." She sighed and her gaze shifted away. "I never wanted to be a burden to anyone."

"The roads won't be passable for some time, so there is no need to rush. Don't worry about being a burden—you're the most interesting event here in years.'' Diana hesitated before succumbing to curiosity. ''Why were you lost in the storm?''

Madeline's eyes closed and she looked sad and tired. Her voice almost a whisper, she said, ''I wasn't lost. I wanted to die.'' When the dark brown eyes opened, she gazed past Diana. ''Then I decided it was too soon . . . I'm not ready yet.''

It must have taken a good deal of strength for her to add in that level voice, ''I am dying, you see. I came back to Cleveden to be with my family, but my sister wouldn't let me into the house.'' She pressed her hand to her breast with the absentness of habitual gesture before finishing less steadily, ''What I have is not infectious. Your household is in no danger from me.''

The words and gesture told Diana all she needed to know about the disease. Instead she asked, ''Why did your sister not want you?''

Madeline paused and Diana wondered if she would refuse to answer, or would lie. Doubt and regret were reflected in the thin face before her expression became resolute, and when she replied, Diana knew the truth had won out.

Instead of answering directly, the visitor said, ''You must have found the pouch I wore under my dress.'' When Diana nodded, Madeline continued, ''Did you open it?''

''No. Shall I get it for you?'' At Madeline's nod, Diana crossed to the oak chest and took out the small, heavy leather pouch Madeline had carried. Diana and Edith had discussed opening it, but decided not to do so unless their visitor succumbed to the lung fever.

''Open it now,'' Madeline directed, waiting impassively as Diana untied the leather thong and opened the pouch to find a number of irregularly shaped objects wrapped in velvet. After glancing at the woman on the bed for permission, Diana unwrapped the package on top, then gasped in awe at the magnificent necklace spilling out of her hand, the interlaced gold chains set with huge rubies that flared blood-red in the sunshine.

The next velvet packet revealed brilliant sapphire earrings with blue fire in the depths. Her eyes wide and startled, Diana continued unwrapping until her lap blazed with barbaric splendor, with diamonds and emeralds and opals and other gems she could not name, all in superbly wrought settings. They were jewels a queen might wear, and after unwrapping them all in wordless wonder, she lifted her gaze to her visitor.

Madeline smiled without humor. "They weren't stolen. Whatever my other sins, I'm not a thief."

"I didn't think you were," Diana said quietly as she studied her visitor, waiting for an explanation.

Madeline's gaze focused on a splash of sunlight on the wall and she said in a voice empty of expression, "I earned those the only way a woman can, though most would say it isn't honest work. My sister didn't want me corrupting her household."

It took Diana a long moment to understand what Madeline meant. Even then, she could not connect what she knew of prostitution with this frail woman whose slim hands knotted on the quilt, who waited bleakly to be condemned. The idea of selling one's body was alien and repugnant, yet Madeline herself was neither of those things. Diana held silence until she was sure her voice would be composed. "Who is your sister?"

"Isabel Wolfe."

"Really?" Diana knew the name, though they had never met; the Widow Wolfe would cross the street if she saw Diana coming, as if proximity would contaminate her virtuous self. Studying Madeline's face, Diana shook her head. "I see little resemblance. Is she much older than you?"

Madeline stared at her, surprised by the mundane question. "Only three years older." She sighed. "It's hard to imagine now, but she was pretty once. She was always rather . . . righteous, though not so bad as she is now. But I really can't blame her for not wanting a whore in her house."

Though the words were said in a matter-of-fact voice, Diana could see the tension in Madeline's body.

Did the older woman think her hostess had not comprehended the earlier oblique reference and was making sure there was no misunderstanding? It was an act of courage and honesty, and Diana warmed to both qualities. She sensed no wickedness in Madeline, no matter what her past. Moreover, Diana was fascinated to meet someone who had lived in such an unimaginable way.

Diana would have asked more questions, but her guest's face was gray with fatigue. Rewrapping the jewels in their velvet, Diana said dryly, "Perhaps you can't blame her, but I can. For a woman who prides herself on her virtue, your sister failed the test for Christian charity rather badly. Someone should remind her of Jesus and Mary Magdalene."

The tension went out of Madeline's face and she smiled faintly. "You are very kind not to condemn me." She sighed. "I will leave as soon as the roads clear."

Diana frowned. Madeline Gainford was in no condition to travel; more than that, Diana was powerfully drawn to the older woman and wanted to learn more about her and the mysterious world from which she had come. "Where will you go?"

"I don't know. Perhaps I'll rent a house in a south-coast village, where the weather is milder. I won't need it for long."

Diana was moved by a flash of pure impulse, impossible to justify but feeling so powerfully right that it could not be denied. "There is no need for you to leave."

Madeline stared, her face openly vulnerable and her brows knit with puzzlement. "Would you have me, a . . . a fallen woman, under the same roof with your child? I am nothing to you."

"Ah, but we have something in common. Your sister will cross the street to avoid me." Diana gave a smile of melting warmth as she reached out and clasped Madeline's hand. "We are all outcasts here. You may stay as long as you wish."

The older woman closed her eyes against the sharp sting of tears, torn between accepting and refusing the offer. Madeline had been turned away by her own flesh and blood; was it really possible that she might find the sanctuary she sought in the house of a stranger?

In the end, she did not have the strength to refuse what she wanted so desperately. Grasping Diana's hand as if it were a lifelife, Madeline whispered, ''God bless you.''

2

TAKING a break from her gardening, Diana sat back on her heels and viewed her former patient with pride. It had been over a year since Madeline had appeared from the storm, and instead of wasting away she had gained in strength and spirit. Now Maddy was a glowing, attractive woman in the prime of life, an integral member of the household who cheerfully performed her share of the chores. Today she knelt on a square of tattered carpet and helped Diana transplant April seedlings in the garden. Diana had the odd fancy that the older woman had also been transplanted, from an unwholesome spot to one in which she could flourish.

Madeline was now so much a part of the family that it was hard to remember life without her. Geoffrey had immediately accepted the newcomer as an honorary aunt, put on earth to dote on him. Edith had been wary at first, but she and Madeline shared a rural Yorkshire upbringing and soon they were friends in spite of their surface differences.

Diana felt the recklessness of spring tingling in her veins, and on impulse she decided the time had come to ask the older woman about her past; with Geoffrey napping and Edith in Cleveden, they had the privacy such a discussion required. Over the last year Maddy had talked freely of the snares and delights of London, of fashion and politics, manners and mores, yet never of her own career as a woman of ill-repute.

Hesitantly Diana asked, "If you don't mind talking about it, could you tell me what it was like to be a . . . a ladybird? I can't even imagine . . ." Suddenly bashful, she leaned forward and thrust her trowel into the earth for the next brussels-sprout plant.

Madeline glanced up, her brown eyes bright with merriment. "I've wondered when you would ask. When I first came here and told you what I was, not only did you not condemn me, you looked as fascinated as if I were a . . . a pink giraffe."

Diana blushed, digging deeper than necessary. "I'm sorry, I didn't mean to embarrass you." She should not have spoken; once again she had betrayed her ignorance of how normal people acted.

"Surely you know by now how difficult it is to embarrass me." Madeline chuckled. "I don't mind talking in the least, if you really want to hear, but I thought it best to wait until you raised the subject." She considered where to begin. "For me it was not a bad life: I was lucky and never had to walk the streets. I was one of the company of Cyprians, the Fashionable Impures, and was usually kept by one man at a time."

She moved her carpet three feet to the left and started on a new series of holes. "Actually, I've bedded fewer men than many of the great society ladies, but they are respectable and I am not, because they sold their bodies with vows in front of a priest."

"How did you come to be a . . . a Fashionable Impure?" Curiosity was rapidly replacing Diana's discomfiture; this was a priceless opportunity to learn more about the mysterious half of the human race that was not female, from a woman who must surely be an expert.

"In the usual fashion," Madeline said wryly. "At sixteen I got in the family way with a lad from the next village. I couldn't believe he would betray me, but he was only seventeen, too eager for life to want marriage. When I told him my condition, he ran away to the army." She shrugged. "Besides, his family didn't like me. They said it was my fault for wearing my dresses too tight and chasing after the lads."

"It's always the woman's fault, isn't it?" Diana heard the bitterness in her own voice as she lifted a seedling and set it in a hole, carefully crumbling the soil to remove lumps and stones before patting the plant into place.

Madeline glanced over, surprised at Diana's tone, but she said merely, "Yes, my dear, it is always the woman's fault, at least in the eyes of the world. My mother always said I had a disposition to sin—something needed only to be forbidden, and I would immediately try it. When I told her I was with child, she threw me out of the house for the parish to take care of. My sister Isabel was angry and disapproving, but she gave me what little money she had saved toward her own wedding." She sighed. "I remind myself that even though she condemns me now, she was kind when I most needed it."

Her voice harder, she continued, "As often happens, the parish didn't want to pay for any more bastards and they sent me to London on the cheapest, slowest transport available. In London, abbesses meet the wagons from the country." Glancing up, she clarified, "An 'abbess' is a woman who keeps a brothel."

Diana nodded, her face averted. She had come across the term in her reading and deduced the meaning.

"I was as green a girl as ever was, and London was bigger and noisier and more frightening than I had imagined. When a well-dressed woman offered me a position in her house, I was glad to accept. I didn't know then what kind of house she meant . . ." Madeline's voice trailed off as she remembered her naiveté and her shock when she learned what she was expected to do.

She sat back on her heels, her hands loose in her lap, the planting forgotten. "I was luckier than most. Madame Clothilde ran a decent brothel as these things go, catering to a wealthy set of men. She kept her girls healthy and well-dressed because it was better for business. I could have fallen into much worse hands. Except . . ." Her voice broke and she stopped speaking.

Diana looked up at the sound, saying softly, "Please, you needn't say any more."

"No, really, it's all right," Madeline said, her voice steady again. "It was a long time ago. It's just that . . . of course Madame Clothilde didn't want any pregnant girls. She called in an apothecary and . . . and they took the baby. I didn't even understand what was happening until it was too late." Her face twisted at the painful memory. "I was very ill then. I almost died. And when I recovered . . . I could never have a child."

Diana reached across, gently touching the older woman's hand in silent comfort. "I'm sorry, I never should have asked."

Madeline smiled, her fingers flexing under Diana's. "No, my dear, I feel better for having said it. It was a great sadness at the time, but like most things, there was a good side to temper the bad. Not having to worry about having a baby was an advantage in my profession."

Diana looked at her searchingly until she was satisfied with the older woman's equanimity. Though adversity did not always improve character, it seemed to have had that benefit in this case. Madeline was a woman of great wisdom and tolerance, both of them Christian virtues. Ironic that her high-minded sister did not share them.

Maddy continued, "The rest of the story isn't very dramatic. Clothilde was quite vexed that I couldn't work for several weeks, but she didn't turn me out, and I was adequately cared for by the other girls. If I had been on the streets, I never would have survived. Of all the sisterhood, the streetwalkers have the hardest lives. They age a decade every year, if they survive at all. But as I said, I was much more fortunate than that.

"I was given a new name when I was recovered. It was one of Clothilde's affectations to give all her girls French names. She was from Greenwich herself, and that was the closest she ever came to France, but no matter; in the world of the demireps, you can be what you wish to be. I was christened Margaret, but since the house had a Marguerite, I became Madeline. I liked it, and later I realized how appropriate it was. Madeline is French for Magdalene, you know, a perfect name for my trade.'' She smiled with genuine amusement. ''After a few months working for Clothilde, I justified her faith in my looks when an elderly banker took a fancy to me and bought me for his own use.''

''*Bought* you?'' Diana gasped as she looked up. She had expected to be shocked, but not in this particular way.

''That's what it amounted to.'' Madeline shrugged. ''It wasn't as bad as it sounds. I was quite happy to go with him, since it was a much easier life. He set me up with lodgings and clothes, everything I needed. Though it sounds like slavery, the payment to Madame Clothilde was merely compensation for loss of my services. Not an unusual arrangement.

''He was very indulgent and treated me like a daughter most of the time, except when he was actually . . .'' Madeline halted, unable to think of a discreet way of finishing the sentence. Hastily she went on, ''He kept me for three years, and at the end made a generous settlement. He was moving down to Brighton for his health, and he said he was getting too old for a mistress anyhow. I quite missed him.''

She looked back for a moment, a fond smile on her face, before continuing briskly, ''After that, I became one of the aristocrats of the trade, able to pick and choose my lovers. I was careful in my choices, and with my money as well, so I never had to go with a man I disliked.''

Madeline's pragmatic words made her scandalous past seem natural, even desirable. Diana asked hesitantly, ''Would you do it over again if you had the choice?''

Madeline's dark brows knit together. ''Do you know, I have never considered that? I did what I had to do to survive. After my fall from grace, my choices were very limited.'' She pondered further before saying slowly, ''Being a fallen woman was a way out—out of Yorkshire, out of poverty, out of a narrow life that never suited me. The great courtesans must have not just beauty, but personality and wit. I had the opportunity to grow, to use my mind to its fullest. I met fine men I could never have known otherwise, and lived a life of comfort and luxury.''

As Madeline fell silent, one phrase reverberated in Diana's mind. *A way out. A way out. A way out of Yorkshire.* The words pulsed with significance for her, a significance she was not yet ready to face. Not yet, but soon, soon. . . .

Diana's thoughts were interrupted as Madeline continued her narrative. ''The first months in the brothel were . . . difficult, but I escaped with my health and sanity intact. After that, since I was a *femme entretenue,* a kept woman, I lived very well. It was rather like having several husbands in succession. The chance of catching some vile disease was slim, and I had much more freedom than a respectable woman. If a man became unpleasant, I could refuse him. Yes, if I had to live my life over, there is little I would change. I felt no shame for what I did. The only shame was in how others saw me.''

She laughed suddenly, her face showing the charm that had made her such a success at her trade. ''Most of the Fashionable Impures had nicknames like the Venus Mendicant, or the White Doe, or Brazen Bellona. Because of my dark hair and eyes, I was known as the Black Velvet Rose. Silly, but rather sweet. It's strange, the influence women like us had. Men who would treat their wives like imbeciles would talk politics with their mistresses. My salon was usually much livelier than the respectable ones, because men would speak so much more freely.''

Madeline gestured expressively. ''Because I preferred being kept by one man, I lasted longer than most Cyprians. Of course, when I was between lovers, I would . . . shop a bit until I found someone who pleased me. I enjoyed all the best aspects of courtship and marriage, without the problems wives have.''

Muffled almost to unintelligibility, Diana asked the

question that burned beyond all others. "Did you actually enjoy the . . . the physical part of the life?"

The strain in Diana's voice confirmed Madeline's
guess that the girl's introduction to sex had been the
sort of crude fumbling that made so many woman despise the act. Carefully she said, "Making love can be
quite lovely. It's best if you care deeply for your partner, but it can be enjoyable with any man you like who
treats you well. Many women never learn that, of
course. We are raised to protect ourselves from all
men's advances, to fear being touched. It becomes difficult to relax and enjoy loving."

Watching Diana to make sure her words did not give
offense, Madeline continued, "It is very agreeable to
know and appreciate one's body as a potential source
of pleasure. A more experienced woman at Clothilde's
told me to explore myself by touch, to take different
textures like silk, velvet, rough linen, cool china, and
to rub them over myself to see how my body responded.

"I followed her advice and found that I was a sensual creature. I would also study myself in the mirror,
trying to understand what made a woman's body desirable to a man. And in time, I learned the kind of
power a woman can have over a man."

Diana had gone beyond wondering at the strange-
ness of this conversation, though she was still too shy
to meet Madeline's eye. She sensed that the older
woman's words were a gift to her, an attempt to explain things beyond Diana's experience. Indeed, there
was an intuitive logic to what Madeline said. Diana
loved to touch, to hug her son's warm body, to express
her feelings with a soft brush of her hand, to evaluate
the fabric she bought or the bread she kneaded by its
texture and consistency. If these other forms of touching were enjoyable, surely the most intimate could be
also?

Madeline hadn't finished yet. "Sex is one of the
most powerful and double-edged gifts God gave to hu-
mankind. It can be a source of pain and for women
even death, yet is also the source of new life. At its

best, it becomes a way of expressing the deepest love a man and woman can share." Her dark eyes were reflective. "It is hardly surprising that sexual knowledge was the loss of innocence that forced Adam and Eve from the Garden of Eden, or so a vicar once said when he was visiting me." She smiled wickedly. "He was not the sort of man of the cloth to preach against life's pleasures."

Her smile faded as she tried to define what she had never spoken aloud. "Sex can be used as a cruel weapon, with one person dominating another. That can work either way, with a woman or a man controlling the partner. It is one of the few ways a woman can hold power over a man, though it is chancy and dangerous. Some people are too cold to be ruled by their senses. Others can be brought to their knees, with all their pride and honor broken by the ones they love. . . ."

She smiled disarmingly. "It isn't usually that way, of course. More often, physical love is a way of giving and receiving pleasure and reassurance. Still," she said, narrowing her eyes as she looked at Diana, "a woman as beautiful as you could become truly powerful if she chose to."

Diana met Madeline's gaze, brushing her forehead with one wrist and leaving an earthy smudge as she asked with grave curiosity, "You really think I am beautiful?"

Madeline nodded. "Yes, perhaps the most beautiful woman I have ever known, and I speak as one who has seen most of the great and notorious beauties of England. If you wished, you might become a duchess, or the greatest of courtesans. Don't you think of yourself as beautiful?"

Diana shook her head. "Not in the least. But I have seen how men look at me, and sometimes wonder what they see. They don't seem to look at other women the same way. Often men . . . try to touch me, as if by accident." She bent over and dug a stone out with unnecessary violence. "I've wondered if that is why so many women glare at me as if I were their enemy."

Madeline sighed. "Beauty, like sex, is a double-edged sword. It can make you a victim, or it can help you acquire what you want from life, whether that is love or wealth or power."

Diana looked up, knowing that what her friend had told her this afternoon could change her life. "You are telling me all this so that I can see myself as others do."

"Yes, my dear, that is the reason." Madeline looked at her with compassion. "You saved my life, in more ways than one, and I would like to repay you in a way more meaningful than jewels, though you may have those too. While I know that you have found a certain contentment here at the edge of the world, I have thought that you are restless sometimes, as I was. If you ever choose to leave, you must understand the power of your own beauty, how to wield it and how to protect yourself. Otherwise you risk being used and destroyed by those who desire you."

She made a wry face. "I, too, have been blessed and cursed with more than my share of the kind of beauty men desire. That fact set the pattern of my life." Her gaze became earnest. "There is nothing shameful in what happens between men and women, and much that is wonderful. Don't be shy of asking me questions."

Diana nodded gravely. "Thank you. Certainly I will have questions later when I have absorbed some of what you have told me. You are right; I have been content here, but I don't want to spend the rest of my life in Yorkshire, both for my sake and for my son's. It wasn't so bad when he was an infant, but Geoffrey needs to meet other children, to study with boys as intelligent as he is, to learn how far he can go in the world." She gave a twisted smile. "He even needs to face prejudice and rejection though I hate to think of that."

She spread her hands outward in a gesture of helplessness. "Until you came, I didn't know how to imagine another kind of life. Sometimes," she said with a return to shyness, "I feel that God sent you to me, to be my teacher and friend."

Madeline smiled a response. There was fatigue in her face, but also gratitude, and a shyness to match Diana's. "I think perhaps he did. I hope so. I would like to give back some of what you have given me."

"Oh, you have," Diana said huskily, her lapis-blue eyes glowing jewel-like with inner light. Madeline was reminded not of a Madonna but of a pagan enchantress, Circe perhaps. "You have given me far more than you can imagine."

The capricious spring weather changed that night, turning cold and damp as gusty winds blew pale clouds across the midnight sky, concealing and revealing the bright passionless face of the full moon. The rest of the household slept when Diana quietly donned her cloak and went into the night. Madeline had been right to sense restlessness in Diana. This was not the first time that she prowled alone across the moors, glorying in the wind whipping against her body, needing to burn away the fierce impatience that would not let her sleep. Restlessness had been as much a background to her life these last seven years as the wind itself.

Madeline's words earlier had struck a chord deep inside Diana, and now they circled in her head as her swift strides carried her across the moor. *Being a fallen woman was a way out—out of Yorkshire, out of a narrow life that never suited me.* It was mad for Diana to consider such a life for herself, even for a moment. Madeline had had no real choices; unthinkable that Diana should follow the same path voluntarily. Unthinkable—and yet she could think of nothing else.

She argued with herself. After all, it was not as if the only two possibilities were living on the edge of the world and becoming a high-priced whore. Diana had occasionally considered moving to some provincial city and presenting herself as a widow of modest means and unimpeachable respectability. Yet the prospect had not inspired her, quite apart from the fact that she hated the idea of living a lie.

She had reached the highest hill in the area, and beneath her gaze Yorkshire rolled away to the south. Moon-touched mist lay in the valleys and dales, the dark hills rising above like floating fairy isles. Diana had found peace here, healing the wounds of the spirit that might have destroyed her if she had not had her child to love and care for. The love that connected her to Geoffrey and Edith had brought Diana back from the brink of pain and despair so great that it was nearly madness; more recently Madeline had come to enrich their lives. But on wild restless nights like this one, Diana wanted more.

Madeline had said that Diana's beauty gave her the potential to become a duchess or the greatest of courtesans. With Diana's unspeakable past she would never be a duchess; even the most modest of respectable marriages was out of her grasp. She could never be respectable, so why not become a courtesan, a woman without shame or apologies? Diana wanted a man in her life; since he couldn't be a husband, then he must be a lover.

The thought was a seductive one. A lover need not know about her past; he would likely not even care. And since she could only hope for an illicit love, why not aim for the best and most profitable liaison possible? The very idea should be abhorrent to a respectable female. Yet what had respectability ever gotten her except pain and loneliness?

Beauty, like sex, is a double-edged sword. It can make you a victim, or it can help you acquire what you want from life, whether that is love or wealth or power. Unfortunately, a woman is more likely to become a victim. All her life she had been the victim of men; they had brought her to the edge of destruction, without even the sweet, passionate lies that had given Madeline pleasure before ruining her. For Diana, there had been only ruination. Now there was something irresistibly enticing about the idea of dealing from a position of strength herself, for power would give her freedom.

She did not want power to punish or to victimize;

her fury had faded over time. The magnitude of love she felt for her son had left no room in her heart for malice or bitterness. If her baby had been a girl, perhaps she would have turned from men forever. But Geoffrey was male and there was no evil in him. And occasionally Diana had seen marriages based on caring; somewhere there existed men who would love and cherish a woman rather than abuse her.

No, it wasn't *men* that she wanted; it was one man, one who would love and protect her in spite of her past, one who could initiate her into the profane, earthly delights that Madeline had described. At the thought, Diana smiled wryly, knowing what a romantic fool she was. It was a sign of how much she had healed that she dared to dream again.

Her cloak billowed out behind her, the heavy fabric snapping from the force of the gusting wind, and she felt almost as if she could spread out her arms and soar far to the south, to the city that was the bright, corrupt heart of Britain. As always, the wind was shredding and dispersing her doubts and confusions, and she gloried in its cleansing strength.

When a drift of cloud darkened the moon, Diana began the long trek back to the cottage. Even in the dark she knew her way across the trackless heights as well as any native Yorkshire woman, though she had been raised far from these moors.

The greatest danger in becoming a courtesan was the risk that her choice might damage Geoffrey, since to leave him behind was entirely out of the question. She would have to separate the two sides of her life in London; surely that would be possible. Quite apart from the fact that she could not bear to be parted from him, London would expand his horizons as much as her own.

The drifting clouds unveiled the moon again as Diana neared Cleveden Tarn, a darkly shining circle of water. Level earth ran up to the edge, as if the tarn was a mirror that some goddess had dropped in the coarse grasses. Impetuously she knelt by the edge and stared into the moon-silvered waters. Though better-

educated than most women, Diana had always been
driven by emotion and intuition rather than logic.
Logic whispered to stay here, where it was safe, but intuition called her to leave, to dare the dangerous, mysterious world that Madeline had revealed to her. The
world where a beautiful woman might have power.

As she gazed into the dark water, calm certainty
flowed through her, dissolving doubts. It was not
chance that had brought Madeline into her life; the
older woman was not only a friend but also an essential link to the future. Somewhere there was a man
who was Diana's destiny, connected to her by a thread
of undeniable fate, a man whom she would find only
if she dared the unthinkable.

Caught in the spell of the full moon, she whispered,
"Great goddess, will you show my lover's face to
me?" then laughed at her own foolishness. That she,
who had been raised in a far-too-godly home, should
indulge in superstitious nonsense!

Her laughter died. As clearly as if words had been
spoken, Diana sensed that it was better not to know
what fate held for her; if she knew the shape of the
future, she might turn away from it. She must go
blindly, trusting that her intuition and the hard-won
faith that guided her life would carry her through.

Diana stood and slowly retraced her steps to the
cottage, pulling her cloak tight around her slim body.
The years of life in the safe shallows were over. Ahead
of her lay her destiny, and that destiny was love.

3

DIANA'S hands were not quite steady as she applied her cosmetics. Madeline had spent many hours training her to make herself as subtly provocative as possible, and Diana could almost do it with her eyes closed, but this time the makeup was in earnest. Tonight they were going to an informal gathering at the home of Harriette Wilson, queen of the London demireps, and for the first time Diana would be offering herself in the market.

Laying down the hare's foot she had used to add subtle color to cheeks paled by nerves, Diana studied her reflection in the mirror. The image that faced her was that of a sophisticated, worldly female whose heart-shaped face and delicate features were too flawless to be real. It was not the face of the young woman who had lived on the moors and baked bread and played with her son in the mud of a streambed.

Half a year had passed since she had hesitantly broken the news to her friends that she intended to go to London and become a courtesan. Not surprisingly, that simple statement had provoked a storm of protest. What *was* surprising was that Edith, the very picture of rural conservatism, had supported Diana's goal, pragmatically saying that the plan had much to commend it.

The real opposition came from Madeline, who had lived the life of a demirep without regret or apology. It was one matter to sell oneself when there was no choice; it was quite another to do so voluntarily. Maddy had mustered every available argument, pointing out that they were not in financial need, asking how Geoffrey would be affected, warning that Diana did not realize what she was getting into. Diana had conceded all her friend's points, her voice faltering when they discussed Geoffrey, but had refused to change her mind.

In the end, Madeline had thrown up her hands in defeat and promised to help Diana in any way she could. Without her aid, her endless lessons about men, society, and how to be alluring, Diana could never have come so far. While it remained to be seen whether she would be a success at her new trade, the fraudulent image in the mirror was a good beginning.

- The low-cut blue silk dress Diana wore was the exact lapis-lazuli shade of her eyes, and her glowing chestnut hair was piled on her head in richly tousled curls before cascading down her back. Not accidentally, the style implied that her thick tresses would fall around her bare shoulders with unrestrained abandon if a man touched them.

As she made a minor adjustment to her hair, a soft knock announced Madeline's entrance. Since coming to London, the older woman had dyed the gray out of her brunette hair, and in the candlelight it was impossible to believe that she was more than thirty years old. Tonight Maddy was stunning in a burgundy-red dress, ready for her role as guide and guard.

Once she had agreed to support her young friend's ambitions, she had shared everything with her adopted family: her income, the fashionable Mayfair house where they lived, her knowledge of London and its ways. She had located the small school where Geoffrey was flourishing, and she had introduced Diana to her friend Harriette Wilson, an introduction which had resulted in tonight's invitation.

Diana turned with a smile, grateful to be distracted from her anxiety. Rising from her chair, she slowly turned around for her friend's inspection, her chin lifted to an angle that conveyed pride without haughtiness. Like every other aspect of her appearance, that angle had been carefully learned.

Madeline studied her, then nodded approval. "Perfect. You have hit the exact balance between the lady and the wanton.''

Diana's smile was crooked. ''In spite of all your thorough and embarrassing lessons on what gentlemen expect of mistresses, I feel more like a lamb pretending to be a lioness.''

''We don't have to go tonight if you don't want to,'' Madeline said gravely.

''But I do want to, Maddy,'' Diana answered, her soft voice resolute. ''Of course I'm nervous, but I'm eager too. Tonight I will enter a world that would otherwise be closed to me. Perhaps I won't like it and tomorrow morning I will be ready to fly back to Yorkshire. Then you can say, 'I told you so,' and I will nod in meek agreement as I embroider by the fire.''

The older woman laughed with loving exasperation as she surveyed her protégée. The girl had never looked lovelier. Though she was twenty-four, older than most aspiring courtesans, she retained the dewy freshness of a seventeen-year-old. At first Diana had found the crowds and clamor frightening after the Yorkshire moors, but after three months in London she had a superb wardrobe and a sense of ease in the bustling metropolis.

Madeline shook her head in admiration. If she knew anything about men, they would be clustered around the girl tonight like bees around a honeypot. Perhaps Diana would dislike the sensation enough to retreat before it was too late. ''You'll do, my dear,'' she said judiciously. ''You'll do very well indeed.''

Harriette Wilson's home was filled with men of the utmost respectability, and women with no respectability at all. All of the males present were rich or titled or fashionable, often all three, while the females were the *crème de la crème* of the demireps. Harriette herself waved casually as Diana and Madeline entered, then turned back to her court. Unlike most of the courtesan breed, ''The Little Fellow'' was confident enough of her own charms so that even Diana's stunning beauty did not make her resentful.

As they paused in the doorway to Harriette's salon, Diana suddenly froze with panic. For months she had worked toward this goal, questioning Madeline, trying to absorb the sometimes shocking answers. She had acquainted herself with her body, done strange exercises to strengthen internal muscles, and learned how to throw a knife for self-defense. But even though she had been a dedicated student, the goal had seemed distant, dreamlike.

Now reality was upon her. Until this moment she could have turned back at any time to safe respectability. But once she set foot in this room, a fallen woman among other fallen women, the die was cast; she would be a whore, even if she never took a penny from a man. For an instant she considered flight; Madeline would take her away and she could abandon her insane ambition.

Diana's fearful pause was as effective as a planned grand entrance. Men were turning to look at her, their expressions running the gamut from simple admiration to naked lust. There must have been at least twenty men staring at her, all of them richer, stronger, and more powerful than she, and Diana was terrified to immobility.

Then Madeline touched her elbow, silently offering support, and Diana's fears ebbed. Her breath eased out, her heart returned to its normal rhythm. Her entrance into this room might brand her a prostitute, but no man could have her without her consent. Lifting her chin, Diana entered the salon, Madeline half a step behind her. Within seconds men were approaching, eager smiles on their faces as they vied to introduce themselves. The voices jumbled together: "I'm Clinton . . . ," Ridgleigh, ma'am, very much at your service . . . ," "Major Connaught, m'dear, may I get you a glass of champagne?"

As she looked into their admiring faces, the evening suddenly seemed so simple, so enjoyable, that she could not imagine why she had been frightened. With a peal of delighted laughter she offered her hand to the nearest one, a short redheaded fellow with bushy side whiskers. "Good evening, gentlemen, I am Mrs. Diana Lindsay, and I would very much enjoy a glass of champagne."

The redhead reverently kissed her hand while a balding gentleman rushed off for champagne. The third man, dark, poetic-looking, and very young, simply stared at her, his mouth slightly open. They really did think she was beautiful, and for the first time in her life Diana felt the power of her own beauty.

The next hour or so passed in a blur. She and Maddy sat by the wall, surrounded by men vying for her attention. She needed to say very little, and every word she did utter was greeted as a brilliant witticism. It was delightful and she felt as bubbly as the champagne, but she was in no danger of forgetting what kind of gathering this was. Across the room, a dark woman and a man in an army uniform were engaged in such astonishingly intimate caresses that Diana was hard-pressed not to stare.

Seeing the direction of her gaze, Madeline whispered that the dark woman was one of Harriette's sisters; the Little Fellow was merely the most successful of a notorious clan. Eventually the couple slipped out together. Half an hour later they returned separately, the woman looking well-used but pleased with herself. Diana forcefully turned her thoughts from what had happened; if and when she did go with a man, it would be as a result of more than fifteen minutes' acquaintance.

"My dear Mrs. Lindsay . . ." The voice in her ear was gruff and a little hesitant, and she turned to look up into the face of the balding man who had stayed very close since she arrived. He was Ridgleigh, she recalled. She smiled with slow promise, the way Madeline had taught her. "Yes, Mr. Ridgleigh?"

He smiled back with fatuous delight. Incredible that her mere existence inspired such a response. After a long, dazzled moment, he said, "Lord Ridgleigh, actually." Clearing his throat, he added hopefully, "Are you looking for a protector, my dear girl?"

She studied him thoughtfully. He was middle-aged and stout, not repulsive, but certainly no Adonis. Still, he had kind eyes. When the time came to take a lover, she could do worse, but Diana was a long way from making that decision. She laid a light hand on his arm. "Perhaps I shall be soon."

Ridgleigh swallowed hard. "When you do . . . pray think of me."

The poor man looked as if he were about to melt, so Diana smiled again. "Would you be so kind as to get me another glass of champagne?"

He hastened off, eager to please her. At the same time, a Gypsy fiddle and a roar of encouraging voices sounded at the far end of the salon. A buxom black-haired beauty leapt onto a table and began to dance, her skirt swishing around her legs and her breasts threatening to burst from their restraints at any moment. A young man who wished to join her on the table was being held back by his friends, who were far more interested in watching the woman than a would-be partner.

During the moments when general attention was fixed on the dancing, Madeline leaned over and whispered, "You are doing splendidly, my dear. You could have your choice of any of these men. Did Lord Ridgleigh offer you a *carte blanche?*" At Diana's nod, Madeline continued, "You could do much worse. He's a pleasant man. Very generous."

Her eyes widening, Diana asked, "Was he one of your protectors when you lived in London?"

"Let me just say that we are not unacquainted." Maddy opened her fan and fluttered it as she chuckled. "You seem to be enjoying the worshipful attention."

"Is that wrong?" Diana said defensively.

"No, but remember that this is only one small part of the game of hearts. Those men don't just admire you, most of them want to bed you, and your presence here gives them every reason to assume you are beddable," Madeline warned. "Be careful. Don't let yourself be alone with any of them unless you are sure that is what you want. Most of these men would not force you, but they will certainly do their utmost to seduce you."

Diana smiled. "I shan't make a proper courtesan if I am too prim to run that risk."

A small line appeared between Madeline's brows, and Diana knew that her friend still doubted the wisdom of this course. However, Maddy knew better than to discuss it further. She stood and said, "Will you be all right if I leave you for a while? I want to talk to an old friend who just arrived."

"I'll be fine, Maddy." Diana gave a reassuring smile. "Truly, I'm a big girl now, well-trained by you to deal with all these mysterious male creatures."

After Madeline left, Diana spent a moment scanning the room. There must be thirty or so men present, and perhaps a dozen women. The crowd around her had eddied between three and a dozen, and four men were staying close in spite of the Gypsy dancer's lures. Lord Ridgleigh brought her the glass of champagne, murmured a fulsome compliment, then subsided into a nearby chair, content to admire her.

Now her attention was claimed by the young Byronic-looking Mr. Clinton. Turning his back on the dancer, he gazed at Diana in a manner much akin to a puppy's. He had said almost nothing to her, but now he managed to stammer out, "You are a . . . a goddess."

Laughing, she replied, "Quite right, Diana was a goddess, of the hunt and of the moon."

His reply was ardent. "You are justly named, for you have captured my heart. I shall call you the Fair Luna."

Diana was absurdly reminded of Geoffrey by Clinton's youthfulness. Despite his handsome face, she felt more like feeding him gingerbread than taking him as a lover. As she sought a reply that would kindly acknowledge his worship without encouraging him further, she felt a prickly sense of unease.

Glancing up, she saw a dark man in the doorway staring at her, his gray eyes as cold and sharply edged as a blade. Perhaps thirty years old, he was broad-shouldered and above average height, with an air of command and a taut intelligence visible clear across

the room. He stood utterly still, and the unwavering
intensity of his gaze was shockingly out of place in
this crowd of light-minded dilettantes.

Diana caught her breath, disturbed by those relentless eyes. She had been a focus of attention ever since
arriving, but no other man had watched as if he wished
to draw out her soul. His concentration was like a
hammer blow, and it struck an answering spark deep
within her, a spark of uncanny connection.

Then, as she absorbed the details of his stern figure,
time stopped. The two of them might have been alone
in Eden and Diana was aware of nothing but the dark
man and her own fiercely beating heart. That austerely
handsome face was as familiar to her as her own nightmares, and in a flash of fear and awe and tremulous
anticipation she knew why intuition had decreed that
it was better not to know her fate.

Just as surely, she knew beyond the shadow of a
doubt that this was the man she had come to London
to find.

The seventh Viscount St. Aubyn had been brought
to Harriette Wilson's much against his will. Two blocks
before reaching her house, he had said abruptly, "I've
changed my mind. I'll let you off and send my carriage
back to wait for you."

His cousin Francis Brandelin grinned. "Oh no you
don't, Gervase. It's taken weeks to get you this far,
and you'll not elude me that easily. You spend far too
much time on whatever it is that you do in the Foreign
Office. The government won't fall if you take an evening's pleasure, and Harriette has one of the best wine
cellars in London."

"I don't doubt that—it's a requirement for a demirep
of her standing," Gervase commented dryly. "However, if it's good wine I want, I can get it at home
more easily."

Francis laughed outright, undeterred by his lordship's attitude. "Perhaps you can get wine, but if you
want a replacement for that opera dancer of yours,
you'll do much better at Harry's than at home."

Though not sure that he agreed with Francis, Gervase did not dignify the remark with an answer. The opera dancer, Colette, had been no great loss. She had made it clear that she preferred more gaiety in her life, then been disconcerted at how quickly Lord St. Aubyn had agreed that he neglected her shamelessly and she could do better elsewhere.

Still, any demirep Gervase found at Harriette Wilson's was apt to have Colette's faults—volatility and greed—in spades. The most successful courtesans were even more temperamental and demanding than society ladies, not at all the kind of mistress he sought. He knew exactly the sort of woman he wanted; she should be reasonably attractive, undemanding, and uncapricious. Perhaps a woman with children who would occupy her attention, so she would not always be pining for her protector's company. He had no objection to children so long as he needn't see them.

Well, it wouldn't kill him to spend an evening sipping Harriette's wine, and he owed it to Francis. The younger man was a sociable sort, and he had undertaken to ensure that the new viscount didn't become a hermit. His cousin was his heir, an easygoing, intelligent young man whose light brown hair and slight, elegant figure came from his mother's side of the family, not the dark, intimidating Brandelins. As a child Francis had looked up to his older cousin, and they had corresponded all the time Gervase had been in the army in India.

When the new viscount returned to England after his father's death, he had felt very alone and Francis' genuine welcome had been like sunshine on a rainy day. It had been gratifying to find someone who cared whether Gervase lived or died. Though they were very different, they had developed a friendship that went well beyond mere blood kinship. Gervase asked idly, "Have you given any thought to marriage?"

In the flickering lamplight Francis' expression was more than shocked, and it was a moment before he replied in a tone whose lightness seemed forced. "What makes you ask that, cousin?"

The viscount said reasonably, "Well, you are my heir and you will inherit someday. Life being uncertain, I would like to know that the succession is assured for another generation."

After a narrow look, Francis said with amusement, "Isn't taking care of the succession your responsibility?"

The carriage halted at their destination and Gervase was glad to let the subject drop. It sounded like Francis was disinclined to matrimony; perhaps it was a family failing. Someday the viscount would have to explain exactly why he himself would never have legitimate heirs, but it was a topic he preferred to avoid as long as possible.

The butler bowed them in without comment since Francis was a regular visitor to the establishment. Sounds of laughter and music floated down the stairs as Gervase followed his cousin up to the main drawing room.

Just before they entered, Francis asked, "Shall I introduce you around, or would you prefer not to stand on ceremony?"

"No need to put yourself out," Gervase replied. "I'm sure I know most of the men, and more than a few of the women."

On entering the large salon, Francis made an immediate line for his hostess, whose curly black head was barely visible amongst her admirers. Gervase lingered in the doorway, scanning his surroundings with the automatic caution of a soldier who has campaigned in hostile territory.

He had met Harriette Wilson before, and privately considered her to have the manners of a rude schoolboy, though there was an undeniable charm in her exuberant vitality. At the far end of the room, a dark Gypsyish dancer stamped and whirled with a young officer of a Highland regiment who should have known better than to dance on a table in his kilt. Or perhaps he was merely advertising himself in the same way that the women were.

Then Gervase's casual gaze reached a cluster of people directly opposite the door and he stopped dead, feeling a constriction around his heart. The girl in the center of the group was half turned away from him, and there was a purity in that flawless profile that answered every man's dream of innocence. Eve before the serpent, the virgin who lures the fierce unicorn to her hand, the loving maiden who comes chaste to her marriage bed. . . .

She was all of those things, and none of them. Even as he stared in helpless admiration, his mind echoed with the harsh words, " *'Tis a pity she's a whore.*"

The emotion he felt was a complex mixture of grief and anger that such sweet innocence was a lie and a delusion. What right had this girl with tumbling chestnut hair to imply that dreams could take flesh? Because, of course, she was a whore; in this company, she could be nothing else. There was no innocence in the lush body alluringly concealed and revealed in clinging blue silk, or in her posture, which made it amply clear that she was available if the price was right.

He put aside anger, reminding himself that he wasn't here to find a dream, a virgin, or a wife, but a mistress. The woman's presence in this place meant that he might have her without any of the complications and disillusion that dreams entail. The primitive male part of him that was so deeply aroused would have carried the girl off like the Romans did the Sabine women. Only slightly more civilized was the impulse to cross the room and ask, "What is your price?"

But the great courtesans were notoriously fickle and would scorn a man who assumed that money alone could buy them. Just as a beautiful woman was a prize that a man could parade before his fellows, the demireps flaunted their own conquests to each other. Gervase had never bothered with such women, having no interest in playing the flirtatious games required, but as he saw the girl lay a graceful, teasing hand on the arm of a youthful admirer, he decided that this time he would make an exception.

Then she turned, her deep blue eyes meeting his with an impact that reverberated through his entire body. A beauty, a whore, and a mystery all at once.

With no further thought he cut across the salon. She watched him come, those incredible blue eyes holding his as if they were the only two people in the room.

Gervase scarcely noticed the men he pushed between. The girl stood as he approached, her posture erect and graceful as she held out one slim hand. He clasped it for a moment, feeling the coolness of her tapering fingers before he bowed and brushed his lips lightly above her knuckles. A slight tremor ran through her hand and he wondered if she too felt something like the tidal wave engulfing him. More likely her silence was merely clever policy, the queen allowing the suppliant to speak first.

Retaining his grip on her hand, he straightened and stared down into her face. She was below average height, the top of her head not quite reaching his chin, and she had a slim waist that emphasized the ripe curves of breast and hip. Close up she was as flawless as she had appeared at a distance, her features exquisitely sculptured, her silken skin begging to be touched. As she regarded him gravely, her full lips were a promise, even though she neither talked nor smiled.

Her cheekbones were high and dramatic under wide, delicately tilted eyes, and one glossy ringlet fell forward to emphasize her bare shoulders and the soft swell of breasts revealed by her low-cut dress. He had never seen hair of such color, a rich shade like polished antique mahogany. She wore no jewels and required none; like a perfect lily, she needed no gilding.

They stood like statues for an endless moment. Gervase saw a pulse beat under the creamy skin at her throat, and her eyes widened, the lapis-lazuli depths showing some emotion he could not identify. Tightening his hold on her hand, he drew her from her circle of admirers, saying only, "Come."

Murmurs of protest, half-amused, half-angry, sounded around him. Without turning his eyes from the woman, he said, "I shall return her shortly." He led her into the relative privacy of a window embrasure, where others could see them but not overhear.

She moved with the effortless grace such beauty deserved.

Gervase still held her hand, and her nearness was playing havoc with his ability to think. Beginning with the most basic of information, he said, "I am St. Aubyn. And you?"

"I am Mrs. Diana Lindsay."

Her voice was as lovely as her face, sweet and musical, unmarred by a provincial accent. She could have been a duchess, except that no duchess had ever been so beautiful. An elusive fragrance of lilac surrounded her, and it reinforced the illusion of innocence that she simulated so well. The part of him that was not quite overpowered by her presence noted cynically that she was going to be very, very expensive, but Gervase didn't care. Instead he asked a more polite version of what he had thought earlier. "What does it take to win you?"

His voice was deep and resonant, equally suited to caress or command. Diana's heart beat with unnatural speed and she inhaled deeply, struggling for the composure that she desperately needed. What had she expected him to do, ravish her? Accuse her of harlotry? Declare love undying? While she had instantly known this man was her fate, clearly the recognition wasn't mutual.

It was better this way. She disengaged her hand without haste. "You may court me and find out."

The strong dark brows arched up. "Court you? I have not come here for a wife."

"Nor did I come for a husband," Diana said blandly. "You and I have simpler aims. If you don't like the word 'court,' choose another. Phrases are unimportant. What matters is that if you want me, you must please me."

Lord St. Aubyn's gray eyes narrowed, the skin tightening over the high, wide cheekbones, and she felt his withdrawal. "So you can amuse yourself watching suitors scramble for your pleasure while you set one against another, like cocks at a fight? No, thank you, madam, I will not play that game."

So he had pride, more than was good for him. That was no surprise; pride was written in every line of the lean body that moved with the deadly smoothness of a hunting cat. There was not an ounce of spare flesh anywhere on him, from broad shoulders to flat waist to muscular legs. Everything soft and unessential had been burned away, leaving only unyielding masculine strength.

Diana wondered if his lordship knew how to smile, and if he did, whether amusement would provide the life that could make those cool, regular features handsome. Commanding herself not to be intimidated by his overpowering closeness, she said calmly, "I have met many men tonight, and you are the only one whom I have invited to come closer."

As he relaxed fractionally, she added, "I will make you a promise, my lord. On further acquaintance I may decide that you will not suit me, but I will never make sport of you."

He smiled faintly and the lightening of his dark features did make him austerely handsome. "I hope that is true. There is a great deal that I will not tolerate, even from a woman of your quite remarkable beauty."

"And there is a great deal I will not accept, even from a man of your no-doubt-remarkable wealth," Diana answered with an edge of irritation in her voice.

Surprise touched his dark face for a moment. Then his smile widened. "You have a high-handed way with you, Mrs. Lindsay."

"It is merely wise commerce, my lord," she said, shifting her weight gracefully from one foot to the other. Motion rippled the silk dress across her body and she could see by his tension that he noticed, and was affected by, that subtle display.

With a mischievous desire to discomfit him further, Diana shifted the conversation to a more intellectual plane. "Like any merchant, I seek to sell what customers demand. Since the market can be a profitable one, I would be foolish not to negotiate the best possible terms for what I sell."

His lordship's mouth quirked with amusement. "But

surely your price is threatened by too large a supply of cut-rate goods? They say that in London, one woman in ten is selling the same product that you are, and that doesn't count women who supply the same service for free, or under lifetime contract."

Diana laughed. "You are confusing two different commodities. Many women sell their femaleness, but women of unusual beauty sell dreams."

There was an odd, disconcerted look in his eye as he murmured, "Not only bold but vain."

Diana raised her brows. "Is it vanity to know one's worth? I am a merchant, with only a few short years to sell my wares before time diminishes the value. Why should I not seek the best price?" St. Aubyn had alarmed her at first, but she was beginning to enjoy the discussion. She had never talked to a man this way, and the combination of intellectual banter and erotic undercurrents was powerfully stimulating. "Money is important, but most of the men here will pay well, so why should I not choose to please myself in other ways?"

"It's a compelling argument," Lord St. Aubyn said dryly, "but if your standards are too high, perhaps I will be unable to meet them. I should regret that very much."

In spite of the lightness of his words, there was an intensity about him that Diana found threatening. It was only the primitive part of her that believed in fate; on the surface, this was a business transaction and the choice to proceed was hers. With a coolness to match his, she said, "Then try to meet my standards, Lord St. Aubyn. Charm me, make me feel beautiful and desirable. Or is charm not an attribute that you have cultivated?"

He reached out one hand and touched her cheek. His fingers were warm and strong, and Diana was acutely aware of his powerful masculinity. Her body responded with a melting warmth that spread and weakened her, that made her wish to open her arms and yield to his wishes. It was utterly different from anything she had ever experienced before, and she was suddenly frightened, not of this dark man with cool eyes and warm hands, but of herself.

St. Aubyn said softly, "No one has ever accused me of charm, but I do have other attributes." Then he lifted her chin with one finger and bent his head to kiss her, his mouth warm on hers, undemanding but infinitely promising. Their bodies did not touch, and the fierce current of mutual attraction was concentrated between their lips with a force like wildfire.

Diana had feared her first kiss, both the intimacy itself and the risk that she would betray her inexperience. Now her heart began pounding. She had not known a kiss could be like this. Oh, no, most certainly she had not expected this. His clear gray eyes were so close and intent that surely he must see her dizziness, must know that she desired to press against him, to discover if that hard body was as warm and welcoming as his lips.

There was no room in her for fear, and Diana was both relieved and bereft when he lifted his head and dropped his hand. She stepped back, wanting to put more distance between them. Grateful that her voice was steady, she smiled faintly, as if such kisses were as common as breathing. "I will set that to your account. It goes some way toward compensating for other lacks."

There was a flash in his eyes and she wondered if she had angered him, but then he chuckled. "When you retire from your present trade, you can become a clerk in the city, keeping accounts and totaling figures."

Amusement still in his voice, he surveyed her lazily. "You are clearly something of an expert when it comes to figures." Before she could respond to the double entendre, he asked, "Do you ride?"

Diana hesitated. "I have, but it was some years ago and I do not keep a hack in London."

"That is easily remedied. I can mount you if you consent to go riding with me."

More double meanings. Diana colored faintly, but

she was determined to be his equal in aplomb. "In that case, I should be delighted to join you."

"Tomorrow morning, then, at seven o'clock?"

Usually Diana breakfasted with Geoffrey before he went to school, but she had known that her new enterprise would cause changes in her domestic schedule. She would compensate by spending more time with him later. "Very well, my lord, seven o'clock tomorrow, number seventeen Charles Street."

He gave a nod of satisfaction. "I shall bring a horse suitable for a lady who has not ridden in some time."

"Thank you, my lord." With a slow, teasing smile, she added, "It is not necessary that the beast be a complete slug."

"I shall bear that in mind: one horse, gentle but not sluggish. Now, let me return you to your admirers."

St. Aubyn offered his arm and Diana tucked her hand into the elbow of his dark blue coat. Even through the layers of heavy fabric she felt the taut power of that arm and she shivered slightly. Madeline had told her that the drug of sexual desire could bring a strong man to his knees, but surely that was not true of a man such as this. His strength was not merely physical; there was determination and quiet control behind those clear, icy eyes. He might desire her, but it was impossible to imagine that he would let any woman hold power over him.

Uneasily she remembered that Madeline had also said that desire might equally bind a woman to a man. Diana had not believed that could happen to her, who had lived so well without physical passion, but now she was not so sure. Glancing up at St. Aubyn's stern profile, she thought of Lord Ridgleigh, with his kind eyes and obvious desire to please.

Diana shrugged fatalistically as St. Aubyn returned her to her chair, then bowed and took his leave. On one level, she had the freedom to choose whomever she wished as a lover, but on another level, she had no choice at all. There was no wisdom or calculation in her response to the dark lord; she knew only that fate had bound them together.

4

SOME of Diana's admirers looked reproachfully at her for having permitted another man a kiss; more attempted to lure her into a quiet corner where they could take similar liberties. Resisting their blandishments, she quickly teased them into good humor again. Getting Madeline into a good mood later in the evening was another matter. The older woman had seen the byplay with St. Aubyn, and as soon as they left in their carriage she gave vent to her feelings. "For heaven's sake, Diana, why did you let him single you out in such a public manner?"

"I'm not a seventeen-year-old with a spotless reputation to protect. Quite the contrary," Diana said mildly. "Besides, I was in full view the whole time."

"Yes, and in full view of everyone, you let him kiss you."

"I didn't precisely *let* him."

A torch outside the carriage briefly illuminated Madeline's exasperated countenance. "That makes it worse. If you wish to succeed as a courtesan, you must be in control of what is happening, not succumb to every passing advance."

"I succumbed to only one."

"But with St. Aubyn, of all people!"

"Is there something wrong with him?" Diana asked curiously. "Did you know him when you lived in London before?"

"No." The shake of Madeline's head was felt rather than seen in the dark. "I made inquiries this evening after he left. He was in India for some years in the army, returning home a couple of years ago when he inherited the title.''

"Well?" Diana prompted. "What did you learn? Is he a gambler who has lost the family fortune, or a scoundrel despised by honorable men?''

"Nooo," Madeline said slowly, "nothing quite so obvious.''

"I am going riding with the man tomorrow morning, so if you wish to persuade me to avoid him, you had better speak more clearly." Diana spoke with a trace of unaccustomed sarcasm.

Madeline sighed. "People react oddly when he is mentioned. He seems to be a cold man, respected, but perhaps not much liked." After a long silence she added, "They say he is the principal spymaster of the government, and that he drove his wife mad and keeps her locked in a castle in Scotland.''

"Heavens," Diana said with a lift of her brows. "How gothic! Is there any evidence for such charges?''

"Not really," Madeline admitted. "I questioned as many people as I could, and no one is even sure that he is married, but since the rumor is persistent it must mean something. St. Aubyn seldom goes out in society, and there was considerable comment when he appeared at Harriette's tonight." As an afterthought she added, "He's very rich.''

"Of the things you have just told me, what makes him an unsuitable choice as a protector? Certainly not his wealth.''

The carriage pulled up in front of the house and Madeline didn't answer as they entered and climbed up to the older woman's rooms. The third floor contained two suites, each with bedchamber, sitting room, built-in closets, and bath chambers with the incredible luxury of fitted tubs. In the past the front suite had been Maddy's, but now she preferred the back because it was quieter. Geoffrey and Edith had the floor above, and the female servants lived in the attics.

Diana felt compunction when she saw the fatigue on her friend's face. In spite of her restored health, Maddy was no longer young, she had been very ill, and this return to her old life must be a strain even without her concern for her protégée. Sitting Madeline down, Diana poured a glass of sherry for her, then pulled the pins from her friend's dark hair and began brushing it out.

When Madeline was more comfortable, Diana asked again, "Why would Lord St. Aubyn be such a poor choice for a lover?"

"Because of the kind of man he is: cold and unloving. Even if he is not a spy and never had a wife, he is unlikely to make you happy." Madeline sighed and closed her eyes. "You will allow that I know more about men and love than you do?"

"Of course I will admit that." Diana unfastened Maddy's dress, then helped her into a soft red wrapper. With a sigh of relaxation, the older woman curled up in the chair while Diana poured a glass of sherry for herself, then sat on the sofa opposite Madeline and began to unpin her own hair. "Now, tell me, why does St. Aubyn disturb you so much?"

Maddy absently twisted the stem of her sherry glass. "My strongest objection to your entering this life is that you are too emotional, too loving. I doubt your ability to let your head rule your heart where a lover is concerned. A successful courtesan must have some detachment. The worst thing she can do is to fall in love with her protector." With a crooked smile she added, "I did that. I can't recommend it."

Diana gazed into the amber wine. "Can love ever be wrong?"

Madeline shrugged wearily. "It may not be wrong, but it is often painful. It won't keep you warm and comfortable in your later years when your lover has discarded you for a younger woman or retired to live piously with his wellborn wife."

Diana had always suspected that something more than illness had driven Madeline from London two years ago. She said with gentle compassion, "I'm sorry. Is that what happened to you?"

Madeline was silent for so long that Diana thought she would not answer. Finally she said, "Not really.

Nicolas was my last protector, for over seven years. His evil-tempered wife lived in the country so we were able to spend much of our time together in London. He was the one who bought this house for me, and he was here more often than in his own home.''

She sipped her sherry, lost in her memories. Then she said bleakly, "He wanted to marry me. Isn't that droll?''

"Not in the least,'' Diana answered quietly, drawing her fingers through her long tresses to loosen the snarls. "You are lovely and kind, a desirable wife for any man.''

The candlelight caught a gleam of tears in Madeline's eyes. "It is not quite unknown for a man like him to marry a woman like me. After all, Emma Harte became the British ambassadress to Sicily by marrying Sir William Hamilton, and she was no better born or behaved than I. Society's high sticklers might have cut Nicolas and me, but that wouldn't have bothered either of us.''

Her face tightened. "But Nicolas was not free to marry. His wife was far too cold a woman to be guilty of misconduct, so there was no possibility of divorce. Still, we were happy until his wife decided to end his relationship with me, threatening to ruin him with his family and their children.

"He was badly torn. He did not want to give me up, but everything in his life was being weighed on the other side of the scales.'' She rotated the fragile stem of her sherry glass between stiff fingers. "I have wondered if my grief at the situation had something to do with my illness. I have seen it before, how unhappiness leads to bad health.'' Lifting the glass, she drained it, and Diana silently rose and poured more.

In a stronger voice Madeline said, "I left London, partly so that he would no longer have to choose between me and the rest of his life, partly so that he wouldn't have to see me die. You know the rest.''

"I see.'' Diana was silent for a moment. "Is your Nicolas still in London?''

Madeline shook her head. "No, that is the first thing

I inquired about once we arrived here. He is living entirely at his estate in the country now. I would not be going out in public if there were any chance of meeting him.'' With sad finality she whispered, ''I couldn't bear to see him again. Nothing has changed. Or at least, I haven't. Perhaps he has. I hope so. It would be easier for him if he no longer loves me.''

Diana's face reflected her compassion. It was typical of the older woman's generous spirit that she wished her lover free of the sorrow that she herself still suffered.

Maddy sighed. ''Do you understand better why a courtesan shouldn't fall in love with her protector? There may be moments of joy, but those are few compared to the pain. There are so many ways in which a grand passion can be disastrous, and almost none in which it can bring happiness. It is far better to have a protector who is a friend, or one whom you love only a little.''

''If St. Aubyn is as cold as you believe, do you really think I could fall in love with him?''

''I think you will fall in love with any man you choose as your lover,'' Madeline said bluntly. ''It is a bad habit women have, and you are more vulnerable than most. You yourself don't know how much you are crying out to be loved, and to love back.''

''But I have a great deal of love in my life . . . Geoffrey, Edith, you,'' Diana stated with maddening calm. ''Why are you so sure I will fall headlong for a man just because we are lovers?''

''Sexual love is very different from love for a child or a friend. No matter how powerful those other loves are, they don't fill the basic need of a woman to have a man.'' Madeline leaned forward a little, her voice earnest. ''Please, trust my judgment on this and don't become involved with St. Aubyn. Choose a man like Lord Ridgleigh. He isn't half so handsome, but he will adore you. Or that lovely boy Clinton, who will write poems to your eyebrows. Even if there is pain at the end, it won't be devastating and you will have some happy memories of the affair.''

She shook her head wearily. "I've known men like St. Aubyn. Certainly he is attractive and can afford to pay generously for the privilege of keeping you. He may even provide pleasure in bed. But he will give you little kindness, and less love."

Diana drew her knees up on the sofa and linked her arms around them, leaning her head forward. Her voice low, she said, "I'm sorry, Maddy. I daresay you are right, but . . . this is something I must do."

"Good God, Diana, *why?*" Madeline exclaimed. "Whenever something really important is at issue, you just look mysterious and say that it is something you *must* do. We are supposed to be friends, yet I have no more idea what is in your mind than if you were a Chinaman. You have intelligence—why the devil can't you use it?"

Diana's face paled and her voice was unsteady when she replied. "I'm sorry, I know this is hard for you, and I know that you are doing your best to save me from unnecessary grief."

She stopped, trying to find some way to explain. Eventually she replied, choosing her words carefully, "It isn't a matter of intelligence, you know. I can read the poets and philosophers and talk about them wittily, but that is just the mind.

"Underneath, I am all emotion and instinct, and they are what rule my life. I can no more understand why there are some things that I must do than I can explain why the wind blows. I knew that I must come to London and try the life of a demirep, and I know now that I must see more of Lord St. Aubyn. I'm sorry." Her voice broke and she finished in a whisper, "I would be different if I could be."

Madeline could feel the younger woman's unhappiness as sharply as if it was her own. She thought of Diana as the daughter she had always longed for, and knew the grief of all parents who wish to save their children from suffering. Maddy sighed. Diana was vulnerable, but she was also strong, with her own deep wisdom. She had already survived grief and loss, and doubtless she could survive another unfortunate love affair. Most women had more than one broken heart in their past.

"I'm sorry, my dear, I'm trying to make you wise, when I failed so miserably at it myself. If you must, you must." She smiled, remembering how the Viscount St. Aubyn had reacted to Diana. "Sometimes men like St. Aubyn have fire under the ice. If any woman can find it, it will be you."

"Perhaps," Diana said quietly. "We shall see." Tightening her arms around her knees, she gazed into space for a time. Maddy was justified in her charge that she hid the inner workings of her mind. Diana had never been able to talk about what was deepest and closest to her heart; only when the issue was resolved could she discuss it. But there were some things that could be shared. "For what it's worth, after months of pondering I think that now I understand why I was so determined to pursue the life of a courtesan in the first place."

Madeline shifted to a more comfortable position. "Yes?" she asked encouragingly.

"You yourself gave me the idea. When you spoke of the life, it sounded . . . free, in ways I have never known," Diana said. "And . . . I didn't want to live the rest of my life without a man. You know how limited the prospects were in Cleveden. In London, there are choices, both in men and way of life, and I found the idea exciting." Her smile flashed mischievously. "I also liked what you said about sex and beauty giving a woman power. I found that most appealing."

"So appealing that you are comfortable exposing your son to this life?"

"You know better than that, Maddy," Diana retorted sharply. Her voice faltered. "That above all concerned me. Success as a courtesan would mean money for his future, perhaps influence if I meet powerful men. He is happier here in his school than he has ever been, and with luck I can retire and return to respectability before he is old enough to realize what I am doing."

She could hear the defensiveness in her voice, and

she ducked her head to conceal tears. If it hadn't been for Geoffrey, becoming a courtesan would not have been the agonizing decision that it was. Not a day went by when she didn't worry about the possible long-term consequences to her son.

"I'm sorry, my dear," Madeline said apologetically. "I shouldn't have said that. It's just that I can't help worrying about how this will turn out for you and Geoffrey. Still, come what may, you know that I will always be here to help you put the broken pieces together again."

Diana subsided wearily into the corner of the sofa, suddenly exhausted by the night's events. For better or for worse, forces had been set into motion that could not be recalled. She could only pray that her intuition was not leading her astray.

Leaving the carriage for his cousin, Gervase chose to walk back to his Curzon Street town house. London at night was not the safest of places, but veterans of the Mahratta Wars were not easily intimidated. As he walked through the cool night air, he wondered why he was reacting so strongly to a pretty face. Francis was right: it was time he took a new mistress.

A pity he could not be free of females entirely, but Gervase needed a regular woman in his life. While temperance in food and drink came naturally to him, his body's other fierce, compelling desires could not be suppressed or ignored. Some men could live comfortably as monks; although the viscount envied them, he was unable to do the same. The deity who had given him so much in the way of worldly goods had also condemned him to a regrettable amount of sexual passion.

In India he had kept a slim native girl with dark almond-shaped eyes and an astonishing sexual repertory. Sananda spoke seldom, waited on him like a servant, and asked nothing for herself. The viscount had supported her and her entire family for years, and left them with enough money to buy two thriving shops. The girl had been properly grateful for his financial generosity, but if she had personal regrets about his departure, she concealed them well.

In many ways, keeping Sananda had been ideal, since she made none of the emotional demands an Englishwoman would. Here in London it would be easy to find a dissatisfied wife of his own class for an affair, but such women required time and effort for wooing, and wanted lying words of love that he had no desire to speak. Gervase disliked the lower grades of prostitutes, both for the possibility of disease and the bleak expression sometimes seen in their eyes, a resignation to pain that reminded him uncomfortably of the pathetic child he had married.

Rationally, he knew that he should look for a mistress who was unfashionable and grateful for financial security. He was a fool to waste time on an exotic, expensive ladybird like Diana Lindsay. Still, as he remembered her sensual body and the flawless face with its deep, beckoning eyes, he acknowledged that one could overdo rationality; what was the point in having money if he didn't indulge in an occasional frivolous luxury? And he had never seen a more attractive frivolity than Diana Lindsay.

St. Aubyn House was a dull but imposing pile, far too much space for a single man. Gervase let himself in with his own key. It had taken him months to convince his servants that he often preferred privacy, but he had eventually prevailed. A lamp waited on a pier table in the vestibule, and he lifted it.

He was restless, not ready for bed, and rather than go upstairs, he stepped into the drawing room. It was a masterpiece of lofty proportions and rich decoration, a room designed for giants or gods. Overhead a coffered and painted Italianate ceiling soared two stories above the giant Oriental carpet that had been custom woven to fit the space, and there was a carved marble fireplace at each end of the room. Scattered about were groupings of graceful furniture that had been built to the designs of Robert Adam.

Crossing the drawing room, he entered the book-lined study. This had been his father's particular haunt, and when Gervase had returned from India the faint scent of the late viscount's pipe tobacco had still lingered. Yet there had been no sense of the man himself. It was not surprising, really; even in life, father and son had touched each other only in fleeting and formal ways.

On impulse Gervase began silently prowling through the house he had inherited. The servants were in their own territory at this hour, and the endless halls and chambers were deserted as he paced their lengths. The high ceilings and hard floors reflected his quiet footsteps as hollow echoes. No denying the place's splendor, with its elaborate molded ceilings and restrained classical detailing. The ballroom was immense and silent, unused since his mother had died fourteen years earlier. The main staircase curved to the ground floor in two wide, opposing arcs and was allegedly the grandest in London. His mother had looked magnificent sweeping down it, jewels sparkling in her golden hair and on her white shoulders.

Though Gervase owned this building and everything in it, he felt no sense of kinship or pride of possession. If this splendid mausoleum truly belonged to anyone, it was to the anonymous housemaids who polished the furniture and sanded the floors and kept it in this state of sterile perfection.

Even after two years, he felt like a stranger here. It had been depressing to return to this cold house under England's damp skies; he sometimes thought that Britain had acquired her colonies so that her citizens could live in warmer climes and still be under the British flag.

On the five-month voyage home, Gervase had toyed with the thought of selling St. Aubyn House and seeking more modest accommodations elsewhere, but had reluctantly decided against it. This house was part of the St. Aubyn inheritance and must be passed to Francis or his heirs when the time came. His cousin had a sunny, uncomplicated disposition; in time he would marry and have a family to warm these cold rooms.

And they were cold, in spite of the carved marble

fireplaces, cold with a chill deeper than the physical. Gervase wondered idly who had built this mansion and lived in it, and whether anyone had ever been happy here.

For himself, the viscount expected neither warmth nor happiness. In India he had learned to expiate his sins with the rewards of work well done, of duty and honor fulfilled, and that must be enough. He had built a useful life for himself, regulating the welfare of his dependents and participating in the affairs of the nation. Much had been given to him, and he had a responsibility to use it well.

Only gradually did Gervase realize his true goal in this late-night prowl: his mother's rooms, which lay behind the master's apartments. Perhaps because he had been thinking about women, he decided that it was time and past time to face his mother's ghost. He had invested the last eight years in developing his strength so that he would not be afraid to face anything in his life.

Medora, the Viscountess St. Aubyn, had been the daughter of a duke. She was as graceful as she was charming, as corrupt as she was beautiful. It was eighteen years since he had seen her, eighteen years since he had set foot in these rooms, yet even now he could almost see her floating across the chamber, hear the echo of her bright, heartless laughter.

As a child he had adored his mother, and was grateful for the casual gestures of affection she sometimes made, despairing when she would turn angry or petulant. He had been too young to realize how little her moods depended on him, and had blamed himself for his failures to please her.

In his mother's sitting room, still decorated with faded panels of the rose silk she had favored, hung the portrait. Gervase stood in the doorway with one hand braced against the frame and studied the painting. It had been done by Sir Joshua Reynolds and was full-size, so lifelike that it seemed Medora could step down from the wall. The viscountess was dressed in figured white silk and had disdained hair powder to let her natural golden hair fall in ringlets around her shoulders.

Gervase was also in the picture, six years old and gazing up at his mother with his dark head in profile. The child's presence lent a false impression of maternal feeling. The real reason Medora wanted him there was for his worshipful expression; she was a woman who needed to be worshiped.

Even after twenty-five years he remembered the sittings vividly, how her friends came to visit and she would laugh and joke with them, to Reynolds' intense disgust. Gervase himself was silent, happy to spend so many hours in her presence and determined to do nothing that might cause him to be sent away. Once one of her friends had complimented Lady Medora on how well-behaved the boy was and she had said carelessly that her son had been born middle-aged. Many times he wondered if that was a compliment or an insult; even now he didn't know. Doubtless it was merely a quip, with no deeper meaning.

For all her look of white-and-gold innocence, Lady St. Aubyn had been a wanton, an expert at indulging her appetites within the broad range permitted the nobility. She had dutifully given her husband two male heirs. The elder had died in early childhood, and the younger now stood and studied his mother's face, trying to understand what had made her what she was.

Medora Brandelin was the only person Gervase had ever loved, and that fact had meant nothing to her. Less than nothing. Thinking back, he believed that her crime against her son had been unthinking and unmalicious, a casual product of curiosity and boredom. It was doubtful that she ever knew or cared what she had done to him.

It was gratifying that he could finally look at her dispassionately, the scars so well-healed that he felt no more than a distant ache. Now he could bury his mother in the same dark well of memory that held the farce of his marriage. That lesser catastrophe had haunted him on and off for years, but he had done what he could to mitigate the damage. According to his lawyer, the afflicted child he had married was alive and in good health.

Even now, he hated to think of what a fool he had been to let himself be trapped into a travesty of marriage; if he had not been drunk, it would never have happened. But in retrospect, the incident was less disastrous than he had thought at the time. The girl Mary Hamilton had gotten an income and probably better treatment than she had known earlier in her life, and Gervase had learned a bitter lesson in self-control. In the years since, he had governed himself with an iron hand, never once overindulging in drink or any other disabling vice.

The marriage was also a perfect excuse for withholding himself from the mating rituals of society. If he were single, Gervase would be considered highly eligible, a tedious and time-consuming fate that he was now spared. While he revealed to no one the true facts of his marriage, a few discreet hints about a mad wife in Scotland had discouraged fortune hunters.

He was tired now, ready for bed, but he took one last look at his mother's portrait and found himself snared by the mocking eyes. Her full knowing lips were slightly parted, as if about to divulge secret thoughts, thoughts he had no desire to hear.

Gervase turned sharply away. Tomorrow he would have the portrait boxed and shipped to Aubynwood. The housekeeper could hang it somewhere, anywhere, as long as Gervase would never see it again.

A night's sleep cleared Gervase's gloomy thoughts, and he was filled with anticipation as he rode through Mayfair, leading a trim gray mare behind him. Briefly he wondered if the mysterious Mrs. Lindsay might have changed her mind; dawn rides were hardly common among her kind, who usually had ample reason to lie abed in the morning.

The Charles Street address she had given him was a handsome, discreet house nestled in a street of aristocratic residences only a few blocks from his own mansion. On the outside there was nothing to indicate

the occupation of the inhabitant; Mrs. Lindsay must
be very good at her trade to have earned such luxury.
Or perhaps a man leased it for her, a thought that
didn't please Gervase.

As he swung from his gelding and looped its reins
over the iron railing, the door opened and she came
down the short flight of marble steps. Gervase had
wondered if she could really be as beautiful as he had
thought the night before, but in the clear morning light
she was even lovelier than he remembered.

If the glow in her deep blue eyes meant anything,
Diana Lindsay had slept the sleep of the just. Her
darkly shining hair was primly pulled back into a chignon and she wore a severe navy-blue riding habit with
a matching hat, its curling cream-colored plume the
only frivolity in her appearance. The very simplicity
of her dress emphasized her stunning face and sensual
figure, and Gervase could feel his loins tighten at the
sight of her. With some effort he kept his voice even.
"Good morning, Mrs. Lindsay. You are very
prompt."

She glanced up demurely. "I guessed that one of
the many things you do not tolerate from your inferiors
is tardiness."

As she stopped three feet away, he found that he
was having trouble with his breathing. If she wanted
a thousand guineas for one night, it would be worth
it. "You are quite right, Mrs. Lindsay, I dislike being
kept waiting." Turning, he gestured to the gray mare.
"Here is your mount."

Her eyes widened, as well they should. The mare
was as fine a thoroughbred as any in Britain. "Oh,
she's a lovely lady. What is her name?"

"She's called Phaedra, but you may change that if
you wish."

Diana turned to him questioningly. "What do you
mean?"

"She is yours." Gervase was gratified by the widening of the woman's eyes; her confusion was a small
compensation for the havoc she was wreaking on him
by her mere existence.

Diana withdrew the admiring hand she had laid on the mare's neck. "I cannot accept her. There is no agreement between us, and I wish no obligation to you before I make my decision."

Gervase was amused by the way she was playing Miss Propriety; she clearly forgot the first lesson of whoring, which was to take any and all gifts offered. "The mare is a gift, not a payment. There is no obligation."

She gave him a long look, level in effect even though she had to look up to meet his eyes. "We shall see. Please help me mount."

Gervase bent over and laced his fingers as Diana put one hand on the second pommel and lifted her skirts to ankle height, then set her left foot on his hands. Lifting her up into the sidesaddle, he noticed that her feet and ankles were as shapely as the more visible parts of her.

It was customary for a man to help a woman adjust her skirts when she mounted, and that simple task was fraught with possibilities. Diana tensed, wondering if her escort would touch her leg or knee. As he hesitated, she could almost see him weighing his desire to do so. She wondered what it would feel like to have those strong tanned hands on her, but he merely adjusted her skirt without brushing the limb beneath the fabric. She was both relieved and disappointed.

St. Aubyn spend a moment shortening her stirrup, then swung onto his own mount. He might be as cold as Madeline said, but he was the model of politeness. He also rode with the unconscious skill of a centaur. Diana resolutely concentrated on her own riding, but could not help thinking that a man on a horse showed to the best possible advantage.

At this hour the fashionable streets of Mayfair were almost empty, which was a blessing for someone who had not been on a horse for years. The mare had beautifully smooth gaits and was a joy to ride, and after they had traversed the short distance to the green precinct of Hyde Park, Diana threw back her head and laughed from pure pleasure. The dark man beside her was as frightening as he was attractive, she was a country girl far out of her depth in dangerous waters, yet it was good to be alive.

Signaling the mare into a canter, Diana enjoyed the wind in her face for half a mile before slowing into an easy trot. St. Aubyn had matched his horse's pace to hers, and she turned to him and said gaily, "Phaedra is perfectly named. It means 'the bright one,' doesn't it?"

The dark brows rose fractionally. "You know Greek?"

Diana hesitated, wondering if she had made a mistake, then decided not. The more of an enigma he found her, the better. She gave him a teasing smile. "Small Latin and less Greek."

"You are a woman of parts, Mrs. Lindsay."

"Even a demirep doesn't spend all her time on her back, my lord," she said with a hint of acidity.

That drew a smile from him. "Of course not. Time must be spent at the opera, being noticed, and driving in the park, being ignored by respectable ladies. There must also be time to pamper your priceless face, and to gossip with the other Cyprians about who is worthy of your attentions."

Coloring slightly at the accuracy of his words, Diana said stiffly, "You seem to know a great deal about women."

"On the contrary, I know nothing at all about them." There was no mistaking the cool withdrawal in his voice.

Surprised at how quickly his mood had changed, Diana studied him unobtrusively as they trotted their horses side by side along the wide path that would be jammed with horses and carriages later in the day. St. Aubyn's profile was as stern and handsome as a marble god's. Madeline was right, it would be far more reasonable to choose a simpler man. A pity that Diana was not a reasonable woman.

It was late September, and the leaves were coloring in the loveliest and most fragile season of the year. As they turned their horses for the ride back, St. Aubyn asked, "How old are you, Mrs. Lindsay?"

"You want to know my age?" she asked in surprise. After a moment's thought she said, "I'm not sure I should tell you. A demirep's age is a professional secret."

"I'm not interested in chapter and verse," he said impatiently. "I merely want to be sure that you are over sixteen. I prefer not to take children to bed."

So he didn't like to seduce children. An interesting fact, and to his credit, since there were so many men who lacked his scruples; a lord had seduced one of Harriette Wilson's own sisters away from home when the girl was only thirteen. Lightly Diana said, "I think I have just been complimented. You need have no fears on that score. I was twenty-four last June 24."

"Midsummer Day?" he reflected. "That would explain it. You must be a fairy changeling, for you have more than mortal beauty."

Diana flushed. His matter-of-fact tone made the compliment more meaningful than any of the lavish words whispered in her ear the night before. "Thank you, my lord, but I assure you that I am quite mortal. Mundane, in fact. If you look beyond the surface, there is nothing at all unusual about me."

"But it's the surface which interests me," he murmured, his gray eyes lazily surveying her, lingering on her breasts and waist. It was the most thorough examination she had ever received, and did nothing to reduce the color in her cheeks. Well, such looks were part of her new life. She had given up the right to wax indignant at a man's insolence, though St. Aubyn's appraisal was not so much insolent as frank. Very, very frank.

"To get the surface, my lord, you must also accept the rest of me," she said in a tone between warning and amusement.

They were leaving the park, and the streets were busier now, as wagons and peddlers began their rounds. "I have a name, you know. Whenever I hear

'Lord St. Aubyn,' I think someone is looking for my father.''

"And what is your given name, my lord?" Diana asked, though Madeline had already told her.

"Gervase Brandelin. I would prefer you to use that . . . Diana."

"I have not given you leave to use my Christian name, my lord, nor am I ready to use yours." Diana's voice was firm, but mentally she considered the name "Gervase." It had a soft romantic sound that didn't fit the hard-edged man who rode beside her. Or did he have a tender side that he showed only to intimates? As they rode into the stableyard behind her house, she decided there was only one way to find out if that were true. But not yet.

It was still early enough that the little yard was empty, the groom inside eating breakfast. Dismounting from his own horse, St. Aubyn went to Phaedra's side and reached up to help Diana down. His hands were firm on her waist as she slid off her mount, and he didn't let go even when her boots were solid on the ground. Tartly, Diana said, "I can stand without aid, my lord."

"I have no doubt of that," he said softly, his voice deep and husky. "But don't you know why men take ladies riding? It creates . . . opportunities."

She was mesmerized by the cool fire of his eyes as he loomed above her. His body was mere inches away, and she felt his warmth radiate through the chill morning air. He bent over to kiss her upturned face, and she permitted it, ready for another lesson in the trade she had chosen.

At first his kiss was as undemanding as the one he had given her the night before, and even so the effect was unnerving. She learned that a hard man could have soft lips. Diana closed her eyes, savoring the pleasure of what was happening and slowly working her mouth against his, tasting its contours.

Her simple response had an explosive effect on St. Aubyn, and his arms slid around her, pulling Diana close as his kiss intensified. The multiple sensations were dizzying and Diana clung to him, captivated by his explorations. She learned now how it felt to press against his muscular body, and the experience was as exciting as it was alarming. Her breasts crushed against his chest with a sweet ache that demanded freedom from the heavy riding habit.

His hand slid down her back, kneading her buttock and pulling her tight against him, and this new intimacy made Diana feel suddenly trapped, helpless in the face of his overpowering hunger. She tried to break free, but his arms held her too tightly. Pure panic set in, and Diana pushed violently at St. Aubyn, shoving at his chest with all her strength.

Releasing her immediately, he dropped his arms and stepped back, then turned away, placing both hands on the saddle of his own horse. His head was bowed and she could hear the unevenness of his breathing as she herself struggled for air, her lungs as strained as if she had been running across the moors.

Finally he turned back to her, his dark face bleak and controlled. "I'm sorry, I didn't mean to frighten you." He inhaled a deep, shuddering breath. "You have a . . . disconcerting effect on me."

She accepted his apology with a quick nod. It had been an excellent lesson in the power of male desire. Remarkable how a simple response on her part had triggered such a reaction from him. However, she had had quite enough lessons for one day. Nervously fingering her riding whip, Diana said quietly, "Please believe that I am not trying to play the coquette. I had not expected events to move so quickly."

His composure regained, St. Aubyn made a quick, impatient gesture with his hand. "Why can't we reach an agreement right now? You know that I want you, and you are not wholly indifferent to me. Name your price. If you want an allowance, tell me how much. Or if you prefer, I will make a lump-sum settlement. But let us waste no more time on preliminaries."

As she stared at him in all his male strength and arrogance, Diana was suddenly furious. "What you see as a wasteful preliminary is essential to me," she snapped. "If that is unacceptable, find another woman. As you yourself said, at least ten percent of the women in London are for sale." Lifting the skirts of her riding habit, she marched away from him. Without looking back, she said, "And take your gift horse with you."

She was almost to her back door when the deep voice called after her, "Wait."

Turning, she watched him tether the two horses before walking over to her. His face was twisted into a scowl, but she felt that his irritation was more with himself than her. He stopped an arm's length away and said haltingly, "I'm sorry; I told you that I know nothing of women."

The clear gray eyes were apologetic as they searched hers. "Until now, there has been no real reason to learn."

Diana softened. It could not be easy for him to apologize twice in as many minutes. Though she had looked forward to holding power over a man, the reality made her uncomfortable.

Encouraged by her expression, the viscount continued, "When and if we become lovers, I promise that some of my rough impatience will disappear." With the ghost of a smile he added, "Even if ten percent of the women in London are available, I don't want them, I want you. And your beauty is no longer the only reason."

If St. Aubyn meant to be disarming, he succeeded brilliantly. Diana released the breath she hadn't known she was holding and smiled in return. "I think we shall reach an agreement in time, my lord. Only, please do not rush me too quickly. I am not a woman of the streets who might earn a hundred guineas in a day at one guinea per man."

A touch of distaste showed on his face: a fastidious man preferred not to think of such things. Raising her eyebrows, Diana said, "Do not show contempt for my less-fortunate sisters, my lord. Remember that when the Empress Messalina challenged the greatest whore in Rome to see which of them could service the most men in a night, it was the empress who won."

He actually chuckled, the lightest expression she had yet seen from him. "I've never bedded a woman educated in the classics. Have you learned anything new from Ovid and Sappho?"

Diana realized that she was getting into very dangerous territory. Primly she said, "In some areas, there is very little new to be learned."

"Are you sure, Mrs. Lindsay?" There was definitely a mischievous glint in his eyes now. "I have lived in India. They are quite imaginative. Perhaps I might even to able to teach you a thing or two, despite your professional expertise."

If only he knew just how little expertise she had! Diana was finding this repartee more than a little alarming, so she said hastily, "I do not doubt that I can learn much from you, my lord." Extending her hand, she said, "If you will excuse me now . . ."

He took her hand and held it, his amusement gone and his dark face serious again. "When might I see you again? Tomorrow?"

She hesitated, trying to remember if she should seem willing or unavailable. Oh, the devil with it. "Tomorrow will do very well. Were you thinking of another morning ride?"

"I was thinking of something a little longer, perhaps a ride out to Richmond. We could make a day's expedition of it."

"I must be back before four, my lord." Geoffrey would be home from school and Diana always spent the late afternoon with him.

"Very well, Mrs. Lindsay, I shall call at ten o'clock." Still holding her hand firmly, he cocked a dark brow at her. "Do you have room for the gift horse in your mews?"

The blasted man was trying to pressure her. With less than total graciousness Diana said, "Since I shall be riding her tomorrow, she might as well stay here tonight. But she is a loan horse, not a gift horse."

St. Aubyn had the sense not to look triumphant as he bowed over her hand. "Until tomorrow, then."

His lips were a light, teasing touch that sent a shiver

up Diana's right arm, leaving a memory of warmth. As she entered the house, she realized that his lordship was not at all what she had expected. Under that fearsome control lurked surprising tenderness and consideration. Would she still feel bound to him if he had turned out to be harsh through and through? Perhaps not, but she was glad that the reality of him was so much more appealing than the first terrifying impression.

Well, Diana thought with wry fatalism as she removed her riding hat, she had wanted a life more exciting than she had led in Yorkshire, and it certainly looked like she was going to get it.

5

WHEN Diana entered the sunny breakfast parlor, Madeline and Edith both eyed her as if she were a wayward child. However, they refrained from questions as the younger woman returned their greetings, then helped herself to the eggs, toast, and tea on the mahogany sideboard. Their forbearance lasted until she had finished eating. Then Madeline asked with admirable restraint, "How was your morning ride?"

"Quite delightful." Diana smiled beatifically. "It is lovely to be up so early, before the city is stirring. Almost like being in the country again."

Knowing that her answer did not address Madeline's real concern, Diana replenished all three teacups, then replied more to the point, "Lord St. Aubyn was very gentlemanly."

Edith, who had a lively sense of humor under her dour exterior, gave a small chuckle as Madeline said with exasperation, "Of course he would be at this stage. But what happened? Did he make you any kind of offer?"

"Yes, but I told him it was premature." Diana poured milk, then stirred her tea. "He also brought a marvelous thoroughbred mare to give me. I told him that was premature as well."

Edith, who knew livestock as well as any man, was disappointed. "You turned down the mare? Pity, I would have liked to see her."

Diana tried sipping the tea, but it was still too hot. "Actually, the mare is in the stables now, but it's only temporary because we're riding out to Richmond tomorrow."

"It would appear that Lord St. Aubyn pleases you." Madeline's tone was carefully neutral.

Diana dropped her levity, knowing that Madeline's questions came from genuine concern. Gazing into her tea, she tried to summarize her impressions. "He is a moody man, but not perhaps as unfeeling as you think. I think he has been very unhappy."

Madeline said gloomily, "It's already too late, then."

Diana took a deep swallow of tea, then raised her eyes. "What do you mean?"

"Once a woman like you starts feeling sorry for a man, you're already on the way to being in love with him."

"Am I so predictable?" Diana's brows arched. "I thought I was looking for a lover, not another child to care for."

"Sympathy is the beginning of caring. Next comes the desire to heal the wounds cruel fate has caused." Madeline gave a wry smile. "It's not too far from there to believing that no one else can possibly love him as well as you do. And then you're lost."

Diana looked mutinous, but before she could reply, Edith said, "Finish your tea and I'll look at the leaves."

Diana obediently drank the rest of her tea in two long swallows, then closed her eyes and twirled the cup gently, thinking of Gervase, Lord St. Aubyn. It was very easy to visualize that taut face, the gray eyes that were usually cool but could warm with humor, the lean, muscular body. . . Hastily she opened her eyes again and handed the cup to Edith, sure that she had given the tea leaves plenty of energy to work with.

Edith gazed into the delicate china cup, her scarred face solemn and her eyes drifting out of focus. She claimed a Gypsy great-grandmother, and when the spirit moved her she would offer a glimpse into the future. While the readings were officially entertainment, they were always heard with great interest.

Her voice was deeper than usual when she said, "Fate," the word drawn out and distant. After a pause

that went on too long, she continued disjointed-
ly, "Anger, a veiled face, secrets that join and divide.
Lies and betrayals." Then, in a whisper, she repeated,
"Lies and betrayals . . . and love."

Diana felt chill fingers on her spine. Though she
chose to make light of Edith's words, in the past they
had been uncannily accurate. Madeline glanced over
and asked quietly, "Are you still sure you want to
become involved with St. Aubyn?"

Before Diana could answer, Edith said in her other-
worldly voice, "The lies and secrets are not all on
one side." Then she shook her head and said in her
pragmatic Yorkshire accent, "Whatever that means."

"I doubt it means anything at all," Diana said
crisply, rising from the table. "And if neither of you
has any more ominous hints or threats for me, I think
I'll go throw knives."

As an exit line it wasn't bad, and it was also the
literal truth. When Madeline had taught Diana what a
courtesan should know, the curriculum had included
many things, one of which was self-defense. Maddy
always had a knife ready at hand in her reticule, in a
sheath on her leg, or concealed near her bed. Three
times the weapon had saved her from great unpleasantness, and once it might have saved her life; the man
who threatened her had later strangled another mistress before killing himself.

The lessons had included how to grasp and how to
stab. *Hold it underhand and stab upward. If you stab
down, you're too easy to block and the blade will
glance off the shoulder or ribs and not do enough damage.* The knife-throwing lessons were intended to make
Diana more comfortable with the weapon; throwing
was not usually recommended for self-defense, since
it left the thrower disarmed. Also, if the distance was
too great, the knife lost force and might not strike hard
enough even if it hit the target.

Even though Diana hated and feared violence, knife
throwing turned out to have a hypnotic fascination. It
required concentration and was a soothing activity
when she felt disturbed, as she did this morning.

During her earlier years in London Madeline had turned a long narrow room on the fourth floor into a practice range. One end of the chamber was covered with soft pine boards to protect the wall, targets of various sizes and heights were fixed to it, and several swinging targets hung in front. The room was used only for knife throwing and the carpet and sparse furnishings were old, but a large window made the place bright and cheerful. Diana and Madeline practiced here regularly, with the room kept locked the rest of the time. Edith had tried her hand at knife throwing but found that the sport had little interest for her.

The special knives were made by an old Syrian man who lived in East London. While shaped more or less like a normal dagger, they were made of one solid piece of steel, with no separate haft. Because of that, the weapons were balanced so that they could be thrown by holding either the blade or the hilt, a most unusual characteristic. Both women had a set of six knives, in three different sizes. The lighter knives were easier for a woman to handle and to conceal, while the heavier ones struck with a more dangerous impact.

Diana thought with amusement how incongruous she would appear to an onlooker. She had changed to a white muslin morning gown, her hair was still primly woven back in a chignon, and she looked as ladylike as anyone could wish. Stepping up to the eight-pace mark, she swung her knife lightly to get the feel, then hurled it at a target. *Thunk!* It slammed dead into the center.

Diana wore strapped to her leg the embroidered sheath Madeline had given her. Turning her back to the target, she whirled, pulling the knife free and throwing it in one motion without stopping to aim. It landed half an inch from the first knife. For the next quarter of an hour she threw from different positions as quickly as possible; if she ever needed to do this in earnest, she was unlikely to have ideal conditions.

Knives spin in midair, and part of the skill lay in learning how to hit the target with the point rather than the hilt or edge. Different distances from the target allowed for a differing number of spins; a throw that might be accurate at five or eight paces would bounce off the target if thrown from six or nine. With time, a good knife thrower learned how to adjust for any distance and could hit the target every time. Diana Lindsay, for all her angelic appearance, was very, very good.

After she had warmed up, Diana started throwing at moving targets, which swung like pendulums and were a real challenge. Nonetheless, she hit nine out of ten in the center circle. When the door opened, she didn't turn until Madeline's amused voice said, "Are you imagining that I am the target?"

"Good Lord, Maddy, don't even joke about such a thing!" Diana went down the range to remove the six knives. It took time to wrench the two largest blades out; the heavier they were, the deeper they struck. Walking back to Madeline, she said, "I do find this relaxing, though I'm not sure I could ever throw a knife at another person, even to save my life."

"Would you be able to throw to save Geoffrey's life?"

"Yes," Diana said without hesitation.

"If a situation ever arises where you are threatened—which, God willing will never happen—just remember how much Geoffrey and the rest of us would miss you." Though Madeline's voice was matter-of-fact, her underlying emotion was apparent. "Save yourself first and make peace with your creator later."

Taking a knife from Diana, she hefted it, then hurled it at the largest target, where it struck quivering three inches from the center. Not pinpoint accuracy, but still a good throw.

Smiling mischievously, Diana took another knife and hit the same target dead center. Madeline chuckled. "I've created a monster. You have the best eye I've ever seen." Taking another knife, she placed it less than a half-inch from Diana's.

Diana laughed. The tension that had existed between them earlier had vanished. "You've never told me how you got started with this. I can understand having a weapon around for self-defense, but why knife throwing? It's such a strange, barbaric skill.''

Madeline smiled wickedly and threw at the moving target, which was swinging back and forth. Her weapon hit off-center and the target spun wildly on its rope, but the knife held. ''I thought the story too warm for your innocent ears. Now that you've entered the trade, I suppose I should enlighten you.''

''How can the story be warmer than some of your other lessons?'' Diana asked in amusement as she sat down in one of the worn chairs at the end of the room opposite the targets. ''I still can't look at a parsnip with a straight face.''

Both women laughed. Madeline had used a parsnip as a teaching aid when describing what a courtesan would be expected to know, reducing first Diana, then herself, to helpless giggles. The lessons had been most enlightening, though Diana sometimes had trouble believing all that Madeline had told her.

''In the past, I talked mainly of what is considered normal.'' *Thunk!* Another of Maddy's knives hit a stationary target. Though she complimented Diana's extraordinary natural skills, she herself was very nearly as good. ''However, some men have tastes that are extremely . . . unusual.'' *Thunk!*

As Madeline went to the end of the range to retrieve the knives, she continued, ''I once knew a gentleman who was incapable of sexual congress in the usual way. However, knives excited him enormously. The first time he visited me, he pulled out two Indian *kukris* and started waving them around. They're wicked, great curving knives, and I thought I was going to be murdered.''

Diana inhaled sharply. Though Maddy was telling the tale with humor, it must have been terrifying. No wonder her friend was so adamant that her protégée learn to protect herself.

Returning to Diana's end of the room, Madeline laid the knives on the side table and sat down. ''After the gentleman threw both of the *kukris* into my washstand, which did it no good, he could perform in quite the normal way.

"The first time that happened, I was alarmed, but he was a pleasant man apart from this oddity." She brushed a tendril of dark hair back from her face. "He suggested that watching me throw the knives would be even more exciting for him. Being an obliging sort, I learned how. It was an interesting and useful pursuit, so I continued even after we parted company."

Diana was round-eyed with wonder. "I hadn't realized quite how far one had to go to please a customer."

Madeline grimaced. "Believe me, this particular idiosyncrasy was harmless compared to some. There are things even the most hardened streetwalker will refuse to do. I'll tell you more about that sometime, so you will be better prepared for what might be asked. Don't ever let a man talk you into something you find distasteful. It isn't worth it."

She chuckled suddenly. "The only real danger in throwing knives for my friend's pleasure was the risk of getting lung fever in midwinter. He liked me to do it naked, you see—I always had the fire built up when he was coming."

"It all sounds very . . . interesting," Diana said faintly. At times like this, she wondered if she was capable of performing as a courtesan. At heart, she was really a conventional creature.

Sobering, Madeline said, "There aren't many men like that, and soon enough you will know how to deal with them. The most difficult part will be your first time. No amount of my teaching will compensate for lack of experience."

"I've been thinking, and I have an idea about how to obscure my lack of skill," Diana said tentatively. In a few sentences she described what she had in mind.

Madeline nodded, impressed. "An excellent idea. You may have a natural talent for this trade after all." She stood and stretched her arms wide over her head. "I'm walking to Oxford Street to look for some plumes. Care to come with me?"

"That sounds delightful," Diana said. "I'll fetch my shawl."

The rest of the day was equally uneventful, with time spent sewing, discussing the week's menus with Edith, and listening to what Geoffrey had learned that day. But that night, after putting her son to bed, Diana once more entered the world of the demirep. Several of Madeline's old friends shared a subscription to an opera box, paying two hundred pounds a year for the privilege of having a shop window for their charms, and Maddy had secured an invitation to join them.

As they entered the first-tier box, Diana saw heads swiveling toward them. She wore shimmering gold silk tonight, a luxurious color that made her hair darkly bright and her skin glow like a peach. The outfit was designed to be noticed, a task it accomplished very effectively. Society ladies ostentatiously turned their heads away, though some took furtive glances, studying the kind of women who lured men away from their homes.

The men were much bolder, staring or squinting through their quizzing glasses in open appraisal. As she slipped into a velvet padded chair, Diana's attention was caught by a man seated directly across the pit in a box on the same tier. He stared with a dark intensity that reminded her of St. Aubyn, but closer study showed that he was a stranger. The man caught her looking at him and gave a slow, knowing smile. She flushed and turned away before remembering that a Cyprian should encourage such interest.

The people in her own box were a merry crew. A regular subscriber, Juliette, was there with her protector, an aging dandy who kept one hand possessively on his mistress's bare shoulder. Juliette had a circle of regular admirers, a fact that afforded her protector great satisfaction.

Some of the men Diana had met at Harriette Wilson's came to pay their respects, and each of them brought friends who begged an introduction and hovered until Diana could scarcely breathe. It was both flattering and alarming. She was learning how to smile and chat with several men at a time, but it was an effort, and she worried about appearing rude by accidentally ignoring someone. Young Mr. Clinton, for example, was so shy that she made a point of drawing him into the conversation.

Diana was beginning to feel faint from the heat and the crowding when a sibilant French-accented voice cut through the babble. "A flower of such perfection will wilt if not allowed air. Would you care to take a turn in the corridor, *ma belle?*"

Glancing up, Diana saw the man who had caught her eye across the opera house. He was darkly handsome, with hooded black eyes, and an exotic, un-English air. Except for his immaculate white shirt and gold-headed cane, his broad, powerful frame was clothed entirely in black, with an elegance just short of foppishness. Inclining her head, Diana said, "Sir, I do not know you."

Without taking his gaze from her face, the newcomer commanded, "Ridgleigh, introduce us."

Lord Ridgleigh, Diana's middle-aged admirer of the night before, performed the introduction unenthusiastically. "Mrs. Diana Lindsay, the Count de Veseul."

"Now will you walk with me, little flower?" the count asked lazily, extending his arm.

Eager to escape the crush for a few minutes, Diana rose and placed her hand on his black-clad arm. "If you gentlemen will excuse me, I will be back shortly," she said with a warm smile that included her entire court. Ridgleigh and the others drooped a bit at her defection, then began discussing horses, that never-failing topic of masculine interest.

Since it was between intervals, the corridors were almost empty. Diana inhaled deeply. "I am grateful for your suggestion, my lord. It is much cooler out here."

"Do you enjoy your first visit to the opera, *ma fleur?*" His voice was sibilant, and for a large man, he was very light on his feet. Though wide and solid, the count gave the impression that his exquisite tailoring concealed muscle, not fat.

Diana glanced up, catching the black gaze intent on

her face. "How did you know this was my first visit, my lord?"

"I attend often," he said, directing his attention to the corridor ahead. After another dozen paces he mused, without looking at her, "You are quite the most beautiful woman I have ever seen. I would surely have remembered you."

"You do me too much honor, Monsieur le Comte."

They reached the end of the corridor, where it curved around the outer edge of the building. No one else was in sight. Remembering Madeline's warning about being alone with a man, Diana felt a touch of uneasiness. Though the Frenchman was attractive, something about him disturbed her. She turned, anxious to go back to other people, but Veseul blocked her retreat, effectively trapping her in a corner.

"Stay a moment, *ma fleur,*" he said softly, his dark eyes examining her in intimate detail. "I have a small matter of business to discuss with you."

His broad, black-clad bulk seemed enormous as he loomed over her, and Diana suppressed a faint tremor, telling herself not to be childish. Veseul was being perfectly polite. Besides, he was hardly likely to attack her in such a public place. Though if he did, the music and conversation were so loud in the opera house that a scream might go unheard. . . .

Concealing her unease, she smiled coolly. "I am listening, my lord. Do you have a proposition for me?" After a mere twenty-four hours as a courtesan, she had already received several such offers and could feign nonchalance.

Sliding his hand to the middle of his ebony cane, he raised the stick and, with the delicate grace of a cat playing with a mouse, caressed her face with the gold knob. The warmth of his hand was still in the metal, and the intrusive intimacy of it revolted her. She tried to withdraw from the cane, but her back was already against the wall. As she stood rigid with distaste, Veseul drew the gold knob across her cheek, tracing the line of her jaw, then ran it across her throat with just enough pressure to suggest what it would be like to have her breathing stopped.

"If you wish to win my approval, stop doing that," she snapped. Ignoring her words, he stroked the cane across the creamy skin exposed by her low-cut gown before pressing it hard into her breast. The knob was skillfully wrought into the head of a serpent, its polished shine almost matching the golden silk of her dress. Diana gasped and shrank back, feeling more assaulted and soiled than if Veseul were mauling her with his hands. Grabbing the cane with both hands, she pushed at it with all her strength, but his wrist was as unyielding as iron.

The count's eyes followed the path of the gold serpent as it traced a circle around her left nipple, but at her angry gesture they flickered up to meet hers. Without withdrawing the cane, he murmured, "I really must have you. What is your price?"

Revolted and furious, Diana snapped, "Accustom yourself to disappointment—it is too late for any business between us. I do not give myself to mannerless men." She stepped sideways and tried to walk around him, but the cane shot out, hitting the wall with a sharp crack and blocking her with a breast-high barrier.

His sibilant voice heavy with menace, he said, "I have not given you leave to depart."

Diana lifted her chin and glared at him. "I am not subject to your wishes or desires, nor ever will be. Let me pass."

He smiled then, a lazy smile all the more chilling for its genuine amusement. "If you dislike me so much, you would be wiser to yield to me immediately. When I was introduced to you, an hour of your company would have sufficed. After just this little interchange, I will want a full night to have enough of you."

Lifting the cane away from the wall, Veseul pressed it above her heart. Diana sucked in her breath, trying to pull as far away from him as possible as he drew the golden serpent down across her belly, then pushed it into the juncture of her thighs in a quick, obscene gesture. The wall was cold against her bare shoulders and she clenched her hands against their trembling.

His musical French accent was quite lovely as he continued, "The longer you withstand me, the more I will want of you. It is quite simple. Come with me now. In the morning you will be the richer, and I will have satisfied my desires."

Diana's breath came in shallow gasps. She was insane to put herself in a position where she must endure this, and a fool for not having one of the knives she had learned to use so well. Madeline's warnings had not seemed quite real to her, but now, for the first time, Diana could imagine doing violence to another human being. The thought of slashing Veseul's complacent, evil face was less unbearable than the idea of submitting to him.

She struggled to sound calm and unafraid, but there was a tremor in her voice as she shook her head and whispered, "No. Not tonight, not ever. I will never give myself to a man I despise."

He laughed lightly, the cane holding her to the wall like a pinned butterfly, his black eyes mesmerizing. "Your wishes have nothing to do with the matter. I promise that I will have you. And the more you despise me, the sweeter it will be."

Diana drew her breath in for a scream, but before she could make a sound, he dropped the cane and stepped back. As calm as if he had not just threatened her, he executed a graceful bow. "Many thanks for your company, *ma fleur*. I look forward to our next meeting."

Diana darted away around him and fled down the corridor. The Frenchman watched her disappear around the curving wall with a faint smile of satisfaction. He was glad that she had resisted him; the more she prolonged the waiting, the more exquisite his ultimate satisfaction.

She really was extraordinarily beautiful, with her Madonna face and perfect, sensual body. He looked forward to savoring every silken, resisting inch of her.

6

STROLLING couples were emerging from the boxes for the interval, and Diana slowed her flight, trying to regain her composure as she mingled with the laughing, flirting crowd. The incident with the Count de Veseul was so bizarre that she wondered briefly if her fear was a wild overreaction to what had happened. After all, he had merely propositioned a courtesan and touched her with his cane. Was that so very dreadful?

Shaking her head, she rejected her doubts. A sense of horror lingered from the encounter, and she had learned more about perverse desires in the last ten minutes than in all Madeline's lessons. She stopped outside the box for a moment, her hand pressed against her solar plexus as she tried to master her nausea. Even now, knowing that she was placing herself in a position where her worst nightmares might become reality, she could not turn back from what she had begun. The intuition that ruled her life insisted that her only hope for a complete, happy life lay in London, pursuing the life of a fallen woman.

Diana's admirers greeted her enthusiastically when she entered the box. With an effort she smiled, trying to appear as if nothing had happened. These men appeared so simple and wholesome compared to the dark depravity of the French count. Clinton gazed at her with his sweet, puppyish adoration and Ridgleigh shyly asked if he could get her anything to drink.

Before Diana could answer, Madeline's clear voice said, "Diana, my dear, would you mind terribly if we left now? I have a bit of the headache."

Madeline looked perfectly healthy, but her shrewd

eye must have seen Diana's distress. Diana willingly seized the excuse to leave, and the full complement of admirers escorted the two women downstairs and kept them company while the carriage was called.

On the ride home, Diana haltingly described what Veseul had done, her voice breaking entirely when she described the horrible violation of his cane. Madeline held her until the trembling ended and Diana could finish, sketching out the rest of the incident in sparse, painful words.

At the end of her recital, Diana said, "I'm being childish, aren't I, to be so frightened?" She craved reassurance and would have welcomed a light dismissal of the incident.

Madeline's response was very grave. "I'm sorry this happened to you so soon, my dear. Six months from now, you would have been better prepared for such outrageous behavior." She tightened her arm around Diana protectively. "As I've often said, sex can arouse dark and dangerous emotions. Veseul sounds like the kind of evil man that is every courtesan's nightmare."

The older woman sighed before continuing with determined optimism, "Still, in spite of his threatening words, Veseul will probably forget your existence quickly, especially if you avoid public places where he can see you and be tantalized."

With a touch of acid, she added, "Demireps go to the opera for admiration and new customers, so there's no need to advertise yourself further if you've set your heart on St. Aubyn."

"I'm not sure yet if I will accept St. Aubyn," Diana said wearily. "At the moment, retiring to a convent looks appealing."

Shrugging with a rustle of fine cashmere, Madeline replied, "While I wouldn't advocate a convent, it's not too late to change your mind about becoming a Cyprian."

Taking Diana's silence as encouragement, Madeline continued with growing enthusiasm, "Returning to the moors is not the only choice, you know. We can take a house in a provincial city where no one will ever know of your flirtation with infamy. We can find Geoffrey another school just as good as Mr. Hardy's. You can make friends, become part of a society that is less grand, but perhaps more honest. Even I might pass as respectable.''

"No, Maddy," Diana said, gently breaking into her friend's planning. "I will continue what I am doing, at least for a while. Veseul is despicable, but he is only one man and I should be able to avoid him easily enough. All the other men I've met have been most kind, not frightening like him.'' She stopped a moment, then added with a note of surprise, "Do you know, I rather enjoy being admired.''

Madeline laughed. "It is pleasant, so long as one doesn't take it too seriously.''

"Never fear," Diana said dryly. "I've heard too many sermons on vanity and how physical beauty is inevitably doomed by the passage of time to let my head be turned.''

Madeline smiled in the dark of the carriage. Perhaps that comment explained Diana's remarkable lack of conceit. If the girl had always been admired and made much of, she might not have become such an unassuming and generous person. Madeline had had her share of both admiration and vanity, and knew very well that she lacked Diana's essential sweetness. But while she herself would never be mistaken for a saint, she could protect her protégée from the wickedness of men like Veseul.

Though Diana's state of mind improved after a night's rest, she was less than enthusiastic about her proposed expedition with Lord St. Aubyn. Still, since she wanted to discover what manner of man lay behind that stern, controlled mask, spending most of the day with him should be very instructive.

When he called precisely at ten o'clock, Diana was waiting in the salon with Madeline, and she thought that the viscount looked singularly grim for a man embarking on a day of pleasure. She was disconcerted, but reminded herself that on the previous day he had become more relaxed and less forbidding as time passed. If he had done that once, he could do it again.

She stood and offered her warmest smile, and his cool gray eyes softened as he bowed over her hand. Good; his lordship was willing to be pleased, although perhaps it was the fit of her riding habit and not her smile that affected him.

"You are very punctual," she said. With a gesture of her hand, she added, "I don't believe you met my friend Miss Gainford the other evening. Madeline, Lord St. Aubyn."

The viscount and Madeline eyed each other rather warily but exchanged polite greetings. Since St. Aubyn might be underfoot in the future, it seemed advisable that they become acquainted. Perhaps if Madeline approved of him more, she would drop her regular pleas for Diana to retreat to respectability.

Outside, the viscount helped Diana mount Phaedra, then asked as he stood by her stirrup, "Are you suffering ill effects from yesterday's ride, Mrs. Lindsay?"

Diana glanced down with a rueful smile. "Some unmentionable parts of my anatomy are reminding me of how long it had been since I last sat on a horse."

The taut planes of his face relaxed a little, and his gray eyes twinkled. "I'm not surprised to hear that. After I'd been five months on a ship, I noticed the same thing myself."

The twinkle became more wicked as he gravely added, "If you think that massage might help any of your unmentionable parts, I will be delighted to offer what assistance I can."

With equal gravity Diana murmured, "A noble and generous offer, my lord, but I prefer to struggle bravely on unaided."

With that, he chuckled and swung onto his own horse. "There was nothing the least bit noble or generous about my offer, and well you know it."

Effortlessly he brought his horse next to hers, so close their knees almost touched. "I should have realized you would be sore today. If you prefer, we can do something other than ride, perhaps hire a boat and go up the river.''

Diana was touched; she wouldn't have expected him to be so considerate. ''You are very kind, but I shall do well enough when I've warmed up. I hadn't realized how much I missed riding until yesterday. My body will just have to become accustomed to it again.''

''Does that mean that the loan horse is now a gift horse?'' he asked as he started his mount down Charles Street.

''No, but riding her does weaken my resolve,'' Diana admitted as they headed west toward Richmond. ''Phaedra is by far the finest horse I've ever been on. I'm surprised you let a rider of unknown skills on her back.''

''So am I,'' Gervase said with more honesty than tact; he had suffered a pang giving Phaedra to a virtual stranger. Too late he realized that his companion might be offended by his doubts of her skill and he gave a questioning glance.

The wonderful blue eyes were brimming with mirth. ''I assume you don't believe in wasting time on fine false phrases?''

''No, I don't, though I try not to be rude.'' He thought a moment, then qualified, ''At least, I prefer my rudeness to be intentional rather than accidental.''

She laughed outright, a chime-sweet sound that made him want to join in. ''That is honesty with a vengeance, my lord. Are you intentionally rude often?''

Impossible not to smile at her. ''No, not too often. I prefer to use rudeness only when I wish to make a point.''

They were riding through a street market, and conversation stopped as they carefully threaded their horses through the crowd. Though Mrs. Lindsay seemed to enjoy his company, Gervase felt off-balance and unsure of himself. None of his previous mistresses had required anything resembling a courtship, but then, he had never pursued a high-level Cyprian like this one, and he had no idea what she expected of him.

For the first time in his life, the viscount wished he had studied the art of flirtation. Did the lady want witty repartee? Florid compliments? Declarations of undying passion? He hoped not; while she certainly inspired physical passion, he had no intention of perjuring himself with lies of love. A major reason for consorting with lightskirts was to avoid untidy emotions.

The streets were less crowded as they headed away from the commercial districts, and Gervase slanted a look sideways at his companion. The woman was so heart-stoppingly beautiful that his brain seemed to go blank whenever he was around her. Riding showed off her profile to great advantage, both the classic symmetry of chin and brow and the less classic but charming little nose. Diana's shining mahogany hair swept back from her face before falling in a riot of curls down her dark blue riding habit, and she looked misleadingly young and innocent. Even in repose, her full lips seemed on the verge of smiling.

Gervase remembered how those lips felt beneath his, then forced his attention back to the road. He would never make it through the day if he didn't suppress his lustful thoughts. She was undermining his prized self-control with remarkable ease, and he didn't like it one damned bit. With the iron discipline that he had been perfecting all his life, he forced his mind into other channels. Fortunately, Diana now offered a topic that helped distract him from contemplation of her charms.

"Where did your five months on shipboard take you?" she asked as they slowed their horses behind a small flock of sheep.

"India. Five months out and five months back—almost a year of one's life just to go and return."

"India!" she said dreamily, her eyes distant. "I've always been fascinated by it. Were you there a long time?"

"About five years. I was in the army under Wellesley." As oncoming traffic thinned, they circled the sheep and moved into a trot. "I returned two years ago, after my father died."

"Did you like India?"

Gervase hesitated before replying. "It's difficult to talk about India in terms of like and dislike. Everything is so very different. Even the sunlight is different, harsh and yellow, not like the cool blue light of England." His voice trailed off as he thought of how much he had changed in those years. He had gone to India in anger and depression, lived with danger and discomfort, and returned to England his own man at last.

When Diana's soft voice said, "Tell me about it," Gervase began to talk. For the rest of the ride to Richmond, he spoke of India's wonders, her killing heat and poverty, her teeming cities, her strange religions with their sometimes moving, sometimes sickening rites. None of his acquaintance, even his cousin Francis, had shown more than a passing interest in India, but Diana's grave attention led Gervase to say more than he would have thought possible. As he talked of his one expedition to the north, where he saw the mountains called the Roof of the World, it occurred to him what a strange conversation this was to have with a whore.

Even as he thought the word, he winced away from it. While the term might be accurate, it was too coarse a description for Diana, who displayed the elegance and erudition of a great lady. Underneath she was undoubtedly as crude and grasping as the rest of her breed, but she concealed it well.

When he came to the end of his discourse, she sighed happily. "I am reminded of the kingdom of Prester John."

Gervase was surprised that she knew the medieval legend. Prester John was the mythical ruler of a fabulous Oriental land of gold and marvels, a Christian king surrounded by barbarians. The story was probably inspired by Ethiopia, but had been romanticized far beyond any earthly kingdom.

"Yes, India is as exotic as any medieval legend," he agreed. "As a boy, I was always fascinated by such tales. I had a book about Prester John and I used to dream about him and his solid gold throne. Perhaps that is one reason I went to India.''

Diana absorbed his words in silence. So the hard-eyed man of the world had been a boy who dreamed of marvels? It was an endearing image, one that made her think of Geoffrey.

They were entering Richmond Park now. A great palace had once stood here, and the forested land had been a royal hunting preserve. Now people came to walk in the woods or gallop their horses with a freedom impossible in the city parks. Autumn marked the trees, where the first leaves glowed yellow and gold in the bright midday sun. Abruptly Gervase said, ''Where do you come from, Mrs. Lindsay? There is a hint of the north in your voice.''

Diana threw him a teasing glance. ''Women like me have no past, my lord, nor a future either. We exist solely in the moment. Shall we see if Phaedra can outrun your horse from here to the end of this trail?''

Without waiting for an answer, she urged the mare to full speed down the open park trail. Gervase was caught unawares and she had a lead of fifty feet before he started after her. As he kicked his horse into a gallop, he felt a mild irritation at the way she had evaded his question. In the past he had never been curious about his mistresses, but he found himself wondering about Diana Lindsay, about what background could produce such dazzling beauty and apparent refinement, about what had led her to practice the oldest profession.

Shrugging off his questions, he concentrated on catching up with her. Diana's long chestnut hair flared back like a banner and she coaxed a very pretty turn of speed out of Phaedra without using her whip. While it was not to be expected that either the mare or her rider could match Gervase and his mount, Diana did surprisingly well, and he defeated her by only a short head.

She was unconcerned at her loss. ''You have the advantage of me, my lord. What shall you claim as your prize?''

"I will think of something," he said absently, admiring the glowing color that the wind had brought to her cheeks. Glancing at the sun, he said, "It's past noon. If we ride down the right fork here, we'll come to the inn where I've bespoken a meal."

Amiably they trotted to the riverside inn. Diana admired the effortless way that her escort had arranged the details, from the private parlor that overlooked the Thames to the excellent food and wine, perfectly chosen to feed active appetites without being too heavy for people who would be riding back to the city.

As she finished the tangy raspberry fool that ended the luncheon, she wondered if he would take advantage of the privacy to press his attentions on her. The thought held more appeal than alarm; she had covertly watched him through the morning's ride, admiring the grace and strength of his whipcord body.

Smiling at one of his remarks, Diana sipped at her wine before making some light rejoinder. Most of her attention was focused on the man across the table. Since she had decided that he was to be her fate, she might as well enjoy what destiny offered. The planes of his face were beautifully sculpted, the cheekbones high and wide. The light gray eyes were clear and penetrating under rather heavy brows, his dark hair too thick to be entirely under control. For all his seriousness and sometimes fierce expressions, she had seen signs of kindness in him, and sometimes laughter as well.

The reality of Gervase Brandelin was tantalizing. She could imagine his deep voice soft with endearments, his hard body fitting against hers, his desire flaming hers. Nervousness laced her anticipation, but that touch of disquiet increased the excitement she felt at the prospect of giving herself to him. The question was no longer *if*, but *when*.

In the same tone that he might have used to a ninety-year-old grandmother, he said, "Would you like to walk in the oak forest before we ride back to London? The trees are some of the oldest and finest in Britain."

Abruptly Diana realized that she was a little drunk. The three glasses of wine must be responsible for her vivid fantasies. How embarrassing; while she was sitting here melting with anticipation, the wretched man was stone-cold sober and perfectly collected. As if she cared a fig for oak trees.

Her daydream crashed into anxiety and her hand trembled slightly as she finished her wine and set the goblet back on the table, sure that she had done something wrong and St. Aubyn no longer desired her. Though Madeline had explained the facts, the essence of what made a woman desirable must lie beyond Diana. The idea that he didn't want her was surprisingly hurtful, and it took an effort to shape her lips into a polite smile. "I would like that. I've never been to Richmond Park before."

The shady woods were as lovely as Gervase had said, a green cathedral of ancient oaks where fallow deer flitted across the trails and drifting motes of dust were illuminated by shafting sunlight. Her wine-volatile spirits lifting amidst such beauty, Diana stooped to pick up a bright yellow oak leaf. Rolling the stem between her hands, she said dreamily, "I half-expect to see a ghostly procession of druids coming toward us."

"There may be some druid shades here, but more likely the ghosts are royal Plantagenets, and Tudors, hunting for deer."

Gervase's voice was prosaic, but her glance showed that his face was not; his usual impassive expression had given way to undisguised desire. With intense relief Diana knew that her fears were unfounded, that he was no more indifferent to her than she was to him. Still a little giddy with wine, she said playfully, "Were deer the only creatures hunted in this forest?"

"Oh, no," he said softly, "there is fairer game than that." He reached out to her, but she lightly whisked herself away behind the massive trunk of the nearest oak, then peeked out at him from behind the tree, laughing and wondering where this unexpected vein of flirtatiousness had come from.

"How do you capture this fair game?" she teased. This was a new Diana, even to her, and she found that she enjoyed abandoning her usual gravity.

St. Aubyn didn't seem to mind her silliness. His eyes rested on her warmly and a faint smile was playing over his lips. Stepping up to the tree, he replied, ''If I knew how to do that, I would have done so already.''

His smile faded as he extended one hand toward her. They were on opposite sides of the tree trunk, partially concealed from each other by the curving bark. His hand caressed her cheek, then slipped into the curls tangled by her riding.

''Did you know that you are being called the Fair Luna?'' As she looked at him questioningly, he explained, ''Because you have the most heavenly body anyone has ever seen in London.''

Diana's eyes widened and she laughed. ''That sounds like young Mr. Clinton's poetic fancy. Still, it is a compliment.''

''It is indeed.'' Gervase's eyes darkened and she could feel the tension thrumming between them. Warm against the side of her head, his fingers made slow circling motions, setting off ripples of sensation that spread throughout her body. Rapt at his touch, her lips parted in unconscious invitation.

''How long must I wait, Diana?'' His voice was barely more than a whisper, but his gaze was hypnotic.

Delicately he toyed with her ear. She hadn't known that such a mundane part of the body could feel so exquisite, and her right hand on the tree trunk was needed to steady her in the face of her body's quickening response. Stroking down her neck, his touch was so light that she could feel the whorls of his fingertips, like the brush of butterfly wings. Who would have thought that a man with such strong hands could be so gentle?

''I can understand that you wish to know me better,'' he said huskily, ''but the more time we spend together, the harder it is to keep my hands to myself. In fact, it is quite impossible.'' Moving around the tree, he captured her, sliding his arms around her waist and drawing her into a kiss.

Dizzily Diana decided that she must be getting the knack of kissing, for the depth and intimacy grew between them every time they embraced. Her eyes closed and she lost herself in the warm interchange of lips and tongues. It seemed entirely natural to explore his mouth just as he was discovering hers, and it was a whole universe of tender, wild touching.

They sank to their knees, their bodies pressed together. He brushed a light trail of kisses across her cheek, finding an exquisitely sensitive spot below her left ear. Sliding his hands down the gentle curves of her back, he caressed her buttocks, hips, and thighs, molding her against him. Her hips began pulsing in a primitive rhythm and she was shocked by her own response.

I shouldn't have had so much wine. Diana realized that if he wanted to take her here, in a public park, she would have no will to stop him. A seductive thought, to have this first encounter take place right now, with no time for her to worry about her limited experience and skill. But even through the haze of wine and desire, she knew that this was not how she wanted to begin. Gervase Brandelin was already too important in her life for casual coupling on the forest floor. She must use her mind, establish some control as Madeline had taught her, not slide into submission like a lovestruck dairy maid.

Besides, she was unprepared to prevent pregnancy. Much as she loved Geoffrey, she had no intention of giving him a younger brother or sister in such a casual, heedless way.

She broke free of Gervase's embrace and sank back on her heels, her knees touching his, her breathing uneven. Before he could embrace her again, she said softly, her voice as unsteady as her breath, "What do you want from me, my lord?"

He hesitated and she continued, unable to resist a smile, "Apart from the obvious, that is."

Realizing that he faced another test, Gervase also sat back on his heels, his hands spread on his thighs as he thought about her question. First he had to cool the fires she raised in him, no mean feat when just kissing her made the blood shout in his veins. What did he want of Diana Lindsay, apart from the opportunity to bury himself in her, to lose all his dark memories and regrets in the immediacy of passion?

An excellent question, one that deserved an honest answer. After his breathing had steadied, he replied, groping for the right words, "I like order in my life, so I want a regular mistress. I would like to know that you would be available when I want you, and would act no angry scenes about my neglect."

She nodded calmly, her lovely face showing no hint of whether she approved or disapproved of his statement. "And what do you wish for me? Long-term sexual intimacy is complicated, as you must know. What pattern would you wish ours to take?"

She had a knack for disconcerting questions; he had never considered how matters should look from her point of view. Gervase set his teeth in his lower lip as he thought about the answer. While their relationship was rooted in commerce, if Diana became his mistress there would be more between them than simple business. The question was, how much more? Slowly he replied, "I want you to be free of financial worries. And I hope you would find our liaison physically satisfying."

Blandly she asked, "And if you don't satisfy me, shall I pretend that you do?"

Stung in his male pride, Gervase retorted, "If you lie, you will have only yourself to blame for dissatisfaction. Even the most skilled of lovers can't read thoughts."

His gaze brushed the lush curves discreetly displayed by her prim dark blue riding habit, then returned to her flawless heart-shaped face, serene in quiet listening. There was too much sensuality in every line of Diana's body to imagine that she would be impossible to satisfy, particularly for a man of Gervase's experience. Her response to his kisses showed that under her ladylike demeanor lay a passionate nature. Having reached that conclusion, he said more evenly, "I know that it is one of a courtesan's skills to convince a man that he is the greatest lover in the history of mankind, but I prefer to think that you will not have to be an actress with me."

Two could play the game of questions, so he continued, "What do you wish of me? You have made it clear that any number of men are willing to pay your price. What more will it take for you to single me out above your other suitors?"

"I never said that I would single you out."

Her musical voice was so matter-of-fact that it took a moment for him to absorb the sense of what she was saying. Then, as angry color rose in his face, he snapped, "You prefer to operate a one-woman bawdy house? That is quite unacceptable to me. I want your exclusive services, and I am willing to pay more than generously for that privilege."

Her wide eyes were still serene, but steel showed in the dark blue depths. "I have no desire to accept all offers, but neither will I promise to be exclusive." After a moment she added, "I do not make promises that I am unsure I can keep."

Gervase stood, his body taut as he brushed leaf mold from the knees of his riding breeches. "If that is how you wish it, then we have nothing further to discuss. I have no intention of waiting in line outside your bedroom door." Trained to be courteous even in anger, he offered his hand to help her rise even as his mouth set in tight, angry lines. Sharing his woman with any rake or footman who took her fancy was insupportable. Quite intolerable . . . and yet his resolve began to waver the moment she laid her hand in his. Her weight was light as she came to her feet with the grace of a forest dryad. She did not release his hand, and the delicate-boned fingers lay within his grasp, radiating a calm that spread through him and soothed his anger.

She stood so close that her breasts almost touched his chest, and he caught the elusive scent of lilac. Her wide innocent gaze lifted to hold his as she asked, "Are you so inflexible that only your way will do? If I am always there when you desire me, why should it matter what I might possibly—only possibly—do in some other hour? What will you lose by that?"

He wanted to say that he was indeed that inflexible. Compromise might be necessary in his public work, but he had found no need for it in his personal life.

Not until now. Just how much did he want this woman with her exquisite face, intoxicating body, and gentle manners? Too much. Too bloody damned much.

His words were cool, but the edge was gone from his voice as he said, "I find it quite unacceptable that you might make sport of me behind my back with other lovers."

She gave a slight shake of her head. "Either you can trust me to be discreet and honorable, or you cannot—that has nothing to do with how many lovers I might have. I promise that what is between us will always be private, yet if I am not honorable, the promise itself means nothing."

An impossible argument to refute: only time would prove if she was worthy of trust. He wanted to repeat that he would never accept her terms, but against his will, reluctant words formed. "I shall consider what you have said."

In spite of the curtness of his answer, in his heart he knew that it was just a matter of time until he capitulated, and from the slight smile that curved her full lips, Diana Lindsay knew that too. If there had been even the faintest glint of triumph in her eyes, he would have wrenched his hand free and turned his back on her forever rather than place his pride in hands that might prove unreliable.

Instead, she turned his hand in hers and pressed a kiss onto it, her lips velvet-warm against his fingers. There was a tenderness in the gesture that he had never known before. Her shining hair fell away from her graceful neck, and the sweetness and vulnerability of that exposed creamy nape struck him so intensely that the shock was physical. It was unlike any emotion he had ever known, an aching dearer than mere sexual pleasure.

Gervase's grip tightened and he lifted her hand and held it against his cheek, rubbing his face against her fingers as she raised her head and gazed at him with deep lapis eyes. In that moment he would have agreed to anything she asked. Bleakly he wondered where this weakness would lead.

7

A distant church bell was striking four o'clock when they reined in their horses in the stableyard behind Diana's house, having ridden back to London in near-total silence. Since he doubted that any whore—or any other woman, for that matter—could be as honest as Diana Lindsay pretended to be, Gervase was suspicious that under her honeyed words she was mocking him.

Diana had been equally quiet on the ride, and as he helped her from her horse he saw signs of tension in her face. Perhaps she feared that she had gone too far in her demands and had lost him. The thought was a satisfying one.

She stood in front of him, her hands lightly touching his arms for balance after her slide from Phaedra's back, her eyes wide and stark. "You wondered when. If you still desire me, you may call tomorrow evening. I will receive you privately."

Gervase relaxed, feeling that the initiative was once more in his hands. Her invitation was unmistakable, and there was no surer cure for sexual fascination than to dispel the mystery. He had known other beautiful women, after all, and shorn of her riding habit and her innocent air, Diana Lindsay would be no different from the others. After they had made love a few times, it wouldn't be difficult to walk away from her if she proved to be more trouble than she was worth.

He made a perfunctory bow over her hand, avoiding any closer embrace. "Very well. Will nine o'clock suit you?"

"Perfectly, my lord. I shall await you then."

He escorted her to the back door of the house, then mounted and rode out of the yard. Diana watched his departure as she waited for the footman to open the door. A prickly man, Lord St. Aubyn, accustomed to having his own way. And why shouldn't he be? As a wealthy nobleman, he could do almost anything he chose.

With wry amusement, she recognized the similarity between him and the Count de Veseul. Both of them were intense, commanding, and they desired her. The difference lay in the fact that the Frenchman wished to plunder her and cared nothing for her consent. In contrast, St. Aubyn, though he might be unused to consider anyone's convenience but his own, seemed willing to learn. He had . . . possibilities. Thank God.

As the footman admitted her to the house, she gave an unladylike snort and lifted her skirts across the threshold. It wasn't anything so abstract as his "possibilities" that attracted her. No, it was other things, such as his controlled strength and rock-ribbed integrity. And, of course, that beautiful, panther-lean body. She wanted to learn the mysteries of love, and his lordship of St. Aubyn should be a most rewarding teacher.

Having taken a full day for personal pleasure, Gervase spent the evening working in the study of St. Aubyn House. In the last two years he had become a key man in the British government, though few people knew what he did. In theory, he held a minor post in the Foreign Office, a sinecure where he worked only the hours he chose and dabbled in dispatches and communications.

In fact, he coordinated the various branches of British intelligence gathering. Short weeks before his untimely death, the Prime Minister, William Pitt, had personally asked Gervase to undertake the thankless task of liaison, based on recommendations Pitt had received from General Sir Arthur Wellesley, the viscount's commander in India. During his years in the East, Gervase had displayed an uncanny talent for weaving fragments of information together to create a larger picture, and now he turned that ability to the critical European theater of war, where Britain had been fighting Napoleon for too many years.

Because the existing intelligence groups were jealous of their information, it was tedious and frustrating work, and a combination of tact and firmness was required to convince them to share what they knew. Gervase also worked with agents and informants on the Continent, evaluating their information and deciding whether their special projects were worthwhile: such spies frequently offered glorious plans that would require them to handle large amounts of British money.

Less tedious and infinitely more dangerous were the occasional trips he made to the Continent when he felt that only his own judgment could be trusted. Since Napoleon had closed all ports to the British, Gervase slipped in with smugglers. Like most of his class, he had been raised to speak French as naturally as English, and he could pass as a Frenchman when necessary. Even so, there was always the chance that his cousin Francis would inherit the title much sooner than expected.

It was an unglamorous business, but vital, and Gervase found it both rewarding and absorbing. Tonight, however, his usually formidable concentration was lacking and everything took twice the time it should. The last report in the pile was from the Decyphering Branch, an odd little group that had been founded by an Oxford don over a hundred years earlier and which was still run as a family business. Frowning, he studied the decoded translation of a secret dispatch to a French agent in London, then gave a sigh of irritation. He had been excited when it was intercepted, but nothing in the message to the mysterious ''Phoenix'' gave a clue as to who the recipient might be. The blasted spy had been a dangerous nuisance for years, and even with this dispatch they were no closer to knowing his identity.

Idly Gervase jotted down the names of half a dozen men who might be the Phoenix, each of them prominent and impossible to challenge without ironclad

proof of treachery. He had had them all watched for
months, but was no nearer to an answer than when he
had begun.

Unfortunately, when he looked at the sheet of fools-
cap he saw not spies but Diana Lindsay in all her sensual allure. Tomorrow night at this time his curiosity
would be satisfied, and he would no longer have to
guess at what lay hidden beneath her elegant clothing.
Tonight, regrettably, he could think of nothing else.
Just the thought of her aroused him to the point where
his brain became useless. How ridiculous and inappropriate that a high-class doxy should come between
him and the work that gave his life meaning.

Finally he crumpled the sheet of names and tossed
it into the fire, since he was making no progress toward the Phoenix. Better to spend the time deciding
what kind of gift to take to Diana tomorrow night as
payment for her favors. He stared at the flames without
seeing them, one corner of his mouth quirked up in
exasperation. The sooner he took the witch to bed, the
sooner his life could get back to normal.

Late that night, Diana was wakened by the nursery
maid with the announcement that Geoffrey was having
another seizure. By the time she had pulled on her
green robe and raced up the stairs, the fit was over and
Geoffrey was lying still on his bed, a sheen of perspiration on his face. Edith sat with him. Besides being
the housekeeper, she had appointed herself Geoffrey's
chief guardian and she slept in the adjoining chamber,
ever alert for sounds that might signal an attack. While
nothing could be done to stop a seizure, Geoffrey's
real and surrogate mothers would watch over him to
make sure that he did not injure himself in his convulsions.

Geoffrey's face was pale, but he struggled upright in
bed at the sight of his mother. "There was no need
for you to get up, Mama," he said matter-of factly.
"It was just another fit."

Diana smiled and climbed up next to him on the
bed, leaning against the headboard and circling her

son with one arm. For all his protests, he snuggled up to her quickly, burrowing against her side. "I was having trouble sleeping anyway, and now we have an excuse for hot cocoa."

"A good idea," Edith said in her deep northern voice. "I'll make some." She left to go down to the kitchen.

Diana felt Geoffrey's forehead. As she expected, it was too warm. The seizures usually came when he was feverish. Now that he was seven, the epileptic fits were less common, but were usually more violent when they occurred. "Perhaps you'd better stay home from school tomorrow."

"Mama," he said, sitting up with an indignant expression. "I like school. I don't *want* to stay home."

"I'm glad you like school, but surely they can manage without you for one day," she said, attempting not to sound too concerned. "Besides, if you have a fever you might have another seizure at school, and that could be a nuisance."

He shrugged his small shoulders with elaborate casualness. "Oh, I had one at school. During Latin. Mr. Hardy made me lie down afterward, but then I went back to class."

"Oh?" Diana's eyebrows lifted, a little irritated that the schoolmaster hadn't informed her of the attack.

Sensing what she wouldn't ask, Geoffrey grinned, mischief wreathing his small face. "The other boys in my class are very impressed. They wanted to know if they can learn how to do it."

After a moment of shock, Diana had to laugh. Now and then she needed to be reminded of how resilient small boys were. "What did you tell them?"

"I said they were out of luck. One has to be born epileptic to do it right," he said loftily.

Diana smiled and brushed her fingers through his silky dark brown hair. She was biased, but anyone would admit that he was a beautiful child. Though small for his age, he had a sturdy, growing body, a sunny disposition, and an outstanding intelligence as well. Surely so many blessings would outweigh his

disability in the eyes of those he would meet as he
grew up.

Her confidence faltered as she saw the way his dark
blue eyes, so much like hers, slipped out of focus for
a moment. The ''staring spells'' came more frequently after he had had a *grand mal* seizure. For a
second or two he would lose awareness of his surroundings and not know it. If he was talking, after a
silent pause he would continue as if nothing had happened.

It was fortunate that they had found Mr. Hardy's
small school, where children could learn in an atmosphere of greater freedom and understanding than was
usual. The schoolmaster has been very matter-of-fact
about Geoffrey's problem, neither impatient nor overconcerned. Judged by how much her son loved school,
the approach seemed to work.

Edith returned carrying a tray with a steaming pot-
tery jug and four mugs. Madeline trailed behind her,
still tying the sash of her dressing gown. Maddy
yawned, covering her mouth with one hand, then said
with a faint air of accusation, ''You're having a party
and didn't invite me.''

Geoffrey giggled and Diana joined in as Edith
poured the cocoa. For the next half-hour it was indeed
a party, albeit a quiet one; it was not the first time the
nursery had seen this kind of impromptu midnight
gathering, and doubtless it wouldn't be the last. Diana
kept a careful eye on Geoffrey's mug since he might
spill it if he had a long staring spell, but he managed
very well. Sometimes she dared hope that he might
outgrow the seizures, but she would be grateful if they
got no worse.

By the time the cocoa was gone Geoffrey was almost
asleep, so Diana tucked him under the covers and prepared to withdraw. His right hand curled under his
chin and his lashes lay dark against his cheek as she
kissed him. At moments like this she loved him so
much that it hurt her heart. She stood and glanced at
her friends. ''Good night, Edith. Thank you.''

Edith gave her rare warm smile, then returned to

her own room. Downstairs, Diana asked Madeline hesitantly, "If you aren't too sleepy, do you have a moment to come in?"

Madeline's shrewd eyes assessed her. "Of course. Is something wrong?"

"Not really." Inside her sitting room, Diana lit several candles from the candlestick she had carried downstairs, then wandered across the room to a window. Pulling back the drapery, she looked down into Charles Street. "I've invited St. Aubyn to come tomorrow night. Or I guess it's tonight now."

Madeline sat down on the sofa and pulled her legs up, tucking her robe under her feet. "Are you sure you are ready for this? You don't look very happy about it."

Diana turned away from the window, letting the drapery fall behind her. "I'm not unhappy. Just nervous."

Madeline eyed her closely. "You don't have to do it, you know, if the idea frightens you. You really haven't had the time to become well-acquainted with St. Aubyn."

Diana shrugged and spread her hands. "I know him as well as many girls know their husbands on their wedding nights, and I have the advantage of not being an ignorant virgin. My experience is very limited, but at least I'm not terrified by the unknown."

"Then what is bothering you?"

Diana sat in one of the chairs, pulling her knees up against her chest and wrapping her arms around them. "I'm not sure, really. I guess it's . . ." She hesitated, searching for the right word. ". . . a kind of melancholy. This seems so . . . so cold-blooded. Such a very long way from the romantic dreams I had as a child."

She smiled ruefully. "You know the ones: Prince Charming and love everlasting. The sort of thing every little girl is raised to expect, and almost none of us ever get."

"You're a romantic, Diana," the older woman said in a kindly voice. "You would like to be in love with

St. Aubyn and you're not. But if you feel that way, why are you going to bed with him? You're under no financial compulsion.''

Diana hugged her knees with a mischievous smile. ''While I'm not in love with him, I find him attractive. *Very* attractive.''

''Well, if you are determined to go ahead with this, that is not a bad place to begin,'' Madeline admitted. ''He has the look of a man who knows his way around a mattress.''

Diana colored and the older woman reminded herself that for all her maturity the girl was still relatively innocent. Well, that would change, and very soon now. Madeline rose and stretched sleepily. ''Well, I'm ready for a bed myself, and it's a sign of my age that I'm glad it's an empty one.''

As Diana chuckled, Madeline crossed the room, but with her hand on the knob of the door she found herself turning to ask once more, ''Are you truly sure this is the right thing to do?''

In the candlelight it was impossible to read Diana's expression, but there was no mistaking the determination in her soft voice as she said, ''Oh, that's one thing that I am very sure of. For all my doubts and dallying, taking Gervase Brandelin as a lover is most definitely the right thing to do.''

Diana forced herself not to stand at the window like an anxious schoolchild. It was five minutes before nine o'clock, and if there was one thing she had learned about Lord St. Aubyn, it was that he was prompt. When he arrived, the footman would escort him to her chambers, and then, and then . . .

She had her hands clenched tight, as nervous as any seventeen-year-old virgin on her wedding night. She had already inserted the vinegar-soaked sponge that Madeline said was the best available protection against pregnancy, and she wore a discreetly provocative gown and robe of translucent silk in a shimmering blue-fire shade that echoed her eyes. Her hair was twisted into a simple style that would fall about her shoulders with the removal of just two pins, and she had set the stage in a manner that was richly seductive without being vulgar. The night was cool, and coal burned merrily in the grates of the sitting room and the adjoining bedroom, where the massive shape of the canopied bed could be dimly seen. Madeline had helped her prepare, then withdrawn, satisfied that her protégée was ready.

Diana had been able to convince Maddy that her anxieties were no more than normal, but now that she was alone she admitted to herself that she was terrified. No matter that intuition urged her forward, that St. Aubyn had treated her with kindness, that she was fiercely attracted to him; in spite of all those things, the thought of trusting herself to him chilled her hands and made her heart beat with the rapid pulse of panic.

Her thoughts returned to the night on the moor when she had decided to try the courtesan's life. Truly, if she had known that the future held Gervase Brandelin, she would never have left Yorkshire. But it was too late to turn back; the tie that bound them was stronger than her individual will.

Just as her mind started to spiral once more into dark fears from her past, a knock on the front door sounded through the quiet house. Her nerves taut as newly tuned piano wire, Diana flinched, then glanced at the ormolu clock on the mantel. Two minutes before nine o'clock. Either the timepiece was slow or his lordship was impatient.

In less than a minute the knock sounded at her own door. Now that the moment had arrived, a fatalistic calm descended and she opened the door. For a moment they just gazed at each other, the air thrumming with tension between them. Gervase was dressed in the dark blue coat and buff pantaloons that were almost a uniform for men of his class, but expert tailoring, a beautifully fit body, and his forceful personality gave him the air of distinction that he wore so casually. His taut, fine-drawn face had the fierce and lonely beauty of a proud hawk, and he was frightening in his masculinity.

Then he smiled and extended one hand to her, and it was suddenly easy to grasp it and draw him inside. She closed the door, and before she had fully turned to face him, Gervase was embracing her, his mouth hungrily pressed to hers and his arms pulling her tight against him. From the feel of his hard body, he had no need for preliminaries, and for a moment panic returned. In most ways he was still a stranger, and though his fire warmed her, she needed more time; Diana knew that if they proceeded too quickly she would be too stiff and fearful to convince him that she was experienced.

She broke away, laying one finger over his mouth. "There is no need to hurry, my lord," she said softly.

He smiled, the clear gray eyes wry. "I'm sorry. I know I'm too impatient, but I have been thinking of you all day. And all last night too." He placed his hands on her shoulders, gently kneading the muscles, and she could feel some of her nervousness depart, to be replaced by a different kind of tension.

"In fact, I've hardly thought of anything else since I met you." His hands slid up her neck into her hair, expertly finding the hairpins and removing them. The thick chestnut masses tumbled down past her shoulders in wanton abandon.

"There. That is how I have been imagining you." He stepped close again and leaned over, kissing her throat through the silken strands of hair. For a moment Diana reveled in the sensation, amazed that so many distant parts of her body would resonate to that gossamer touch.

It was time to put her plan into effect. Stroking the dark head that lay so close to hers, she whispered, "Gervase, there is something I would ask of you."

He tensed, thinking that it was a singularly inappropriate time to discuss money. Still, she had a right to raise the issue, since their relationship was one of business. But it was hard to think of anything other than how ravishing she was, clad in blue silk so sheer that the curves and shadows of her body were clearly visible beneath it.

He stepped back and reached into his pocket for the velvet jewelry box and handed it to her. She opened it and gasped, as well she should. The sapphire pendant was magnificent, of a deep lucent blue, and the setting and chain were beautifully wrought. He had spent some time in selecting the gem, and it was lavish enough to pay for a good deal of her time. "It is almost the color of your eyes, though less brilliant."

"It's beautiful! I've never had anything like this." She looked up shyly. "Shall I put it on?"

He lifted the gem from the box, then circled behind her to fasten the chain around her neck, careful not to pull any of the delicate hairs at her nape. A mirror hung between the windows and she walked over to it, lifting one hand to touch the pendant admiringly. Gervase stood behind her, and her gaze met his in the mirror. "Thank you. It is very lovely. You chose well."

Her voice was soft and inviting, and the cynical part of him commented on how expensive presents had that effect on women. "I'm glad you like it," he said, then parted her hair again to unclasp the chain. When she looked at him questioningly, he smiled. "It will be in the way and could be rather painful."

She nodded in acknowledgment, then turned to face him as he replaced the pendant in its box and set it on the pier table. In the candlelight her eyes were almost black. "Actually, that was not what I wanted to discuss."

While her expression was calm, her words came hesitantly and her clasped hands betrayed tension. He found it odd that a woman of her calling was so nervous. "You will think that I am foolish, but . . . there is only one first time for any pair of lovers." Her face was earnest and very young as she lifted it to him. "I want tonight to be special."

He laid one hand on her waist, feeling her slim warmth through the layered silk. "It will be. I promise that."

She smiled briefly, but it didn't reach her ey "There are only so many ways of making love

makes it special is what is here''—she reached up and
touched his forehead—''and here.'' She laid her hand
on his heart.

Speaking carefully, as if using words she had rehearsed, she continued, ''Tonight, let's pretend that
we are young lovers, coming together for the first time.
I will play the maiden, and you the man who guides
and teaches me.''

Lifting her hand to caress his cheek, she said softly,
''In a way, it is true, since this is our first time, so
why shouldn't we enjoy the fantasy? Let us imagine,
just for an hour or two, that the world is a simple place
and that we can rediscover the wonders of first love
and the awakening of passion.''

Then she smiled with deep promise. ''Best of all,
we can capture some of the wonder without the fear
and awkwardness that curse real innocents.''

Gervase hesitated. While taking one's time increased the pleasure, it hardly seemed necessary to
playact as well. Diana was so exquisite that he needed
no layer of dreams to increase his desire. But as he
studied her hopeful, anxious face, it seemed no great
chore to act such a role. Women were different from
men, and if it pleased her to spin a fantasy, it would
cost him nothing to indulge her. With her Madonna
face and air of gentle refinement, it was easy to imagine her a maiden giving herself for love, yet because
she was a woman of experience, there would not be
the fear of hurting her.

As he thought about it, the idea became exciting and
he began to smile. ''Your wish is my command. Since
I have never had quite the experience you describe, I
shall have to think a moment how I would begin.'' He
clasped his hands below her shoulders, his thumbs
making slow circling motions through the silk on the
tender flesh of her inner arms.

''I would start with talking,'' he said thoughtfully,
''perhaps over a glass of wine. Would you happen to
have some wine?''

Her eyes sparkled up at him. ''Will brandy do, my
lord?''

"It will do very nicely." As she crossed the room to where a decanter and goblets waited, he added, "Next, I would insist that you use my name. Titles don't lend themselves to intimacy."

She carefully poured three fingers of brandy into a goblet, then glanced up. "Very well . . . Gervase."

He hadn't realized how musical his name could sound. Before she could pour a second goblet, he took the decanter from her hand, replaced the stopper, and set it on the sideboard.

"We need only one. Also, it would be time to introduce a note of greater informality." He peeled off his coat and untied his cravat, tossing them casually over the back of a chair. Under the white shirt his shoulders were very broad, a striking contrast to his narrow hips and waist. A few strands of curling dark hair were visible at the open throat of his shirt.

Lifting the brandy glass, he guided her to the sofa with a light hand on her back, and they sat, their bodies close but not quite touching. He offered her the goblet and she sipped from it, her eyes holding his over the rim, then handed it back. He turned the goblet so that he drank from where her lips had touched. "We would begin slowly."

He rolled the brandy around in his mouth, savoring the smoothness of it before he swallowed, then held the goblet up to her mouth, tilting it so she could drink. "I would encourage you to drink enough that you would relax, but not so much as to make you unwell or unsure of what you are doing."

He watched the column of her throat flex as she swallowed, a motion he had never consciously noticed, but which was now deeply erotic. Drinking more of the brandy himself, he stretched his arm along the back of the sofa and toyed with her hair, running his fingers through the dark glossy strands. "Then I would tell you how deeply beautiful you are."

"Would I believe you?" she asked, a smile in her eyes.

"I would be prepared to swear on any number of Bibles." He set the goblet in her hand and reached out to sketch her features as he described them. "I would extol your night-blue eyes, your satiny skin, your ruby lips."

Diana's face sparkled with appreciative humor. "Do lovers never use more imaginative metaphors?"

He chuckled. "I doubt it. If they did, they would be poets. Lovers are more involved with each other than with fine phrases." He took another mouthful of brandy, no longer able to distinguish its fire from his own. "Since you are young and modest, I would avoid talking about your enticing breasts, your slim tantalizing waist, your rounded inviting hips."

A becoming hint of rose colored her face as his fingers lightly followed his words. "Quite right not to mention them—a modest maiden would find such talk too suggestive."

"Perhaps about now," he mused, "I would think it time to make different use of the brandy." He pulled aside the top of her robe, exposing the low-cut gown underneath and an expanse of gently swelling flesh. Dipping his forefinger in the brandy glass, he trailed it from the pulse point at the base of her throat toward the shadowed valley between her breasts. Then he leaned over and kissed along the brandied path, his mouth hot and firm against her.

As his lips moved to the edge of the gown, Diana's body quivered and she gave a shuddering gasp. "An innocent maiden would find this all very surprising." He paused and she hastened to add, "But not unpleasant. Not in the least."

He raised his head and smiled, his mouth mere inches from hers, his eyes soft and amused. The deep timbre of his voice a caress, he murmured, "Then I would retreat a little, to give you time to accustom yourself to the newness. But I would not retreat too far."

He leaned forward, closing the distance between them. This time his kiss was not hungry and demanding, as when he had first arrived, but leisurely and probing, bent on exploring every surface and texture of her yielding mouth.

With such a myriad of things to learn just about kissing, Diana wondered if she would ever live long enough to master all the other subtleties of making love. Since they had eased back against the arm of the sofa, balance no longer required her attention and she lifted her hands and buried them in the thick springiness of his dark curling hair.

After an endless, delicious embrace, Gervase pulled back and smiled, brushing a lock of hair from her cheek. "An innocent maiden might not know how to kiss that well."

So far, so good. He found her convincing, and even if her mind held doubts, her body seemed to know what to do. Diana laughed rather breathlessly. "Surely kissing would be one thing we would have practiced before now?"

"Mmm, doubtless you're right." He lifted her away from the sofa and slid the robe from her shoulders to pool on the cushions. Above her waist, the wisp of gown covered scarcely more than her breasts, and the silk was so sheer that the dark areolae were faintly visible.

Gervase's breathing was no longer even when he bent forward and took her right nipple in his mouth, the heat of his kiss scorching through the gauzy fabric. With his right hand he cupped her left breast and began to tease the nipple between thumb and forefinger. The combined assault created sharply pleasurable sensations and Diana's body tightened in response. Deep within her there was spreading fire, and her breath was a low moan as she pulled his head closer.

His own breathing uneven, Gervase stood and scooped her into his arms, her pliant body molding to his chest. "About now I would decide that you were ready for the next step." She felt the vibrations of his deep voice as she put her arms around his neck and pulled his head down for another kiss. His muscular arms held her effortlessly, and the kiss lasted as he carried her through the door and laid her on the high bed.

Sitting on the edge of the mattress, he stroked the

silk-clad curves of her body, the coolness of the fabric belied by the warm body beneath. Diana lay back against the pillows, one slim arm entwined with his, her fairness a dramatic contrast to his dark skin. She might have been a shepherdess, giving herself trustingly to her beloved in some Elysian field where fear and betrayal would never be known; her lapis eyes held exactly the shadow of anxiety that might be found in an innocent girl who both yearned for and feared the act of ultimate intimacy.

A five-branch candelabrum burned on the bedside table, and with a hand that trembled slightly, Gervase reached over and began pinching the candles out. "Now," he said huskily, "it would be time to extinguish the light so that your maidenly shyness would not be offended." After snuffing four candles, he stopped. "Here, I think, I will diverge from the script. It would be a crime to hide your beauty in the dark."

The candle left burning was sufficient to illuminate the scene. Diana's blue eyes were vulnerable and intimate in the candlelight, bidding him enter an unknown world of warmth and welcome. Her lips were parted and the rapid rise and fall of her breasts testified to her response. One of her knees was drawn up, and shadows played suggestively under the skirt of her gown.

As Gervase absorbed the grave sweetness of her gaze, he was suddenly and completely overwhelmed by emotions unlike anything he had ever felt before. He had never been in love, his only experience with a virgin had been a searing disaster that haunted him still, but now Diana's fantasy came alive for him. Her gentle, sensuous beauty touched a vein of romanticism so deeply buried that he had not known it existed, and fiercely he wanted to believe in innocence, that one could begin again.

Bending over, he cupped her face in his hands and kissed her with a hunger that went far beyond the physical. For once in his life he would throw away the guilty chains of living and imagine that he was worthy of loving and being loved. In reality such joy was for-

ever unattainable, but for this handful of moments he
would dream. "Oh, God, Diana, don't ever let me
hurt you," he whispered, his voice rough with tenderness and passion. "You are so rare."

Her arms encircled him and he came down full
length beside her for a kiss in which each of them gave
and received equally. Only the thought that too much
clothing separated them enabled him to eventually release her and sit up. As he undid his cuffs, she reached
up to unbutton his shirt.

"Am I acting too boldly for my role?" she whispered as her hand slipped inside the shirt to caress his
chest. Her palm brushed his softly bristling hair as her
fingers made delicate explorations.

"Perhaps," Gervase gasped, "but don't stop."
Amazing that such a light touch could excite him so.

Her face showed a mischievous pleasure in his reaction, and it took a major act of will for him to stand
and remove the rest of his clothing, leaving it in a
heedless pile on the floor.

He slid one arm under her thighs to raise her as he
removed her gown, leaving her fully exposed for his
admiration. Her loveliness made him grateful that he
had left the candle lit; such beauty deserved to be savored.

Lowering himself to her side, he laid one leg across
hers to keep her close, then gave her breast the attention it deserved now that it was free of all restraint.
The tautness of her nipple teased his tongue. When he
was sure that it could be roused no further, he lifted
his head to murmur, "I would be very careful that no
part of you would feel neglected," before giving the
same thorough treatment to her other breast.

Diana whispered, "You, too, are beautiful," stroking his wide chest, caressing the hard planes of muscle
and bone, the ridged battle scars. There was no spare
flesh on him anywhere, every part of his lean body
honed to taut strength. As her hands glided over his
head and shoulders, her hips began an involuntary
pulsing against him.

His hand stroked down her body, kneading and caressing her waist and stomach before reaching the silky triangle of hair at the juncture of her thighs. Gervase raised his mouth to kiss her lips at the same time that his fingers delicately penetrated to her sensitive, hidden depths. Her legs tensed and her sharp inhalation was so convincing that he could almost believe she was as innocent as the maiden of her fantasy. Lost in his own role, he murmured, "Just relax. We will take as long as you need." Raising his hand to her knees, he caressed her silken inner thighs, slowing massaging his way lower until she opened to him.

He summoned all his skill to bring her to the final readiness, and when her body was hot and moist and her breath rough and urgent, he moved between her legs and slowly, gently entered. She had acted the virgin so convincingly that it was almost a surprise that no barrier blocked his passage.

Diana gasped and her muscles tightened around him with such fierce sweetness that it took all of Gervase's will not to culminate immediately. Instead he held very still, his arms supporting him so that his weight wouldn't hurt her. Remembering the roles they played helped him maintain his control. "Now I would give you a few minutes to get used to how it feels to have a man inside you," he said with a teasing half-smile, "and for me to calm down."

Diana shivered in delight and pressed her hips upward, rotating them to deepen the sensation. She had not known how empty she was until he filled her, and it was impossible to get enough of him. He inhaled sharply. "And I would warn you not to do that unless you are impatient to be done."

Diana stilled, whispering, "Oh, no, not yet, I most certainly do not want this to end." Gervase's dark hair tumbled over his forehead and she could see a film of perspiration on his face and torso. She had never dreamed that his dark face could show such openness and intimacy, and she lifted one hand to caress his cheek and the corded strength of his neck.

Even the touch of her hand inflamed him, and it took time to regain his control. Only when he was sure did he begin moving inside her, exploring her secret depths. Still careful to be gentle, he murmured, "Now I would tell you to move against me as we find a rhythm together."

She obeyed, and he started deepening his strokes, pushing harder and longer, his eyes searching to catch every nuance of feeling as it rippled across her face.

She moaned and her eyes closed, the better to savor the sensations consuming her. For all that Madeline had told her, Diana had never dreamed that pleasure could be so exquisite and tormenting. She drew him as deep into her as was humanly possible, her nails digging into his back as her thrusting hips took on an uncontrollable rhythm of their own.

It was unbearable and she pleaded incoherently, "Please, Gervase, please . . ." without knowing what she asked for. And then, just when she could endure no more, her body convulsed in a series of shuddering explosions. She cried out, her voice drowned in his as he plunged and erupted within her, their bodies joined in ultimate closeness.

They lay tangled in each other, the only sounds their deep, uneven breathing. Diana's arms were wrapped tight around his torso, unwilling to release him even now, and she could feel tears seeping from beneath her closed eyelids.

Gervase raised his head from the pillow as he eased his weight from her. As he did, she felt him brush the tears from her cheek. "Did I hurt you?"

She shook her head, opening her eyes to smile reassuringly at him. "No, not at all. It was just that it was so . . . so wonderful. I'm afraid that I cry at everything that makes me feel deeply, whether I'm happy or sad."

He relaxed, then rolled onto his side, holding her tightly so they were still joined. Cradling her head, he said softly, "I've never experienced anything quite like that. Your suggested fantasy was brilliant—it added a whole new dimension." He chuckled. "You were very convincing. It was easy to believe that you were an innocent, until the very end."

"Oh," she asked, wondering if she had somehow betrayed herself, "did I act wrongly?"

"Say rather that you forgot to act, and responded quite unlike a virgin." He kissed her lightly on the forehead. "Do you think you will have to pretend satisfaction with me?"

Diana laughed and snuggled against him. Madeline had devoted quite a bit of time to explaining masculine arrogance. Well, he had earned a bit of arrogance. "You are very cocksure about your performance, Gervase," she teased.

His gray eyes narrowed in amusement. " 'Cocksure'? That sounds like the right word."

Diana laughed so hard that their bodies separated, leaving her with a sense of regret for the loss. "It is quite a talent to be vulgar and clever at the same time."

He grinned, then pulled the bedcovers over them. The fire was dying down and there was a chill in the air that they hadn't noticed earlier. Diana was content to lie against Gervase, her head on his shoulder, her arm across his waist. Her lover; what a marvelous reality the words had taken. Once more intuition had guided her truly. The thought of this joining had been terrifying, and only faith that they were meant to be together had given her the strength to accept him.

Now, like mist on the moors, her fears had vanished, and not just because passion had burned them away. Deeper than desire lay some inexplicable quality in Gervase that made her feel peaceful and protected with him, a kindness that had disarmed all her buried angers. She sighed and snuggled closer. Dark secrets might still lie between them, but tonight they had begun a journey together that must surely, in time, lead them to light.

They lay languid until he said, "We still haven't determined how you are going to be compensated. If you thought that offering a sample would raise the price, you are correct." She rolled over on her back and he raised himself on one elbow, playing with her long hair. In the dim light it looked black, with only an occasional hint of chestnut richness.

"Do you want to have all your bills sent to me? Or would you prefer to have a regular allowance, perhaps three hundred pounds a month?" He formed her hair into patterns on the pillow, arcing out like willow leaves.

Diana felt a flash of irritation at his assurance. It was a very generous offer, but . . . did he assume that after a satisfying tumble, she would automatically fall in with his wishes? Maddeningly, his confidence was not far off the mark, but she wasn't going to let him know that. Far better to keep him off balance. "Need we be so formal? Bring me presents instead. Surprise me. If I satisfy you and you pay a just price, that will work well enough."

He frowned, his dark brows drawing together as he looked down at her. The comfortable intimacy was fading. "I prefer that matters be settled."

"I am not a 'matter to be settled,' my lord." Diana let her lashes flutter down over her eyes, consciously casual, as if what he did was of no account to her. "Have you never learned that with people you must be flexible or you will be infuriated?"

He snorted, caught between irritation and amusement. "I want a mistress, not a philosopher."

"You have both, and a thousand other things as well. If that does not please you, you are quite free to look elsewhere."

"Perhaps I will in time, Diana. But not yet." He laid one hand on her breast and moved it in slow circles, teasing the nipple as he captured her mouth with his. "Definitely not yet."

Catching her breath, Diana was surprised to find herself responding; she would have thought that she had had quite enough for one night. But apparently she hadn't, and by the growing pressure against her thigh, Gervase hadn't either. He whispered, "Once more I will diverge from the script. If you had really been a virgin, a gentleman would refrain from doing this again so soon. Fortunately you are not the former, so I need not behave like the latter.''

Diana learned that knowing what to expect added to the pleasure. This time their lovemaking was shorn of the pent-up desire that had driven them earlier, and it lasted for an endless, languorous time, with Gervase bringing them both to the edge again and again, then retreating. The prolonged buildup led to a powerful, long-lasting climax, subtly different from the earlier one, but equally intense.

After, Diana lay with her head on his chest, her hair spilling across them both like a veil as their slow breathing matched in rhythm. At this rate, her lack of experience would be eliminated in no time. His strong hand cradled her neck and he was so still that she wondered if he slept. It would be very easy to drift into dreams, but she preferred not to. With an effort, she lifted herself so she could look down into his face. ''Gervase?''

''Yes?'' His eyes opened and there was a very strange expression in them, one she could not analyze. Contentment? Satisfaction? Doubt, or perhaps even fear? Diana was usually very good at sensing others' emotions, but this was too complex a blend to define. She reminded herself that while sex was in some ways a simple act, this was not a simple man.

''I think it is time you left. It is very late.''

She felt his hand tense on her neck. Had he expected to stay? According to Madeline, some men liked to sleep with their mistresses, whereas some did not; it was an individual taste.

His voice was cool and detached, remote from the intimate tangle of their naked bodies. ''How fortunate that you reminded me. I prefer to sleep alone myself.''

If that was true, why did she feel that he was angry at being asked to leave? Though Diana had never spent the night with a man, she didn't doubt that she would enjoy having Gervase's warm, solid body next to hers. But occasionally Geoffrey came down in the early morning, and she would not risk her son finding a man in her bed.

As he pulled his pantaloons on, Gervase asked curtly, "What are your other rules?"

Though his withdrawal hurt, there was nothing she could do about it. Lifting her chin a bit, she said calmly, "Always inform me in advance when you wish to visit."

"So you can chase your other lovers out of your bed?" His voice was definitely hostile as he tugged on his wrinkled shirt.

"If that is what you choose to believe." Diana felt shy about climbing naked out of the tumbled bed, but modesty seemed ludicrous after what had passed between them. She got up quickly, then retrieved her silk robe from the sitting room. Wearing it could be justified by escorting him downstairs.

"What other explanation could there be?"

His gray eyes were chilly and his height and broad shoulders made him an intimidating stranger as he loomed over her. It was hard to remember how close they had been short moments earlier. Diana quailed inwardly, but didn't drop her gaze. "You might try believing that I have a life apart from my . . . work. I might be out, I might be busy with something not easily interrupted. If I am expecting you, it will be more convenient for both of us."

Her logical answer relaxed him. Crossing the room, he put on his coat, shoving his cravat into his pocket. At this hour, there would be no one to criticize his mode of dressing.

Lifting a candlestick, Diana led the way downstairs and unbolted the front door. The rest of the household was long since asleep, and in the distance she heard a clock strike three times. The deepest, darkest hour of the night.

Before she could open the door, he took the candlestick and put it on a table before embracing her, making his good-night kiss as thorough as any they had yet shared. Her arms went around his neck as he pulled her close, his strong hands shaping her soft curves. In spite of her fatigue, she realized that if he was ready for another round, she would be more than willing to cooperate.

Even as he kissed her, Gervase knew how foolish it was to try to claim a woman of her kind, to attempt to move her so thoroughly that she would accept none of the other men who desired her. There might be an expression of dazed delight on her face when he lifted his head away, but she was, after all, a whore.

Even as he told himself that she was not worth the effort, an inexplicable surge of possessiveness came over him. Seeking the entrance to her robe, he slid his hand between the silken panels, low, between her thighs. "I want you to be mine, Diana," he whispered, caressing her most secret places with the edge of his hand. "Only mine."

She shook her head wordlessly, her flawless face mysterious and unreadable even as he felt the hot, involuntary response of her body. He wanted to take her again, right there, with only the thin Oriental carpet between them and the cold marble floor. Since Diana wanted that too, perhaps his purpose would be better served by not satisfying their mutual desires. Releasing her, Gervase turned, opened the door, and went alone into the night.

Diana shivered as she bolted the door, feeling the dark side of what joined them. In her bedchamber she changed to a high-necked, long-sleeved flannel nightgown, the antithesis of eroticism, then crawled into bed. She had slept here for three months, but never before had the bed seemed so large or so empty.

Tired though she was, sleep proved elusive. *Sex is a double-edged sword.* Madeline's long-ago words haunted her. Diana had thought she understood, but only now was the meaning clear. Never having experienced passion, she was now unprepared for its power. The night had been a shattering experience for her, not just because of the new physical worlds revealed, but because of the emotions stirred. She had given and received pleasure, and so had Gervase, and that magical sharing created a closeness quite different from her feelings for her son and friends.

Clearly the viscount desired her, but she desired him

equally. She wanted to yield to his wishes, to promise to be only his, to talk and laugh and love with him so that the hard lines of his face would soften into the irresistible tenderness he had shown her tonight. The only power she wanted over him was the power to make him happy.

It would be treacherously easy to center her world around him and his demands, but that was not what she had come to London for. Diana already understood some of the complex currents that lay between them, and sensed that there was far more beyond her comprehension. Like her, Gervase had been gravely wounded by life, and he had done less healing than she had. Until she understood the origins and depths of his pain, there could be no worthwhile future for them.

She drew herself into a tight little ball, her arms wrapped around herself in an attempt to regain the warmth she had felt earlier. No matter how hard it was, she would resist that insidious desire to surrender. Someday, God willing, she could safely surrender to Lord St. Aubyn, but much must change first. She wanted them to be equals in their loving, not master and slave.

Diana shivered uncontrollably, knowing that it was not simple fate that had joined them, but the goddess Nemesis herself. Nemesis, the goddess of retributive justice. Had Diana known what was to be, she would have stayed at High Tor Cottage, but it was far too late for retreat. The thread that joined her to Gervase was now too powerful to be denied.

In the days ahead, she would play the role of independent woman and he could accept that or not, as he chose. Even as she made the silent vow, she wondered if she could keep it. As she had told Gervase, tears came easily to her, and when she buried her face in the pillow, she was unsure whether she wept from joy or sorrow.

8

THE dinner hour was long past and Whitehall nearly deserted when the British foreign minister paid Lord St. Aubyn a visit. George Canning was brilliant, unpredictable, and very, very ambitious. Ever since William Pitt, the guiding spirit of the Tory party, had died a year and a half earlier, the party had been fighting bitterly over who among them was most fit to wear the great man's mantle. Virtually the only thing the Tories agreed on was the necessity of defeating the French, but more of their energy went into fighting each other. It was a battle Gervase had little taste or patience for.

He had been deep in a pile of reports from Portugal when Canning's entrance caused him to look up, then narrow his eyes thoughtfully. Politics is a matter of personalities, and Gervase's army service and friendship with Sir Arthur Wellesley in India had allied him with the war minister, Castlereagh, one of Wellesley's closest friends. The foreign minister and the war minister had overlapping responsibilities, and there was fierce, covert rivalry between them, so Canning automatically regarded Gervase with suspicion. Usually the two dealt indirectly; this was the first time Canning had sought him out.

Gervase stood, glad of an opportunity to stretch, and offered his hand. "Good evening, Canning. You're working late."

Then he stiffened. Behind the foreign minister was another man, a Frenchman who was one of the viscount's chief suspects for the spy called the Phoenix.

After shaking hands, Canning waved casually at his companion. "I'm sure you two know each other."

The Count de Veseul, elegant in black, gave a debonair smile. "But of course we do, though it is a thousand pities society does not see more of Lord St. Aubyn."

Gervase accepted the Frenchman's proferred hand without enthusiasm. There were other men who might be the Phoenix, but Gervase rather hoped Veseul was the culprit. He despised the man, with his unctuous charm and his air of secret amusement. The count moved freely in the upper levels of British society as well as the court-in-exile of the French monarch, perfectly placed to hear things he shouldn't. Gervase suspected that the Frenchman had the audacity, intelligence, and viciousness to dare anything. His face reflecting none of his thoughts, the viscount asked blandly, "Have you come to work here in Whitehall, Veseul? Heaven knows we are understaffed."

The Frenchman waved his gold-headed cane gracefully. "Work? *Moi?* I am a lily of the field. I toil not, neither do I spin. I leave such things to diligent fellows like you."

Raising his brows, Gervase murmured, "You underrate your accomplishments. Surely the tying of such cravats is a life's work in itself."

"Ah, but that is not work, that is art," Veseul said soulfully. "I am a master of many obscure forms of artistic endeavor."

The count's black eyes gleamed with amusement, confirming Gervase's suspicion that this conversation took place on two levels. The Frenchman knew what kind of work the viscount did, probably guessed that he himself was suspected of spying, and took private, smug satisfaction in this sparring.

Canning broke in. "Veseul and I will be dining at White's. Care to join us?"

Gervase shook his head with feigned regret. "Sorry, I've several hours' work ahead of me."

"In that case, there is a brief matter of business I'd like to go over with you before I leave."

When Gervase looked pointedly at the French count, Canning said impatiently, "We can speak freely in

front of Veseul. No one loathes Bonaparte like an exiled royalist.''

Gervase said nothing, just continued to look at the
count. Unfazed by that cool regard, Veseul smiled broadly.
''I'll wait downstairs for you, George. Suspicion is an
occupational hazard in St. Aubyn's work.'' Touching his
fingers to his brow in a mocking salute, he left.

When they were alone, the foreign minister scowled
at Gervase. ''You were bloody rude to Veseul.''

Gervase settled back behind his desk. ''The man is
almost certainly a French agent. Strictly off the record, I'd advise you to be careful what you say in front
of him.''

Canning looked startled as he settled in the one
straight wooden chair that the small room offered
guests. ''That's a damned serious accusation. Can you
prove it?''

''If I could, Veseul wouldn't be wandering around
loose,'' the viscount said dryly. ''I may never have
proof. I am merely suggesting that you mind what you
say in front of him.''

After a moment the foreign minister nodded
thoughtfully, then turned to the business that had
brought him here. ''The information you provided
made the Copenhagen campaign a success.''

Gervase's brows rose fractionally in surprise. ''I just
coordinated it—the information came from a number
of sources. But military intelligence doesn't win bat-
tles—soldiers do.''

''Yes, but *lack* of military intelligence can lose a
battle.''

''True,'' Gervase agreed, curious where this was
leading.

''You're very good at what you do. Getting you to
take this post was one of the best things Pitt did.''
Canning's voice was clipped and his compliment
sounded grudging.

''I'd be surprised if that is all you came here to say.''

''Quite right.'' Canning's eyes wandered a bit, then
came back with a snap. ''They say that you have the

best information files in the country. Do you also keep them on Englishmen?''

"No.'' Gervase's voice was flat. "If you want ammunition to use on your opponents, look elsewhere.''

Canning grimaced. "More concerned about someone having ammunition to use on me.'' His pale blue eyes studied Gervase shrewdly, trying to decide if the viscount was telling the truth.

Gervase pushed himself back from the desk, crossing his long legs in front of him casually. "Canning, I am here for one reason only: to contribute what I can to sending that Corsican bastard to the hell he so richly deserves. I'm not a politician and have no interest in becoming a minister or gathering power for myself. That's why I survived the fall of Addington's government last spring, and I fully intend to survive the fall of Portland's administration, and as many other governments as we have between now and the time Napoleon is defeated.''

Canning smiled crookedly. "With the amount of laudanum Portland takes every day, he probably won't even notice when his government collapses.''

Gervase glanced at his visitor sharply, wondering if Canning was trying to provoke him into saying something indiscreet. Perhaps not; Canning was notoriously plain-spoken and he was related to the aging Duke of Portland by marriage.

The minister continued, "Came here to thank you, St. Aubyn. I took a lot of criticism over the Danish campaign. Public opinion was on the side of the Danes, and we came off looking like thieves and bullies. If it weren't for you, we might have been losers as well, which would have been far worse.''

Gervase sighed. The Copenhagen business had left a bad taste in his mouth. "I didn't like it either, but you were right to invade Denmark. If you hadn't, Bonaparte would have taken the Danish fleet and used it against us. Without our superiority at sea . . .'' He shrugged eloquently.

The last statement needed no completion. One by one the Continental powers had fallen, until only Brit-

ain held out. It was a stalemate: the French could not
defeat the British at sea, and Britain was unable to take
the battle to Napoleon on land. If the British ever lost
their marine superiority, Bonaparte would invade
and the long war might be over, with Britain one more
nation bowing to the emperor.

The direction of the conversation caused Gervase to
mention something that he had been considering. "The
action you took to secure the Swedish fleet should keep
the Baltic Sea a British lake, but there's another neutral navy at risk: the Portuguese."

Canning nodded glumly, the weight of affairs falling
heavily over him. "I've been thinking of that. Do you
have reason to believe the French will try to annex
it?"

Gervase gestured at the pile of papers on his desk.
"I'm piecing together information now. The full report should be ready for you in two or three days, but
my guess is that if the Portuguese aren't persuaded to
remove their fleet within the next few weeks, Napoleon will have it."

Canning pursed his lips is a soft whistle. "That
soon?"

"I'm afraid so."

The foreign minister frowned for a moment, then
smiled wryly. "Well, I guess it's time I made myself
even more unpopular. At least the Portuguese are more
likely to listen to us than the Danes were." He stood
indecisive for a moment. "Thank you. Been told to
be wary of you, but I expect that was just politicking.
I think you look sound, and your recommendations
have always worked out."

Gervase stood also and murmured, "How satisfying
to know that I have your approval."

Ignoring the sarcasm, Canning gave him an assess-
ing glance. "Could use a man of your abilities. If you
throw in your lot with me, you'll go far."

His voice cool, Gervase said, "My hereditary seat
in the House of Lords is quite sufficient. You may
comfort yourself with the knowledge that I will not let

my information sources be used by anyone else for political purposes.''

"Suppose I'll have to settle for that."

For the first time Gervase smiled. "Yes, you will."

Canning nodded acknowledgment, then left, pulling the door closed after him as Gervase subsided behind his desk, feeling very tired. Canning was not the first politician to try to subvert the viscount, and doubtless he wouldn't be the last.

Pulling out his gold watch, he saw that it was after nine o'clock. It had been three days since that incredible night with Diana Lindsay, and there wasn't a waking hour when he hadn't thought of her. He had resisted the urge to see her again too soon; while Gervase reluctantly conceded that he needed women in a general way, he certainly didn't need any female in particular. Having proved his willpower, he now had an overwhelming desire to see her again, to bask in her warm, sweet sensuality.

Scribbling a quick note, he found one of the porters still on duty and paid the man a guinea to take the message to 17 Charles Street and wait for a reply. Then the viscount returned to his endless reports, balancing the honesty and accuracy of one agent or informant against another, laying the basis for recommendations that might influence the life or death of hundreds of people he would never meet. He became so absorbed that it was almost a surprise when the porter came into the small office and handed back his original note, which had been resealed with the imprint of a cupid holding a finger to its chubby lips.

In spite of the amusing seal, for a brief, miserable moment Gervase was sure that she had rejected him because she was occupied with another man or for some inexplicable female reason. Schooling himself to impassivity, he broke the wax and unfolded the sheet, then felt his face relax into an involuntary smile. Across the bottom of the paper, in a flowing elegant hand, Diana had written, "Come and be welcome."

* * *

Diana had been getting ready for bed when the message came from St. Aubyn, and she felt a burst of gladness that he was coming. For three days she had wondered if she had done something to give him a disgust of her, either by her refusal to grant him exclusive rights or by the way she made love, though he had had no complaints at the time.

Another full-scale seduction scene didn't seem appropriate, so she hastily dressed in a simple apricot-colored gown and pulled her hair back, tying it with a matching velvet ribbon. She was very aware that if he decided to visit her regularly, tonight would do much to set the tone of their meetings.

All of the servants had retired for the night and she let him in herself. For a moment Gervase took her breath away. She had thought him an attractive man from the beginning, but now that she was intimately aware of the muscle and bone that lay beneath the restrained tailoring, she could hardly keep her hands off him. Well, perhaps she shouldn't; Madeline said that gentlemen liked a woman to take the lead sometimes.

Shyly she made herself step forward, placing her hands on his shoulders and lifting her face to kiss him. A warm, unexpected smile lit his face and he returned her kiss with interest, encircling her with a hug that threatened her ribs. Eventually Diana laughingly broke off. "I'm sorry, my lord, I need to breathe."

"I suppose I do too," he agreed. He released her, then reached into his pocket. "You said you wanted to be surprised," and he laid a small brass figurine in her hand.

Diana examined the delicate Oriental workmanship with fascination. The figurine was about four inches high and depicted a graceful, voluptuously feminine woman with a serene face and a flower blossom in her hand. "How beautiful, Gervase. Is she an Indian goddess?"

He nodded. "Yes, she's Lakshmi, the Hindu goddess of fortune and prosperity, the consort of Vishnu. That's a lotus blossom that she carries. I kept her in my office at Whitehall, on the off chance that she might bring good luck. Since it was late, I could think of nothing else to bring you. I'm sorry—the figurine isn't worth much, but since you were interested in India, I thought she might please you.''

She gave him a glowing look. "She does, but I didn't mean to rob you of something that you cherish.''

She tried to return the figurine, but he folded it back into her hand, his fingers warm and firm on hers. "Lakshmi is the Hindu goddess of grace and womanly beauty as well as wealth. Clearly she belongs with you.''

He really had the most disconcerting knack for compliments, Diana decided. She gave him a dazzling smile and he reacted visibly, showing her a face quite different from his more public aspect. She almost kissed him again, but the practical side that had developed in her years of motherhood took the upper hand. "You said that you came from Whitehall. Did you eat dinner?''

The viscount looked blank. "I had breakfast,'' he offered.

Diana rolled her eyes in exasperation, then took his hand and led him downstairs to the kitchen. "You're under no obligation to feed me,'' he said mildly as she sat him down at the long scrubbed deal table.

"Perhaps not, Gervase,'' she said with an impish look. "But it is in my own best interest that you keep your strength up.'' While he laughed, she went to take stock of the larder. After a quick survey she said, "There is some cold sliced ham and bread and cheese. If you would like something hot, I could make an omelet in a few minutes.''

Gervase hesitated. He hadn't even known he was hungry, but now he felt ravenous, and the thought of hot food sounded wonderful. "If it's not too much trouble, I'd like that.''

"No trouble at all.'' To keep him from starvation for the next five minutes, Diana set bread and cheese on the table, then poured two beakers of ale, tangy and cool from the pantry.

Gervase felt an amazing sense of well-being as he watched Diana move gracefully around the kitchen, stoking up the coal fire in what looked like a very modern cooking range, snipping the ends of a chive plant that grew in a pot below the high, narrow window, then mixing them into the beaten eggs with slivers of ham and cheese. He'd had no idea Cyprians knew how to cook.

He admired the intentness of her face as she concentrated on her omelet. Strands of dark chestnut hair had escaped to curl around her neck, and she looked utterly delectable. He would let that part of the evening wait; as desirable as she was, he was enjoying this fragment of domesticity. Was this kind of comfort what life was for most people? If so, perhaps being a lord was more a liability than an asset. But common men didn't have a Diana Lindsay tending their hearths; they couldn't have afforded her services.

Remembering the nature of their relationship took some of the pleasure out of the scene. Of course it was in her interest to keep him happy, and obviously she was richly schooled in satisfying the many forms of male appetite.

Impossible to maintain the cynical thought as she served him the steaming omelet, the fragrance of chives scenting the room. Gervase said, "Aren't you going to have some? This is enormous."

She hesitated. "It does smell good. If you're sure there will be enough for you?"

"I think that half of this will ward off starvation a little longer," he said gravely.

She chuckled and got another plate, taking a quarter of the omelet for herself, and sat on the opposite side of the table. Having much the smaller portion, Diana finished first and thoughtfully sipped her ale as she admired her visitor, glad to see the lines of fatigue disappearing from his face. "What do you do at Whitehall?"

He shrugged and carved off a thick slice of bread. "Mostly I move papers from one pile to another."

"That doesn't sound very exciting."

"It isn't."

Driven by a random imp of curiosity, Diana asked,

"Are you really the chief spymaster of the British government?"

Had she not been watching so closely, she would have missed the slight hesitation as his fork paused in midair. Finishing the omelet, he said casually, "Who on earth told you that?"

"Madeline. When she asked about you, that is one of the things she heard. Apparently it is commonly said."

Gervase looked at her, his gray eyes cool. "A great many things are said commonly, most of which are not true. Why would you be interested in such matters?"

She shrugged. "I'm not interested in them for themselves, but I'm interested in you."

He eyed her rather warily over his ale. "All I do is move papers around. People may interpret that any way they choose. What else did Madeline hear about me?"

Narrowing her eyes as she tried to remember, Diana said, "That you are very wealthy. That you keep much to yourself, though you could enter any level of society you chose. That you have a mad wife in Scotland." She listed the items as if they were of equal importance.

Gervase didn't reply directly, merely raising his eyebrows ironically. "With such an intelligence network, she accuses *me* of being a spymaster?"

Diana shook her head. "She accuses you of nothing. Like any good merchant, we were concerned with gathering the facts needed to make a decision."

"How very rational of you."

She smiled then. "Not really. No matter how logical the process, in the end I make all of my decisions for emotional reasons. I'm not a rational person, you know."

"Good," he said, his voice very soft as he stood and rounded the table behind Diana, pulling her into his arms. "By a strange coincidence, I don't feel very rational myself just now."

She gasped as he kissed her neck, then made one

last hostess remark. "Do you wish to end your meal
with a sweet, my lord?"

"Exactly."

She lifted her face for a kiss, thinking that it would
be very easy to get used to this. The thought was a
flippant one, and she was unprepared for the surge of
passion she felt when his lips met hers. Raising her
arms, she clung to him, feeling Gervase's own shocked
and hungry response. Dimly she sensed that he was
equally startled at being seized by desires as unruly as
a river torrent, but neither of them had the will or the
desire to pull back. Doubt and caution would come
later.

It was very late when Gervase left. Diana had fallen
asleep, and after tucking the down quilt under her chin
he simply stood, feasting his eyes for long minutes
before he could bring himself to leave. He had never
met a beautiful woman who was devoid of vanity and
the arrogance that beauty brings, yet Diana, who was
the most beautiful of all, seemed without those flaws.
She was generous in her lovemaking, her responsiveness was a man's deepest dream, and the mere sight
of her could still rouse a flicker of desire in his exhausted and sated body.

Reality returned downstairs, where Madeline Gainford placidly awaited him. She had been sewing, but
she put her workbasket aside to intercept him in the
hall. Gervase had stiffened warily as the shadowed figure came from the salon, and he relaxed only slightly
after identifying her. What on earth could the woman
possibly want at four in the morning?

If she was aware of his suspicion, she ignored it.
"If you've a moment, my lord, I would like a few
words with you."

"Of course." He followed her back into the salon
and they both seated themselves, Gervase stretching
his legs out wearily. He had paid little attention to
Madeline Gainford when Diana had introduced them,
but now he saw that she was very attractive, with the
calm expression of one who has seen the best and worst

the human race can offer. If he hadn't just taken another mistress he would have wondered if she was available, but at the moment it was hard to feel interest in anyone other than Diana.

The wide brown eyes were scrutinizing him with the same thoroughness that he was exercising on her, and the staring match might have gone on indefinitely if Gervase weren't so tired. "At the risk of sounding impatient, what do you wish to discuss? It is rather late for socializing."

She reached into her workbasket for a piece of embroidery stretched over a hoop, then looked up. "I am interested in business, not socializing, my lord. Diana told me she refused your offer of a monthly allowance in favor of random gifts."

"Yes, and what business is it of yours?" he asked, his deep voice balanced on the edge of irritation.

"Diana is my business, Lord St. Aubyn. Since you are willing, I would like to see the arrangement regularized."

Glancing down, she made a tiny, precise stitch as she prepared to expand on her statement, but Gervase cut her off, his voice rough. "So pimping is your trade, and you wish to extract the last farthing of profit out of her. Very prudent. You'll not find another wench so valuable anytime soon."

The older woman flinched a little at his words, but her soft voice was level. "You mistake the matter. I wish to speak to you because I love Diana, not because I'm a panderer."

That was even worse. Gervase knew there were courtesans who preferred their own sex. Some men found the idea exciting, but the thought of Diana and this woman as lovers revolted him. "I see. Rather than trying to extract more money, you want to warn me off because you are jealous."

Disconcertingly, she laughed. "I express myself poorly. I love Diana as the daughter I never had, as a friend, and as a woman who saved my live in several ways. Not," she said with a gleam in her dark eyes, "in the fashion you luridly imagine."

She shrugged expressively. "Diana is too inexperienced to know what she is turning down. It's all very well to be romantic and quixotic when one is young, but twenty years from now she will be glad to have savings to ensure a comfortable old age."

She set another stitch in her embroidery. "To a courtesan, having 'money in the Funds' is rather like the holy grail. Diana may not appreciate what she turned down, but I do. I intend to see that she earns all the security she can."

Gervase closed his eyes briefly, wishing this interview was taking place at a time when his brain was in normal working condition. Was she really trying to protect her younger friend, or merely being greedy on her own behalf? Probably the latter, unless Diana had set Madeline to this task. Opening his eyes, he said, "Every month Diana is my mistress, I'll have two hundred pounds deposited in an account in her name. You can tell her about it or not, as you choose, but you will not be able to touch a penny yourself. Is that satisfactory?"

He expected anger that the money was out of her reach, but she smiled serenely. "Perfectly satisfactory, my lord. A very gentlemanly thing to do."

He stood, saying with heavy irony, "Will there be anything else, Miss Gainford?"

"Yes. Please don't mention this arrangement to Diana."

His mouth twisted. "Do you really expect me to believe that she doesn't know what you are doing?"

She gestured gracefully, the candlelight glinting from the needle in her hand. "You should believe it. It's the truth."

"Ah, yes," he said, unable to avoid bitterness as he remembered the innocence on Diana's sleeping face. Diana, the consummate actress. "Everyone knows how truthful whores are."

There was some satisfaction in seeing the dull flush on her cheeks, but it was nowhere near strong enough to counter the dark mood that dogged his heels on the walk home.

* * *

The next morning it was easier to accept Diana's duplicity in having her companion demand more money. Doubtless the viscount's new mistress had her full female share of volatility and illogic; he supposed that after grandly refusing his offer of a regular allowance, she had changed her mind. Since she wouldn't admit to her *volte-face*, he devised a method to compensate her at exactly the level he had initially offered: no more, no less. When he joined her for a morning ride the day after, he went prepared.

Diana was waiting in her salon and she greeted him with a blithe kiss as the morning sun burnished her chestnut hair. Did she ever look less than ravishing? After bowing over her gloved hand, Gervase handed her a small item of filigreed gold.

Diana studied it in puzzlement, then gave him a smile that began deep in her lapis-blue eyes. "Should I recognize this? Perhaps it is too early in the morning and my wits are begging."

When she smiled like that, Gervase felt the usual enchanted delight begin to steal over him and his lingering resentment over her request for more money dissipated. "That is the beginning of a series of payments to you."

"Oh, I'm to be paid in little bits of worked gold?" she asked with interest.

"It's the catch of a pearl necklace," he explained, "a rather beautiful double rope of pearls. I had the jeweler disassemble it." He dug a tiny object wrapped in velvet from an inner pocket. "Whenever I visit you, I'll bring another pearl. Then, when the necklace is complete, I'll have it restrung."

She examined the flawless, lustrous sphere, its silvery sheen marking it as a pearl of the highest quality, then said with a mixture of admiration and amusement, "Now, this really *is* imaginative, my lord. In one stroke you have surprised me while efficiently saving yourself from having to think about the subject again for months to come."

The viscount's face grew more than usually expressionless, but there was no criticism in her chiming laughter. Placing one hand on his arm, she stood on her toes to brush a velvet-soft kiss on his cheek. "Thank you, Gervase. You are most kind."

Even that light touch was enough to make him consider forgoing their ride for indoor sport, but the morning was bright and beckoning, and there would be few more as fine before winter set in. They walked back to the stables, where Phaedra had taken up permanent residence. Since Diana was now her mistress, the loan horse had become a gift horse.

As they rode the short distance to Hyde Park, Gervase felt some remorse about the pearl necklace. His midnight chat with Madeline had resulted in a commitment of two hundred pounds a month, to be deposited into a bank. Based on the cost of the pearl necklace, if he visited Diana an average of three times a week, she would receive one hundred pounds' worth of pearls each month, which would equal his original offer of a monthly three hundred pounds. He had thought that he was being ironically clever, but she had accepted the idea with such good grace that he was a little ashamed of having calculated so closely. Since she provided such superior service, he would rather be generous than haggle over every pennyworth of value.

Shrugging guilt aside, Gervase gave himself to enjoyment of the brisk autumn air and the teasing conversation of his mistress. Diana was surprisingly well-read, and they became involved in a discussion of Restoration dramatists, a light topic for a bright morning. They had thrice circled the park and were heading back to Charles Street when Diana's words broke off in the middle of a dissertation on the female playwright Aphra Behn.

Gervase's mount was a step ahead of hers and he glanced back when her voice broke. Diana had unconsciously tightened her hands on the reins, pulling Phaedra to a stop, and her face was white and strained as she looked down a small cross street. "Is anything wrong?'' he asked quickly, responding to an automatic protective instinct.

She swallowed hard and shook her head, but her voice was uneven as she signaled the mare to move forward. ''Not really. I just saw a man who . . .''— she searched for a phrase, then ended lamely—''was once rather unpleasant to me.''

Gervase felt his face harden at her remark. So she had seen an old lover; doubtless London was full of them. His voice cool, he said, ''If you placed yourself entirely under my protection, I would have the right to deal with any man who bothers you, but your present position leaves you open to insult.''

She lifted her head, quick color flaring in her cheeks. ''I have not asked for your help, my lord.''

''No doubt the dragon who guards you chases off unwanted suitors,'' he said acidly.

''The dragon . . . ?''

''Your friend Miss Gainford.''

Diana laughed. ''I never thought of her as a dragon, but she would make an elegant one. Or would she be a dragoness?''

Gervase smiled back, his momentary irritation forgotten. Diana had a near-magical ability to disarm, and as they rode on, debating the merits of Aphra Behn, he was calculating how much time he could afford to spend with her before going to Whitehall.

By the time they rode into her stableyard and he had helped her from Phaedra, his hands tarrying on her supple waist, he had decided that Whitehall could damned well wait.

The Count de Veseul had no trouble following Diana Lindsay and Lord St. Aubyn the few blocks to Charles Street. It was mere chance that the count had happened to see her as he returned home from a long night of illicit business. He had thought about the trollop a great deal since meeting her at the opera and had made discreet inquiries, but she seemed to have disappeared from view after the briefest of appearances on the courtesan scene. He had been on the verge of instituting a serious search when luck had thrown her right in his path, but then, he had always been lucky. Amusing to see how quickly she had recognized him, and how the blood had drained from her face. She was no less beautiful for being frightened; quite the contrary.

And to think St. Aubyn was one of her current lovers; if that didn't prove his luck, nothing did. The count knew a great deal about St. Aubyn, and respected the cool, analytical brilliance of the Englishman's mind. Indeed, St. Aubyn was the only man in Britain that Veseul feared might expose him, and he was delighted to see the viscount looking like a daft youth with his first woman. How satisfying to know the Englishman was prey to vulgar emotional weakness; the Frenchman had no such frailty.

After the couple entered the elegant town house, Veseul lingered in an alley opposite, imagining what the two were doing upstairs behind that proper Mayfair facade, images flickering through his brain like a lewd dream. It aroused him to think of another man possessing that beautiful wanton; knowing that man was the British spymaster added a *soupçon* of decadent excitement. When the count finally took Diana Lindsay, it would take a very long time indeed to satisfy the desire that was accumulating.

The detour made Veseul late for his rendezvous back at the rooms he leased in a large block of flats, a busy place where comings and goings at odd hours were unremarkable. Waiting impatiently was his associate Biron, a weasel-faced man of no style or elegance, but most useful.

After they had discussed the usual business, Veseul pulled a cigar from his desk and trimmed the end as he said casually, "I want you to put someone in the household at 17 Charles Street."

Biron regarded him suspiciously. "Who merits such close investigation? Our resources are not unlimited."

Veseul lit the cigar, then exhaled, watching Biron flinch back from the stream of smoke. "Just a whore, but she has interesting guests. Make sure that whoever you put there is observant, reliable, and of unquestioning loyalty.''

Biron glared, suspecting that his superior's motives were personal, but he nodded his head stiffly. ''It shall be done.''

Biron was an orthodox revolutionary, bound by dogma, and it chafed him to obey an aristocrat of the *ancien régime*. Veseul took malicious amusement in knowing that Biron thought the count should have been sent to Mme. Guillotine in the heady days of the Reign of Terror. The weasel-faced man had a small, unimaginative mind, and for all his revolutionary fervor, he had done less for the cause of France than the aristocrat he despised.

After Biron left, the Frenchman mused for a moment, pleased by the thought that the snare was beginning to tighten around Diana Lindsay, so slowly that she would have no inkling of what lay ahead of her. The count was not like other men, a creature of impatient lust that must be gratified instantly. A connoisseur knew how to wait and savor. He imagined how she would look with her limbs bound to the posts of a bed, her flawless face distorted by the knowledge that there would be no escape.

But he had more important things to do than contemplate what he would do to a whore, be she ever so lovely. Veseul began to write a summary of the information Biron had brought, adding his own comments about the implications before translating the report into a cipher and recopying it.

When he was finished, he folded the sheet very small, then took the heavy brass seal that bore the reversed incisions of the arms of Veseul. Unscrewing the handle revealed a second, secret seal in the form of a bird rising from flames: a phoenix.

9

DIANA moved through her daily rounds with a cat-in-the-creampot smile on her face; no amount of intellectual knowledge of loving could match the reality. Gervase was constantly in her thoughts, and not just because of the passion they shared. Though the mere thought of making love with him produced a quickening deep inside her, his unexpected tenderness drew her most. He was a warm and witty companion, seldom laughing but with a wry, self-mocking smile that was irresistible. With her, he was a different man from his usual cold, commanding presence, and she took pride in the fact that she created that difference.

Diana wanted Gervase in her life with a fierceness similar to what she felt for her son: she wanted to be his woman publicly, to sleep all night in his arms and be accepted by his friends. It was a cruel paradox; becoming a courtesan may have tainted her forever, yet they would never have come together had she not entered the harlots' world.

Sometimes, with chill despair, she remembered what Maddy had told her: *He has a mad wife in Scotland.* Those flat words represented a conundrum she had no idea how to solve. She knew that he desired her, at least for now, but a mistress was an object of lust, not love. While she had a place in his life, it was a small, dishonorable one. Was this what she had come to London for? Surely, somewhere ahead there would be a solution.

Whenever her thoughts reached that point, she resolutely turned her mind to other things, laughing with her son and friends, practicing her knife throwing. She did her domestic chores, she hired a French cook who had a tale of woe, and she fought a running battle with Geoffrey about riding lessons.

The issue was an old one. Her son had always loved horses, and Phaedra's residence in the stables caused him to redouble his pleas for a pony. Diana felt deeply ambivalent about the subject. The life she wanted for Geoffrey meant that he must someday learn to ride, because a gentleman who didn't was a freak, and a freak was the last thing she wanted her son to be. However, riding could be dangerous even for the best of horsemen, and if Geoffrey suffered a *grand mal* or even a *petit mal* seizure, he might be seriously injured or killed in a fall.

For the last three years she had taken cowardly refuge from his desire for a pony by saying that she would consider it when he was older, but she knew she could not put him off much longer. To compensate for her refusal to let him ride, Diana let Geoffrey keep a scrawny kitten he had rescued from a gang of street boys. But few beings are as persistent as young children, and Diana knew that the subject of riding would surface again.

When he recalled the autumn of 1807 in later years, Gervase knew that rain must have fallen, the London skies must have grayed, a hundred minor irritations of living must have occurred, but he remembered none of them: the weeks passed in a haze of golden days and fiery nights. The affairs of the nation, if not prospering, at least became no worse. The Portuguese were persuaded to remove their fleet to safety in Brazil. His own work went well as his network of informants grew ever wider and deeper, and government officials of all political stripes came to accept that his recommendations were untainted by self-interest.

But it was Diana that cast the enchantment over his life. Warm and welcoming, she was always there when he wanted her, sensing his moods, knowing when to talk and when to be silent; when to melt in his arms and when to take the lead with a gentle sexual aggres-

sion that was richly stimulating. Diana was so much
the perfect woman that she couldn't possibly be real;
only a paid mistress with a flair for acting could be so
wholly responsive. Gervase sometimes wondered what
was the real woman and what was pretense. The
warmth and sensuality couldn't be entirely false or she
would not be so convincing, yet she had a maddening,
elusive air of mystery that veiled the central core of
her.

He seldom wasted time with such thoughts. It was
easier to accept her as she appeared, and he glided
through the days on a strange emotion that he neither
recognized nor named. Only much later, when those
perfect days were history, did he realize that the emotion was called happiness.

More than three pearls were being delivered every
week; he should have bought a triple-strand necklace,
not a double. Diana kept the pearls in a crystal goblet
on her dressing table, and the level visibly rose as the
weeks passed.

The goblet itself was a gift from him, one of a set
of heavy Venetian cut-glass vessels. He found he enjoyed giving things to Diana, and she took the same
pleasure in the armload of flowers that he impulsively
bought from a street vendor as she did in the priceless,
exquisitely wrought mantel clock said to have belonged to Marie Antoinette. In fact, she may have liked
the flowers better, judging by the way she buried her
face in them before giving him a brilliant, pollen-
dusted smile.

A routine soon developed. Several nights a week
Gervase came by after working late and they shared a
supper, talking and laughing before making love.
Sometimes they rode very early in the morning, when
Rotten Row was as quiet as the viscount's own country
estate. Gervase offered to take her to more public gath-
erings, such as the theater, but she always refused, and
he was secretly pleased. He knew most men would
flaunt the fact that they had won such a prize as Diana,
but he preferred the magical bubble of privacy that
they shared. Their seclusion also saved him from hav-

ing to speculate on what other men present might be enjoying her matchless charms.

Then the golden age ended. The changes were subtle, though the event that triggered them was not.

Gervase had been in Kent talking to smugglers for six days, and he had missed Diana with a constant ache, much as a missing limb was said to haunt its former owner. He had returned a day early just to see her, and his first act had been to send a footman the short distance to her house to ascertain if she could receive him. He was not sure what he would have done if she had refused or had been otherwise occupied; probably gone to her house and kicked her other company out of bed.

It was almost ten o'clock when he arrived and she let him in. He wasted no time before kissing her, at the same time checking that every curve was just as he remembered it. Though Diana was laughing when she emerged from his embrace, he saw that she looked tired; beautiful, but not quite as flawless as usual.

"I shouldn't have left you," he said teasingly, his forefinger brushing the hint of shadow under her eyes. "You look like you missed me."

"I did." She accompanied her words with a long hug, her arms wrapping his waist while she laid her head against his shoulder. It was a simple request for comfort with no undertones of passion, and Gervase felt oddly touched as he held her, feeling her tension diminish as he stroked her. After a few peaceful minutes he asked, "Is something wrong?"

She hesitated, then stepped away, shaking her head. "Not really. I'm always a little sad at this time of year. Everything is so bleak. The whole of winter lies ahead, and spring seems so far away."

Laying his arm around her shoulders, he steered her downstairs, where they had gotten into the habit of eating. He liked the hominess of her kitchen, so different from the lethal formality of the official St. Aubyn dining rooms, where sixty people could eat cold food in high state. "English winters are certainly a dreary affair. Still, they don't bother me too much, perhaps because I was born in winter. It's my season."

"Oh, really?" Diana went to the oven to remove the pheasant pie she had put in for warming when Gervase's footman had called to announce that he was back in London. Using heavy mitts, she pulled it out and placed it on the pine table, where she had set two places, an open bottle of red wine, and an assortment of homemade pickles. "When is your birthday? I'm ashamed of myself for not asking before."

"Good Lord, Diana, what does it matter?" he scoffed as he poured wine into the goblets and served the steaming hot pie. "But for the record, I was born December 24."

"Christmas Eve! What a lovely present that was for your mother." Ignoring her own plate, Diana sat on the bench next to Gervase, enjoying the feel of his thigh against hers.

"On the contrary, she said that being in the straw wrecked her holiday." The dryness of Gervase's voice did not quite conceal the remembered pain. His mother had made that statement in her characteristic manner, the barb concealed under languid honey as she beckoned and rejected at the same time. He moved on quickly, before Diana's thoughtful glance could become a question. "It's interesting that our birthdays are exactly opposite, each at the end of the solstice, after the sun has paused for three days and is on the verge of turning."

She nodded. "When I was little, I thought it rather special to have been born on Midsummer Day. The solstices were honored in all pagan cultures. What is Christmas but our own version of the Saturnalia, the celebration that the sun is returning and life will continue instead of dying in endless night?"

Gervase looked up from his pheasant pie and pickled onions with amusement. "Where on earth did you learn that?" Diana's magpie assortment of knowledge never ceased to amaze him.

She colored slightly. "Oh, I read it somewhere. Do opposite birthdays mean that we are also opposites?"

"Of course," he said softly, his clear gray eyes flaring with the intensity she had come to recognize. He laid his fork down and turned sideways on the bench to face her. "I am male and you are female. How much more opposite can two people get?"

He put one hand under her chin and lifted it for a warm, pheasanty kiss. "Haven't you ever heard that opposites attract?"

"What do they attract?" she asked in a voice as husky as his. Undoing a button on his shirt, she slid her hand inside, feeling his quickened breath.

"If you've forgotten so quickly, it appears that I must remind you." He wrapped his arms around her, his weight carrying her back until she was lying on the bench beneath him, laughing.

Because the bench was hard and narrow and the stone floor would be cold, they adjourned to her bedroom before matters proceeded much further. Six days of separation had fanned the flames of desire to a bonfire and they made love at fever pitch. Gervase couldn't get enough of Diana, wanting to bury himself in her, to know every secret of her body and mind. Diana's own kisses were equally fierce and she clung to him with a fervor that went beyond passion to deep need.

After the explosive climax, there was a lazy interval when Diana retrieved the abandoned supper from the kitchen, bringing it upstairs for cold consumption in bed. When they made love again, it was a slow savoring as she lay on top of him, controlling the tempo with the gentle pulsation of her hips.

Later they lay curled up together, her back nestled against his stomach, his hand cupping her breast as the slow rhythm of his breathing stirred tendrils of her dark hair. Outside, raw wind whistled down the streets of Mayfair, but Gervase couldn't remember when he had felt happier or more content. If six days resulted in such a spectacular experience, he wondered lazily what kind of reunion they would have if separated for a fortnight; it might be beyond his powers of survival. Still, one could hardly ask a better end. . . . He dozed off, hoping Diana would fall so deeply asleep that she would forget to send him home. At that moment, the height of his ambition was to spend a full night with her.

When the faint tapping on the door came, he was so relaxed that he didn't stir as Diana stiffened to alertness, then slipped from his arms. He heard the faint rustling as she donned robe and slippers, but the low-voiced conversation with the person at the door was unintelligible.

Contentment shattered when she left the room, closing the door quietly behind her. Gervase came fully, angrily awake. Good God, could she possibly have another lover calling at this hour? Perhaps some damned gamester who had just left the tables was stopping by to complete the evening's entertainment. His fury left no room for common sense and he dressed swiftly, yanking on his clothing by the ruddy glow of the coal fire.

Stepping into the hall, he heard the distant footsteps of Diana and the servant and he followed, driven by a sick need to learn who had the influence to rouse her at this hour. In the shadowed silence, he easily located the stairwell she had climbed and he took the steps two at a time, quiet as a hunting cat. Odd that she would meet someone up here, but she could hardly bring another man into her regular bedroom with Gervase there. Bitterly he wondered how many beds she kept in readiness. The upstairs hall was dimly lit by a partially open door halfway down the length, and he softly went to gaze in, even as he damned himself for pursuing an action that could only cause pain.

The sight that met his eyes was indeed shocking, though not in the way he had expected; convulsions are a terrifying sight, particularly in a child so young. The little boy's body arched, shaking the whole bed, and his desperate gagging sounds filled the corners of the room. Diana was beside him, her face anguished, her hands deft and gentle as she steadied his body from twisting onto the floor. Gervase registered the fact that a stern-faced older woman and a young maid were also in the room, but his attention was riveted by the drama on the bed.

Then the seizure ended. The silence was profound as the child's body relaxed and his desperate breathing returned to normal. Diana leaned over, holding him with infinite gentleness.

Gervase was immobilized by a contradictory blend of relief that she had not come to another lover, and pure infantile jealousy; seeing her lavish so much tenderness on another person left him feeling diminished. He knew how contemptible he was to begrudge a child love, but the part of him that ached at the sight was also a child: a wounded child.

Invisible in the dark of the hall, he could have taken his small-minded resentment and faded away to nurse it alone, burying it so deeply that he could deny its existence. Instead, after hovering on the brink of flight, he stepped into the room.

Everyone turned to him, but he saw only the two figures on the bed as they stared with identical lapis-blue eyes. The boy's face was questioning, but Diana, gentle Diana, who always welcomed and never reproached, was gazing at her lover with furious vigilance, like a tigress whose cub was threatened. If looks could kill, Francis Brandelin would be a viscount. Gervase was momentarily rocked by her hostility, wondering why his entrance caused such antagonism. Was this virago the true Diana and the gentle mistress only the practiced mask of a courtesan?

In spite of his internal questions, Gervase continued walking toward the bed. The tension in the room had a gelid, explosive quality, and only the child was oblivious of it. Secure within Diana's arms, he asked, "Who are you?"

Gervase sat sideways on the bed opposite his mistress. The bed was so low that it must have been custom-made, perhaps to save the boy from a dangerous fall if a seizure hurled him to the floor. "My name is St. Aubyn. I'm a friend of your mother's."

The child gravely offered his hand. With those vivid blue eyes, it was quite unnecessary to hear, "Good evening, sir. I'm Geoffrey Lindsay,'' to know that this was Diana's son.

The boy's small hand gripped firmly. Looking the visitor up and down, he asked, ''Why are you calling so late?''

He saw Diana's body grow even more rigid, if that were possible. Did she think that Gervase would call her a whore to her own child? That would explain her anger. Directing his words to Geoffrey, Gervase answered, ''I know it's past the fashionable hour for calling, but I've been out of town. I stopped by hoping your mother would feed me.''

Geoffrey grinned. ''Mama likes feeding people.''

''She does it well.'' As one would expect of Diana's child, the boy was beautiful, with dark hair, a bright intelligent face, and a maturity in his eyes unusual in one so young. From the looks of that smile, he'd inherited her charm as well.

Geoffrey's face darkened. ''Did . . . did you see what happened?''

Gervase nodded. ''Yes. That was quite a seizure you had. A wretched nuisance, isn't it?''

The expressive eyes widened. ''Do you have fits too?''

''Not now, but I did sometimes when I was a boy.''

Now both pairs of blue eyes were studying him intently. Even though she kept a protective arm around Geoffrey, Diana's hostility was lessening. Her eyes shifted from Gervase to someone beyond; then she nodded in response to a silent question. Behind him he heard the other two women withdraw from the room, leaving Diana alone with her son and her lover.

With cautious excitement Geoffrey asked, ''You mean . . . I'm really not the only one who has seizures?''

Speaking for the first time, his mother said, ''Of course you aren't, darling, you know better than that.''

Geoffrey shook his head stubbornly. ''You *say* that I'm not, but I've never met anyone else who has them.''

So the boy thought that he was the only one, some

kind of freak or monster? It was an emotion Gervase understood all too well. "It's not that uncommon. When I was in the army, I had a corporal who had seizures occasionally. A physician once told me that anyone can have a seizure under the right—or rather wrong—conditions. I had them when I had fevers."

Geoffrey almost bounced on the bed, fascination written on his face. "That's what happens to me! Mama hates it when I'm ill, because I have more fits."

Gervase glanced up, but Diana was avoiding his gaze. If her son had been ill, that might explain her fatigue and tension when he came earlier. "I can see why it would upset her," he said in a matter-of-fact voice. "They say my mother wouldn't come near the nursery when I had even the mildest case of sniffles."

Geoffrey was inching toward his visitor, the blankets a tangled drift around him. "What did it feel like for you?"

Gervase cast his mind back twenty years. "I never felt anything during the actual seizure—it was like being asleep. But I remember that when one began, it felt like . . . like someone had tied a strap around my forehead and was pulling it backward."

"That's it exactly!" the boy exclaimed. "Like a giant, tugging at me. Sometimes I fight him off and don't have a fit."

"What?" Diana stared at her son in surprise. "Sometimes you can stop the seizure from starting? You never told me that."

He fidgeted, glancing askance. "It doesn't work very often."

Shaking her head, she straightened and said, "I guess a mother is the last to know." She still wouldn't look at Gervase.

Another memory surfaced now, and the viscount said abruptly, "The worst of it was the eyes. I'd blank out, then the next thing I knew I was lying on the ground. People would be gathered around, staring at me. All those eyes . . ."

He stopped speaking as he saw that Geoffrey's face was very still, and etched with more knowledge than a child should have. Any epileptic knew those stares, the eyes avid with curiosity, or fear, or disgust, or perhaps the worst of all, pity. Geoffrey knew, but would not speak of it in front of his mother.

Instead the boy said after a brief hesitation, "Did you learn to ride even though you had fits?"

"Of course."

Geoffrey gave his mother a speaking glance. Diana headed off the "I told you so" hovering on her son's tongue by saying briskly, "Isn't it time you got to sleep, young man?"

"No! Not tired at all." His remark was undercut by a wide yawn. As if it were a signal, a young tabby cat jumped on the bed. Geoffrey lifted the little animal in his hands. "When I had the seizure, Tiger was frightened and jumped off. I've only had her a few weeks, and she's already learned to sleep on my bed."

"Clever cat," the viscount said, suppressing a smile.

"It wouldn't be a bad idea if you tried sleeping on the bed too, young man," Diana said firmly as she pressed her son back, then tucked the blankets around boy and cat. "This is not the right time for a lengthy discussion. Besides, Lord St. Aubyn must be getting home himself."

The blue eyes flew open. "He's a real lord?"

Gervase almost laughed out loud; he couldn't remember when he'd impressed someone with so little effort. "Yes, a real lord. A viscount, to be exact."

The boy eyed him doubtfully. "Where's your purple robe?"

"I only wear that on special occasions, when I can't avoid it. Usually it's a nuisance, always getting stepped on and knocking vases off tables," Gervase said gravely. He stood and proffered his hand. "A pleasure to meet you, Mr. Lindsay."

This time Geoffrey's grip was a good deal less firm, but he still had the energy left to offer the kitten's paw for shaking.

Gervase accepted the thin striped forepaw with fair aplomb. The cat appeared to have no opinion. Then the viscount looked more closely and said in surprise, "Good Lord, the cat has thumbs." Tiger had a long extra toe that projected almost exactly the same as a human thumb, though it was less flexible.

Geoffrey smiled mischievously as he fought a losing battle to keep his eyes open. "Mama says that it is scary to think what cats will get into once they've developed the opposable thumb."

Gervase gave Diana an amused glance but she was looking down at her son, her expression obscured. Even with his eyes closed, Geoffrey was unready to call it a night. His voice blurred with fatigue, he asked, "Will you tell me about the army sometime?"

"If you wish."

Diana glanced up sharply, then thought better of what she had intended saying. As she leaned over to kiss her son's cheek, Gervase withdrew and waited outside. In spite of the lateness of the hour, he had a great many things to say to his mistress.

10

DIANA felt the door panels digging into her rigid shoulder blades as the anger she had suppressed in front of Geoffrey emerged as a glare. Her temper was not improved by the glint of amusement in Gervase's eyes. Her voice low and hard, she said, "Clearly the rumors of your spying activities were accurate."

Unalarmed by her expression, the viscount said, "I admit I was curious where you were going at such an odd hour. If he's been ill, I suppose that explains why you look tired tonight."

"It's time you left."

"It *is* very late," he agreed, "but not yet quite time to leave. If we're going to fight, let's do it downstairs. This corridor is freezing and you must be too."

The blasted man was right; her shivering was as much from cold as from anger. Taking the candlestick from her hand, he wrapped one warm arm around her unyielding shoulders and led her back to the bedroom. A few minutes later she was ensconced in a wing chair by the fire, a cashmere shawl wrapped around her and a glass of brandy in her hand. Pampering was a novel and pleasant experience, but she refused to let herself be mollified.

Gervase knelt by the hearth, stirring up the fire and adding more coal until it was burning bright and hot. He had already poured himself a brandy and now he took the opposite chair, lounging back and crossing his long legs at the ankles. In the dim light it was impossible to read his expression; his face was a collection of elegant shadows, hawklike and distant. She didn't want to be affected by how he looked, and she certainly didn't want to think of what they had been doing with such pleasure earlier in the evening, so she stared into the heart of the fire. If he wanted to talk, let him say something.

He regarded her thoughtfully. "Why are you so angry?"

"Need you ask?" she said. "Following me upstairs was an unforgivable intrusion. I have been very careful to keep Geoffrey in ignorance of what I do. Until tonight, I have been successful. Now . . ."

It would have been much easier if he had met anger with anger. Instead, he said after a moment, "You're quite right. I've always had more curiosity than is good for me. It didn't occur to me that I was putting you in an untenable position, and I'm sorry if that has happened. Still, I doubt any damage was done. He's young enough to accept my story without questions."

"He believed it now, but when he's older, he'll remember and wonder." She pulled her legs up under her in the chair, her body tight as strung wire. "How do you think it will make him feel if he deduces that his mother was a whore?"

"Since my mother was one, I know exactly how he would feel." His bitterness was unmistakable, and she glanced at him, startled. Gervase never spoke of his life before India.

With obvious effort he said in a milder tone, "Actually, it would be more accurate to say that whoring was her pleasure, not her vocation. No, I don't suppose Geoffrey would be happy to think that of you—boys have very high standards for their mothers—but surely you must know that he is bound to learn the truth eventually, unless you send him away."

She said tightly, "I hardly intend to do this forever. In a few years my . . . market value will have diminished considerably. By the time he is old enough to start wondering, this life should be behind me. One reason I prefer to live quietly is so there will be few people to connect me with my disreputable past."

It gave him a sharp sense of loss to think she might not always be there in the future. It would be very easy to carry on with her like this forever; even though her spectacular beauty would fade with time, there would still be passion and comfort.

But this was not the time to discuss her future. "I doubt that one night's encounter will make Geoffrey think the worse of you. If you don't want me to see him again, I won't."

She gave a brittle laugh. "You don't know much about children, do you?" she said, then subsided into silence again.

"No, I don't," he agreed. "Enlighten me."

She sipped her brandy, then wearily leaned her head against the back of the chair. "The first thing he will do tomorrow is ask when you'll call next. Then he'll chatter about how you had seizures too; it's a great event in his life to meet someone who had a similar affliction. He will also rehearse, in excruciating detail, all the questions he wants to ask about the army, and he will end by telling everyone how you shook Tiger's paw."

Gervase laughed out loud. "As bad as that?"

After a moment, Diana had to smile too. In spite of her motherly qualms, the situation was not without humor. Trying to maintain her righteous indignation, she looked up and said ruefully, "It may seem funny to you, but you don't have to deal with the consequences. Pandora's box has been opened."

"You're right, I don't know much about children," he admitted, "but he's a fine boy. You must be proud of him."

He had found the perfect way to disarm her, and for a man unused to children, he had done a surprisingly good job of conversing with one. It was getting harder to maintain her irritation, so she changed the subject. "The seizures—I gather you don't have them anymore?"

"Not since I was twelve or thirteen." He shrugged, his shoulders wide in the firelight. "While seizures were a feature of my childhood, they were rare, most of them when I was under six. One physician told my father that fits are not uncommon in small children and often go away as they grow up, which was what happened to me. I gather that your son's problem is more severe.''

She nodded, staring into the glowing coals. ''Yes. He has fewer *grand mal* seizures than when he was an infant, not even one a week unless he's ill, but they seem to last longer. He also has *petit mal* seizures, the staring spells, and they occur more often. They last only a few seconds and aren't usually a problem, but if he were doing something dangerous . . .'' Her voice broke. When it was even again, she continued, ''I've asked physicians, but no one can say what will happen to him in the future.''

Almost against her will, she found herself speaking her worst fear. ''If he gets worse . . .'' She swallowed, then finished almost inaudibly, ''They put dangerous epileptics in madhouses.''

''Geoffrey is unlikely to end up in a madhouse.'' The calmness of his tone was a balm. ''There is obviously nothing wrong with his mind. While it is possible that his condition will worsen, he is likely to stay the same or even improve. It is a hard uncertainty to live with, but all life is uncertain. An accident can turn the healthiest of men into an invalid in an instant. Geoffrey will have to live within limits, but not intolerable ones.''

Gervase swirled his brandy as he mused half to himself, ''I remember how ghastly it was, knowing my own mind was betraying me, but Geoffrey seems to have adjusted to it. There is no reason to assume that he can't have a satisfying life—other epileptics do. They say that Napoleon himself has seizures.''

''I'm not sure Bonaparte is the best example of a successful life. Still, I take your point.'' Diana sighed. His words were nothing she hadn't thought a thousand times, but it was good to be reminded by someone more detached. Her son's lively mind and good nature had gained him acceptance in his school; surely he could do as well in the wider world as he grew. ''I know I worry too much. I try not to flutter over Geof-

frey, but I'm not always successful. It's fortunate he
has Madeline and Edith as well.''

"Edith?''

"The older woman who was in his room when you
came in. She takes care of Geoffrey, the household,
and everyone in it. I suppose she is rather like his
grandmother, and Madeline his favorite aunt.'' She
examined the amber depths of her brandy as she voiced
one of her secret concerns. ''We all adore him, but
there aren't enough men in his life. That's one reason
he was so interested in you.''

"Is his father alive?''

He knew immediately that it was the wrong question
to ask. In a voice that could have cut glass, Diana said,
''I do not wish to discuss Geoffrey's father.''

Gervase certainly had his secrets, and she had a right
to hers, but he was intensely curious about the boy's
father. Diana might be a widow. More likely Geoffrey
was illegitimate, which would explain why Diana was
a member of the oldest profession rather than respectably married. In a vague, general way, Gervase had
resented all the anonymous other men in her life, but
now Geoffrey gave him a more specific focus of jealousy. The boy was a link to his mother's earlier lover;
every time she looked at her son, she must think of
the man who had seduced her. She would have been
scarcely more than a child herself.

Gervase was very good at extrapolating a whole picture from scattered fragments of information, and his
past observations, plus what he had learned tonight,
suggested that Diana had been raised the protected
daughter of some prosperous merchant or was even of
the minor gentry. Then she had fallen in love with
some handsome, smooth-talking scoundrel who had
casually impregnated and abandoned her, and her
family had cast her off.

It didn't bear thinking of. Gervase found he was
holding the cut-glass goblet so tightly that it left
grooves in his hand. Suddenly he understood in a vis-
ceral way why Diana had wished to keep her life in
separate compartments. She had played flawlessly the

role of the perfect mistress, with no past or conflicting loyalties, and he had accepted and enjoyed her on those uncomplicated terms.

Now that was no longer possible. As she stared into the glowing coals, her beautiful profile sad and remote in the firelight, she defied the labels of "mistress," or "whore," or anything else that could be casually described and dismissed. She was simply Diana, who pleased him more than any other woman he had ever known. Her anger and hostility this evening were curiously endearing. She was no longer the perfect illusion, but a real woman, one who grieved for the child she loved and who must have gone through hellishly difficult times before achieving the gentle tranquillity that characterized her now.

Sitting half a dozen feet away, Gervase felt closer to her than he had earlier, when their bodies had been so intimately entwined. Impulsively he said, "Come to Aubynwood for Christmas."

Her head came up in surprise and she turned to face him. In the shadows, he could no longer see her expression. "You would have me stay in your own house?"

"Why not? It would cause comment in London, but 'gentlemen' can be as indiscreet as they wish on their own estates."

A smile hovered around her lips at his cynical words, but she shook her head. "It's a tempting offer, but I can't accept."

"Of course." Finishing his brandy, he set his goblet down on the side table with a little more force than necessary. "I had forgotten that your other customers would be unwilling to forgo your services for a fortnight." Gervase was surprised to hear just how caustic his words sounded.

"That isn't the reason," she said. His irritation seemed to increase her calmness. "Much of the fashionable world will be away from London at the same time, so I could leave without being missed. But I am hardly going to leave my son alone for Christmas. He and Edith and Madeline are my family."

"Bring him along," Gervase said recklessly. "Bring Madeline. Bring Edith. Bring the French cook if you want. Aubynwood is large enough to absorb your whole household."

"Are you serious?"

He felt absurdly pleased at the startled note in her voice. "I am always serious," he stated. "It's my besetting sin."

With the warm, intimate laughter he loved, she rose and came to sit on the arm of his chair, brushing a feather-soft hand over his hair. "I will have to discuss it with Madeline and Edith, but if they agree, I would be very happy to come."

"Does Geoffrey get a vote?" He raised his hand and laid his palm on her cheek, feeling the flex of bone and tendon under her satiny skin as she spoke.

"I know he'll be delighted to be in the country again."

So they had lived in the country. He added the fact to his slender file on Diana even as he drew her head down for a kiss. Her lips were soft and yielding, all trace of her earlier anger gone, but after a leisurely interval she lifted her head, doing her best to suppress a yawn. "It's too late to be starting that again, my lord. While I am properly impressed by your stamina, I am so exhausted that I could fall asleep sitting up."

He smiled, sliding his hand under her velvet sleeve to caress her smooth arm, not wanting to go. "I have an ulterior motive for inviting you to Aubynwood. Maybe there we can spend the whole night together." When she hesitated, he added, "I assume that you won't do that here because of Geoffrey."

Diana nodded. "Exactly. Geoffrey may have accepted that faradiddle about you happening by at two in the morning for a snack, but it would be impossible to explain having you in my bed." After a moment she added with a questioning note, "You said that you preferred to sleep alone."

"I lied," he admitted, "and the colder it gets, the less appealing I find the ten-minute walk home in the middle of the night." He stood and enfolded her in his arms. "I understand that you can't do it here, but a full night should be possible at Aubynwood. The house is so large that if Geoffrey decided to come visit you, it would be lunchtime before he could make his way from the nurseries to the master's bedroom."

Her soft laughter tickled his ears as he lifted her from her feet and tucked her into the bed, velvet robe and all. Looking not much older than her son, she smiled up at him, her eyes barely open. "Do you know, Gervase, you really are a nice man."

He gave her a wry half-smile and dropped a light kiss on her forehead. "You needn't sound so surprised when you say that."

The sound of her sleepy laughter followed him from the room.

Lord St. Aubyn's invitation to his country estate was the subject of a lively breakfast discussion the next morning. Edith demurred at first, saying that a plain Yorkshire woman staying with a lord was like a pig pretending to be a guest at Sunday dinner, rather than the main course. Under the scoffing, Diana could see Edith's curiosity about what a great house was like, and it was not hard to persuade her that she could spend all her time with Geoffrey in the nurseries if she chose.

Geoffrey was delighted by the prospect, talking about it with such enthusiasm and stamina that his loving keepers could only be grateful when he was well enough to go to school again. Madeline, after her initial astonishment, agreed readily, but the odd glances she gave Diana indicated that she would have a number of questions to ask on some future occasion.

That occasion arose several days later, when the two women were at a draper's choosing fabrics and trimmings. Diana had decided that her Christmas gift to Edith would be a new dress in something brighter than the older woman's usual brown and navy blue, and now she was studying the racks of fabric bolts that reached to the ceiling of the Bond Street shop.

"Maddy, what do you think of that red wool for Edith?"

Madeline eyed it appraisingly. "It's not quite the right shade. Look for something more scarlet and less crimson."

Since Madeline's color sense was infallible, Diana dutifully continued her search. It was a quiet afternoon and the shopkeeper left them alone to ponder the choices slowly. Soon they were surrounded by bolts and ribbons, choosing cloth not just for Edith but also for themselves. Comparing an emerald silk lustring with a light moss-green wool, Madeline said casually, "I must admit you were right about St. Aubyn. I thought he was a hopeless cold fish, but the man must be besotted, or he wouldn't have invited you bag, baggage, and family to his country seat."

"Mmm, you think so?" Diana asked noncommittally. "He has estate business to take care of, so perhaps he just wanted a bit of company over the holidays, since he had to go there anyhow."

Madeline gave her companion an exasperated glance; Diana was getting that deliberately obtuse look in her slanting blue eyes. Nonetheless, the older woman persevered. "More likely St. Aubyn decided he couldn't make it through two weeks without you. He sees you five days out of seven, and if he didn't work such long hours at Whitehall he would be camped on our doorstep."

"What do you think of this wool for a morning dress for me, Maddy?" her companion asked, holding a smoky fabric by her face.

"You should never wear that shade of gray, and don't try to change the subject."

"But it feels so wonderful and soft that I don't want to put it down." Diana smiled mischievously. "And why shouldn't I change the subject? It's your subject, not mine, and it isn't one I wish to discuss."

"You are making that abundantly clear," Madeline said acerbically. She looked at the gray wool and shook her head. "You are the only woman I know who buys fabric by feel rather than by color." Narrowly watching Diana's expression, she said in an offhand way, as if the thought had just occurred to her, "I wouldn't be surprised if St.Aubyn asks you to marry him."

Blandly ignoring the latter statement, the younger woman said, "Why shouldn't I choose cloth by feel? After all, it goes against my skin, and if I must choose between being comfortable and looking stunning, I will choose comfort every time."

"The secret of good dressing is to keep looking until you find something that looks as wonderful as it feels, and that gray wool is *not* it." Madeline took the fabric from Diana and rolled it up again, then pulled a bolt of rich teal-blue wool from the bottom of the pile and held a length up by her friend's cheek. "There. That's just as soft and it makes your skin glow like cream and your eyes shine like sapphires."

Diana fingered the material, delighting in its softness. "You're right. This feels just as lovely and the color is marvelous." She laid the bolt on their "to buy" pile.

Madeline said hesitantly, "I don't wish to nag you, but you really must think about the future. You seem to like St. Aubyn a great deal. He treats you very generously and you've been purring ever since you started sleeping with him." She looked across to see a faint flush coloring Diana's elegant cheekbones. "If he does ask you to marry him, would you accept?"

Her voice sharp, Diana finally met her gaze. "Very well, if you insist, I will tell you what I think. While he finds my body pleasing, he is far too much the aristocrat to marry a whore, even one with pretensions to gentility. Yes, he has been good to me, but he is pride right to the marrow and I would never suit his notions of consequence. He might like to keep me as a mistress indefinitely, because it saves him the effort of finding another, but that is a very long way from an offer of marriage."

Madeline noted Diana's vehemence with interest. "Even the most prideful of men can behave in unexpected ways when their hearts are engaged."

Diana gave an unladylike snort. "The part of Lord
St. Aubyn that is most engaged is *not* his heart."

Madeline grinned. Listening to Diana trying to be
vulgar was like watching Geoffrey's cat trying to be a
tiger. "Don't count on it. The piece of anatomy you
refer to often does have a mysterious connection to the
heart."

As she rolled a length of red velvet with careful
precision, Diana said flatly, "You seem to forget the
mad wife in Scotland."

"I haven't forgotten, but I'm not convinced any such
person exists." Madeline lifted a spool of Belgian lace
and stretched a piece against the velvet. "I've made
more inquiries. While there is a vague rumor about a
wife, no one knows anything definite. I wouldn't be
surprised if St. Aubyn spread the rumor himself to
keep from being pursued. Has he ever mentioned a
wife?"

"I made a reference to the subject once," Diana
admitted.

"And . . . ?"

"He didn't answer me."

Madeline suppressed a smile. It was poetic justice
for Diana if St. Aubyn also evaded topics he didn't
wish to discuss. "Interesting that he didn't confirm the
rumor. If there was a wife, one would think that he
would have informed you, in case you were getting
ideas of marriage."

"Talk about making bricks without straw!" Diana
said with exasperation. "When the man can fit me into
his busy schedule of government service and managing his extensive property, he stops by for a few hours.
He probably likes the efficiency of being fed and ser-
viced under the same roof, and that is all there is to
it. Remember? He and I have a purely business relationship."

Diana's voice broke on the last sentence and her hand
on the edge on the counter was trembling. Madeline
laid her own hand over it, saying softly, "Are you in
love with him?"

Her voice unsteady, Diana looked down at the

counter, not meeting Madeline's eyes. "Do you think I would make such a mistake after you so carefully explained why a courtesan should never fall in love with her protector?"

"That's not an answer."

"What do I know about love?" Diana said in a frail attempt at humor. "I've only just discovered lust."

Madeline squeezed the slim fingers that lay under her own. "The two are related, you know. Sex bonds two people together, and since you are seeing no one else, I'm sure that you must be at least halfway in love with him, if not more. If he loves you enough to ask you to marry him, would you accept?"

There was a long, long silence before Diana answered in a voice husky with unshed tears, "Perhaps matters will work out. I truly hope so." She shook her head with weary regret. "But I don't see how."

11

THE December weather was unusually dry and the trip to Warwickshire passed with smooth speed. Lord St. Aubyn had provided his own luxurious coach, complete with hot bricks and a hamper of delicacies to stave off starvation. He himself had ridden up to Aubynwood three days earlier, ostensibly to take care of some business, though Diana suspected that was merely an excuse to avoid making the trip with three women and a child.

Not that she blamed him; ten hours in a fast, jolting coach with Geoffrey was enough to strain anyone's nerves, quite apart from the fact that the coach would have been crowded with five people. The servants had been given the time off to be with their own families, though the French cook, who had no near relations, had offered to come and help with Geoffrey. However, Gervase claimed he had more than enough underemployed servants to take care of guests, so Diana brought none.

Geoffrey was in high good spirits, enjoying all the new sights, envying the postilions, burrowing into the depths of the stables when they made brief stops at posting inns. As the early winter dusk fell, Diana dozed in a corner of the coach and questioned the wisdom of taking him to Aubynwood. For the moment, the thread of intuition that led her was thoroughly buried by the concerned parent. Was she making a grave mistake letting her son and Gervase become better acquainted? Having known only affection in his life, Geoffrey would expect the same from the master of the house. While she wouldn't allow her son to be too much in the way, the paths of the two men in her life were bound to cross occasionally during the visit. Gervase had been patient the time he had met Geoffrey, and Diana didn't think that he would be intentionally unkind, but it was hard to imagine the viscount having much interest in the doings of a child.

In a way, it would be worse if Gervase took an interest in the boy; Geoffrey yearned for a father and would eagerly adopt any adult males who showed an interest in him. If the barriers between Diana and her lover proved insurmountable, Geoffrey might be crushed by the loss. Diana sighed and braced against a deep lurch of the coach. After consciously deciding to let events take their own course, she had spent the last week worrying. As Madeline would be quick to point out, the only results of such behavior would be wrinkles. Bless Maddy for her common sense.

Diana's first impression when the coach swept up in front of Aubynwood was that Gervase had been understating when he said the place could absorb her entire household; it looked like a good part of Mayfair could have been housed in comfort. Aubynwood had been a convent originally and much of the original building and cloisters survived, sprawling in both directions in the dusk. Pale golden stone had been the building material, and the great house's medieval character was romantic in the extreme.

As they unpiled their stiff bodies from the coach, Geoffrey's hand slipped into Diana's, a sure sign of awe at his surroundings. Madeline and Edith were made of sterner stuff, their faces composed as they shook out their skirts and prepared to enter. Then Gervase came down the steps to greet his guests and Diana found her eyes riveted on him. The near-darkness eliminated detail and made her very aware of how beautifully he moved, light-footed and confident, the unconscious arrogance of his breeding in every line of his body. And Madeline thought he might consider her as his wife? Ridiculous.

Then he was in front of her, bowing over her hand

before giving her a smile that began deep in his eyes,
and suddenly, breathlessly, the idea that he truly cared
for her did not seem so preposterous. That intimate
smile lasted only a moment and then he was greeting
his other guests, impeccably polite. He and Edith had
never formally met and Diana could see Edith giving
him the same frank inspection she would have bestowed on a piece of livestock. Geoffrey, amazingly,
was remembering his manners rather than swarming
all over his host, or perhaps he found the man as intimidating as the manor.

The house was entered through a giant two-story
hall done in the mock-Gothic-revival style of the mid-
eighteenth century rather than the true Gothic of the
original convent. Still, it was charming, with carved
wooden statues of baroque saints set in niches high on
the white plaster walls and a great ox-roaster fireplace.
Gervase suggested that they might wish to rest from
the journey before dining, and the housekeeper, Mrs.
Russell, led them off to their rooms. Geoffrey and
Edith, as promised, got the nursery suite, cozy but far
removed from the main apartments. Madeline and Diana were also given rooms some distance apart; there
would be no shortage of privacy.

Diana's rose-hued chamber was luxurious, and a
welcoming fire awaited her. She went to stand in front
of the fireplace, glad of the warmth after a day spent
in an unheated coach. It helped counter her sense of
depression; Aubynwood was a stark reminder of the
unbreachable social distance between her and Gervase. The physical distance was quite another matter;
that was breached very easily indeed. . . .

As the thought ran through her mind, she turned at
a slight sound to see Gervase emerge from an alcove
in the far corner of the room. After a moment's surprise, she began to smile; she should have expected
something of this nature.

He stood in the concealed doorway without speaking, his face controlled but his eyes voracious, as if
she were the love of his life and he hadn't seen her in
years. Then in half a dozen swift strides he crossed

the room and cupped her face in his hands, staring at her with scorching intensity. "Lord, Diana, how I've missed you."

He bent over and kissed her with great deliberation, his mouth demanding. Her own passion flared, fueled by the depression she had felt on arriving as a stranger in his home. She raised her hands to his lean waist and his arms slid around her in a crushing embrace, his hands roving her body as if seeking to relearn every inch of it. Her fatigue dissolved as contact with him revitalized her, and she kissed back without restraint, craving the taste and touch of him.

"I wanted to make love to you on the marble steps. I want to lock the door and keep you in here for the next fortnight." As he spoke, he unclasped her cloak, letting it fall to the floor in front of the fire, then reached behind her to untie the sash on her demure high-necked dress.

"Shall we start with locking the door and think about the fortnight later?" she asked breathlessly, not quite able to forget that someone might walk in at any minute. He indulged her by turning the key in the lock, then continued what he had begun.

Diana found herself fumbling with the buttons of his pantaloons, her hands clumsy with haste. Perhaps her frantic desire had something to do with showing this grand house that she, too, had a place here, even though it was a furtive, unadmitted one.

Gervase undressed her with as much skill and much more haste than a lady's maid, his lips searing the tender flesh of her throat and breasts as they were bared. She felt the heat of the fire against the back of her bare legs, then the soft scratchiness of the thick Chinese carpet as he laid her on it, his hand probing and teasing her to readiness.

As she lifted her hips to receive him, there was no subtlety, only an aching passion that demanded fulfillment. She wrapped her arms around his rib cage, pulling him into her, reveling in the sweet, familiar weight of his body, his hips thrusting against hers in the intoxicating rhythm that swept away all thoughts of the

house and her responsibilities and anything else but
the rising fire inside of her.

Then desire flared and consumed them both. It was
only after the sound of her cry had long faded that she
thought to be grateful that the rooms adjacent were
unoccupied. Gervase's body still enfolded hers and she
could feel his pounding heart before he rolled onto his
side next to her. His dark hair was tangled and the
firelight cast highlights on the film of perspiration on
his face. After he had caught his breath, he said, "I'm
sorry, Diana. I had every intention of being a good
host and letting you rest from your journey. But when
I saw you there . . ." He let his head fall back on his
arm, his eyes shadowed.

Turning her head until her face was only inches from
his, Diana said, "I'm not sorry. You have quite cured
me of travel fatigue." Though he wore most of his
clothing, she was wholly naked, and she shivered as
the chill air struck that portion of her damp skin that
was turned from the fire. Seeing the motion, Gervase
reached for her cloak and pulled it over her.

In spite of their physical nearness, he was remote
from her, his expression harsh and withdrawn. Diana
leaned across the short gap for a light kiss, asking
softly, "Is something wrong?"

His expression was obscured, and he was silent for
too long. When his words finally came they were reluctant, as if saying something he was loath to admit.
"You're like . . . an addiction. The more I have of
you, the more I crave you."

"And you dislike that?"

"I don't want to need anyone. Ever."

In the face of such uncompromising words, Diana
wondered whether she should even try to reply. She
could feel the chill of his mood dispelling her satisfied
contentment and she sat up, wrapping her cloak around
her. Without true intimacy, it seemed wrong to be naked in front of him.

She stared into the fire, wondering what one could
say to a man who preferred aloneness, who wanted to
be sufficient unto himself. "You need air to survive,

and food and drink and sleep. To be fully human, one also needs other people. Why do you find that so unacceptable?''

Even to discuss such matters was to betray vulnerability, and there was a long interval before he replied. ''Needing objects is safe enough—one kind of food can easily replace another. To need people is dangerous because . . . it gives them power over you.''

Still looking at the fire, she drew her knees up and wrapped her arms around her legs, folds of cloak spilling around her to the rug. ''Sometimes that is true, but why do you assume that others will always use their power against you?''

With a hard, brittle laugh he said, ''Experience.''

She turned then to face him. ''Can you truly say that *everyone* you have ever cared about has abused your trust?''

Silence. Then, ''No. The risk increases with the level of caring. If one cares only a little, there is only a little danger. The real risk is in . . . caring greatly.''

She felt pity that he couldn't even bring himself to say the word ''love.'' What had happened to him, that the very thought of loving was so frightening? She stood and said, her voice gently mocking, ''Then you are in no danger from me. I can see what a bother it must be that your lust is temporarily out of control, but sex is just a 'thing,' like the need for food and drink. Take comfort in the fact that soon I will not be a novelty and you can easily replace me with another woman.''

Turning away, she wished he would go so she could give way to tears. Now she understood why Madeline had warned her against Gervase; it was a mistake to love a man who daren't love in return. Even if fate was on her side, she could only do so much alone; if he could not transcend his fears, there would be no future for the two of them.

Gervase stood also, coming behind her and wrapping his arms around her waist, pulling her against the length of his body. His voice soft and sad, he asked,

"Can I replace you that easily, Diana? Is that all that is between us, intemperate lust that will soon wane?"

She held her body rigid, fighting the desire to melt back against him. "I can't answer that. Only you can."

"But I don't know the answer. I don't even understand the question."

Speaking from her own hurt, she said, "You don't pay me enough to teach you the questions."

His arms dropped away, and when he spoke, it was in a voice of cool irony. "Good of you to remind me what is really between us. Since it is only vulgar money, there can be no danger."

She turned to face him, her slanting blue eyes stark with unhappiness. "You said that, not I. If that is what you choose to believe, then of course it must be the truth. After all, the customer is always right."

He flinched back at her words. "If only it were that simple." With his Indian mistress Sananda, it *had* been that simple. Only their bodies connected, never their minds and spirits. He put his hands on Diana's shoulders and drew her to him. "But even after that spectacular sexual exchange has discharged physical desire, I still want you. And so I fear you."

She softened then, wrapping her arms around his waist and resting her head on his shoulder. "Do you really think I would ever hurt you?"

He laid his cheek against her tangled hair, the scent of lilac poignant around her, and replied so softly that she could barely hear the words. "I don't know. I really . . . just . . . do not know. And that is what frightens me."

His heartbeat was slow and strong beneath her ear. It was impossible to be angry with Gervase when she could feel his pain and confusion as sharply as her own. Despairingly she knew that she wanted to embark on the ultimate folly: to try to heal him with her love. She was a fool, a helpless, gullible fool. Perhaps it would be better for both of them if they ended it right now. Fighting to keep her voice level, she asked, "Do you want me to leave Aubynwood?"

His arms tightened around her. "I don't want you

to leave. I just . . . want you. And that's the hell of it.''

After he left Diana, Gervase went outside without stopping for a coat, hating himself both for needing Diana and for hurting her. The ground was stone hard in the cold and he found himself taking the path he had always followed as a child when he was escaping his keepers. It led upward through dark trees to the top of a hill behind the house. A stranger to the terrain would have seen nothing, but Gervase's feet still knew the way.

There was a belvedere on the top of the hill, a charming folly built in his grandfather's time, and it offered shelter from the biting wind. Too tense to sit on the carved stone bench inside, he stood with a hand on one of the Doric columns that framed the entrance. A waning moon lent pale, silvery light to the scene, and the openness of the empty night helped dispel his haunted confusion. Below, he could see the dark bulk of the main buildings and the gardens that had been laid out in medieval times. All the land visible in every direction belonged to him.

His word was law at Aubynwood and half a dozen other manors, he had been a soldier of uncommon bravery and skill, and when he spoke, the most powerful men in Britain listened. That being the case, why did he fear one small, soft woman? A woman, moreover, who had never been anything but warm and undemanding. He knew the answer, of course; even now, he would rather not think of his mother and his wife. When he had told Diana that deep caring caused deep betrayal, it was Medora Brandelin that he had had in mind. As an example of perfidy, she was more than enough.

The deep chill of the stone column numbed his bare hand. It was December and in a few days he would be thirty-one years old. The first part of his life had been dominated by what he felt about his parents: anger, despair, and rejection.

In India he had grown beyond anger to detachment

and cool efficiency. Usually he was satisfied with the man he had become, but now he saw clearly just how his disastrous past had crippled him. It had been easy to overlook that deficiency in himself when his relations with women had been purely physical, but with Diana there was more than lust, and caring had triggered this firestorm of doubt and confusion. Good God, it was grotesque to be afraid of his own mistress, yet the past held him with such heavy chains that he was unable to accept the gentle warmth and affection she offered him.

Sorting slowly through the jumble in his mind, he realized that the core of his distress was the fear that he would become dependent on Diana, needing her warmth as desperately as he now craved her body. Then, when he was at her mercy, she could betray him. Yet the fear was not a reasonable one. Diana was not a helpless innocent like his wife, and could never induce the lethal guilt he still felt about that incident.

Nor would she ever be able to wound him as severely as his mother had. Lady St. Aubyn's worst crime had been her betrayal of her son's trust; since Diana did not occupy a comparable position of trust in his life, she could never inflict the same kind of damage. Moreover, he could not imagine Diana deliberately hurting any living creature; he had never heard her say an unkind word about anyone. Though she plied the courtesan trade, she was warmer and more honest than any woman he had ever known.

He had been creating problems where none existed. There was no real cause to fear Diana, no reason to forgo her enchanting company. Hurting both of them with his misgivings had been childish nonsense. She could never be his wife and they both knew it, and that simple fact established boundaries that safely defined their relationship. In time the extraordinary passion he felt for Diana would fade to a more comfortable level, though he could not imagine that he would ever stop desiring her. Meanwhile, there was no reason not to enjoy what gave them both such pleasure; not just the passion, but also the affection.

That simple realization made him feel so light and free that he could almost have flown back to the house. Instead he plunged down the hill through the woods, reaching the house within ten minutes, his body warmed by his energetic passage.

Gervase was not surprised to learn that his guests, tired by their journey, had declined a formal dinner. His butler informed him that Mrs. Lindsay was taking a simple supper with her son and his nurse in the nursery and Miss Gainford had decided to join them. He was glad of it; he preferred not to act the host with his other guests until he had seen Diana alone.

By the time he himself had eaten, it was past nine o'clock and he entered Diana's room through the secret door again. She was sitting in front of her vanity table, wearing a high-necked green velvet robe and brushing the thick hair that fell to the middle of her back. She glanced up, her eyes meeting his in the mirror, but she said nothing. He came to stand behind her, taking the silver-backed brush and gently pulling it through her hair. The heavy tresses crackled like a living being under the brush and he caught up a handful, savoring the silky feel of it.

Musingly he said, "I've never seen hair the color of yours before, yet I can't imagine you with anything else. Blond would be too frivolous, red too flamboyant, black too harsh, brown too common. Instead you have hair the color of a ripe chestnut, or of polished mahogany. By candlelight it's very dark, yet it glows both red and gold."

A faint smile acknowledged the compliment, but her voice was very grave. "I wasn't sure that you would come back."

As he resumed brushing he hit a snarl and concentrated on untangling it as he replied, "I'm sorry for what I said earlier. I shouldn't have spoken."

Her head made a slight impatient movement. "You meant what you said, didn't you, about not wanting to need anyone?"

Gervase hesitated, then said, "Yes."

Her night-deep eyes were stark in the mirror, but

her soft voice was steady. "Then don't apologize for your words. I would rather have your honesty than your silence."

"Even when honesty is painful?"

She held his gaze without flinching as she answered, "Yes. Pain is inevitable, but it isn't all there is to life. I would rather suffer sometimes than feel nothing. If one tries to eliminate the hard times, the good times are lost too."

He moved his hand to her throat and caressed it through the fine-spun chestnut strands, stroking the edge of her jaw with his thumb. "You seem so fragile, yet you are stronger than I am."

Her smile was wry. "There are many kinds of strength. Mine is the woman's strength of emotions, of yielding and enduring. I am not so strong in other ways."

"You are strong enough to teach me through your example." Gervase set the brush down and laid his hands on her shoulders, wanting to feel her reactions through her body as well as to watch them in the mirror.

Choosing his words slowly, he said, "I am tired of living in fear. I do care about you and it is foolish to try to deny that." Even with his new resolution, it was difficult to add, "I'll try not to run away from you again."

He felt the faint tensing of Diana's body as she absorbed his statement; then she raised one hand to cover his where it lay on her shoulder, saying simply, "I am so glad."

Her face shone with happiness, and the warmth of her smile began to melt the defenses he had so carefully built around his heart. Gervase was not yet ready to speak of that, nor to give a name to what he felt, but he knew that things had changed between them. He bent over to kiss the slender fingers that still covered his. "So am I."

Diana raised her face to his and they shared a kiss of great sweetness. He was very different from the man who had first attracted and frightened her, and she was awed by his bravery. She lived in her emotions and understood their highs and lows, but for a man whose soul had been scarred in ways she could only guess at, it was an act of supreme courage to let himself be vulnerable.

It was a very short step from sweetness to passion. They made love slowly, knowing they had all night. There was a new kind of intimacy between them, and at the height of ecstasy Diana felt that their souls briefly joined, that she felt the fierce splendor of his spirit within hers, and that neither of them was alone anymore. It was a transcendent moment, and in its aftermath Diana wept, both for the beauty of their sharing and for the fact that it was too soon over.

Half-hoping that he would not hear the words, she performed her own act of courage, whispering, "I love you."

For just a moment she feared that she had gone too far, too fast, that he would interpret her declaration as a demand and he would withdraw again. Instead he kissed her with exquisite tenderness before laying his head on her breast, his arms tight around her. She stroked his dark head, glad that there was enough light to see the peace and happiness on his face and to savor the trust between them.

Diana's instinct urged her to tell him all about herself, about Yorkshire and how she had come to be there, about Geoffrey and why she had chosen to become a courtesan. Though she had never actually lied to Gervase, she had certainly not told him the whole truth, and now she longed to put an end to all deception. But in spite of the closeness between them, she feared how he would accept the full story, and she could not bear to shatter this perfect moment.

And so the time for truth-telling slipped away in soft laughter, sweet embraces, and deep silence. Later Diana would be bitterly sorry that she had not followed her intuition to lay bare her past, but she could never have dreamed what a high price she would pay for her weakness.

12

GERVASE'S speculation proved correct: it was a great pleasure to spend a whole night with Diana. He was vaguely aware that through the night they shifted positions, fitting their bodies to each other in new ways, and this morning he awoke more contented that he could ever remember. He lay on his back now, Diana burrowed under his arm, her own arm lying across his waist. As he stirred, she moved in response, her drowsy hand moving down his body to rest more intimately. He grinned; this was a splendid way to wake up.

It was the shortest day of the year, the morning dawning late and pale. Since the door had been locked the night before, no maid would be coming in to build the fire, so Gervase reluctantly slid from the warm bed to perform that chore himself. Diana murmured a protest, coming more awake at his withdrawal. He brushed her hair back, amazed at how lovely she could look this early, her face free of artifice and her hair tangled. "Don't worry, I'll be right back."

He suspected that he had an idiotic smile on his face, a smile that lasted through the time it took him to add coal to the remnants of the fire and ensure that it was burning strongly.

The room was still bitingly cold, and when he returned to bed a sensible person would have kept away until he was warm again. Diana, however, rolled over and embraced him. "Mmm, you've gotten chilled." As she bonelessly cuddled against him, she chuckled softly. "I just found something that isn't cold."

Laughing, he moved under the covers, his lips seeking her breast. "If you'll cooperate, I should warm up very quickly."

Making love in the morning had its own special lazy flavor as drowsy bodies came awake, the breath and blood quickening with passion. Gervase enjoyed watching as the pearly light brightened and Diana became more visible, her face exquisitely mirroring her responses. Amazing how every time they came together, it was different and special. Perhaps his desire for her would never wane; it was a measure of how far he had come since the night before that the thought pleased, not alarmed him.

Afterward, as they lay twined together, Gervase said regretfully, "I must get up soon and return to my room."

Diana laughed. "Do you really think that there isn't a servant in the house who hasn't guessed why I am here?"

He gave her a teasing smile. "They can guess, but they don't know. Perhaps Edith is the target of my wicked ways."

Her languorous eyes had a smile in their depths. "You prefer a woman old enough to be your mother?"

Something must have shown on his face, because he saw a flicker of question in her eyes, and she spoke on a different topic. "Does the secret passage run to your bedchamber?"

The room was warmer now and he pushed the covers down his chest as he replied, "This was called the mistress's chamber. I don't think my father ever used the passage—illicit lust was not his style. The master's suite is at right angles to this room and the distance is quite short. Since the chambers are connected, it seems reasonable to come and go as unobtrusively as possible."

She raised herself, resting her head on her hand and looking at him curiously. "Do you actually care what anybody thinks about what we are doing? It doesn't seem in character for you."

Gervase folded his hands behind his head and thought about it. "I don't really give a damn what

most people think. At the same time, privacy means a
great deal to me. I suppose that is a contradiction.''

Her eyes twinkled at him. ''If not precisely a contradiction, at least it's a very fine distinction.''

With her exquisite face and tumbling chestnut hair,
she looked as delicious as the first strawberry in spring
and he leaned over for a quick kiss. ''If I don't leave
now, it will be another hour before I do, and unfortunately I promised to inspect the barn of one of my
tenants. Care to come with me?''

She subsided gracefully back under the covers until
only her mischievous face showed. ''Will I be sunk
beneath reproach if I decline this morning?''

He laughed and swung his feet to the floor. ''Slug-
abed.''

''Guilty as charged. It was a long journey,'' then,
with a wicked smile, ''and I was not allowed much
rest last night.''

''Very well, you're forgiven this time.'' He pulled
his clothes on casually, since he would be changing to
riding dress back in his room. ''I should be exhausted
myself—after all, I was doing most of the work—but
instead I'm full of energy.''

She extended one hand from the bed toward him.
''If you still have an excess of energy when you return,
why not stop by and see if I'm still here?''

He laughed and caught her hand, pressing a kiss in
the palm before unlocking her door and returning to
his own room. He was beginning to understand why
people married. So great was his sense of well-being
that even that thought didn't disturb him.

The sense of well-being lasted as he changed, his
valet, Bonner, blandly ignoring the bed that hadn't
been slept in. After a quick cup of coffee, Gervase
headed to the stables. It was a gray day, and the heavy
air promised rain or snow later. The whole estate
drowsed, as if no one felt like stirring outdoors.

He saddled his own horse and was leading it out
when he discovered the small figure outside one of the
stalls. The viscount checked his stride a moment, then

recognized Diana's son, Geoffrey. The boy was standing on tiptoe against the half-door, one hand reaching over to offer a piece of carrot to the horse inside. As Gervase watched, the horse delicately lipped up the carrot, then permitted the boy to stroke its soft muzzle.

Geoffrey was so raptly intent on the horse that he hadn't noticed the viscount's approach, and he jumped when Gervase uttered a cheerful "Good morning."

Turning quickly, the boy wiped his hand on his trousers and bobbed his head. "Good morning, sir." Then, with a look of uncertainty he asked, "Or is it 'Good morning, my lord'?"

Gervase grinned; this morning, everything amused him. " 'My lord' is correct but 'sir' is simpler, so perhaps you should use that. What do you think of my stables?"

His eyes shining, Geoffrey said, "They're wonderful, sir. I've never seen anything like them."

When he had first met the boy, Gervase had been struck by his resemblance to his mother, but now he was more aware of the differences. The wide, intensely blue eyes were Diana's, but the jaw was squarer and the hair a dark brown, without any chestnut tones. The viscount's good humor chilled a little as he wondered once more who the child's father was, or if Diana even knew. He put the thought aside. "I'm going to ride out to one of the tenant farms. Would you care to come with me?"

As he spoke, he resumed leading his horse outside, Geoffrey falling in by his side. At Gervase's words, the boy looked up, then said woodenly, "I'm sorry, sir, I don't know how to ride."

"I suppose you haven't had the opportunity. Still, you're going to be here for several weeks. Would you like to learn how?" Remembering the yearning look on the boy's face as he had fed the horse, Gervase expected an eager acceptance.

The small face blazed with excitement before the light died. He shook his head. "I don't think my mother would let me, sir."

"Why not?" They had reached the stableyard and
Gervase mounted, holding his horse in as he gazed
down at the boy.

With matter-of-fact acceptance Geoffrey said, "She's
afraid I'll fall off and kill myself."

Of course; Gervase had been forgetting the seizures.
He could understand Diana's concern, but he could
also see the boy's longing. "Has she said that she
doesn't want you to ever learn?"

Geoffrey shook his head. "No, she says to wait until
I'm older." After a moment he added, "It . . . upsets
her to talk about . . . what's wrong with me."

Geoffrey's expression was oddly mature when he said
the words, as if he knew that his mother was not quite
reasonable but accepted that she couldn't help herself.
Perhaps coping with his disability had made him wiser
than his years.

Gervase knew better than to comment on what was
none of his business, but as he lifted his reins in readiness to depart, he couldn't bear the wistfulness on the
boy's face. On impulse he reached his hand down.
"You can ride with me if you like. I'll take the blame
if your mother disapproves later."

Geoffrey's momentary hesitation vanished under a
wave of eagerness and he reached up and grasped the
viscount's hand. Gervase lifted the boy easily and settled him in front of the saddle. It wasn't the most comfortable of positions, but Geoffrey didn't mind; as his
hands grasped the horse's mane, he was almost vi-
brating with excitement.

They headed east toward the tenant farm at an easy
trot, Gervase trying to remember if he had ever ridden
with his father like this. Probably not; he had received
his first riding lesson from a groom when he was three
and had had his own pony at four. Besides, the late Lord
St. Aubyn had never ridden for pleasure, nor had he
had much interest in the company of a child.

In spite of his interested gazes at everything they
passed, Geoffrey at first kept a respectful silence, as
befitted a well-brought-up child. Then he asked
whether the straightness of the road they traveled

meant that it was built by the Romans, followed by a question about the sheep in an adjacent pasture, and soon the words were tumbling out one after another.

Diana had not exaggerated about her son's ability to chatter and ask questions. However, Geoffrey listened to the answers intently, then made intelligent comments before asking new questions. His wide-eyed enthusiasm made the long ride to Swallow Farm pass quickly; the boy was surprisingly good company.

Gervase's tenant, Robbins, greeted his landlord respectfully but without groveling; the Robbinses had been on this land as long as the Brandelins. However, Gervase was irritated to see Robbins' eyes flicker to Geoffrey's face, then back to his own. Probably wondering if the boy was the viscount's bastard; doubtless Robbins would manage to find a resemblance. Gervase should have known this would happen; nothing that the landlord did would pass unnoticed. As he had told Diana, he didn't much care what others thought, but he despised prying curiosity.

Leaving Geoffrey proudly walking the horse around the stableyard, Gervase inspected the barn, agreeing that the roof needed repair and that an addition would permit an increase in the milking herd. The farm was one of the most profitable Gervase owned, and worth the new investment. Declining an offer of tea, he and Geoffrey were soon on their way back to Aubynwood.

Gervase wondered whether his young companion would run out of questions, but there seemed no danger of that. At a convenient pause, the viscount himself asked, "Is this country different from what you are used to?"

As he said the words, he realized that he was hoping to find out more of Diana's past—not the action of a gentleman. Nonetheless, he was disappointed as Geoffrey hesitated, then said neutrally, "It is rather different, sir."

Spymaster or not, Gervase couldn't bring himself to probe further. "It isn't necessary to say 'sir' in every sentence."

"No, sir," Geoffrey said obediently, but Gervase

caught the trace of laughter in the words. It was obvious that the boy had a lively sense of humor, and the viscount wondered briefly what it would be like to have a child of his own. He had never had much to do with children, thinking of them only in terms of heirs, not regretting the thought that he would never have one.

Now he was suddenly, achingly aware that he had forsaken not just heirs to St. Aubyn but also the reality of children, with their curiosity and joyfulness. He would never carry a son of his own before him like he carried Geoffrey, or have a little girl with all the world's sweetness in her smile, like Diana. . . .

Instead, he had a wife who was no wife at all, and he would never have the chance to remake the past by giving a child of his own what he himself had craved when he was young. When he had left the island of Mull, he had felt a sense of doom, a belief that he would be punished for his crime against the afflicted innocent he had married. Now he saw clearly what his punishment was: at twenty-two, he had never imagined finding a woman who gave him the pleasure Diana did, or that he would feel the lack of children. He had lost far more on Mull than he had realized, and now he felt a new and piercing grief for that old loss.

There was the possibility of illegitimate children, but the usual precautions had proved effective so far, and he would wish bastardy on no child of his. Treacherously, his mind speculated on whether his wife would live to a great age. Perhaps in the drafty cold cottages of Scotland she would take a chill, and leave him free. . . . He frowned, appalled at thinking such a thing. The girl had been an unfortunate pawn, caught between two men, one drunk and one mad; she did not deserve his ill will.

Deducing something from the viscount's dark silence, Geoffrey asked no more questions. The damp chill was increasing, and Gervase was glad the ride was almost over.

As they came in sight of the stables, they both recognized Diana's waiting figure as she stood in front of the double doors, a deep blue cloak falling in graceful folds around her. After a practiced inspection, Geoffrey announced, "Mama is not happy."

Gervase also saw the tension in her stance. "I'll talk to her. I didn't mean to get you into trouble."

"It will be all right," Geoffrey said tranquilly. "Mama says it isn't natural to expect someone to be good all the time."

The philosophical words sounded so exactly like Diana that Gervase's black mood broke, and he was smiling as they pulled up in front of her. "Good morning, Mrs. Lindsay," he said, as if they hadn't been sharing bed and bodies three hours earlier. "I hope you will forgive me for forcing your son to accompany me. It was a long ride, and I wished for company."

Diana nodded, her expression unreadable. Gervase dismounted, then lifted Geoffrey to the ground, where the boy hurled himself at his mother, grabbing her hand and chattering about the marvelous time he had had and the things he had seen and how horses were even finer than he had imagined.

Interesting that even though he knew he had displeased her, Geoffrey went to his mother so trustingly, with the confidence of a child who had never been rejected. Gervase realized that he himself was painfully jealous, envious that the boy received so much love that he never doubted its existence; and he was jealous of Diana's affection, for surely if she gave so much warmth to her son, the amount she had for her lover would be diminished.

For one of her lovers. The words echoed harshly in his mind. Gervase assumed that he had favored status, but he was merely one of the men in her life. Of course she loved her son more; lovers might come and go, but children stayed. It was grotesque to be jealous of a child, a boy who was probably a bastard, who had a serious affliction, one whose mother was only a high-grade whore, and who faced a doubtful future.

And yet he was jealous. What would it have been like to run to Medora Brandelin knowing that he would always be welcome, sins and all? Not to have to wonder about his mother's moods, about whether she would be so absorbed in her latest lover that she had no time for her son, or whether she would have one of her brief attacks of maternal feeling, and would demand homage of him?

Such thoughts had no place in the mind of a grown man, and Gervase hated himself for the weakness. His face rigidly controlled, he handed the reins of his horse over to a groom.

As Geoffrey paused for breath, Diana smiled at him. "Edith is looking for you, my dear. Remember, Mr. Hardy said you must do lessons every day or you will get behind in school."

Geoffrey wrinkled his nose but said obediently, "Yes, Mama."

She brushed her hand across his hair tenderly. "Run along, then. I'll join you for tea. I want to talk to Lord St. Aubyn."

Blithely unaware of undercurrents, Geoffrey took his leave of the viscount and scampered across the stable-yard toward the house. Gervase watched him go, and as silent penance for his own irrational jealousy, vowed to help the boy get what he wanted.

Diana turned to him, her face grave. "Shall we walk in the gardens? Even at this season, they look quite beautiful."

He nodded and offered his arm, and they strolled around the house to the vast and varied gardens. Though the flowerbeds slept in winter and the ground was iron hard beneath their feet, the Aubynwood grounds were still lovely. They passed the maze, then the topiary garden, where yew bushes were sculptured into whimsical shapes. As they walked, Diana's hand on his arm relaxed. "I'm sorry Geoffrey disturbed you. I'll try to keep him out of your way."

"No need to apologize," Gervase said. "I found him to be very good company. Please don't be angry with him for riding. He said that you wouldn't approve, but I persuaded him."

Her fingers tightened again. "I'm not angry." She glanced up, her lapis-blue eyes obscured beneath her long dark lashes, then said in a rush of words, "I know that it's wrong of me to be so protective of Geoffrey. It isn't right that he always be surrounded and pampered by women. But I am so frightened when I think of what might happen . . .''

While Gervase couldn't possibly know the full depth of fear that came with being a parent, she saw understanding on his face as he considered her words. As they passed from the knot garden to a section of parterre, he said, ''Everyone who rides gets thrown occasionally, and there is some chance of injury. Still, since you say Geoffrey has very few fits, the danger for him is not much greater than for other children learning to ride. I survived, in spite of my occasional seizures.''

''I know that you're right.'' Diana swallowed and looked down at the gravel path that crunched beneath their feet. ''And I know that if he doesn't learn to ride and do the other things that boys do, he will never have the kind of life I want for him. Even so . . .'' She stopped, then said, ''It isn't just the *grand mal* seizures. They are uncommon, but the staring spells are more frequent. He might easily fall from a horse then.''

''Then he must learn to fall properly.''

Diana turned to Gervase, her face indecisive. He stopped also and took her hands, holding them between his. ''You'll be here several weeks—let him learn the basics of horsemanship. I'll teach him myself if you like. There will never be a better time. He's a good age to begin learning, and your fears aren't likely to be any less in the future.''

As she hesitated, he added persuasively, ''There is some risk, but life is full of risks. Even though he is obedient now, eventually he will resent you if you try to hold him too close. Isn't that a danger as great as any physical one?''

She bowed her head and nodded, staring down at their joined hands as her chilled fingers warmed between his palms. Gervase's words forced her to face thoughts she would rather ignore. Would it be a blessing or a disaster to let the most important males in her life get to know each other better? She consulted her intuition, but her emotions were too involved for her to get a clear answer. Geoffrey might be hurt riding, yet he craved the attention of a grown man so much; how could she deny it to him when Gervase was willing?

Sensing that she was wavering, Gervase said softly, "I won't let any harm come to him, Diana."

"You are very good," she said in a low voice. "Much better than I deserve."

"On the contrary," he said, his voice dispassionate. "I am the one who is undeserving."

She glanced up then, wondering what thoughts lay behind that austerely handsome face. When she had first seen him at Harriette Wilson's, she had been both attracted and frightened by his aura of tightly focused power. She had soon discovered that he was quite different from what she expected, that behind that cool mask lay a man who could be both generous and sensitive. Even so, she was always surprised by his kindness, perhaps because she never expected kindness from men.

He might never speak words of love, but his deeds, his protectiveness and reliability, were far more precious. She was glad that he was worthy of love, for she could not help loving him. Standing on her toes, she kissed him lightly. She lingered a moment, feeling his lips warming under hers, then withdrew and whispered, "Thank you, Gervase."

He had such beautiful eyes, light and clear like winter sky. Gervase was an honorable man and she was behaving less than honorably to him. Once more, she considered revealing her past. Once more, in her fear of destroying the sweetness of the moment, the opportunity passed.

13

SINCE time was limited and the weather unlikely to improve, the riding lessons began that very afternoon. After consulting with his head groom, the viscount arranged to borrow a well-trained, docile pony from a tenant whose own children had outgrown it. His face taut with excitement, Geoffrey was thrilled speechless, a state Gervase didn't expect to last long.

On the viscount's advice, Diana was not present for a lesson that could only be nerve-racking for her. They started in the barn, with hay piled belly-deep around the pony. As Dapple munched in contentment, Geoffrey practiced falling, learning how to tuck his body and roll, how to relax and minimize the chances of injury. The boy took it as great good sport, hurling himself down into the hay with squeals of delight, until tumbling into a ball started to become habit.

The next stage was learning to hold a secure seat, and Gervase made the boy bend, twist, and turn in every direction. The trick was to stay in the saddle without touching the reins. Inevitably Geoffrey sometimes bent too far, which gave him more chances to practice falling.

After an hour and a half, Gervase judged that his hay-covered student had had enough for the first day, and they repaired to the nursery for tea with the rest of the party. The next day they progressed to walking the pony around the paddock, with part of the path through an area padded with hay. Gervase would unpredictably push the boy off on some of the circuits. The hay was thinner than it had been inside, and the

falling not as soft, but Geoffrey took it all with undiminished enthusiasm.

The viscount had originally offered the lessons as a
way of expiating his guilty conscience, but he found
he enjoyed them almost as much as Geoffrey. It was
impossible not to respect the child's resilience and
good nature, and Gervase was beginning to appreciate
him in his own right, rather than just as Diana's son.
It was even possible to forget the nagging questions
about the boy's father, and what that man had meant
to Diana.

Watching his student carefully, Gervase observed
several of the staring spells, when Geoffrey's eyes
would slip out of focus and his words would stop in
mid-sentence if he was speaking. Fortunately for his
riding future, his body didn't slacken and his knees
and hands remained firm through the duration of the
spells. Unless he was moving at a gallop, the *petit mal*
seizures might never cause a significant problem. Perhaps not even then, though jumping would be a different story.

With a mixture of pleasure and embarrassment, the
viscount realized that the boy was starting to develop
a kind of hero worship for his teacher, striving to
please, repeating his words to others, even copying
gestures and movements. Since Geoffrey had no father, it was natural for him to become attached to a
man whom he saw much of. Gervase felt heartily unfit
for a pedestal, but supposed he could appear worthy
for three short weeks.

The first lessons were held in the early afternoon,
when the day was apt to be warmest, but the day before Christmas they went out in the morning so Geoffrey could help gather greens later. That session gave
Gervase a brief, horrifying glimpse of what Diana had
lived with for years.

Geoffrey was making rapid progress, and this morning Gervase held the pony with a long rein, directing
it in circles first to the right, then to the left. They
were halfway through the lesson when Geoffrey said,

very distinctly, "Damn!" He pulled on his snaffle reins, then slid from the pony's saddle as it halted.

Before Gervase could question why he had stopped, Geoffrey's body arched back in the first stage of seizure, hurling him onto the soft ground as he made horrible gagging sounds. The other time he had been present at a seizure, Gervase had been a spectator. This time, he was the only person around, and responsible for the boy's welfare.

Yelling for a groom, he released the startled pony and raced across the paddock to Geoffrey's side. Although he knew the fit was unlikely to harm the boy, it was impossible not to feel primitive panic at the sight of the violent convulsion. There was nothing he could do but wait until the seizure was over, and ensure that Geoffrey didn't hit anything that would injure him.

After a minute of so, Geoffrey relaxed and his breathing returned to normal. The change was so dramatic that it was easy to understand why seizures had been considered demonic possession in the old days. The deep blue eyes were dazed, but the boy knew what had happened. Apologetically he murmured, "I'm sorry, sir." The long dark lashes, so like Diana's, fluttered. "If you help me back on Dapple, I'll do better."

As an example of pluck, it was hard to beat. Swallowing the tightness in his throat, Gervase brushed at the dirt on the boy's face, then said casually, as if having a lesson interrupted by a fit was perfectly normal, "I think that's enough for this morning, old man. If you don't get some rest, you might miss the Christmas Eve celebration."

Still hazy, Geoffrey nodded agreeably as the viscount scooped him up and carried him back to the house. The boy had slipped into a doze by the time they reached the nursery. As Gervase was laying him on his bed, Diana arrived, alerted by a servant, her eyes wide with apprehension. Gervase said reassuringly, "Nothing to worry about. He just had a seizure, not a riding accident. A little rest and he'll be fine.''

Relaxing, Diana took charge of preparing her son for bed as Gervase left to wait for her in the old schoolroom next door. After ten minutes she emerged, no longer alarmed but with signs of strain in her face. The viscount took advantage of the fact that no one was around to give her a quick comforting hug. ''Something very interesting happened. Apparently Geoffrey knew that he was going to have a fit. He reined in the pony and dismounted before it began. If he can always do that, riding may be no more dangerous for him than for anyone else.''

''Really?'' Diana's eyebrows shot up. ''He seems to be telling you things about his seizures that he never told me.'' A slightly querulous note was in her musical voice.

''Perhaps he thinks he has already told you.'' Gervase paused, remembering what Geoffrey had told him. ''Or perhaps he hasn't spoken because he knows you don't like talking about his epilepsy.''

Diana's jaw tightened as she faced the idea that her son was unwilling to discuss something with her. Gervase added gently, ''Not because he is afraid of you, but because he doesn't want to hurt you. It's common to try to protect those one loves.''

It was very tactfully put. Diana slid an arm around his waist and leaned her head against his shoulder for a moment. ''You're perceptive for a man with little experience of children.''

His arm tightened. ''I don't know about children in general, but Geoffrey and I seem to understand each other tolerably well.''

''I'm glad.'' Without looking up at him, Diana asked hesitantly, ''Do you ever think about having children yourself?''

He stiffened and pulled away from her. ''I sincerely hope that this is a theoretical discussion?''

It took a moment for her to realize what he meant. Then she laughed and crossed the schoolroom to perch on one of the battered birch desks that generations of Brandelins had occupied.

"No, I have no reason to suppose that I'm breeding. Whenever I am near you, I take precautions." She gazed through her long eyelashes flirtatiously. "I have learned from experience that anything might happen, at any time, and I had best be prepared."

He relaxed at her teasing words. Then, because she was very interested in the answer, Diana returned to her earlier question. "Have you never wished for children of your own? At the very least, most men in your position want an heir to carry on the name; some men even want children for their own sakes."

His face shuttered instantly. "There is no place in my life for children." Briefly she saw a flicker of expression that she couldn't interpret—anger, perhaps, or regret?—but his voice was flat when he said, "My line is flawed and deserves extinction. There are other heirs, more worthy ones."

His words were as harsh as his face, and they chilled her. What could cause him to repudiate the very thought of children? Was there madness in his family, or some other affliction that had skipped him but which might reappear in his offspring?

Quietly she said, "As you told me two days ago, there are risks to all living. Is your blood so tainted that you would forgo the chance to discover what a child of yours would be like? Have you never wished to share your experience, or to rediscover the world through young eyes?"

A spasm of uncontrollable emotion crossed his face, and it was a moment before he replied. "I do not choose to discuss this with you," he said brusquely. "Now or ever."

His words could not have been clearer, and it was a line she dared not cross. But though he might try to withdraw into his practiced detachment, she sensed some of his feelings through the invisible bond that connected them. That connection thrummed with tension, like a tether drawn too tightly, and Diana felt his pain, both the hurt of their conflict and an older, deeper wound she could not begin to understand.

There was nothing to be gained, and much to be lost, by pursuing the point, so she bowed her head in submission. The desk she sat on had been carved by generations of bored students, and she skimmed her hand over the corner, where the words "St. Aubyn" appeared in precise letters that slanted downward. Carved by Gervase, or a more distant Brandelin? What had Gervase been like as a child? Grave, certainly, and conscientious.

She said musingly, "Did you know that bees in their hives are said to hum the Hundredth Psalm on Christmas Eve? And they say farm beasts speak of the glorious coming among themselves, but woe betide the human who tries to overhear them."

The atmosphere eased. Gervase was no more fond of discord between them than she was, and he grasped at the change of subject. "I never heard about the bees. I always thought that during the winter they hibernated or some such."

He strolled over to the window set low under the eaves, glancing out at the sunless morning. The grayness of the light gave his face the cool tones of a marble statue. "Here in Warwickshire, the story is that on Christmas Eve the farm animals turn east at midnight and bow in homage to the newborn king."

Diana gave a ripple of laughter. "What wonderful things to have happen on the night of your birth."

He glanced back with pleased surprise. "You remembered."

"Of course." Then, tentatively, "I have birthday presents for you. I was going to wait until tonight, but it will be late when we retire, and it won't be your birthday anymore."

Gervase looked startled, as if far more used to giving than receiving. "Perhaps now would be best."

"Very well," Diana said, glad to have those moments of strain so easily set aside. "Shall we go down to my room?"

Downstairs, she checked to be sure that the corridor

was clear before beckoning her host into her bedchamber. He had always entered by the secret door before, and this seemed rather daring. Once inside, she went to her wardrobe and brought out a man's dressing gown, a richly luxurious one in dark blue velvet, nearly floor-length to protect against drafts.

As he accepted it, she said, "I made it from this fabric because it's marvelously soft. I expect that you never pamper yourself much, so I wanted to."

He smiled and thanked her as he stroked the velvet, feeling its sensuousness on the sensitive skin of his palm. Diana was right, he would never have chosen this fabric himself, but it had a welcoming warmth, much like Diana herself. And he was deeply pleased that she had made the robe with her own hands.

She continued shyly, "I thought . . . it might be convenient for you to keep it at my house. Since you are there so often."

It was a backhanded confirmation that he had a regular place in her life, and it made the gift even better. He thanked her with a kiss, the folds of robe crushing between them. Her mouth welcomed him, but before he could get too involved she pulled away. "There is something else."

She went to the wardrobe again and brought out a flat rectangle about two feet square, wrapped in silver paper. Gervase undid it carefully, then caught his breath when he saw what lay within. He held a framed map of the Kingdom of Prester John, beautifully detailed with fanciful beasts and tiny drawings of imagined wonders. The map was very old, exquisitely drawn and colored, and must be valuable, but it meant much more than that, and for a moment he was too touched to speak. That she should have remembered that conversation about boyish dreams . . .

He glanced up to see her regarding him anxiously, hoping that she had pleased him. "It's beautiful, Diana. More than that . . ." He stopped, then said slowly, "These are the two most personal gifts anyone has ever given me. Thank you."

Her smile was as lovely as the dawn. "I'm so glad.

I wanted to give you something that would be special.''

Laying the map on the table, he drew her to him for another kiss, one hand cradling the back of her neck, the other firm on her lower back as he felt the delicacy and strength of her. After a long, languorous interval, he said in the intimate voice he used only in the bedroom, ''There is another present you can give me, which will be very special indeed and could only be given by you. We have almost an hour until luncheon is served.''

Her rich laughter filled the room. ''Lock the door, my love, and I shall rejoice in giving it to you.''

That evening was a family Christmas, unlike any Gervase had ever known. Diana and her entourage could have been a closed circle, excluding him even in his own home; instead, in subtle ways he was drawn in and made welcome. The women had decorated the morning room with greens, male mistletoe and female ivy, prickly holly with bright scarlet berries. A Yule log burned in the wide fireplace and Diana had made a kissing bough, the traditional centerpiece of the Christmas festivities. It hung from the ceiling, its twined double hoops covered with greenery and adorned with candles and tiny ornaments cut from gold foil.

Geoffrey had made ''Christmas pieces'' for each of the adults, including the viscount. They were a traditional schoolchild project, and the bright bits of colored paper offered compliments of the season in the boy's best copperplate script. Gervase was unexpectedly moved both at the thought and at the boy's pleasure in having his work well-received.

After the formal dinner, the servants retired to their own celebration in the servants' hall, leaving the lord of the manor and his guests to play Christmas games such as snapdragon. In his lavish, lonely childhood, Gervase had never discovered the simple pleasures of sitting in a darkened room and trying to pull raisins drenched in brandy from their bed of low blue flames

without hurting one's fingers. Geoffrey was delighted
to teach an ignorant adult the "Song of Snapdragon."
*(With his blue and lapping tongue, many of you will
be stung, Snip! Snap! Dragon!)*

Simple pleasures to most people, but entirely new
to Gervase. They sat and laughed and told stories as
they drank hot lamb's-wool and ate tiny mince pies,
fragrant with spices, the rich, warm crusts crumbling
in the fingers. Edith had unexpected skill as a story-
teller, holding the others rapt with tales from the old
mummers' plays, acting out characters such as St.
George, the Turkish Knight, and Ginger Breeches.

There was no bedtime on Christmas Eve, and Geoffrey finally succumbed to sleep with his head on his
mother's lap. It was Gervase who carried him up to
his bed in the nursery, waiting while the boy was
tucked into his bed, his face angelic and trusting. Afterward the viscount also carried Diana to her bed,
but with her he stayed, and they laughed and pleasured
each other in the most ancient of all celebrations of
life.

The days passed swift and timeless. Diana had never
seen Gervase so relaxed. When they first became lovers he had been reserved, touching her only with desire, but now he was becoming affectionate in private,
though he maintained complete propriety in public.
He liked to have her near, and mornings when he studied dispatches delivered from London, she sat at the
far end of the library within his sight as she went over
lessons with Geoffrey. The viscount worked with great
concentration, but sometimes she felt his gaze on her
and would look up to see those clear gray eyes watching, no longer cool and guarded. Even across a long
room, she felt as if he reached out to caress her. Other
times, when she played the pianoforte in the music
room, she would look up and see that he had found
her, and was taking pleasure in both her and her music.

When the weather was dry, they rode together, and
after a fortnight Geoffrey, glowing with pride, joined

them on his pony. Edith was pleased to be in the country again, and Madeline, with her ability to take each moment of life as a gift, was serene and happy. All the people Diana loved best in the world were at Aubynwood. She wished they could stay like this forever and never return to the pretenses and obligations of London, but in spite of her wishes the days glided inexorably past, one by one.

The twelve days of Christmas passed, with a small mince pie eaten on each to bring luck for the coming year. Then the greens were taken down and ceremoniously burned, and too soon they were packing to leave. The night before their scheduled departure, snow began falling, not the brief occasional flurries of early winter but a gentle, steady cascade of flakes. Geoffrey had been put to bed, and Madeline and Edith had also tactfully withdrawn. Both Diana and Gervase were restless, reluctant to end the last day, and at his suggestion they decided to go for a walk.

They strolled through high-hedged gardens, her hand tucked securely under his arm. The shrubbery was black against the white earth and their slow steps were soundless. The stillness of the air kept the cold from biting deep, and the silence was pure and complete. They might have been a north-country Adam and Eve, alone together at the world's beginning. Gervase had always loved the fresh loveliness of falling snow, particularly at night, when every trace of light was caught and amplified by whiteness and a gentle glow suffused the dark.

Diana wondered aloud if the weather would prevent them from leaving Aubynwood. Gervase shook his head. "Probably not. There are only a couple of inches on the ground, and the storm seems to be diminishing. The snow might stop by midnight. It feels like it will stay cold, so the ground will be hard for good carriage travel."

Diana sighed regretfully, then turned her face up into the snow, laughing with a child's delight at the drifting crystalline flakes. In the dim, uncanny light he was struck once more by how beautiful she was, so lovely that his heart ached at the sight. Her heart-shaped face was framed by the hood of the wine-red velvet cloak he had given her for Christmas. The garment had been made specially to his order, with a lining of rich, costly Russian sable, as warm and exquisite as Diana herself.

For three weeks she had belonged to him alone, and suddenly the thought of sharing her in London was unbearable.

They were deep in the gardens now, utterly private, and Gervase stopped walking and turned to her, pulling her fiercely into his arms. He had thought that with time, familiarity would diminish passion, but the opposite was true. After three weeks of being with his mistress day and night, he wanted her more than ever. The silken welcome of her mouth, anticipation of the hidden delights of her body, the intoxication of her response, were greater aphrodisiacs than novelty could ever be.

The first night they had ever made love, he had wanted to bind her to him with passion, but had retreated from that, accepting that she was a courtesan who bestowed her favors where she chose. Now he was no longer willing to accept that, and he would use all the weapons at his disposal to make her his.

Diana clung to him, her kiss as hungry as his own, as if she too could not bear to end this enchanted country interlude. Her eyes were closed and ice crystals starred her long dark lashes. The night was cold, but where they touched was fire.

His arms were around her, and behind her back he peeled the leather glove from his right hand. They stood so close that no stirrings of chill air could come between them, and he reached down, slipping his hand into the folds of her cloak, under the soft luxuriant fur. Diana's body was warm and pliant beneath the flowing silk of her dress, and he cupped his hand around the fullness of her breast. She caught her breath and pressed against him as her nipple hardened beneath his hand. He caressed her slowly, feeling her tremble with reaction before he stroked lower, over the sweet curves of waist and hips until he reached the sensitive juncture of her thighs.

She yielded to him wholly, and her willingness made

him more than a little mad with wanting. The light
dress was easily raised and he found the waiting secret
depths of her. Her lips broke free of his as she inhaled
with a low cry and he whispered into her ear, "I want
you to be mine, Diana, only mine."

His embrace was support and protection, and without
it she could not have stood alone. The coolness of his
skilled fingers against her heated flesh was deeply erotic,
and his husky voice was urgent as he commanded,
"Promise me, Diana, that there will be no one else."

She had just enough awareness left to know that
Gervase was using passion as a weapon to persuade
her to a promise she did not want to give, and anger
stirred under her desire. It was not enough that he
dominated her physically and sexually; he wanted
more. Did he really think he could enslave her through
her love and need for him? As Madeline had said, sex
was a weapon, one she could use as well as he.

Without answering his words, she stroked the well-
loved contours of his hard body, feeling him shiver at
her touch. Deftly she undid buttons, then knelt on the
snow-softened earth, reaching up to grasp his hand
and tug him down to join her. Catching his mouth with
hers, Diana kissed him lingeringly, with all the skill
she had learned from him. Then, when he had no more
breath for words, she lay back, pulling him against her
so they lay full-length together in the wintry garden.

The snow made a pristine bed, and the spread of her
rich cloak protected them below as the folds of his
long coat fell around them from above. Too aroused
to resist her gentle guiding hand, he entered her, and
for just a moment they were united, their bodies perfectly attuned. Then he inhaled, a long shuddering
breath, and when he had achieved a measure of control
he withdrew. Her loss was so acute that she cried out
with longing. He was poised above her, his arms and
legs shielding her from the cold as he demanded
harshly, "Promise me."

Even now, as desperately as she wanted him, she
would not yield. Instead she whispered, "Love me,
Gervase, as I love you." Her arms circled his chest

beneath his coat and she slid them down his body, feeling the lean muscle and hard bone, the straining tension in his back as he fought both his desires and hers. When her hands reached his taut hips she pulled him into her, murmuring once more, "Love me, please."

She thrust up against him, and he could no longer withstand her. He was beyond words now, beyond demands. The snowy night, the garden, the fact that they were fully dressed yet as intimate as man and woman could be, raised them to a white heat of passion, their bodies clashing and joining in a rhythm that could not be controlled or denied.

Such intensity culminated quickly, and she cried out with the mingled pleasure and pain of ecstasy. He gasped and drove into her one last time as his body convulsed, and then there was silence again, broken only by ragged breathing and the soft sibilance of wind through the high, circling hedges that protected their tryst. They lay close and still for long moments, Gervase's cheek next to hers, the gossamer softness of sable warming their faces, the slowing tempo of their hearts beating together. Each was reluctant to speak, knowing that words would pierce the physical harmony of their lovemaking.

Finally, his body still covering hers, he lifted his head and shoulders and cupped her cheek, his fingers lying gentle and passionless along her temple. His face was a pale oval above hers, his expression unreadable. When he spoke, his voice was as light and cool as his touch, as if the question was of no great importance to him. "Why do you need to see other men, Diana? For money? If you want more, you have only to ask."

The anger she had felt earlier returned as she remembered how he had attempted to use the sweetness of passion to control her, in a perversion of what should be most honest and true between them. She tried to master her resentment, reminding herself how different he was from her in his actions and beliefs, but she still felt his actions as a breach of trust.

With too many thoughts conflicting in her mind, she didn't speak, and after a long pause he asked, "If it isn't money, is it that I don't satisfy you?'' His tone was still light, but they were so close physically that his body's tension revealed how much the answer mattered to him.

It is difficult to speak of serious matters when bodies are intertwined; besides, Diana was beginning to feel the chill earth even through her warm cloak. Her light push signaled him to roll away, and he stood, leaving her cold and alone even as he helped her rise. He brushed the snow from her cloak with quick, impersonal strokes, and when he finished, he captured her hands in his own warm clasp. "You must answer me, Diana."

"I know," she said in a voice as soft as shadow. "You asked why I want to be free to see other men and suggested two possible reasons, but neither is the correct one."

"If it isn't money and it isn't lust, what does that leave? Promiscuity for its own sake, because you need the variety, or because you like to have men in your power?"

This time his voice was sharpened to wound. With sudden clarity she saw that they were engaged in a covert struggle, and if she agreed to be his exclusively, he would win. She would be in the neat little niche of mistress, comfortable and convenient, and he would be free to concentrate on important masculine things, not wasting deep thought on a mere woman.

Their relationship might be rooted in sex and money, with other, deeper reasons she was not yet ready to confront, but Diana knew beyond doubt that what she wanted from him was love. If he loved her as she loved him, all other barriers could be surmounted; if she yielded now, they would both be the losers.

She and Gervase each carried dark scars on their souls, scars only love could heal. In the language of the heart she must be the teacher, for she knew something about giving and receiving love, while Gervase could scarcely bring himself to say the word aloud. If they were to have a future together, she must fight him; she must compel him to explore his own heart, and to let her in.

She wanted no other man, had not once considered

it since she met Gervase, yet she would not give him the promise he desired. If he was uncertain of her, was forced to question what she meant to him, perhaps he might grow to the point where he would offer her love, and it would set them both free.

Her hands tightened on his and she bent her neck briefly to rest her forehead on his firm shoulder. *A courtesan should never fall in love with her protector.* What she was going to do would hurt him, and his pain would grieve her as well. It was also dangerous, for love might be too alien and threatening an emotion for him to accept. Gervase had his pride and his formidable other defenses, and he might leave her rather than admit to feelings that would make him vulnerable. Yet once again instinct whispered that denying him was the right course. If she was a coward now, she would stay forever on the edge of his life. The thought of losing him terrified her, yet only by taking that risk was there a chance that she might truly win the man she loved.

After a moment's more thought, she knew what to say, words that would be honest, and which might show him the way. Raising her head, she tried to see his clear gray eyes, but the darkness defeated her. "No, not money, not sex, not power or promiscuity."

Snowflakes fell silent and weightless between them, and her breath moved them in a slow dance. "My deepest wish is for a man who truly loves me, and whom I can love in return." She thought a moment, then added, "Ideally, I would like marriage, more children, an honorable place in the world."

His hands around hers were absolutely still. "I can give you none of those things."

"I am not asking them of you." She drew in her breath, then continued steadily, "I want nothing that you will not freely give." Her hands tightened on his. "I love you, but I will not spend the rest of my life in the shadows of yours, waiting for you to weary of me. You desire me, but passion without love will surely fade. As I grow older, every time you come I will wonder if it is the last. I will not live that way."

When he opened his mouth, she laid a gentle finger on his lips. "You are the most important man in my life, but I see no advantage in promising you the fidelity a wife owes her husband."

Her cheeks were moist, not with cool melted snowflakes, but with the warmth of tears. It would be so much easier to give him what he asked. In a voice no longer steady, she said, "If you cannot love me, so be it. But I will not make a promise that I do not intend to keep, nor will I give you faithfulness when it might prevent me from finding a man who would truly love me."

His tone sharp, he said, "In other words, you will give your body to any man you fancy until one becomes so besotted with you that he will offer marriage?"

"That is not what I said." She shrugged, her gesture lost in the darkness. "Still, men sometimes marry their mistresses. Do you think that no man could want me except as a whore?"

He released her hands then, stepping back. "On the contrary, all men who see you want you, and apparently you are willing to let them all have you." His deep voice was rough now. "But your strategy is poor. A fool who is mad with longing will be more likely to offer you marriage, so you would be better off refusing him until the ring is on your finger."

"It is not marriage for its own sake that I want." She spoke as directly as she knew how. "I am not a complicated woman, Gervase. What I want is simple: love. Unfortunately, while the idea is simple in essence, finding it is not easy."

"So if I could say the words you want to hear, you would no longer accept other lovers?" She was not sure if it was bitterness or mockery in his voice.

"If you spoke from the heart." Her words fell into silence, and after a long pause she said gently, "Even now, in the abstract, you can't say 'I love you,' can you?"

His silence was colder now than the night air, and it hung between them for endless moments. Finally she took his arm and they retraced their way back to the manor. Courteous as always, he escorted her to the door of her chamber. Dropping his arm, he stepped back, scrutinizing her face as if she was a complete stranger. His expression was cold and still, as if it had frozen in the winter night. He looked painfully different from the man he had been these last three weeks, and it hurt her to see.

Standing on tiptoe, Diana laid her hands on his shoulders and pressed her lips to his. ''Come to bed, love,'' she whispered.

When she touched him, there was one slight, involuntary tremor of response, then nothing. He inclined his head briefly, his mouth opening as if to speak. Then he shook his head and walked away. Despairing, she watched his wide retreating shoulders until he turned the corner out of her sight.

Diana prepared for bed mechanically, then lay awake for hours, hoping he would come through the passage and join her, but he didn't. For the first time at Aubynwood, she slept alone. She had done the right thing, but the tight, anguished knot at the center of her being was so painful that if he had come and asked her again to promise fidelity, she might have agreed.

The first night at Aubynwood, Gervase had retreated from her before deciding to allow himself nearer, and then there had been three weeks of comfort and joy. Now, war was joined between them, a subtle covert war, and by her own actions she had pushed him away again. Was the bond between them strong enough to withstand his fears? Or would her need for him cause her to surrender, condemning them both to less love than they were capable of? She had no idea, and her emotions were far too turbulent for her to hear the frail voice of intuition.

As she waited through the endless night for the dawn, Diana feared that she would pay any price rather than lose him.

14

THE morning came late and heavy and Diana woke unrefreshed from restless slumber. The room was cold, with neither Gervase nor a maid to build the fire, and she shivered as she added fresh coal to the faintly glowing embers herself. Even though it was nine o'clock, her chamber was dim in the gray half-light, and from the window she saw that the storm had deteriorated to a near-blizzard, with a hard east wind whipping the snow into drifts. It was like a high country storm in Yorkshire, and the sight pleased her. If they were forced to stay at Aubynwood, there would be time to heal the breach with Gervase.

But her hopes were frustrated; only Madeline was in the breakfast parlor. The footman gave her a note from Gervase. He wrote that he could no longer linger in the country, that he would be able to reach London on horseback, but conditions were quite unsuitable for a carriage. She and her party should avail themselves of Aubynwood for as long as they wished, and he recommended that she heed his coachman's advice on when the roads would be safe for travel. It was a brief, impersonal note, such as could be written to anyone. Only the last sentence held any comfort: *I will call on you on your return to London.*

She folded the letter slowly. As careful as the viscount was with words, he would not have added that last line unless he really intended to see her again. Perhaps she refined too much on what had happened last night, and there had been no fundamental change between them. But in her heart, she did not believe

that. Last night battle had been joined, and it would
end with them truly united, or forever apart.

For five long days Diana and her party waited
through snowing, blowing, and finally thaw. Even a
house as large as Aubynwood began to seem too small,
and they were all ready to leave as soon as the St.
Aubyn coachman allowed that a carriage could manage. The roads were muddy and slow, quite unlike the
journey north, and they had to spend one night at an
inn.

Diana was tense with anticipation when they arrived
back in London, longing to see Gervase, but her hopes
were dashed again. This time is was her own servant
who handed her a letter, and for a long, heart-stopping
moment she feared that it would say good-bye, that
the viscount had no desire to put up with her moods
and demands any longer, that she had already been
replaced by any one of hundreds of more satisfactory
mistresses.

Given her black imaginings, it was some relief to
tear open the envelope and learn that the worst had not
happened, though the message was bad enough. In
another polite, passionless note, Gervase said that he
found it necessary to go to Ireland on business, and
that he would be back in several weeks.

As she stared down at the heavy, cream-colored sta-
tionery, she wondered if this was another skirmish in
their undeclared war. He had made no mention of an
upcoming trip to Ireland; was his business really that
urgent, or was he giving her a demonstration of what
it would be like to live without him?

He needn't have bothered, because she already
knew. The weeks ahead stretched as endless as eternity.

The winter trip to Dublin was difficult and exhaust-
ing as Gervase stopped and talked with various raffish
men to discover what they knew. The other, more important part of his task was to visit his former commander from India, Sir Arthur Wellesley, now Chief
Secretary of Ireland. Wellesley was a lean man of mid-

dle height, with a great hooked nose and an air of quiet
self-possession. The two men had always gotten on
well, and they could be friends now that Gervase was
no longer a junior officer. They had an amiable private
dinner, keeping the talk general until the meal was
over and the servants dismissed.

Each had a glass of port, though both men were
abstemious in their habits, and Gervase idly fingered
the goblet. If he hadn't been so absorbed with Diana
during the autumn, he would have visited Wellesley
earlier. He had come to make an offer, something
against his usual practice, but which needed to be
done. He began with a question, one for which he
could guess the answer. "How does governing Ireland
compare with life in India?"

Wellesley grimaced. "I'd prefer an honest battle any
day—Ireland is too heartbreaking. I can effect a few
mild reforms, but attempting major changes would
make matters worse."

"Does the fact that you were raised here make your
task easier or harder?"

"Harder, I think, because I see more of the com-
plexity. If I'd grown up in England, I would be more
sure that I knew the answers." Wellesley's voice was
sardonic as he studied his port, swirling the goblet
absently. "When I think that I might spend the rest of
my life doing this sort of thing . . ." He shook his
head, not completing the sentence.

"This is only temporary," the viscount said. "The
campaigns you conducted in India, the Battle of As-
saye—there isn't another man in the army who could
have done what you did. It's just a matter of time until
you receive another command."

Wellesley leaned back in his chair wearily. Though
he was not yet forty, a man at the height of his powers,
he looked old tonight. "You know something of how
they think at the Horse Guards, St. Aubyn. The commanders of the army are suspicious of Indian victo-
ries, as if they render a man unsuited to fight in
Europe. And my brother's politics are held against me
as well."

The viscount was silent, acknowledging the truth in the statement. Wellesley was a brilliant military man, not with the charismatic flair of a Napoleon, but with a calm, precise skill that would not permit defeat. As a junior officer, Gervase would have followed him to hell itself. With Europe almost totally under the sway of the French emperor, Britain needed military brilliance, and to waste such talent was insane. But it was true that army headquarters looked askance at Indian army experience, and that Sir Arthur's politician older brother had created many enemies through vanity and imperiousness. The two men could not have been more different, but Sir Arthur was loyal to his brother even though their close relationship injured his own ambitions.

"You have your supporters. As minister of war, Castlereagh is doing everything he can to get you a command. And . . ." Gervase took a sip of port. He had come now to the real reason for this visit. "I might be able to help. I am not without some influence, though it is of a subterranean kind."

Wellesley's brows lifted. He had heard rumors of the work St. Aubyn now did. "Are you saying that you will assist me?"

The viscount nodded. "Several of the ministers owe me favors. It is time I collected." There had been the matter of the Treaty of Tilsit between France and Russia, for example. Gervase had discovered what the secret articles were and how they affected Britain. He had given the information to Canning, and the foreign minister had been most grateful. There were other incidents, other ministers. Much could be done.

Wellesley looked startled, and the light blue eyes sparked with hope. "You would do that for me? You have a reputation for avoiding politics."

"Generally I do," Gervase agreed, "but what is the point of having influence if it is never used?" He tilted his goblet back and finished his port. "For years we have been stalemated, with Britain controlling the seas and France the Continent. Sooner or later, a crack will show up in Napoleon's Fortress Europe. When it does, you must be there to turn the crack into a chasm. That won't happen if you are an administrator in Ireland.''

He stood, offering his host a hand. ''Don't get too comfortable here in Dublin. It won't be for much longer.''

Wellesley stood also. His handshake firm, he said, ''I most sincerely hope you are right.'' He gave his rare, charming smile. ''I am fortunate in my friends, St. Aubyn. Whether or not you are successful, you have my deepest gratitude.''

The meeting with Wellesley was the high point of Gervase's journey. The rest was the routine business of spying, talking to sailors and smugglers and scoundrels of various stripes, receiving pieces of information, and sending inquiries back along the chain of informants, hoping answers would eventually return.

He worked long hours, as he always did on such journeys, but this time his concentration was broken. He had hoped absence would loosen Diana's hold on him, but instead he was haunted by images of her. He would see a woman make a graceful gesture and his heart would constrict, even though he knew it couldn't be her. When he transcribed his notes on what he had learned, her flawless face would come between him and the paper; he would see the intensely blue eyes and the slow smile that always welcomed, as if there were not another man in the world.

Worse than the images were the memories of touch. At night he would waken with his hand curved as if her soft breast were cupped within, or he would feel the warmth of her silken skin. He was obsessed with her, and he hated it. Gervase had asked what she wanted, she had answered—and she might have been speaking a foreign language. Why couldn't she have asked for something comprehensible, like jewels or carriages? But if she had desired something obvious, she wouldn't have been Diana.

Despising himself for his weakness, he tried to hurry his business, knowing that the longer he was away, the greater the danger that she would accept other men, one of whom might promise her whatever it was she craved. Not a day or night went by that he didn't imagine her accepting another man's advances, welcoming him to her chamber with that intimate smile, then opening her arms and offering more. . . . The thought of someone else possessing that matchless body made Gervase ill.

The last night at Aubynwood he had attempted to establish complete dominion over his mistress, and he feared that his failure had shifted the power to her hands. She said power over men was not her goal, but he doubted that; her beauty was power, and he could not believe that she didn't enjoy wielding it.

His doubts deepened after a nightmare he had in Bristol, when he dreamed that Diana was a cat, all sleek, sensuous grace, and that she was playing with him. He was a helpless, broken-winged creature attempting to escape, and whenever he nearly won free, she would lazily reach out a paw and drag him back, the cruel needle-sharp claws stabbing just deep enough to draw blood, but never enough to put him out of his misery.

He woke in a cold sweat, his heart pounding, fear and despair vivid in his mind. As he tried to remember the cat, it had a dual nature, seeming sometimes like Diana, sometimes like his mother. Was he wrongly confusing the two women, or was the dream a warning that all women were alike; that no matter how gentle and accepting Diana pretended to be, once she was sure of her hold on him she, too, would use her power to torment?

He didn't want to believe it. She had shown no signs of wanting to bend him to her will, or to wound and destroy for no reason. But if he was wrong, he feared he would not know until it was too late, when she was already exacting a subtle, excruciating emotional price that he would be unable to escape.

He had decided to make this overdue journey on impulse, knowing that he needed time to think, but he had not realized how grimly unpleasant those thoughts would be.

* * *

It was early evening when Gervase arrived back in London. During the last stages of his journey he had debated whether he should stop seeing Diana for the sake of his own sanity. He knew he had enough will-power for that, though the mere thought of never see-ing her again was gut-wrenchingly painful. But when he went to India he had decided not to live a slave of his past, and if those demons were discounted, there was nothing about his mistress that should make him shy away. And the rewards of keeping her were so infinitely satisfying.

As soon as he arrived at St. Aubyn House he sent a message to Diana, asking if it were convenient to call later, and his footman had returned with her agree-ment immediately. It had been almost a month since he had seen her, and a voluptuous sense of anticipation made him move slowly, savoring the prospect as he bathed and shaved, then walked the short blocks to her house. London lay passive under one of its famous thick fogs, and the eddying mists veiled the city like a dream.

The maid said Mrs. Lindsay would be with her son for a little longer, but that he could wait in her rooms. Now that she was so close he was impatient, and when the maid left him in Diana's sitting room he set the small gift he had brought on a table, then paced rest-lessly. He had never been alone in her rooms like this. They were spacious chambers, with high ceilings and classic proportions, well-furnished but not over-crowded. Fine moldings crowned the walls, deep Per-sian carpets lay soft beneath the foot, and the colors were harmonious for a total effect both stylish and soothing, rather like Diana herself.

He wandered into the bedchamber, where his gaze fell on the crystal goblet of pearls standing on her dressing table. He walked over and lifted the half-full goblet, admiring the lustrous spheres within as he dropped in another pearl. Then he halted, his fingers stone-still on the goblet. Though money was some-thing he thought about very seldom, now he wondered how Diana paid her day-to-day expenses. The pearls were very valuable, but they weren't cash. The money he deposited for her every month was untouched, and he was not absolutely sure that she knew it existed. Did she have savings, or did other men support this fashionable household? The thought shattered the unnatural calm that had carried him through the last few hours.

Suddenly, in a terrifying surge of jealousy, he had to know what secrets were concealed here. He stalked to the graceful marquetry desk and rifled through, but its drawers contained no illicit messages, nor any clues of her life before she had appeared in London. Turning to a wide wardrobe with shining satinwood veneer, he threw open the doors. Elegant gowns in the rich, subtle colors she favored hung before him, dainty kidskin slippers lined up below.

The dresses were like silent shadow Dianas and he thrust his arms among them, smelling the fragile aroma of lilac as he pushed garments impatiently aside. A gossamer blue shawl shot with silver thread flowed over his wrist and slid to the floor. As he hung it again, he brushed the soft nap of velvet and discovered the cloak he had given her, its dark red surface giving no hint of the sable richness within.

Without knowing what he sought, he plumbed the wardrobe's depths as if concealed somewhere within was the intoxicating, elusive essence of Diana herself. The only trace of male presence was the luxuriant blue robe she had made for him to keep here. He stared at it, abashed, then straightened her clothing meticulously, not closing the doors until he was sure there was no sign of his trespass.

Unsatisfied, he opened the top drawer of the chest that stood by the wardrobe. Inside lay neatly folded intimate apparel, delicately embroidered shifts and petticoats, fine silk stockings. There were no corsets, for Diana needed none, but there was a pair of rather daring lace-trimmed pantalets that he had never seen her wear. The sight twisted the knife of his jealousy as he wondered if someone else had seen them.

His heart pounding as if he had been running, he scooped up a fine lawn chemise and buried his face in it. The scent this time was a potpourri blend with lavender. The cool touch of the fabric against his face helped bring him to his senses. He closed his eyes, shuddering. Diana would think he was mad if she came in now. Perhaps he was.

He folded the chemise and laid it back in place, smoothing the garments to their original order, his fingers clumsy and coarse against the sheer material. He had just closed the drawer when the sitting-room door opened. He was in full view of that door and he turned to see his mistress, her gentle beauty enhanced by a forest-green robe, her glossy chestnut hair falling in loose waves around her throat and shoulders.

The cat whisked in and vanished under a chair as Diana halted, her gaze meeting and holding his across the distance separating them. He wondered if she had seen what he was doing, and if she had, what she thought of his invasion of her privacy.

Her lips curved in an uncertain smile, and at the sight he swiftly crossed both rooms and embraced her. Even though he ached with desire, making love was less important than simply holding her tight, feeling the soft curves of her body fitting against the hard angles of his. His hands roamed over her back and waist and hips, and he rubbed his cheek against her silken hair as the haunting sweetness of lilac surrounded them.

She raised her face for a kiss and he obliged, thinking that her mouth alone could rouse him more than the whole of any other woman's body. After a long satisfying embrace, he held her away from him. "I've missed you."

"Good!" she laughed, her face bright again. "I would hate to think I was the only one who noticed how long it has been."

Gervase smiled at that, and she was glad. His face had been closed and wary when she first came in, and for a moment she had been terrified that he had come to say that he could live without her quite easily. Then he would have casually given her the rest of the pearl necklace as a parting gift; Madeline said that was the sort of thing gentlemen usually did. Instead, he ignored that last night in the garden. She knew the issues raised then were buried, not resolved, but she was too much a coward to raise them again tonight. Well, she had never claimed to be brave.

Gervase wrapped his arms around her shoulders and steered her to the small sofa, pouring a brandy before he sat down and pulled her close. She cuddled under his arm, thinking how strange it was that she felt so wonderfully safe and protected with him, in spite of all that lay between them.

He offered the brandy goblet to her. "I trust you weren't with Geoffrey because he was ill?"

"No. Actually, I was reading him a story and we both wanted to see how it ended. I'm sorry for keeping you waiting."

"No matter."

His hand brushed the side of her breast, and warmth began to uncoil deep in her body. She knew he liked a little boldness, so she unfastened two buttons on his shirt and slipped her fingers inside. A little breathlessly she said, "I'm thinking of buying him a pony. He had a birthday last week, and insists he is now old enough for a mount of his own."

Gervase chuckled. "There's nothing wrong with his logic. I'll get him the pony he rode at Aubynwood. It's a good animal, and the owner's own children have outgrown it."

She slid her hand down his thigh, feeling long, hard muscles beneath her palm. "He'd like that. How much will it cost?"

The viscount shrugged. "I'll pay for it."

Glancing up at him, she said, "No, I will."

He gave her a reproving glance. "Diana, you have not yet mastered the trick of being a mistress. You're supposed to accept whatever gifts are offered, and wheedle for more."

She said acerbically, "Would you prefer me like that?"

He raised his hand and delicately toyed with her ear. "Actually, I like you very well the way you are."

"Then let me pay for the pony. It's for Geoffrey, after all, not for me." It was hard to remember her principles when he was doing such delightful things to her.

"You mean I can give presents to you, but not your son?" He paused, then said, "I like Geoffrey for his own sake, you know."

His words were deeply gratifying. Relaxing against his side, she said, "In that case, I accept on my son's behalf. Geoffrey will be delighted—he fell in love with that pony."

"Good. I doubt he would appreciate what I brought you." He reached over to the table that stood by the sofa and lifted a small flat package. "I found this in Dublin."

She sat up to unwrap the gift, then gasped at what she found inside. "Gervase, it's exquisite! I saw a *Book of Hours* once as a child, and I've never forgotten it."

In her hands she held one of the medieval prayer books that marked the cycles of the days and the seasons. Every *Book* was an individual work of art, with hand-lettered text and illustrations that were miniature masterpieces. This one opened to an Annunciation scene in the Hours of the Virgin and she brushed her fingertips reverently across the page, imagining the devotion the book had inspired over the centuries.

"I'm glad you like it. The dealer who sold it to me said it was Flemish, about four hundred years old." He finished the brandy and set the goblet on the end table.

Diana looked at him, her eyes shining. "You find the most marvelous, unusual things. I don't know how to thank you."

His smile was deep and intimate. "I can think of a way." Putting his hand behind her head, he drew her down for a kiss. The slow courtship of talk and touch was over; now they were both ready to carry what they had begun to its magnificent conclusion.

They made love like a tropic storm, a whirlwind of

heat and turbulence. Afterward they rested in lazy contentment, knowing the night was young. Three candles cast a soft glow, since Gervase insisted on seeing her. Diana had come to agree that light was better. She loved the beautiful lines and planes of her lover's body, the soft vibrations of his voice, the way his face would relax into the peacefulness he showed only with her. He lay with his head pillowed on her breast, his arms enfolding her, his breath soft and even.

The tranquillity was interrupted when a small body thumped onto the bed. Gervase was instantly alert, and she was reminded that he had been a soldier. Then he relaxed as the tabby cat stomped her way up the mattress, each footfall a small quake. Diana tried to sit up but Gervase held her tight. "I'm sorry," she said apologetically, "I don't know how the cat got in here."

"She came in when you did." He scratched the furry head, getting a delighted purr for his efforts. "I don't mind if you don't. I rather like cats. They're contrary beasts. That's probably why she isn't sleeping with Geoffrey."

Tiger had rolled over on her back and was letting the viscount scratch her stomach, a sign of rare favor.

"Usually she does," Diana said, "but I'm afraid that I've been encouraging her to sleep with me since we got back from Aubynwood. It's been lonely here."

Smiling with satisfaction, Gervase transferred his stroking from Tiger's stomach to Diana's. She could see why the cat enjoyed it so much; if she had been equipped to purr, she would have done so.

"What kind of a mother lures her son's pet away?" he teased.

Diana felt the muscles in her midriff tighten. "*Please* don't say that, even in jest. I wonder all the time if I am doing the right things for him."

"I'm sorry. It's hard to joke about what is most important to us." He propped himself on one elbow as he lengthened his caresses. "From what I've seen, you're doing a wonderful job. Geoffrey is intelligent and happy and confident." After a moment's thought he added, "He's not afraid of you."

It was an odd sort of remark; she put it aside to ponder it later. "I try so hard to do what is best for him. In fact, I'm afraid I try too hard. It was easier when he was small, but as he gets older he needs so much more than I can give him. That was one of the main reasons I came to London."

"And the other reasons?"

She looked deep into the clear gray eyes that could be both ice and fire. "Why, to find you," she said slowly, "although I didn't quite realize it at the time." It was the exact truth, more so than Gervase could possibly know.

Suffering from neglect, Tiger hopped up and stood on Diana's chest, mittened forepaws firm. She stroked the sleek feline body. "Have you ever studied a cat hair, Gervase?"

"I can't say that I have." While he liked cats, he wasn't keen on having one come between him and his mistress.

She held up two long hairs that had come off in her hand. "Look at the alternating bands of color."

Curiously he examined the hairs she held in her fingertips. One had five distinct color changes between the pale shank and the dark tip; the other was mostly dark except for a white dot below the tip. "In order to create these tabby stripes, every single hair on that cat's plump body is different," she mused. "Have you ever wondered how God keeps it all straight?"

He laughed. "No, I've never thought of it in those terms."

She looked at him, serious now. "Do you believe in fate, that there is an underlying pattern to our lives?"

He drew himself up until his head was level with hers. "You're raising all sorts of questions I've never considered."

Her intense blue gaze caught his. "But think of it. I had never been to one of Harriette Wilson's evenings, nor had you. Don't you believe there must have been a reason, something drawing us both to that point in time and place?''

He hesitated, remembering the irresistible pull he had felt when he first saw her, the absolute desire. But that was, after all, simply desire. ''No. It was only chance.''

She laid one hand lightly over his heart. ''I think it was meant to be.''

Her touch aroused him but he still disagreed with her words. ''If we hadn't met, I would have found another mistress, you would have found another protector. That would have been my loss, but perhaps your gain.''

Her lapis eyes were deep with ancient feminine mystery. ''No other man would have been right. It had to be you.'' As he watched her uneasily, she smiled. ''Poor love, I'm making you uncomfortable again. Never mind. Perhaps someday you will think differently. Tonight is not for philosophy.''

With gentle firmness she pushed the indignant cat over the edge of the bed, then bent down and feathered kisses down Gervase's torso. He leaned back on the pillows, his breath quickening as her soft lips moved slowly down his abdomen. He believed in chance, not destiny, but he would not deny that meeting Diana was one of the luckiest chances of his life.

On the surface, nothing had changed. Since Parliament was in session and Gervase sat in the House of Lords, he was busier than ever, but he still visited Diana often. He would leave before dawn and she would ache at the loss, but neither of them ever suggested that he stay. The barriers that had lowered briefly at Aubynwood were now firmly back in place.

They rode early in the mornings when weather permitted, Geoffrey joining them if it was not a school day. They might almost have been a family. Diana was delighted at how well they got along, even though she feared future consequences to Geoffrey if Gervase disappeared from both of their lives.

On the surface all was tranquillity, but Diana felt

the tensions building beneath the calm. When he thought she was unaware of it, Gervase would stare at her, his expression dense and unreadable. The thread of emotion that connected them drew tighter, and she sensed a dark, deep mood in him. His lovemaking was urgent and demanding, and he would raise her to such heights of passion that she would almost lose her sense of who she was.

Almost, but not quite. A deep, primitive part of her being wanted to let go, to melt and let him shape her to his will, but self-preservation was stronger. She dared not trust him unless he loved her, and he dared not admit to love.

Diana drifted, taking each day as it came, treasuring each moment with her son and her lover and her friends. She knew it was cowardly of her not to force the crisis that must come, but she had a fatalistic belief that matters would resolve in their own time. She could only pray that when the hidden tensions exploded, in the aftermath she and Gervase could be free of their dark pasts—free to love each other.

15

IN the spring of 1808 the first faint cracks in Napoleon's empire appeared on the Iberian Peninsula. The emperor forced the popular Spanish king, Ferdinand VII, to abdicate and placed his own brother Joseph on the throne. Infuriated, Spain burst into flames of insurrection. Gervase, in his small office in Whitehall, gathered and evaluated information and rejoiced.

In April, Sir Arthur Wellesley had been promoted to lieutenant-general and assigned troops to aid a Venezuelan revolutionary. But then Spain and Portugal sent delegations to Britain asking for aid against Napoleon, and Wellesley's destination was changed to the Peninsula. Gervase had used what influence he had on his former commander's behalf, and had no doubt that the general would justify the faith of his supporters.

Wellesley was in London now, and tonight he had requested a private meeting with the viscount to discuss a matter that concerned them both. For privacy's sake, the general came to St. Aubyn House. Gervase received his visitor in the library and poured them both glasses of port. After sitting and taking a nominal sip, Wellesley went straight to the point of his visit. "You know about the Marquess de la Romana?"

Gervase nodded. "One of Spain's most respected generals. He's in Denmark now, doing garrison duty for Napoleon."

Leaning forward for emphasis, Wellesley said, "Romana is a Spanish patriot. If he knew the situation in Spain, he would no longer serve the emperor, nor would most of his men." The general was by nature reserved, but his light blue eyes sparkled at the prospect of military action, and he looked years younger than he had in Dublin. "If someone can reach Romana and tell him Napoleon has removed the King of Spain, the Royal Navy will carry the marquess and his army home to fight the French."

Gervase made a frustrated gesture. "I know all that. We've been doing our damnedest to get a message through to Romana."

"Should have guessed you were already involved." Wellesley gave a short bark of laughter. "And the results?"

"Four good men have died trying," Gervase's voice was clipped. He had known all four agents, and their deaths weighed on him, even though they had known the risks and gone willingly.

"I'm sorry." Wellesley paused a moment, his expression grave. "But we must try again. The force I'm commanding isn't large enough to defeat the French troops on the Peninsula without help. Romana has nine thousand trained soldiers. If they return home, together we might break the French army in Spain. And after that . . ."

The sentence did not need completing. If the French were pushed out of the Peninsula, the long stalemate would be over. The war could be carried into France, to Napoleon himself. There would be peace in Europe only when the emperor was defeated.

"I know what's at stake," Gervase said shortly. He settled back in his chair, sipping his port while his thoughts went around in a familiar circle. In the last weeks, he had thought of only two things: of the situation in Europe and what Britain could do to exploit it, and of Diana. Always and everlastingly, Diana. Because of her, he had been reluctant to reach a conclusion that had been inescapable from the beginning. Briefly he hesitated, knowing that once the words were spoken there would be no turning back. "I'm going to go to Romana myself."

Wellesley's brows rose in sharp surprise. "Think you have a better chance of success than one of your regular agents?"

"Perhaps. I can hardly be less successful."

"An officer has to accept that men serving under him will be killed," Wellesley said obliquely.

"Yes, and I did that in India." Gervase's gaze rested on his glass of port, whose blood-red depths reminded him of things he had seen in the army, things he would rather forget. "But I am no longer an officer. I will not ask anyone else to undertake a task that has already killed four men."

Wellesley looked at him measuringly. "As you wish. Do you have a plan?" He was too practical a soldier to argue with a man whose mind was made up, particularly when success might make all the difference in the upcoming battle for the Iberian Peninsula.

"A fishing boat can take me to the Netherlands. After that, I'll travel overland to Denmark. I've done this sort of thing before, though not when the issues were quite so critical." He shrugged. "I speak French well enough to pass as a Frenchman, and I have the necessary identification papers."

"You make it sound simple," Wellesley observed. "But I imagine the other agents were equally well-qualified."

"They were, but it takes luck as well as skill. Perhaps I'll be luckier."

"Let us hope so." Wellesley lifted his glass in an informal salute. "Do your damnedest to come back alive."

Gervase smiled faintly. "Believe me, I am even more interested in that outcome than you are."

After Wellesley left, the viscount sat in his library thinking of what he must do before he could leave for the Continent. He kept his affairs in good order and little was required; he could leave for the coast by tomorrow evening.

So tonight would be his last with Diana. A year ago, he had been fatalistic about the occasional dangerous mission his work required, hoping for success but not overconcerned by the prospect of failure. His life was much richer now, and he cared about whether he survived. The thought of leaving Diana was acutely painful, and he wasn't sure which aspect was worse: the separation itself, or the gut-twisting fear that she would find someone else in his absence. It had been bad enough when he went to Ireland in January, but this journey would be longer and infinitely more hazardous.

It was ludicrous to be so concerned about a mistress. Before he met Diana, he had felt a contemptuous superiority to men who let women lead them around like lapdogs; now he had much more understanding of how that was possible. Not that he would ever let his mistress make a fool of him; if she even tried, he would sever the ties between them instantly, but part of Diana's charm was that she never threatened or demanded. The perfect woman, and at the same time, an utter mystery.

He sighed. At the moment, the time was better spent in visiting Diana than in speculation about what she would do in his absence. There would be time enough for brooding on his journey.

Gervase arrived earlier than usual, and the deviation from normal worried Diana. Her anxiety was increased by the remote expression on his face when she went down to greet him in the drawing room. She had learned that even when he was at his most withdrawn, affection from her would soften his sternness, so she lightly crossed the room and embraced him, lifting her face for a kiss. He held her tightly, his mouth demanding, and she sensed that his tension was not because of her, but for some other reason.

Leaning back in his arms, she asked, "Is something wrong?"

His clear gray eyes were searching, as if trying to memorize every line and curve of her face. "Would you like to go out somewhere this evening? It's early yet."

It was an unprecedented suggestion, since they valued their time alone together for both the passion and the peace. Wondering what lay behind his words, she replied, "If that is what you would like, I'd be delighted. What did you have in mind?"

He thought for a moment. "How about Vauxhall? The gardens opened for the season a fortnight ago and there is always something amusing going on. Have you ever been there?"

"No. Would I need to change into a different dress?

He surveyed the soft rose-colored muslin dress she wore. It was simple, but the lines were elegant. "Just a shawl. The evening is a little cool."

One of his carriages was waiting outside, and within minutes they were on their way. Gervase said little, but he held her hand firmly, the length of his forearm hard against hers, their fingers intertwined. Something was clearly amiss, but Diana, as was her custom, preferred to let him speak in his own time.

Vauxhall had flourished for almost a hundred and fifty years, a pleasure garden south of the river where people from all ranks of society went to enjoy music, entertainments, dancing, fireworks, and most of all, to watch other people.

Rather than take a boat across the river, Gervase had his coachman drive them over London Bridge. After he had paid seven shillings for admittance, they strolled the lantern-lit walks, Diana holding his arm and enjoying herself immensely. Music from the concert filtered through the cool night air, and the atmosphere was festive. Young couples in love held hands, aspiring dandies eyed the crowds through quizzing glasses, wide-eyed shopgirls in their best gowns brushed elbows with jewel-spangled ladies, and some who were not ladies, like her.

Eventually they took a small round table and two chairs in a quiet alcove formed by tall shrubbery. While Gervase went for refreshments, Diana enjoyed the passing parade. It was all quite amusing, until she noticed a still figure, unusual in a place of constant motion. She turned her head, and found herself staring at the Count de Veseul. He was no more than twenty feet away and his dark face regarded her with languid amusement from the edge of the flowing crowd. With insulting deliberation the count stared at the soft, curving flesh exposed by her low-cut gown, then raised his cane in a mocking salute.

Diana flinched. She was too far away to see the cane clearly, but she had a vivid memory of the serpent head, and how he had used it that night at the theater. It had been months since she had seen Veseul, and she had almost forgotten his existence. Now the menacing glitter in his eyes brought back the terror she had felt then, and she stared at him, unable to break her gaze away. Even though she was safe with so many people around, she felt alone and helpless without Gervase at her side, and the terror would not abate. She shivered and pulled her shawl around her shoulders against a sudden chill.

Time hung suspended as she stared at Veseul, willing him to go away. Then suddenly Gervase was walking toward her, and she was able to wrench her eyes away from the Frenchman. After the viscount deposited plates and glasses, she grasped his hand and pulled him down next to her, feeling safer for touching him. "That man there, do you know him?"

Surprised, he followed her glance. Veseul bowed his head ironically, touching his hat in acknowledgment of the viscount. At the same time, he was joined by a woman, a glorious golden creature dressed in the height of fashion, who stared at Gervase and Diana, but especially Diana, with cold pale eyes. Then the pair turned and walked away, disappearing swiftly in the crowd.

"He's the Count de Veseul, a French royalist who escaped to England during the Reign of Terror," Gervase answered. "He often acts as a liaison between the British government and the Bourbon court-in-exile. Why, does he take your fancy?"

There was an edge to his voice. Shuddering, Diana said, "No! He frightens me. The way he was staring . . ." She shook her head, unwilling to explain further. With Gervase beside her, her fears seemed petty and unreasonable.

His momentary jealousy assuaged by her words,

Gervase covered her cold hand with his. "I'm sorry, I shouldn't have left you. Any woman alone here will attract unwelcome attention, especially a woman as beautiful as you."

Beginning to relax, Diana took a forkful of the paper-thin ham that Vauxhall was famous for. After swallowing the salty fragments, she asked, "Did you recognize the woman with Veseul?"

"Yes. She's Lady Haycroft, a widow," he said briefly.

Surprised at what sounded like embarrassment, Diana asked, "Do you know her well?"

Shrugging, he said, "I've met her occasionally at those government social functions that I can't avoid. She's looking for a rich husband. I suppose that is why she is here with Veseul. There are few eligible men of wealth that she hasn't attempted to . . . further her acquaintance with."

It didn't take a genius to read between the lines. Since no one seemed to know if Gervase was married, his wealth and virile good looks would certainly attract predatory females. Diana found her brows drawing together in a definite frown. Seeing the expression, Gervase grinned. "Yes, she has cast out lures, and no, I haven't taken them. Lady Haycroft is all ice and hard edges, not what I look for in a mistress."

Clearly the connection that helped Diana sense his feelings ran both ways. He seemed gratified at her reaction, so perhaps it was not a bad thing. Blushing a little, she applied herself to her plate, washing the ham down with a sip of burnt wine, then wrinkling her nose. The drink was a Vauxhall specialty, but perhaps it was a taste that needed to be acquired. Outside, someone announced that the fireworks were about to start, and she heard the sound of people moving to find vantage spots.

Setting his fork down, Gervase said, "There's something I have to tell you."

His voice was serious, and Diana glanced up at him, stricken. "You are tired of me and want a new mistress. You brought me here thinking that a public setting would prevent me from making a scene.''

''Good Lord, of course not.'' He clasped her hand under the table reassuringly. ''Do you really think that I would set you aside so casually?''

She looked away, not able to meet his eyes for fear that her incipient tears would start. ''I don't know. I don't understand how men think, either men in general or you in particular.''

His grip tightened. ''Well, I don't know how your mind works either, but I promise I wouldn't dismiss you in a public place merely to save myself some discomfort. If it ever comes to that, I'll tell you in private, so you can throw things if you like.''

The hard rat-a-tat-tat of firecrackers announced the start of the display. Flinching at the unexpected noise, Diana smiled tremulously. ''I'm afraid that I'm a cryer, not a thrower. You would probably prefer throwing.''

''You're right about that,'' he agreed with feeling. ''But all this is quite apart from what I wanted to tell you.'' He stopped, as if thinking about how best to phrase it, then said simply, ''I'm going away for a while.''

''Like your trip to Ireland?''

He shook his head. ''Not exactly. I'll be gone longer, and . . . there's a chance I won't come back.''

Her eyes widened as she stared at him, trying to make sense of his words. In a hushed voice she asked, ''Are you going over to the Continent on some secret business?''

In the red flash of a skyrocket she saw an approving nod for the shrewdness of her guess, but he said only, ''I can't discuss it, Diana. If all goes well, I'll be back in a few weeks.''

''And if all doesn't go well?'' Her fingers were clenched hard over his, as if that could prevent him from leaving.

''You needn't worry. I'm going to send a note to my lawyer in the morning. If I don't come back, you'll be provided for.''

''That isn't what I meant,'' she said fiercely, fighting tears. "You can't go and get yourself killed. There is too much unsettled between us."

An unearthly flash of violet light lit up the alcove, and in its coruscating brilliance she could see a subtle shift in the muscles of his face before he said softly, "Then you'll be waiting for me to return?"

"Of course." Three rockets boomed outside, one after the other, as she swallowed hard, trying to dispel the lump in her throat. "Why did you bring me to Vauxhall?"

His eyes slanted sideways as he thought. "Perhaps I thought that if tonight was different, you might remember me better."

"Does that mean you are leaving tomorrow?" He nodded, and she stood abruptly. It was difficult to breathe. He was not a man to mention a trivial danger, and if he was warning her that he might not return, the hazards must be great indeed. "Then why are we wasting time here? Please take me home now. I know a better way to create memories."

He stood also. The leafy alcove was nearly private, and in the unsteady light he studied her, his face shadowed, before he pulled her into a crushing embrace. "Oh, God, Diana, you are so beautiful, and I want you so much . . ." he whispered before he lowered his head to claim her lips, rendering words impossible.

A whole series of fireworks exploded above, shattering the air like cannon fire while the alcove filled with flaring sheets of light in orange and green and cold, uncanny blue-white. As hot and furious as the sky over their heads, desire blazed between them. Outside, people cheered and applauded the fireworks show, while Diana strained against Gervase, her mouth and tongue and hands as demanding as his, her body driving into his, as if the barriers of fabric that separated them could be overcome.

Finally he pulled away, his breath coming hard, and took out a handkerchief to gently blot the tears on her cheeks. His voice husky with passion, he said, "Come, it's time to go home. I want to make love to you with every minute that is left."

Closing her eyes for a moment, she nodded, then raised her hand and brushed her hair back as she schooled her features. His fingers lightly touching the back of her waist, Gervase guided her out, seeking the quickest route to his carriage.

Behind the alcove, hidden from view by the shrubbery but able to hear every word that had been spoken, the Count de Veseul stood quite still, his hands lightly laced on the gold head of his cane, his face impassive except for the trace of satisfaction revealed by the bursting fireworks. So St. Aubyn was going to the Continent on some nefarious business. Doubtless he would cross the Channel with smugglers, landing in northern France or the Low Countries. A little thought would reveal which European affairs might require the personal attention of the British spymaster; then it would be a simple matter to issue descriptions to the guards and patrols that kept Bonaparte's empire secure.

The viscount was clever, but he would have to be a good deal more than clever to escape the net that he would run into. Removing him would simplify Veseul's own work, with the added benefit of making that beautiful, wanton mistress of St. Aubyn's amenable to others who might wish to sample her charms.

Negligently lifting his cane to push back the brim of his hat, the Frenchman strolled back toward the main rotunda. Amenable or not, he would have her. He was a patient man, but he had waited long enough and grew weary of it. Besides, he had found no other woman in Britain that he wanted half so much as Diana Lindsay. A pity that she wasted that flawless beauty on an Englishman. The French agent in the Lindsay household reported that the whore was quite amazingly faithful to her lover, but such fidelity would hardly outlast his demise.

As the final pyrotechnics exploded above his head, Veseul stopped and glanced up into the light-slashed darkness. His breath quickened as he watched the fading streaks of fire and thought of Diana Lindsay, of her perfect beauty, and of her disdain.

With sudden savagery he stabbed the golden serpent's head viciously into his left hand.

It was dawn when Gervase left Diana's, and she had been right: Vauxhall was already half-forgotten, but he would remember the night just past whether his life lasted a week or a century. She came downstairs to say good-bye, her soft arms clinging, her chestnut hair a lilac-scented tangle against his unshaven cheek. Then she had resolutely stepped back, her eyes stark but her chin high, refusing to say a word to stop his departure. He admired her for that; at that moment, if she had begged him to stay, it would have been almost impossible to resist her.

Since he had had no sleep at all, it was fortunate that his preparations to leave were simple. He gave instructions to his personal secretary and to his assistant at Whitehall. He wrote a note to his lawyer directing him to make a settlement on Diana if he should fail to return. He wasn't sure why he bothered; if something happened to him, she could find another protector in an hour, perhaps even a man who could marry her. No, Diana wouldn't need the money, but the bequest would be a sign of what she had meant to him, even if he had never been able to say the words she wanted to hear.

He had an hour free in the afternoon and thought briefly of going to her again, but he couldn't subject either of them to another farewell. Instead, almost against his will and hating himself for what he was doing, he put into effect an idea he had been considering for months.

Across the street from Diana's house was a small, genteel apothecary's shop, the only business on that block of Charles Street. Gervase had had the owner investigated and knew the man was discreet and knowledgeable, willing to do many things if the price was right. The apothecary put in long hours at his job, and he recognized the viscount as a regular visitor to the house across the street. He never even raised an eyebrow at being paid such a large sum of money to keep note of what gentlemen called on the beautiful Mrs. Lindsay.

16

GERVASE had been gone nearly three weeks and Diana's days were a test of quiet endurance. It didn't help that half of Geoffrey's conversation revolved around Lord St. Aubyn, and riding, and questions about when the viscount would return. At night she would hold the small brass statue of Lakshmi he had given her, rubbing it for luck as she prayed to any god that would listen to bring Gervase back to her.

Fortunately it was early summer, for it made the loneliness and uncertainty easier to bear. She turned twenty-five on Midsummer Day and her household gave her a party, with melt-in-the-mouth pastries made by Edith and a sweetly singing music box shaped like a nightingale from Madeline. Geoffrey gave her a scarf that was so perfect that it must have been selected by Maddy, and an irregular bouquet of flowers that were clearly chosen by him. She hugged all three of them, not knowing what she would do without her friends and her son.

The morning after her birthday dawned with the sky a cloudless blue bowl of light, the sort of summer day that came only once or twice a year in the damp islands of Britain. It was a day when it was easy to believe that Gervase would return soon, intact and passionate and as glad to see her as she would be to see him. Geoffrey was delighted to accept her invitation to accompany her to the market, and they set off together, Diana carrying a basket and a list from Edith. *(If you find raspberries, buy several quarts and I'll put up preserves. Be sure the chickens are young.)* In spite of their French cook, Edith would not let herself be driven entirely from the kitchen.

Geoffrey was in high spirits as he wove his way between pedestrians and vehicles with the jauntiness of a natural city dweller. Diana watched him with pleasure; she was sure that in the last six months he had been having fewer seizures. Some days she even dared dream that he might outgrow them altogether, though she kept the hope firmly buried in the back of her mind, as if examining it too closely would be unlucky.

As they walked to the market, Geoffrey laughed and chatted, skipping back and forth so that he covered twice as much ground as she did. Slowing by her side, he asked, as he did at least once a week, "Do you think Lord St. Aubyn will be back soon?"

"I'm sorry, Geoffrey, I just don't know. He could come back tomorrow, or next month, or . . ."—she inhaled before saying something she had avoided until now—"or perhaps never."

"Never?" Geoffrey glanced up at her, his deep blue eyes startled. "Why wouldn't he want to come back?"

"It isn't that he wouldn't *want* to, but travel is dangerous. Sometimes ships sink, accidents happen. And there is a war going on." She waved her free hand vaguely.

Her son considered that for a few steps before asking, "Are you going to marry him?"

"Why do you ask that?" she countered, uncertain how to answer. If he was thinking of her and Gervase in man-and-woman terms, the complications could be just beginning.

Geoffrey kicked a pebble across the cobblestones. "When we were at Aubynwood, you were together all the time." She glanced at him, wondering if he knew just how much time they had spent together, but he didn't seem to realize how literally accurate his statement was. "You seem to like each other."

"Liking each other doesn't always lead to marriage." She felt her way carefully, wanting very much to know her son's opinions. "Would you like to have Lord St. Aubyn for a father?"

His face furrowed in an expression of deep thought before he finally shrugged. "I don't know."

"You like him, don't you?"

"Yes, but . . ." His voice trailed off and he stopped to scratch an undistinguished but friendly dog. The dog gave a soft canine moan and leaned against Geoffrey's leg. Her son looked up hopefully, but Diana said, "No, we do not need another pet. Besides, he looks well-fed and must have a home already."

Geoffrey tousled the floppy hound ears, then walked on while the dog sat and looked after them with regret. Continuing his previous thoughts, he said, "Lord St. Aubyn is a great guy, but . . . when he's around, you pay him too much attention."

She sighed. Well, she had always known that jealousy was a possibility, even though she had done her best to make sure her son received a fair share of her regard. But having been raised by three adoring women, anything less than total attention was likely to feel like deprivation. She was glad that he was aware of how he felt, and could articulate it rather than just sulking.

Taking his hand, she stood on the street corner till a heavy dray passed, then crossed, not relinquishing his hand on the other side. "I'm sorry you feel that way, Geoffrey. I am very fond of Lord St. Aubyn, but that is separate and different from the way I feel about you. A thousand Lord St. Aubyns couldn't make me love you any less."

Deciding that it was appropriate to touch on another issue, she added, "It would be the same if I ever have other children. You are my firstborn, and no other son or daughter could ever take your place." He glanced up, his fingers tight around hers, but didn't reply. It was a lot for a small boy to think about, even a boy wise beyond his years in some ways.

The market was just ahead, and a sudden burst of voices sounded. Grateful for the distraction, Geoffrey pulled away and scampered up to a small crowd that was forming. Something about the voices and the way her son's body went rigid warned Diana, and she lifted her skirts and hastened to join him.

In a circle of gaping onlookers, the proprietor of an egg stall was having a seizure. The middle-aged woman writhed on the ground, her body arched back and her tongue protruding as inhuman rasping sounds came from her mouth. Her flailing arms had knocked over baskets of eggs and she lay among smashed shells, bright yellow yolks running across the ground and staining her plain gray gown. A man by the egg stall waved people back, saying gruffly, ''Her'll be right enough soon.'' The bystanders watched with varying degrees of curiosity, pity, and revulsion.

After a quick glance at the woman, Diana turned to her son, seeing his trembling lips and the expression of horror and loathing on his face. Suddenly he turned and bolted away, fleeing blindly down the crowded street. She half-expected this, and followed, but it took two long blocks to catch up with him, and only then because his wrenching sobs demanded more breath than he could spare. He slowed to a halt in front of a confectioner's shop, gasping for air, tears running down his face. Dropping her basket, Diana knelt and wrapped her arms around him, as if he were much younger than eight years old.

Through his gasps for breath, he managed to ask, ''Is that . . . what happens to me?''

She hesitated a moment, then admitted, ''Yes.''

Shaking his head violently, he said into her ear, ''It's dreadful, like being an animal. No wonder they stare. . . .'' He struggled against his tears, then buried his face against her neck. ''It isn't fair! What did I do that God made me like that?''

She held him tightly, aching that she could do no more. To see a seizure for the first time was shocking; to know that he himself could be so terrifyingly out of control was far worse. Ignoring the people walking around them, she rocked him in her arms, crooning, ''It's all right, darling, it isn't that bad.''

The trembling diminished, but his voice was anguished, no longer that of a child. ''It *is* that bad.

There's something wrong with me, and I'm different. I'll always be different.''

Diana sank back on her heels, holding his hands as she watched his tear-smudged face. ''Yes, you are different. It may seem unfair, but God's reasons are not easy for us to understand. *Every* person is different, sometimes in good ways, sometimes in hard ways, but it is our differences that make us what we are.''

He dragged a sleeve across his eyes, trying valiantly to master his distress. ''I . . . I'm not sure I understand.''

She thought rapidly, trying to find a way to explain, to help him understand and accept without bitterness. ''Your schoolmaster, Mr. Hardy, says that you notice things that most of the other boys don't, and that you are always kind to boys who are new or who aren't good at making friends. Isn't that true?''

''Y-yes.''

''I am very proud you are like that,'' she said softly. ''Would you be as considerate of others if you had never known what it was like to be different yourself?''

''I . . . I don't know.'' He thought, his attention no longer on his own misery. ''Probably not.''

''You see, being different may be difficult sometimes, but hasn't it helped make you a better person?''

He considered gravely. ''I see. Yes, maybe it has. Does that mean I should be glad that I have fits?''

She smiled, and dug a handkerchief out for her son. ''You don't have to be glad, but it is good to accept it and not be angry. Being angry at God for being unfair doesn't help at all.''

Geoffrey wiped his eyes and blew his nose, then looked at his mother curiously. ''Have you ever been angry at God?''

The question cut too close to the bone. Her voice a bit unsteady, she said, ''Yes. And it didn't do any good, either. It didn't make me happier, and it didn't change what was wrong. The only thing that helped was when I changed myself.''

She saw that he was about to ask for clarification, which she would just as soon avoid. Rising, she

brushed at her sprigged-muslin dress, decided that it
would survive its harsh treatment, then said cheerfully, "Shall we see what the confectioner has this
morning? I think we both deserve a treat."

Geoffrey's face became that of a small boy again,
and he gave a whoop before dashing into the confec-
tionery. Diana followed with more restraint. She had
always known that someday her son would realize what
happened during those moments when his body went
out of control and he lost consciousness, and she was
grateful he had accepted it so well. On the whole, she
thought, he was dealing with life's injustices better than
she ever had.

When he ran into French troops so soon after landing in the Netherlands, Gervase had thought it was bad
luck. He had talked his way out of the first encounter
with false papers, officiousness, and an aristocratic
French accent, but the next time he had been less fortunate. The guards checked his description against a
broadside, agreed that he was surely the Viscount St.
Aubyn, notorious British spy, and had arrested him.
He managed to escape from the flimsy local jail, ac-
quiring a shallow wound from a bullet along his upper
arm in the process.

After that the hunt was on, and he would never have
gotten clear if he hadn't found a small band of Gypsies. Gervase had worked with Gypsies before, and
spoke some of their language. The nomads hated Napoleon because of the barriers he put on their free way
of life, and for an only mildly extortionate amount of
gold they were happy to take in the Englishman and
wend their way north toward Denmark. They traveled
more slowly than he would have preferred, but at least
his chances of reaching General Romana were good.
And during the journey, he had ample time to think
about who among the handful of people aware of his
mission might have betrayed him.

Each week passed more slowly than the one before.
The earliest time Gervase might have returned passed,

and anxiety was a tight, constant knot inside Diana.
She spent more time than usual at knife throwing, not
because she needed the practice but because the concentration required kept fear at bay. There was satisfaction in the familiar weight of the weapon in her
hand, the narrow focus on the target, then the solid
thunk! as the blade buried itself.

On this dull July morning, she had been throwing
for half an hour or so with only Tiger for an audience
when Madeline entered and sat down to watch. After
observing for a while, the older woman asked, "Does
this make you feel better?"

Diana smiled wryly. "Knife throwing does relieve
tension." She walked down the narrow room to collect her weapons.

Madeline asked hesitantly, "It isn't just that St. Aubyn is away, is it? You have been . . . edgy, uncertain
ever since we stayed at Aubynwood. Is something
wrong between you, or shouldn't I ask?"

Diana tugged at an embedded knife. As usual when
her deepest emotions were involved, she hadn't been
able to discuss them, even with her closest friend, but
she owed her an explanation. In a brittle voice she
said, "Everything was fine at Aubynwood until the
end. Then he wanted me to forsake all others, and I
refused, and talked about love, and he went off in a
huff."

Freeing the blade, she returned to the upper end of
the range. "As you know, he came back, but ever
since February, he has been watching me like Tiger
watches birds in the back garden. For months I have
felt as if something is waiting to happen. And then he
went away."

A fan of knives in her right hand, she shook her
head. "I don't know what to think, Maddy. I know
that he wants me, and I'm sure it is more than just
lust, but I don't understand him, or what is going on
between us."

With a trace of humor, Madeline said, "Sometimes
I think men and women are two entirely different spe-

cies that just happen to be able to mate and produce offspring.''

Diana gave a twisted smile. ''Perhaps you are right.'' She hefted a knife, then flipped it underhand and missed the bull's-eye by a handspan, a poor throw for her.

Madeline sighed. Diana was suffering, and even her best friend could offer little in the way of comfort. Except, perhaps, by distracting her a bit. ''Have you ever heard of the Cyprians' Ball?''

''The *what?*'' Diana asked with astonishment.

''Obviously I never mentioned it. It's just what the name implies—a ball given by courtesans for their favored clients. Parliament will be ending soon and society will be heading to Brighton or the country, so this is a way of reminding the gentlemen of what they will be missing.''

Intrigued, Diana said, ''A gathering of famous men and infamous women?''

''An apt description,'' Madeline agreed with a smile. ''It's usually held in the Argyle Rooms. This year's ball is tomorrow night, and I'd really like to attend. It's been so long since I've been out. Will you go with me?''

Diana hesitated. ''What will the men present expect?''

''Oh, you won't have to do anything you don't want to,'' Madeline assured her, ''though it might be better to leave before it gets too late, since some men always drink too much.'' She leaned forward hopefully. ''Will you come? I do want to go, but not alone, and I doubt Edith could be persuaded.''

''If you want to, of course I'll go with you,'' Diana said. Absorbed in her thoughts of Gervase, she hadn't considered how dull Maddy's life was. And getting out would be better than staying home and brooding for still another evening.

The Argyle Rooms were very splendid and, most of the time, very respectable. Tonight, however, decent women kept their distance to avoid contamination;

also, perhaps, to avoid the horrid possibility of seeing their own fathers, husbands, or sons join the Fashionable Impures, ''a company more fair than honest.''

Madeline was lovely in a bronze-colored dress cut modestly in deference to her years. In a mood to be admired, Diana wore a blue silk gown which she thought rather dashing, but which was positively prudish in this company, where the most daring exposed their breasts completely. There were many young bachelors, since they were the Cyprians' best customers; men were not expected to live without sex until they wed. The women were uniformly attractive, and far more flamboyant than respectable ladies. The dancing was also far more intimate, and some of the activities in corners caused Diana to turn her eyes quickly away.

But Maddy was right: it was good to be among people. Concern for Gervase was a weight on her heart, but the music was gay, the dancing lively, and high spirits abounded. She and Madeline quickly attracted a group of admirers, several of whom she had met on her previous excursions into the world of the demireps. Naturally Harriette Wilson herself was present, and gales of appreciative laughter came from the circle around her. Diana relaxed, chatting and listening and even dancing with some of the shyer young men, who seemed unlikely to be too demanding. Seeing that her protégée was doing well, Madeline wandered off in mid-evening to talk with old friends.

The night was well advanced when Diana found a quiet corner by the musicians' platform to catch her breath and watch the dancing. After a few minutes, a group of young men stopped nearby. From their rowdiness it was obvious that they had been drinking heavily, and Diana edged away, not wanting to catch the young bucks' attention. As she did, she noticed an elegant young man with light brown hair several feet in front of her. He seemed familiar, and after a moment she recognized him as Francis Brandelin, Gervase's cousin, whom she had met briefly the same evening she had met the viscount. Like her, he was watching the dancers and minding his own business.

One of the group of drunken revelers said in a voice pitched to carry over the music, "Look! Who would believe that Brandelin would be here? From what I remember of Eton, I wouldn't have thought women were his preference."

A coarse burst of laughter greeted the remark, and Diana saw Francis Brandelin's lips tighten to a thin line as his face paled. Another drunken voice said, "But he's such a pretty fellow, maybe he wants to rival our Harriette."

Diana caught her breath at the cruelty of it. What they implied was the most vicious of slanders, an allegation of a crime punishable by death. Their target looked stricken and unsure, as if torn between confronting his accusers, ignoring them, or walking away.

Moved by pure impulse, Diana came forward from her corner to stand in front of Gervase's cousin. Laying a hand on his arm, she said in a throaty, seductive voice, "Francis, darling, I'm so glad you came. I've been looking everywhere for you."

He stared at her, his expression strained and confused. As the jeers from the neighboring group died away, she linked her hands around his neck and said reproachfully, "You've been neglecting me, darling. It's been three days." She sighed, then added huskily, "That last time was *such* a night."

Standing on tiptoe, she pressed a light kiss on his lips, saying softly as she drew back, "Don't look so surprised. Smile at me as if you mean it, then we can walk away from them."

Understanding flickered in his eyes and he smiled down at her and offered his arm. "It has been much, much too long," he said clearly. "I trust you have saved tonight for me?"

She cuddled close, looking as provocative as she knew how. "Of course, darling. Tonight, and any other night you wish."

Leaving dead silence behind, they walked away. When they had circled halfway around the room and were out of sight of the group that had been baiting him, Francis drew her into a vacant alcove and examined her carefully, his expression puzzled. "You're Diana Lindsay, aren't you? The Fair Luna who appeared once, and has hidden her face since."

"Yes." Diana released his arm. "I'm sorry, I hope I didn't embarrass you."

"On the contrary, you helped me out of an unpleasant situation. Why?"

Diana glanced at him; then her eyes slid away as she sat on the small sofa. It was easier to act than to explain. "I guess I didn't like the odds—six of them and only one of you."

His voice edged with bitterness, he said, "Would you aid me if what they said was true, if I was guilty of 'abominations'?"

Startled, she raised her eyes to his. Madeline had once explained in a matter-of-fact way how some men preferred their own kind, and were greatly reviled for it. It seemed bizarre to Diana, something entirely outside her experience, and she had no idea how to respond. But as she stared at Francis Brandelin, she could feel the anguish in him. Choosing her words carefully, she said, "A woman in my trade is hardly qualified to speak of abominations. I prefer to live and let live."

His face eased and he sat down next to her. "Then you are very unusual." Francis' gaze was appraising. "That time you appeared at Harriette's, my cousin St. Aubyn reacted to you like . . ." He paused, searching for a suitable simile, ". . . like Galahad seeing the Holy Grail. I asked once if he was . . . seeing you, and he just *looked* at me, then changed the subject."

His voice held a questioning note and Diana almost laughed aloud. She knew all about how Gervase could *look,* and it was comforting to know that he was the same with his nearest relative as he was with her. Shaking her head, she said, "Would you expect me to be less discreet than he?"

"No, I suppose not," he said with regret. "I hoped that he had made some arrangement with you. He works too hard. I'd like to think he found time for some enjoyment.''

''You and your cousin are close?''

He shrugged expressively. ''I suppose I'm as close as anyone. He was the nearest thing I had to a brother. When I started at Eton, he kept the other boys from bullying me too much. After my father died, he was one of my guardians until I came of age, though he was in India much of the time.''

''You sound fond of him.'' Diana knew she should end this conversation, but she couldn't resist talking about Gervase.

''Oh, yes, he's the best of good fellows.'' Francis' tone was briefly enthusiastic; then the expression of strain came back to his face and he looked down at his hands, which were twisting restlessly. ''If you do see him, you won't tell him what happened tonight— what they were saying about me?''

Diana felt a surge of compassion. If this young man indeed had unorthodox preferences, he must be terrified at the thought that those he loved most would hear, and condemn him. Resting her hand on his, she said gently, ''Of course not. Who could possibly be interested in the ramblings of drunken louts?''

His face eased at her words. There was little physical resemblance to Gervase, but he was pleasant and attractive, with a vulnerability that reminded her of Geoffrey. Though Francis must be near her own age, she felt much older. He looked up and said with a faint smile, ''You are a very restful woman. Would you . . . may I call on you sometimes? Just to talk?''

She suspected that he needed to talk rather badly. ''Of course. I live at 17 Charles Street. Late morning and early afternoon are the best times.'' She smiled and stood. ''I suppose that we should leave together if we wish to maintain the charade, but I must find my friend Madeline first.''

He stood also and said with his first real amusement, ''Leaving with not one, but two, beautiful women would do my reputation no end of good.''

Madeline was located, and was quite ready to leave

and to accept Francis Brandelin's escort. After introducing them, Diana excused herself to go to the ladies' retiring room upstairs. Three Cyprians who had been very active about their trade earlier in the evening were resting, and their bawdy forthrightness made her blush to her ears. Even after her months as a mistress, she clearly had much to learn about what might occur between men and women, so she took care of her business and left hastily.

The hallway and stairs to the lower floor were empty and dark, and many of the candles in the wall brackets were burned out or guttering. At the bottom of the grand staircase she turned to go back to the main ballroom, not even seeing the man who waited under the stairs.

The first she knew of his presence was when a pair of strong arms seized her from behind and dragged her under the staircase. Before she could cry out, her arms were pinioned and a hard hand was clamped over her mouth as her captor pulled her back against his body. The man was tall and broad, and she guessed who he was even before the menacing French-accented voice whispered, "What a pleasant surprise, *chérie*. I did not expect you to appear in public with your own kind."

Diana could smell spirits on Veseul's breath, and there was an uncontrolled note in his voice more frightening than the cool ruthlessness she had seen in him before. He nipped her ear, his teeth sharp and painful. She struggled, trying to free her arms, but was helpless against his size and strength.

"Ah, you're a lively wench." Then, his breath quickening, he said hoarsely, "My God, but you can stir a man's blood. Come home with me now, and I will show you how a Frenchman makes love." She felt his hard arousal against her buttocks, and he began rubbing against her, thrusting his hips rhythmically as one hand slid across her body. He fumbled at the bodice of her low-necked gown, sliding his hand inside to grasp her breast.

She felt a torrent of revulsion that once more he was

violating her, and she bit furiously at the hand across
her mouth, managing to sink her teeth into one of his
fingers. She tasted the metallic sweetness of his blood
as he swore and tightened his grip on her face, at the
same time squeezing her breast painfully, his fingers
digging deep into the soft flesh. His voice harsh and
angry, he snarled, ''Your lover won't be back, you
know. St. Aubyn will never escape the Continent alive.
He is almost certainly dead already.''

He pinched her nipple viciously, but that pain was
nothing compared to the agony his words caused, and
for a moment she froze, numb with shock. Above their
heads she heard footsteps, and she took advantage of
Veseul's momentary distraction to twist free of his
grip. He could have recaptured her easily but he hesitated when the Cyprians from upstairs came down the
steps and passed within three feet. Diana darted over,
putting the bypassers between her and the count, gasping, ''Please, help me.''

One of the women gave a scornful, half-drunk snort.
''What's the matter, muffy, is 'e too much man for
you?''

Diana shook her head, unable to speak, then made
her escape, not looking back at the shadowy figure
beneath the stairs. When she reached the ballroom,
she paused for a moment, automatically straightening
her gown and running a hand over her hair while she
tried to compose herself.

Could the French count really know if something
had happened to Gervase? Diana would not, could not,
believe it. If disaster had befallen her lover, surely she
would know it, would feel his absence from the emotional bond that linked them. Veseul merely knew that
the viscount was away and used that knowledge to
throw her off balance, perhaps hoping confusion would
make her more easily swayed. But she was not quite
the innocent she had been the first time she had en-
countered the Frenchman and his dark demands, and
she would not allow herself to break down.

Both Maddy and Francis Brandelin looked at her
oddly but made no comment on her flushed face or

breathlessness. Instead, Francis offered both women an arm and led them outside to the carriage, covering Diana's silence with witty gallantries.

None of the three noticed an older man coming late to the ball. The gentleman stopped and stared as the group passed him on the stairs, so close he knew he could not be mistaken in his identification. He didn't stay long at the ball, and on his return home he wrote a note before retiring. It was very short, and began with the words: *The Black Velvet Rose has returned.*

Raging, the Count de Veseul left the Argyle Rooms and went to an expensive brothel he sometimes frequented. Even though he had desired Diana Lindsay from the moment he saw her, he had not expected to feel such virulent, ungovernable passion when he actually held her in his arms. She had caused him to make a fool of himself, and he was grimly determined that someday she would pay for that humiliation.

At the brothel he demanded that the madam parade all of her available girls, as attractive a group of prostitutes as could be found in London. None had Diana Lindsay's refinement or stunning beauty, but one called Meggie was the right height, with chestnut hair and blue eyes, and in dim light she would do well enough.

He chose her with a curt gesture. Upstairs in the sumptuous candlelit bedroom, he ordered the girl to strip her clothes off and lie on the bed. After locking the door, he removed his cravat and used it to tie her wrists to the bedposts. Unsurprised, Meggie said, "This'll cost you extra, my lord," in a harsh cockney accent quite different from the musical, educated tones of the woman who was becoming his obsession.

His eyes rested on Meggie without expression as he lifted his cane and stroked her with the gold serpent head, drawing it across the curves and valleys of her body, teasing and jabbing with increasing intimacy. Experienced in the ways of men, she gave practiced little moans of pleasure, as if all her life she had been waiting for a man to make love to her with a cane.

But it wasn't cooperation that he wanted, it was fear.

Swearing with vexation, he withdrew the cane and twisted the gold head off to reveal the thin, glittering blade of a swordstick. As candlelight reflected along the bright edge, he said with silky threat, "Will you enjoy this as much, little *putain?*"

Meggie's eyes were blue-gray, not the deep lapis lazuli of Diana Lindsay's. They opened now and the bored compliance of a prostitute was replaced by horror as he laid the blade on her breast. The tip was so sharp that only the lightest of pressure was required to break the skin and draw a shallow slash from nipple to navel. She screamed, a high-pitched shriek of pure terror as he raised the sword over her, paused to let her fully understand her danger, then lunged forward to stab the blade into a mattress a bare inch from her throat.

Her terror was everything he could wish for. With leisurely unconcern, the Frenchman unbuttoned his breeches and covered her, thrusting into her body as she continued to scream and fists began pounding on the door. He allowed himself the luxury of pretending that the writhing body and panic-stricken face beneath him belonged to Diana Lindsay, and his violent assault relieved some of his angry frustration.

Hissing a string of French profanities, he culminated, his arms holding him fastidiously above the woman's bleeding torso. Then he withdrew from her and stood, pulling the swordstick from the mattress and screwing the head of the cane on. He was buttoning himself, once more in control, when the door burst open and a gigantic footman crashed into the room, followed by the hard-faced madam with a pistol in her hand.

As Meggie's hysterical sobs filled the room, Veseul said calmly, "Your whore is not seriously injured. She is not worth the effort." Ignoring the pistol aimed at his heart, he dug gold coins from his wallet, dropping them negligently on a table. "For her cooperation, and for the temporary loss of her services."

The madam's eyes were narrow and angry; much was allowed a rich nobleman, but even in a brothel

there were limits. As the footman untied the weeping
woman, the madam scooped up the gold and waved
the Frenchman out of the room with the pistol. "Get
out, and don't ever come back. We don't want your
kind here."

Shrugging, he left the bedchamber. The little epi-
sode had restored his habitual calm by relieving the
worst of his frustration. It had also been a pleasant
rehearsal for what he would do to Diana Lindsay when
he finally had her in his power.

17

ANOTHER week passed and there was still no word from Gervase. For the sake of her sanity, Diana clung to her belief that Veseul had just been trying to frighten her. Madeline had agreed when she had heard the story, though her brown eyes clouded with concern and she warned her younger friend to be very wary of Veseul. The warning was quite unnecessary.

Francis Brandelin began calling regularly and Diana guessed he was debating whether to confide in her. Whatever he decided, she enjoyed his company. He was amusing and intelligent, and had a sensitivity rare in men. Besides, though he was very different from his cousin, talking to him made Gervase seem closer.

This night was cold for July, and a steady drenching rain was falling when Diana was woken from a restless sleep by a soft footstep. Drowsily she asked, "Geoffrey?"

"No, damn you, not Geoffrey."

The answer was harsh and angry and adult. Frightened awake, Diana sat bolt upright in the bed. An image of Veseul and his threatening black eyes flashed across her mind and she drew in her breath to scream for help. Her cry was cut off as the intruder seized her, one hand gripping her shoulder and the other clamping across her mouth as he said furiously, "It's only me. The man who gave you this house. Or have you forgotten that?"

Perhaps he was mad, and that thought was even more terrifying. As Diana struggled, he continued, "I'm going to light a candle. Don't scream when I let you go. If there is anyone in bed with you, I suggest he leave while I'm striking the flint, or by God, I'll break his neck, even if he is half my age.''

When he released her, Diana slid across the bed away from him, her body tense with fear. The intruder took only a moment to strike the light, then turned to her with the candle in his hand. He was tall and thin, with the weathered face of a man in his late forties. His saturated greatcoat dripped onto her bed, and gray streaks showed in his wet dark hair.

As she clutched the blanket around her, he recoiled, as shocked by her as she had been shocked by his stealthy entrance into her bedchamber. "Who the devil are you?" he snarled.

He might be angry, but he didn't appear mad. His surprise caused her fear to subside a little and she said with creditable calm, "Surely that is what I should be asking you.''

"Where is Madeline?"

"Here, Nicolas. I no longer sleep in this room.'' The cool voice came from the doorway, where Maddy was a barely seen shape in the dim light, her dark hair in a heavy braid and her scarlet robe tightly belted around her. She spoke into the charged silence. "I heard you cry out, Diana. Are you all right?''

Diana forced herself to reply calmly, "Yes.''

Madeline's attention was on the intruder, and the room pulsed with tension. He took a step toward her, his voice a blend of complex emotions. "So there you are—''

She raised a hand, cutting off his words. "If you wish to speak to me, this is not the place to do it.''

"If I wish to speak to you!" He closed the space between them with furious strides.

Maddy glanced at the bed. "Go back to sleep, Diana. There is nothing to fear.'' Then she led the man from the bedchamber.

Sitting with her arms wrapped tensely around her knees, Diana gazed at the closed door as her mind raced. *A courtesan should never fall in love with her protector*. Her friend never spoke of the man who had inspired those words, but as Diana lay back against the pillows and tried to relax, she guessed that the mysterious protector had come back into his mistress's life.

It was a short trip across the hall to Madeline's chamber, and after they entered she took the candle from Nicolas' hand and lit a lamp, then knelt on the hearth, adding fresh coal to the fire. As she stirred the glowing embers, he said explosively, "Damn you, Madeline, look at me!"

Still kneeling, she raised her eyes to his. He was glaring, fury plain on his face. Fury, and desire. There had always been that between them. It was a struggle to keep her voice calm. "How did you find me?"

"Melton saw you at the Cyprians' Ball and wrote. He said you left with a boy young enough to be your son. I came to London as soon as I got his letter. I still have the key to the house." He paused, then added with bitter accusation, "It was the only thing of yours I did have."

"You frightened Diana."

He crossed the chamber and bent over to grab her arm, lifting her to her feet. "To hell with Diana. Where have you been these last three years?"

Three long and lonely years. . . . She tried to pull away, fearing the response his touch aroused, but he had her securely by both arms. His grip hurt, though not half so much as her heart. Still not meeting his eyes, she said evenly, "I left London. I wouldn't have come back last autumn if I hadn't heard that you never came to town now."

He put a hand under her chin and forced her to look at him. "Everyone said not to fall in love with a whore, but I always said you were different. I even believed it."

She could no longer avoid his green eyes, and her heart twisted at the pain she saw as he asked harshly, "Where were you, and with whom? Or were there too many men to count?"

"No, Nicolas, there were no other men."

His expression was disbelieving, but he released her,

unbuttoning his wet greatcoat and throwing it across a
chair. The last years must have been difficult ones for
Nicolas, Lord Farnsworth. He was thinner and grayer
than when she had last seen him, and he looked haggard in his black clothing.

Madeline knew he would not leave without making
love to her, and she craved that, even though the problems still lay between them, even though scars that had
partially healed would be ripped open again. She stood
very still, trying to collect her thoughts. So thoroughly
had she believed that he was gone from her life that
she had never imagined such a scene, never rehearsed
it in her mind, and she was unsure how to proceed.

His intense gaze holding hers, he said slowly, "I
couldn't believe you would leave like that without telling me. I came back from Hazeldown and you were
gone, the servants dismissed, the furniture in holland
covers, not a single personal thing of yours in the
house. Your man of business wouldn't tell me anything, even though I had referred you to him myself."
The anger was leaching out of him, leaving the pain.
"Why, Maddy?"

The truth was far less hurtful than what he imagined, and there was no more need for secrecy. She
took his hand and drew him to the sofa, sitting at the
far end from him. "I left because I was dying, and I
didn't want you to see."

His expression tightened at that, and he studied her
thoroughly. "You appear healthy enough."

"I am now." She pressed one hand to her breast in
the old reflexive gesture. "There was a lump . . . it
was growing rapidly. The physician said it was just a
matter of months."

His anger returned. "Did you trust me so little that
you thought I would abandon you to die alone?"

She shook her head and said gently, "No, love, I
knew that you wouldn't. That is why I left."

"I don't understand." His voice was flat, but his
eyes were naked and vulnerable.

"Have you forgotten what was happening then? Your

wife threatened that if you didn't give me up, she would ruin you.''

His face worked for a moment. "Of course I haven't forgotten. But I chose you. I was prepared to let Vivian do her worst.''

Madeline leaned back against the sofa, her face deeply sad. "Her considerable worst. Your children would have been torn in their loyalties, your family ripped apart, your reputation ruined. Even Hazeldown might have been threatened." His arm lay along the sofa back, and she reached over to take his hand. "It was too high a price to pay for a few months with a dying woman.''

He turned his hand and caught hers, gripping convulsively. "You should have let me make that decision.''

She looked into his beloved face. He was not what the world called handsome, but his craggy features had distinction and they were inexpressibly dear to her. "Can you honestly say you did not feel any relief when I left?''

He hesitated, unable to deny her words. After a long silence he said slowly, "I wondered at the time if you left because of some misguided impulse of nobility. I did everything I could to find you, but you might have vanished from the face of the earth. Where did you go?''

"Yorkshire, to the village where I was born." She gave a wintry smile. "My sister wouldn't have me under her roof.''

He swore again while she continued, "Diana, the woman you terrified in my old bedroom, saved me from a blizzard and gave me a home. More, she made me part of her family. It was a peaceful life, and it was good to be accepted, not condemned.''

Madeline closed her eyes briefly, remembering. "I grew stronger and the lump gradually disappeared. When I came back to London, I visited the physician who had treated me. He said such tumors are unpredictable. Usually they kill, but sometimes, inexplicably, they go away.'' Opening her eyes again, she said,

"And that is all that happened. It was very simple, really."

"Why did you come back to London?"

"Diana wanted to live here." She caught her breath as his grip on her hand loosened and he caressed her arm under the sleeve of her robe, his fingers light and knowing. A delicious, melting sensation flowed though Madeline's body, and they both knew that she was his for the asking, at least for this night.

He slid down the sofa and took her face between his hands. The anger was gone, leaving gentleness and desire. "Why didn't you let me know you had returned?"

Her pulse was quickening and it was hard to remember what had been so clear. "My health has improved but your wife still has the power to ruin you. And so much time had passed . . . time enough for you to forget me."

His green eyes were tender now. "Do you think that only women know how to love?" And then he kissed her.

She moaned, hungry for the familiar touch and taste and weight of him, and her arms went around his neck, pulling the hard length of his body against her. There had always been rare passion between them, and the years of separation had fanned it to inferno heat. As his lips moved to her throat and he opened her robe, she found that she was crying. Through her tears she whispered, "Oh, Nicolas, I love you so. Your wife will eventually find out and we will have to separate again, but let us make the most of what days or weeks we have."

In the drama and intoxication of reunion, he had neglected to tell her the fact that made all the difference. "Vivian is dead."

Madeline gasped, her body stiffening as she stared at him. He smiled wryly. "Don't look like that, I didn't murder her." He slid his hand into her robe and circled her breast, holding it with gentle possessiveness. "In one of God's little ironies, she died six months

ago of the same disease that you had. Didn't you notice that I'm wearing mourning?''

She shook her head, her face stunned.

As a gentleman, he had told his mistress very little
about his wife, but now he wanted Maddy to understand. "When my father died, the estate was bank-
rupt. I married Vivian for her dowry; in return, she
became Lady Farnsworth. A common arrangement.''

His hand tightened unconsciously on Madeline's
breast. "I never dreamed how high a price I would
pay for Hazeldown. I treated Vivian with the respect
due my wife, I gave her a position she could never
have achieved as a merchant's daughter, I gave her
children, but it wasn't enough. She tried to own me,
body and soul, and when she couldn't, she made my
life hell. It wasn't because she loved me, but because
she needed to dominate. She wanted me to give you
up because she couldn't bear to think that I had found
some happiness.''

Madeline laid her hand over his, her brown eyes
warm with silent sympathy. Choosing the words carefully, he said, "For eight years, you made my life
worth living. You were wrong to leave like that, without telling me, but . . . it was so like you to act from
a generous spirit.'' Her heart was a steady throb under
his palm. "Don't ever leave me like that again.''

He leaned forward and claimed her lips, and this
time she made no attempt to resist the rising swirl of
passion. She kissed him fiercely, glorying in the re-
discovery of every remembered inch of his body, still
not quite believing they were together again. If lightning were to strike her dead in the morning, she would
die content for having loved Nicolas one more time.

Later, when desire was temporarily satisfied, they
lay in each other's arms and talked as they had so often
in the past. She spoke of Diana and Geoffrey and
Edith, and how she had learned to pluck a chicken
again. He talked of Hazeldown and his children. She
had watched their growth at second hand, and delighted in knowing that his daughter had married and
presented him with a grandchild, that his younger son

enjoyed life in the army, that his heir had become a
keen agriculturist.

She was dozing with her head on Nicolas' shoulder
when he said, "When shall we be married?"

She turned her face up to his. "It is quite unnecessary that you marry me. With my past, it would cause
something of a scandal. I'm content to be your mistress."

"Well, that's not what I want for either of us." Her
braid had long since come undone and her hair drifted
across his chest. He stroked the thick dark strands,
then leaned forward to brush a kiss on her forehead.
Like him, Maddy was no longer young, and the lines
of living in her face made her all the more dear to
him. "All my life I have done my duty to Hazeldown
and the Farnsworth family. Now I'm going to do something for myself."

She chuckled and snuggled closer. "If you still feel
that way when you are out of mourning, we can talk
about it then." As she sank into sleep, she reminded
herself to tell Diana that falling in love with one's protector was not always a bad thing.

In the years that Diana had known Madeline, she
had seen her friend go from despair to resignation to
a deep, unshakable serenity. Now, for the first time,
she saw Maddy radiant with joy. For the next week
Lord Farnsworth was at the house constantly. Since he
acted as his own land agent, he could not be away
from his estate for too long during the summer, and
he made the most of the time before he had to return
to the country. Farnsworth was a mercurial man, quick
with words and laughter and occasional impatience,
and he watched Madeline in a fashion that made Diana
wish that Gervase regarded her that way, rather than
with the dark, puzzled wariness she seemed to inspire
in him.

After Lord Farnsworth left, the house seemed quieter than ever, and Diana welcomed a visit from Francis Brandelin. Though he was as polite and charming
as usual, he was edgy, and she guessed that he had

been drinking. For courage, perhaps? They talked of commonplaces over tea, with Francis crumbling the cook's excellent cakes without eating any. He reminded her of Geoffrey when her son had something regrettable to confess.

Deciding it was time for a bit of coaxing, Diana poured herself more tea. "Is there something you wish to discuss, Francis?" They had gotten on a first-name basis quickly. Leaning back in her chair, she added with grave reassurance, "You know that anything you say to me will go no further."

Carefully setting his own cup in the exact center of the table, he said in a low voice, "I know that. But . . . it is still almost impossible to speak."

"Because words have power, and once you say them, what you fear will become true?"

He considered a moment, then gave her a fleeting smile. "I suppose that is it. You're very perceptive."

"Not perceptive," she said with regret. "Experienced at not being able to say what should be said."

He gave her an inquisitive look, but today was not the time to talk about her problems. Instead she said, "Because words have power, saying them can also set you free."

He stood up then and crossed the room in quick, nervous steps, coming to a halt in front of a window, where he stared out, his hands linked behind him. "I know that, Diana. I suppose that is why I want to tell you about . . . about my weakness. Because talking to you may be the beginning of freedom."

She rose and walked quietly to the window, standing to the side so she could see his profile. "What those men said about you at the Cyprians' Ball . . . it was true?"

"Both true and false." Francis swallowed hard, the tendons in his neck drawing taut. "Young boys are separated from everything they know and sent to school, thrown together without privacy, tormented by older boys. Intense friendships can develop. Sometimes they behave in ways that the world considers . . . unnatural." He turned to face her, his light blue eyes as bleak as the hinges of hell. ''Most men outgrow such things, pretend that they never happened. Despise the very thought, despise those that behave that way.''

''But you did not?'' Her voice was very gentle.

''But I did not,'' he answered flatly. ''I hoped, prayed that I would outgrow my . . . unnatural desires. As an adult, I have never acted on them, but it doesn't matter. The desire is still there.'' Francis shrugged, then gazed across the room, his eyes distant. ''It's ironic, you know, I'm the exact opposite of most men. I like women, I really do.''

He glanced at her a little shyly. ''I like you a great deal.'' His eyes slid away again. ''But I don't want to . . . to make love to women. It wasn't just Eton . . . I think I was born this way—I'll never be what the world considers normal.''

Diana had a flash of insight. ''Something has changed recently, hasn't it?''

''You really *are* perceptive.'' He turned back to the window, absently watching a curricle pass. ''Ever since I came down from university, I have behaved like a proper young gentleman, doing all the proper social things. I've gone to balls and met young misses, always taking care to avoid raising expectations. I hoped I would meet a girl I could fall passionately in love with and everything would be all right, but it never happened.''

''And then?'' Diana prompted.

''I have fallen passionately in love.'' A muscle jumped in his jaw. ''But not . . . not with a woman.''

It was all so very far from Diana's experience. She sensed the desperate pain in Francis, and prayed that she would say the right words. ''Does he . . . return your feelings?''

''We've never talked about it.'' He played with the edge of the blue brocade drapery, his fingers stiff with agitation. ''He's a few years older than I, more experienced. I think we are . . . the same kind. When we are together . . . nothing happens that could not be seen by anyone. But the way I feel . . . and what I see in his eyes . . ." His strained voice broke off.

It was at that moment that she truly understood and accepted. The love in Francis' voice was not essentially different from her love for Gervase, or Maddy's for Nicolas; Diana could not believe that such love was evil. Speaking her thoughts aloud, she said with deep compassion, "It is tragic that neither of you can speak for fear that you are wrong, and the other may hate and revile you."

His slender fingers clenched on the drapery. "It is worse even than hate and revulsion. What we are speaking of is a capital crime. Men are hanged every year for it. The mere accusation can wreck a man's life."

If only she knew more of the world. Tentatively she asked, "Is the same true in all countries?"

His hand eased. "No, I think Britain is the least tolerant place in the world. The ancients did not believe that love between men was a sin. Even today, Italy and Greece are said to be . . . less condemning. I've heard of Englishmen who have exiled themselves there, and wondered if that might be an answer."

"Perhaps you should ask your . . . friend if he would like to go on a tour with you," she suggested. "To Italy or Greece."

He let his breath out in a long sigh that held both sorrow and relief. "Perhaps I should." He turned to face her then, his eyes deeply sad. "That might solve some problems. Not all. I think, in time, I can learn to accept myself."

"If you can do that, the hardest battle has been won." Diana fell silent, admiring his hard-won wisdom. Then she searched his face, wondering. "Why did you choose to talk to me? You hardly know me."

"That is part of the reason," he said slowly. "It is easier to talk to someone who has not known me for years. Also . . . you remind me of a Madonna, all warmth and understanding. I thought that if anyone could accept me, it would be you." A spasm of pain flickered across his face. "But what of my family? My mother and younger sister, my cousin Gervase. If they should learn—will they despise me?''

He shook his head, as if trying to deny the reality of his life, then cried out with despair, his control on the edge of shattering, ''You are a mother, Diana. Tell me, how would you feel if you learned that your son was . . . like me?''

Diana closed her eyes against sudden hot tears. It was not difficult to feel compassion for a newly made friend, but his words brought tragedy unbearably near when she considered how she would feel if it were a full-grown Geoffrey standing before her. She took a deep breath, then opened her eyes.

Francis stood directly in front of the window, his light brown hair shining in the bright shafts of afternoon sunlight. His handsome young face was nakedly vulnerable as he braced himself for her judgment, without hope.

Softly she said, ''I can't speak for your mother, Francis, or for anyone else. I can only say that there is nothing Geoffrey could do, or be, that would make me stop loving him. And my son could do far worse than be like you.''

She stepped forward and placed her hands on his shoulders, giving him a light, affectionate kiss as a tangible sign that she was not repelled by him. Francis' arms came around her convulsively, so tight that she could barely breathe, and she felt him shake with tears and anguish that had been too long denied. She returned his embrace, offering comfort as if he were Geoffrey, though he stood half a head taller than she.

As the emotional storm subsided, his embrace relaxed and he whispered his gratitude, ''Thank you, Diana. For being what you are, and for letting me be what I am.''

18

AFTER leaving the Gypsies, Gervase had made his way through the French army disguised as a dealer in cigars and chocolate. When he finally reached General Romana on the Danish island of Fünen, it had taken time to convince the Spaniard that he was a genuine representative of the British government.

Once convinced and apprised of the situation in his homeland, Romana lost no time in accepting the Royal Navy's offer to return his army to Spain. Making the arrangements gave Gervase a profound sense of satisfaction; this one act had justified his entire life. Deep in his bones he knew that the Peninsula was Napoleon's Achilles' heel. It might be years before the French emperor was defeated, but his end had begun.

The viscount could have joined Romana's army on the voyage to Spain, but preferred to return the way he had come. It would be faster, and on his journey he had learned things that should reach Whitehall as soon as possible. Besides, he had personal reasons for wanting to go home. The sight and sound and feel of Diana haunted him, both waking and sleeping. Traveling through one dark and dangerous night, he had stopped dead in his tracks mere yards from a French patrol, immobilized by a sudden flood of feelings about her. It had taken time and painstaking analysis to realize that the bush he hid behind was lilac, and that its fragrance was bringing his mistress irresistibly to mind.

Every time they were separated, he wanted her more. But this time, threading through his desire and longing was a dark strand of suspicion. The French had been expecting him; Diana was one of the four people who knew anything about his journey, and the other three were government officials. Though it was hard to reconcile her sweet loving with betrayal, on this he would not allow his emotions to cloud his judgment.

Fearing the worst, he racked his brain to remember what he had told her about his work, but doubted there had ever been anything of significance. For that he was grateful; it would hardly be surprising if a woman who sold her body would also sell information if the price was right. If she had done so, he would learn the truth from her. What he had not yet decided was what he would do about it.

The passage across the Channel was slow and hazardous as the brandy-laden boat was buffeted by heavy summer storms. Gervase was already bone-weary when he arrived at dawn in Harwich, but he immediately hired a post chaise and set off for London, rain, muddy roads, and all. It was a slow journey, and toward the end he was so exhausted that he hired a postilion rather than drive the final stages himself.

It was late in the evening when they reached London, and he had intended to go directly to the cold grandeur of St. Aubyn House. Instead, surrendering to an impulse impossible to deny, he directed the postilion to Diana's house, even though he was asking for trouble, even though he was breaking her rule of always asking permission to call.

Climbing wearily out of the chaise with the small shoulder-slung pack that was his only baggage, he paid off the postilion. The rain had diminished to a damp mist that saturated clothing and chilled the bones in a manner more like November than August, and the streets of Mayfair were almost deserted. Light showed in Diana's window and he wondered dully if she was entertaining another man, and what he would do if she were.

He climbed the marble steps slowly, hoping she was alone, for even the short blocks to his own house

seemed too far to walk. The housemaid who eventually answered the door said to wait in the drawing room
while she went to see if the mistress was receiving.
Dropping his pack by the door, he wandered aim-
lessly, refusing to sit because it would be too hard to
stand again.

And then Diana was standing in the doorway, one
hand on the frame for support as her wide lapis eyes
encompassed him. She was fragile and lovely in a blue
dressing gown, her hair loose as if she had been preparing for bed. Was that shock on her face, surprise
that he was alive? Perhaps dismay?

Before he had finished his despairing thoughts, she
had covered the short distance between them, embracing him with such force that he staggered back a pace
before he enclosed her in his arms. Diana was everything that was soft and warm and clean, fresh and fragrant as a spring morning as she tried to wrap his tall
body with her small one. The dense core of exhausted
tension that had been winding tighter and tighter since
he left England began to dissolve, and as he rested his
cheek against her sleek burnished hair he felt like
smiling for the first time in two months. "You'd best
be careful, Diana. Too much enthusiasm and I may
collapse on you."

She turned her face up to his, and he was shocked
by the tears coursing down her face. "I was so worried," she whispered. "It's been so long since you
left—I was afraid something must have happened."

When was the last time anyone had been this concerned about his fate? Even weeping, she was so beautiful it hurt to look at her. Words fled and he was
content to stare, feasting on the sight and feeling of
her pliant body against him. She was so warm. . . .
Eventually he remembered another of his failings. "I
didn't bring you anything," he said apologetically.

"Idiot," she said, her deep blue eyes bright through
her tears. Then, with a teasing smile that caught at his
heart, she said, "I think that I can extend you credit
for tonight. But you'll have to kiss me as surety."

Even for an exhausted man, it was an irresistible

invitation. Her soft lips were welcoming, and he fully savored the familiar shape and taste and pressure. She made a soft sound in her throat as she responded, and his world narrowed down to the woman in his arms. There was no past or future, no one and nothing but Diana, and she was more than enough.

His energy was reviving in her presence, and when the kiss finally ended he stepped back. "I'm sorry to call in such a disgraceful state. I've been traveling steadily for weeks and have had these clothes on longer than I can remember."

She didn't dignify his remark with an answer. Instead, she rang for a maid, then came back and slipped an arm around his waist. Abandoning his pack in the drawing room, Gervase circled her shoulders with his arm and willingly surrendered to her guidance. Diana ordered the maid to bring food and wine to her bedchamber; then they climbed the stairs, linked together in a manner inefficient but rewarding. As they entered her rooms she said, "You're in luck. I was just about to bathe so the hot water is already here."

"That sounds like a good idea, but I warn you, I may fall asleep in the water."

She smiled impishly. "I'll make sure you don't drown." Diana's suite of rooms included a small chamber with one of the only fitted baths Gervase had ever seen. The long, deep tub was large enough to accommodate a full-grown man, and was full of steaming water with a faint floral scent.

Working with the efficiency she had learned raising a son, Diana began to undress Gervase. He accepted her actions with amusement, content to be passive. "You've lost weight," she commented, her hands skimming his ribs as she unbuttoned his battered shirt.

"The meals were not always regular."

Then she stopped and sucked her breath in, her fingers poised just above the raw, barely healed scar on his left arm. "Your journey must have been as dangerous as you expected," she said with a catch in her voice.

"It was."

She touched her lips to the scar, butterfly-light in case it still hurt, and he saw that there were tears in her eyes again. He completed his undressing in silence, too moved by her tenderness to speak, but feeling the stirrings of desire in spite of his utter exhaustion.

None of Gervase's houses ran to the sybaritic luxury of a fitted tub, and the unaccustomed pleasure he felt on sinking into the hot water was so sharp that it was almost pain. The maid knocked at the door of the sitting room and Diana left to exchange his filthy clothes for a tray of food and a bottle of wine. She poured a glass of the wine and handed it to him, and he sighed with unmitigated bliss. "I think it is entirely possible that I have died and gone to heaven."

Laughing, she said, "Your body is reacting in a way that they say is denied to angels."

He smiled and laid his palm briefly on her cheek, then sipped the wine and tilted his head back against the wall. The hot water loosened sore muscles he hadn't realized he had, and he felt weak as an infant. Tomorrow he would think about his government and personal responsibilities, and the question of who had warned the French of his coming, but for now he would mindlessly absorb the pampering Diana gave so well.

She had taken off her dressing gown and wore only a sleeveless low-necked shift made from a fine cotton that was far from opaque. With facecloth and soap in hand, she knelt by the tub and began washing him, the feel of rough fabric like a massage. Her deft touch was not overtly erotic, but she was gently thorough and the effect was seductive in the extreme.

As the wine warmth spread through his veins, he observed that it was impossible for her to be ungraceful, no matter how she moved or bent or turned. She was scrubbing his legs now, her bare arms plunged deep in the water. Knowing the words inadequate, he said, "I haven't felt this well since I left your house in May. Not even then, because I was leaving you." Reaching out, he brushed her slim neck with his fingertips as she leaned over the tub, saying quietly, "You are a pearl beyond price."

She looked up with a brief shy glance, her face glowing with pleasure at his words, then returned to her self-appointed task. He finished the wine, tucking the glass into the corner between tub and wall, luxuriating. When the rest of him had been roundly scrubbed, Diana moved to the top of the tub to soap his hair, her strong fingers giving his scalp pleasure undreamed-of. Her full breasts were tantalizingly revealed by her water-splashed shift, and as she leaned over him Gervase surrendered to temptation and took one into his mouth, feeling the immediate hardening of her nipple through the sheer fabric.

Her eyes widened and met his as she trembled under the warm movement of his mouth. Abandoning her task, her fingers tightened spasmodically in his hair, then relaxed with pleasure. Her arms slid down to lie loosely around his neck as her eyes closed and her breathing quickened. Raising both hands to her slim rib cage, he held her steady as he moved his lips up above the low neckline of the shift to the cleft between her breasts, brushing kisses to the hollow at the base of her throat. The warm steamy atmosphere of the bath chamber gave her skin a moist, delicate tenderness, and the desire that had been a low smolder became flame.

As their mouths met in mutual hunger, Gervase slid his hand up her shapely leg to the hem of her shift, raising the gauzy fabric. He had to break the kiss to lift the shift over her head, but that deprivation was justified by the uncovering of Diana's full, stunning beauty. Her glossy chestnut hair tumbled loose in wanton tresses and her slender waist emphasized the rich womanly curves. Of their own accord his hands reached out to touch and caress as he tried to touch every silken inch of her.

As he gathered her in his arms to draw her into the tub, she laughed, torn between amusement and misty desire. "Do you really think this bath is large enough for two people?"

"It's a subject that deserves investigation," Gervase replied as she joined him, her body resting lightly on his in the buoyancy of the water. Her taut nipples teased his chest and their thighs brushed before her legs settled outside his. Her wet skin was sleek and smooth as satin, and he understood why sailors dreamed of mermaids.

When kisses and closeness were no longer enough, he cupped her round buttocks in his palms and lifted her easily onto him, sliding deep, deep into her body. She gasped and melted bonelessly against his chest, her long chestnut hair floating fanlike across the surface as their bodies pulsed together in a slow, exquisite underwater dance unlike anything Gervase had ever known. For these moments they were one in body and mind, their feelings so attuned that as they catapulted to rapture he was unsure which of them led the way and which followed, or if there was any difference.

They came down from the peak slowly, still joined while their rough breathing caused ripples in the water. What Gervase felt was far more than satisfaction, or even ecstasy; it was as if he had crossed into some strange new country with Diana, and his emotions were too new and profound to understand.

It was safer to say, "I'm surprised we didn't raise the water to the boil." One arm tight around her shoulders to support her above the surface, he brushed wet hair from her face tenderly as her cheek nestled against his collarbone. "I'm going to have fitted tubs installed in every house I own."

He could feel the vibration of her laughter as they lay breast-to-breast. Raising her head, she replied, "I hadn't realized how enjoyable a bath could be." Cautiously standing up, she climbed from the tub, wrapping herself in one of the large towels folded in readiness. "There seems to be almost as much water on the floor as in the tub."

The water was cold and lonely without her, so Gervase ducked under the surface to rinse his hair, then climbed out and they dried each other with towels and laughter. With both affection and lust satisfied, he was almost unconscious with fatigue. His last memory before falling into the deepest, most restful sleep of his life was enfolding Diana in his arms to hold her by his heart through the night.

As the young mistress and her lover slept, the French cook efficiently examined the contents of the viscount's abandoned pack with an experienced eye, carefully copying his cryptic notes before returning everything to where she had found it. After months of time wasted here, she finally had something of value to report. Most of what she wrote meant nothing to her, but she did not doubt that the Count de Veseul would understand.

When Diana woke, it was early morning and Gervase was still sleeping soundly. The gray stranger's face he had worn when she first saw him the night before was gone, and he looked young and peaceful. It pleased her enormously to have that effect. She didn't have the heart to wake him, so she broke another rule, letting him sleep while she had breakfast with Geoffrey.

After her son had gone, she went to her chambers and found Gervase beginning to stir. When she ventured close to see if he was awake, he seized her and pulled her into the bed for a morning greeting that left them both flushed and laughing breathlessly. Afterward they lay face-to-face, his hand cradling her head as he drifted toward sleep again. Then, abruptly, his gray eyes snapped open. "What time is it?"

"About ten o'clock."

"Good Lord, half the day is gone." He sat up and ran one hand through his dark hair, which was in dire need of a cut. Then he slid out of bed and located his clothing, which had been cleaned, pressed, and left neatly folded on a chair.

Diana sighed and got up also. She should have known it wouldn't last. She put her rumpled dress into some semblance of order, then pulled the bell twice as a signal for breakfast to be brought up. She enjoyed watching Gervase dress. Even his shabby clothes couldn't hide the beauty of his lean body. Wide shoulders, narrow hips, long muscular limbs, and that lovely masculine grace of movement. . . . She gave a sigh of pleasure.

"What are you smirking about?" he asked with a quick smile as he buttoned his shirt.

"I do not smirk," she said with dignity. "I was merely admiring your body."

He rolled his eyes. "I shouldn't have asked."

She chuckled, delighted to see him in such a light-hearted mood. He pulled on his worn jacket, looking every inch a man of distinction. She supposed that when he was skulking around Europe he changed his manner, but now he was unmistakably on his home ground. Breakfast arrived and the smell of hot country sausages persuaded him to stay long enough to eat. In fact, he ate ravenously, having been too tired—or busy—to eat the night before. Having breakfasted with her son, Diana wasn't hungry, but she had tea to keep Gervase company.

When he finished eating, he scooped her up in a playful hug, lifting her off her feet in sheer exuberance. "I'm sorry I have to leave, but as you can imagine, I've a thousand things to do after being away so long."

"Are you sorry you lingered here?" she asked, hoping he wouldn't say yes.

He grinned. "I should be, but I'm not."

"Will you come tonight?"

"Yes. Late, but I'll be here." He put his hands on her shoulders and pulled her toward him for a quick kiss that momentarily threatened to get out of hand. Then he was gone.

Diana had her own day's tasks ahead of her, but for a few minutes she curled up in one of the wing chairs with a contented smile on her face. No matter what Gervase said or didn't say, this morning she felt like a well-loved woman.

Gervase's feeling of well-being was short-lived. He had intended to go directly to Whitehall to find the foreign minister, but his eye fell on the apothecary shop whose owner had watched Diana's house. After the warmth of her welcome, it seemed absurd that he had set a spy on her; time to pay the fellow off.

The shop was empty at the moment, and the apothecary, a dusty little man, greeted the viscount without surprise. "Good morning, my lord. I trust you enjoy good health." Then, with a knowing look, he added, "Yon ladybird is a popular wench."

The words were like a solid blow, puncturing Gervase's warm glow. Schooling his face to blankness, he said coolly, "Indeed?"

"Aye. Mind, I can't vouch for the nights, after I've gone home. During the day, things were quiet at first, but the last few weeks, she's had a fair number of visitors." Malice glinted in his colorless eyes. "Gentlemen visitors."

Gervase reminded himself that it was the apothecary's gossipy interest in his neighbors and his knowledge of prominent Londoners that made him so well-suited to spying; that and his location. And a caller was not necessarily a lover. "Did you recognize any of them?"

"Oh, aye. There was a gentleman we don't see much in London nowadays, Lord Farnsworth. He scarcely left the house for a week or more. And there's a young fellow, comes by in the afternoon. Saw them kissing in the window myself, bold as brass."

Gervase felt ill. Had she taken other lovers from boredom, or because she had reason to believe that he wasn't coming back? It hardly mattered. "Do you know who the young fellow was?"

"Aye. Lad called Francis Brandelin." The apothecary's gaze was voracious as he looked for a reaction; he was a man who fed on the griefs of others. Though Gervase had never identified himself by name, he didn't doubt that Soames knew who he was, and that Francis was his cousin. He'd be damned if he gave the old vulture the satisfaction of a response. "Was there anyone else?"

Soames scratched his head. "Well, in a manner of speaking."

"What does that mean?"

"There's a fellow I've seen hanging about when I've left for the night, a Frenchman."

"Why is he only 'in a manner of speaking'?" Gervase asked, unable to stop twisting the knife in his gut.

"Never actually saw him go in. I expect he was waiting till he was sure she was alone. He'd want her to himself." Soames gave a lewd chuckle. "He's a lord, the Count de Veseul."

Gervase had thought nothing could be worse than hearing that his best friend was one of Diana's lovers, but he had been wrong. The Count de Veseul was his own best guess for the French spy known as the Phoenix, a man of power and depravity. So he too visited Diana. Had he come as a lover, or as a French agent buying information about Gervase? Or both? If she had told Veseul that Gervase was heading to the Continent, she might very well have been shocked by his return.

Blindly Gervase reached into his wallet and took out his last gold pieces and set them on the counter. He was grateful that a customer came in, for it spared the necessity of comment.

As he turned toward Whitehall, he wondered what in all the holy hells he was going to do about Diana.

Gervase had said it would be late when he came, and the rest of the household was already in bed as Diana waited in the drawing room. She felt a nagging sense that something was wrong, even though he would surely have sent a message if he was unable to visit her. When the knock finally came, she set down her book and flew eagerly to the door. But her welcoming smile chilled at the sight of him. Checking her usual greeting, she looked at him searchingly, trying to decide what was wrong. The exhaustion of last night was gone, and so was the lighthearted openness of the morning. Instead, Gervase was remote, with the cool

distance he maintained when matters between them
were strained.

"May I come in?"

She had been staring rudely, she realized. "Of
course."

She stepped aside and he walked past her. He was
in his normal well-tailored attire, a London gentleman
again.

"Have you eaten?" She faltered, trying to reestab-
lish the pattern that had been between them for so
long.

"Thank you, but I am not hungry." He walked into
the drawing room and she followed.

"Then . . . do you want to go to my room?" she
asked uncertainly. Over the months they had been together, food was optional, but the bed was constant.

"Again, no, thank you. I wish to talk to you, and a
bed might interfere with that." He stayed on his feet,
prowling, as if using one of her chairs would be a
commitment.

"Gervase, what is wrong? Is it something I've
done?" With growing dread Diana wondered if the
crisis she had been anticipating was at hand.

"Perhaps." He leaned against a heavy mahogany
table, his hands resting on the edge and one knee bent
with a casualness at odds with the tension that radiated
from him.

Under her defensive fear, Diana felt a stir of irritation. Choosing a chair, she sat and said crisply, "It's
late. If you wish to pick a quarrel, please begin before
it gets any later."

"It's not really a quarrel I'm after. It's just that . . ."
He paused, searching for words. "Matters cannot continue as they have been. Whenever I have asked that
you accept my protection, you have always refused, so
I really have no right to complain that you have been
seeing other men. I could live with the idea of . . .
sharing you, as long as it was just a possibility. Now
that I know it for a fact, I find it quite unacceptable.

"In the past you have laid down the ultimatums, and
after due consideration I always accepted them. But

this time the ultimatum is mine: if you will not promise me fidelity, I will have to end our arrangement."

Such cold words for what had been so warm. It was only when she looked deep into his ice-gray eyes that she saw the passion and the pain under the surface calm. Linking her trembling fingers together, she said carefully, "Why are you so sure that I have been seeing other men?"

He shrugged. "You were being watched in my absence."

"What!" Her hurt and confusion were burned away by pure outrage. "You set spies on me?"

"Not seriously, the way I would have done if I thought you were a foreign agent." He was so impossibly calm. "Just a casual surveillance that noted several men, though I suppose there could be a good number more, since you were not watched at night. Considering the length of my absence, it's hardly surprising that a woman of your passionate nature felt the need for . . . diversion. Perhaps I should be glad that you were sleeping with several men rather than becoming deeply involved with one, but I find myself curiously ungrateful."

For the first time his voice was uneven, an edge of pain appearing. "But you were quite straightforward about wanting what I couldn't give you, so I can hardly blame you for pursuing your goals. Since Lord Farnsworth's wife died recently, and newly widowed men are often very persuadable, you might well become Lady Farnsworth. That would have the advantage of being immediate, but the disadvantage that he already has heirs, so a child of yours would be unlikely to inherit."

A china shepherdess sat in the center of the table and he lifted it, studying the detail as if fascinated. "In most ways, my cousin Francis is a much better choice. He is young and attractive, of an age to be romantically in love, far more personable than I, and he is my heir. But you might have to wait thirty or forty years to become Lady St. Aubyn, and you will never be that if he dies before I do."

He set the shepherdess back on the table. "Actually, I've never quite understood what you see in me. There's the money, of course, but you've never seemed overconcerned with that, especially not for a woman of your calling.

"Then there's the sex—you certainly seem to enjoy it, and I don't think it would be possible to counterfeit such responsiveness—but any number of men would be delighted to give you as much sex as you want. Of course, you know that already."

"Stop it!" Aghast, Diana stood abruptly. "Gervase, have you gone mad? You are talking rubbish about so many things that I have no idea how to reply."

His eyebrows arched eloquently. "Oh? I thought that I was being perfectly reasonable."

She felt like swearing, but lacked an adequate vocabulary. "That is exactly the problem! You are talking about matters that are inherently emotional with all the passion of . . . of a watchman calling the hours. More than that, you are wrong about almost everything you are saying."

"Am I? I stand willing to be corrected."

Her hands balled into fists of sheer frustration. "To begin with, neither Lord Farnsworth nor Francis is my lover. Farnsworth was with Madeline."

"Really?" After a moment's surprise, he said consideringly, "I suppose that is possible. She's an attractive woman."

"*Possible* has nothing to do with it," she snapped. "It's the truth. They have loved each other for many years. They had to separate, but now that his wife is dead, I don't think anything short of death will ever part them again."

He smiled faintly. "I suppose that pleases your romanticism."

"Yes, damn you, it does!"

"Why are you so angry?" he asked, genuinely curious.

She shook her head and turned away, pacing nervously across the drawing room. How could she prop-

erly convey how much his every word and attitude
mocked what was most important to her? How much
his spying violated her cherished privacy? How his
cool, detached reasoning infuriated her emotional nature?

She stopped and pressed her hands to her temples.
Gervase could no more help being rational and detached than she could help being emotional and intuitive. And, God help her, she loved him, even though
at the moment she had trouble remembering why.

Turning to face him across the length of the room,
she tried to match his calm. "We have joked about
being opposites, my lord, but it is sober truth. We
speak different languages, even when we say the same
words, and I don't think I can explain my anger. At
least, not without thinking about the reasons for a few
weeks, then translating my thoughts into words you
might understand. Since you seem to prefer facts, we
will confine ourselves to them. Lord Farnsworth is not
my lover, nor is your cousin Francis. We are friends,
no more."

He looked so skeptical that her anger began rising
again. "Do you assume that no man could possibly
have any interest in me when I am not on my back?
Don't judge everyone by yourself."

His lips thinned. "Oh, I don't doubt there are men
willing to talk with you and no more. But since you
and Francis are given to embracing each other in windows in broad daylight, I may be forgiven for thinking
your 'friendship' an unusually warm one."

His words jolted her. So someone had seen that embrace, that innocent gift of comfort. A simple thing,
yet not easily explained, given Francis' circumstances.

"Is my information wrong?" he inquired gently.

"It is not wrong, but it is . . . misleading. If you
don't believe me, ask your cousin. No doubt you will
believe him sooner than me."

"I really would like to believe you," he said bleakly,
the yearning in his voice unmistakable.

She lifted her hands in a gesture of helplessness.

"Have I ever done anything to make you doubt my word?"

"Not that I know of." The qualification was an insult, yet Gervase's voice was matter-of-fact. "That is what has stopped me every time I considered leaving you. I knew I wanted you more than was sane or wise, but you have always been so sweet, so undemanding, asking only for love. And moderate remuneration, of course. Whenever I pulled back, I would remember that you had given me no cause to doubt your honesty, and would return to become more besotted than ever."

Settling his weight on the table, he crossed his legs in front of him. "But there is another matter that raises a few questions in my mind. You guessed I was going to the Continent. Did you sell the information to a French spy, or merely mention it to another of your lovers without knowing he was a spy?"

Diana gasped, stunned by his words. "What on earth are you talking about?" she gasped. "Although I have reserved the right to take other lovers, I did not do so in your absence. And I don't know any French spies. I told no one where you were going, though I think Madeline and Edith might have guessed."

He cocked his head to one side and appeared to consider. "I suppose that is a possibility—that one of them casually mentioned something to someone else. I am constantly amazed at how far and fast information travels."

His gray eyes met hers again, as clear and cold as a winter sky. "I would much rather think the information got out by accident than that you sent me off with that touching farewell to what you knew would be certain death. If I had not been very lucky, I would not have returned. In that case, cultivating Francis could have made you Lady St. Aubyn very soon."

He paused to let the import of his words sink in before continuing. "Perhaps it was my imagination, but you seemed quite surprised to see me alive last night, though afterward you managed to allay suspicion most effectively."

Diana felt caught in a nightmare, unable to assimilate the sheer, cold-blooded cynicism of his words. Her voice shaking, she asked, "Do you honestly think I could make love with you, then sell your life? That after arranging your death, I could set out to seduce your heir in hopes of achieving a title?"

He lifted his wide shoulders in a shrug. "I hope not, but that may be just my wishful thinking. I really do not know."

It was incomprehensible that he could stand there and coolly say such wounding words. Diana's knees would no longer support her and she sank into a deep chair, gripping the arms with numb fingers. "If you think me capable of such vileness, how can you sit there and talk so calmly? How can you bear to be under the same roof with me?"

"I don't know what I believe. That is why I am here. So, Diana, what is the truth?"

She buried her face in her hands, saying dully, "What is the point of saying anything? If I could deliberately betray you, my protests of honesty are worthless. If I did not, you have only my word on it, and you appear to value that very little."

"Actually, I prefer to give you the benefit of the doubt."

"How generous of you, my lord," she said without raising her head. She wished he would go, but even worse than the pain of his presence and his accusations was the fear that if he left, he would never come back.

She did not hear his soft footsteps, and it was a surprise to feel his warm hands take her shivering ones as he knelt before her. "Diana, I'm sorry," he said quietly. "It has not been my intent to hurt you, simply to learn the truth. Whether or not you have had other lovers in the past, the way the French learned of my journey—those things are less important to me than whether you will promise not to see other men in the future."

She raised her head and looked at him wearily. His face was a scant foot away, the sculpted lines and planes more familiar than her own features. In some ways she knew him better than she knew herself; in others, he was alien and incomprehensible. "Why does it matter so? Is it because you are so possessive that you can't bear to think of another man playing with your toys?"

His hands tightened on hers, but he didn't look away. "It matters because . . ." He drew a steadying breath, his gaze locked to hers, ". . . because I love you."

She had wanted desperately to hear those words, and now she was so drained that she wasn't sure what they meant. Trying to suppress her tears, she whispered, "How can you love me if you don't trust me?"

She was so close that the anguish in his eyes was unmistakable. After a long pause he said, "I didn't know that love and trust had anything to do with each other."

"They do to me." Gently disengaging her hands, she sat up straight. "Do you really mean what you said, or are you just saying that you love me so I'll do what you want me to?"

His dark skin drew sharply taut over his high cheekbones. Sitting back on his heels, he said, "I suppose I deserved that."

She had no more intended to hurt Gervase than he had intended to hurt her. The fact that neither of them wished to wound did not make it any less devastating.

"I spoke the truth, Diana. I love you as I have never loved any other woman." His sincerity was too raw to be feigned. "If it were possible, I would marry you. Since it is not, I hope love is enough to hold you, because it is the most I can give."

The room was utterly silent. Diana felt faint as the blood drained from her face. He had come the entire distance that she had wanted, and now that he had, she was terrifyingly uncertain how to proceed. Finally she said unevenly, "It is a compliment that you contemplated marriage, but of course a man of your position and consequence could not possibly take a courtesan to wive."

His detachment shattered and he stood, looming over her as he gripped her chin with one hand and forced her to look at him. All the passion she knew he was capable of burned in his eyes as he swore, "Consequence be damned! Make no mistake, Diana, if I could, I would marry you tomorrow."

As Madeline had said, passion was dangerous, a double-edged sword, unpredictable in its consequences. Diana had wanted to break through Gervase's hard shell of control. Now, terrifyingly, she had. He had always been gentle, careful with his formidable strength, but now he was frightening in his intensity. His clear gray eyes were no longer like ice, but were windows to the fierceness of the emotions burning inside him.

"I would most certainly marry you"—his grip tightened convulsively, and a dozen heartbeats passed before he could continue—"because that would give me the right to kill any other man that touched you."

19

HIS fingers tight around Diana's jaw after those too-revealing violent words, Gervase felt the pulse in her throat. She closed her eyes for a moment, the thick dark lashes shadowing her delicate skin, then opened them again. She had been bewildered and defensive, but now she challenged: "If you feel that strongly, then why *won't* you marry me? A wife swears fidelity, and I would honor my vows."

He let go of her and spun away. Nine years ago he had known that someday he must pay the penalty for his unforgivable crime against an innocent, and now the price was being exacted from his very marrow. He kept his back turned to Diana to conceal how difficult it was to answer. Taking a deep, deep breath, he replied, "I can't marry you because I have a wife."

The silence stretched, unbearably empty, until finally he turned to Diana. She was curled tightly in the chair, her knees drawn under her, her face unreadable but her body tense and rejecting. "So the rumors of the mad wife in Scotland are true?"

Except for the barest explanation to his lawyer, he had never once spoken of that black night in the Hebrides, but he owed Diana the truth of why he could not make her his wife. Besides, he felt obscurely that having to confess his crime to the person he cared most about was part of his punishment. "She is in Scotland, but she's not mad. She's . . . simple."

Diana's beautiful eyes widened in astonishment. "You mean . . . you married a girl who is mentally deficient?" At his nod, she continued, "Why on earth did you do that?"

His fingers raked his dark hair in agitation; then he sat opposite Diana, knowing he must tell her the full damning story. "I married her at the point of a gun, or close enough."

As she sat in waiting silence, he leaned forward and braced his elbows on his knees, his head bowed over his linked fingers. "It happened nine years ago. I was touring the Hebrides and stopped at an inn on the Isle of Mull. One of the barmaids was easily persuaded to visit me after she finished work."

His fingers tightened. "I'd had too much to drink, and when I went to my room I didn't realize that the woman in my bed was not the barmaid. The girl who was there started screaming and her father burst in. He was certainly mad, a crazed, sex-obsessed vicar named Hamilton who insisted that I had compromised his daughter and must marry her."

"I suppose this is where the gun comes in," Diana said in a voice of studied neutrality.

"Yes, although I was drunk enough and angry enough that I took the pistol away from him." The viscount stared down at his interwoven hands, remembering the hoarse voice and compelling eyes of the mad vicar, who believed his witless daughter was an irresistible temptress luring men to sin. The mad vicar, who had been his father-in-law for all these years.

"Why do you say the girl was simple?" Diana asked, curiosity overcoming her detachment.

"She could hardly speak. The few words she said were almost incomprehensible. And her eyes and face were . . . wrong. Empty. As if there was no one there."

More wondering silence. Then, "Under the circumstances, why on earth did you go through with the ceremony?"

Gervase shook his head. "I'm not really sure. I didn't realize something was wrong with her until later. At first I believed Hamilton and his daughter had arranged it all to trap me, and perhaps they did—I still don't know. But then I found out he was a clergyman, a gentleman of sorts, so his daughter could be considered gently bred.'' He shrugged helplessly. "Even though it was unintentional, I *had* compromised her. And so, because I was confused, uncertain of the right thing to do, raised to be a 'gentleman,' I married her.'' With bitter humor he added, "I have never gotten drunk from that day to this.''

Diana still sat in that tight withdrawn knot, her eyes hooded and inscrutable. Ironic that they were reversing their earlier roles; now she was composed but he was distraught. Her gaze strangely intent, she asked, "When you had had time to think clearly, why didn't you have the marriage annulled? After all, it took place under coercion.''

Shaking his head, he returned his gaze to his hands. "I never thought I would want to marry, so an annulment didn't seem important.'' He gave a twisted smile. "I never imagined that a woman like you existed. But even if I had wanted it, an annulment was impossible.''

"Why?'' Her gentle voice was relentless.

"Because . . . the marriage was consummated.''

"So you seduced a girl of feeble mind? I suppose it wouldn't have been difficult.'' Her cool voice had a knife-sharp edge. "Few women could resist you when you are in a persuasive mood.''

"I didn't know then that there was anything wrong with her.'' The blank child's face, slack and swollen with tears, was vivid to his inner eye. Then his guilt forced him to add, "And I didn't seduce her.''

"Oh, she seduced you?'' Diana said, caustic now.

"No, that isn't what happened.'' Gervase was unable to sit still any longer and he stood, his agitation needing physical release. "I was angry, she was my wife . . . and I forced her.'' He turned to Diana, willing her to understand, to extend some of her infinite compassion to help him, but she simply stared at him, wearing the blind mask of Justice.

"She was scarcely more than a child, she didn't really understand what was happening, and I raped her.'' His anguished voice rose. "In my anger and wounded pride and drunkenness, I overpowered and injured a helpless innocent.''

He closed his eyes, trying to block out the memories of the girl's pain and panic as the walls reflected echoes of his guilt and self-loathing. Hoarse and low, he said, "Don't bother to say anything. I've already said it to myself a thousand times."

He whirled away again, covering the length of the room in angry strides, wishing as he had so often before that he could repeal that moment of time, that he had left the girl without touching her, that he did not have to admit such base behavior to the woman he loved.

Diana's caustic voice followed him. "How nobly you are suffering for your sins. I'm sure your guilt has been a great comfort to the child you ravished and abandoned."

Gervase swung back to face her, shocked by the bitter condemnation of her words. Defensive, he said, "I couldn't undo my actions, but I made a settlement on her behalf, contingent on her being properly cared for. I could do no more."

"Oh?" Diana inquired with a mockery of sweetness. "You have visited her, seen to her welfare, made certain that her mad father hasn't abused her?"

He flushed at her sarcasm. "I went to India within a fortnight. My lawyer took care of the arrangements. He would have informed me if anything was wrong."

"And of course you didn't want to know more. You signed over some money, then left her to *rot.*" Her voice was a whiplash. "Or does your lawyer visit her, to see for himself that she is well-treated?"

"I don't think he has ever gone in person," was the reluctant acknowledgment.

"All your guilt and regret are for *your* unhappiness, *your* failure to live up to your own standards of honor." Diana uncoiled from the chair, her slim body radiating fury. "Nothing you have said shows genuine concern for the girl you married. *Nothing!* Her mad father may be keeping her locked in a stinking cell. He may have sold her to a brothel. She may be dead. How would you or your precious lawyer know?"

"Why the devil are you so outraged?" Gervase said incredulously. He strode across the room, stopping a scant arm's length away from her. "I should think you would be praying that she's dead. Then you could be a viscountess. Isn't that what you want—position, security, comfort?"

In their months together, he had never seen her truly angry, and it was shocking to see such rage in the woman who had won him with her gentleness. In a voice that trembled on the edge of hysteria, she cried, "In a world where men rape innocents and abandon them without another moment's serious thought, you wonder why I am outraged? Ask any woman who has ever been victim of a man's selfishness and violence why she is angry. Ask Madeline. Ask Edith. Ask the child you married."

Gervase had wondered how a woman like Diana had turned to harlotry, and now he knew, not in detail, but in essence. She, too, had been grievously injured, and her grief and hard-earned compassion made her a champion of all women's anguish. Her fury came from some well of torment buried deep inside her. Understanding that, he could not return anger.

And Diana's accusations were just; the thought of what he had done to Mary Hamilton had tormented him, but more because it was proof of his own deeply flawed nature than because of empathy with his victim. After making a minimal reparation, after handing over money he would scarcely miss, he had thought no more about the girl's welfare, not really.

No matter that their marriage was a mockery; the girl was his responsibility, one he had not properly discharged. He closed his eyes, shuddering; he had dismissed her as barely human. In its way, that was a crime as wicked as the initial act of violence. God only knew what kind of life she lived with that evil father of hers.

Gervase had faced black truths about himself before, and he did not let himself turn away from this one. He took a deep breath, then said flatly, "You are right. I have behaved as badly over the last years as I did at the beginning."

Diana had been staring at him, her fists clenched

with the force of her feelings, but his words undercut
her anger. Calmer now, she asked, "Are you going to
do anything about it?"

"I'll find out from my lawyer where she is living and
visit her myself. I imagine I will know what to do when
I see her condition." He thought a moment. "The
sooner it is done, the better. I can leave the day after
tomorrow. I suppose I'll be gone a fortnight or so."

Even though she was under control again, Diana still
looked unapproachable, her face set and remote. Now
more than ever Gervase wanted to hold her, to forget
his transgressions in the sweet depths of her body, but
there was still too much anger in the air. Nor did he
deserve comfort or reward until he had discharged the
debts of the past.

Instead, he picked up his hat and left. As he went
out the front door, he humorlessly considered the irony
of having a mistress who was so concerned about the
welfare of his wife.

As the door closed, Diana sank back into her chair,
her shaking body huddled in the circle of her arms as
the scene with Gervase replayed in her head. *You were
watched in my absence. . . . Did you sell the information to a French spy, or casually mention it to one
of your other lovers?* Did he really think that she could
betray him? Or give herself to another man when there
was such intimacy between them?

*I have a wife . . . she's simple. . . . She was scarcely
more than a child, and I raped her.* Diana had known
that some crisis was imminent, that long-buried secrets would erupt from the depths like lava, but still
his words astonished her. She had never anticipated
such a confession, nor had she expected the shattering
fury that had possessed her.

Because I love you . . . because I love you. The
words she had longed for with hope and uncertainty
echoed in her mind, and she let the tears she had been
fighting flow unchecked. The crisis was far from over,
there was still much to be resolved—but he loved her,

as she loved him, and surely that would be enough to carry them through what lay ahead.

Exhausted though she was by emotional storms, when Diana returned to her rooms she began to pack.

Gervase made no attempt to sleep that night, knowing that his feelings were strung too tightly to permit rest, and that he had much to do before he headed north. He wrote a short note to his lawyer, asking for his wife's current direction, and no more; it would be better to learn everything else himself.

Through the rest of the night and into the day, he swiftly dealt with the most urgent of his business. Though all of it was important, nothing unexpected appeared until late in the afternoon, when he received a dispatch from one of his agents. Enclosed were documents taken from an enemy courier captured in Kent just before embarkation to France. Under the seal of the Phoenix, Gervase found a neatly coded summary of the information that he himself had just brought back from the Continent.

He stared at the tiny, cribbed notations on the thin sheets of paper as a wave of nausea broke over him. He had been back in England for less than three days, and already the Phoenix had learned what he had discovered and was alerting his masters. Perhaps the information had been sold by a spy at Whitehall, but with cruel clarity Gervase recalled leaving his pack in Diana's drawing room. He had slept late the next morning, and when he woke his cleaned clothes and pack had been waiting by her bed.

There had been ample time for her to search his belongings, to copy the terse notes he had made. *There's a fellow hanging about, a French lord, the Count de Veseul.* He had asked her about Farnsworth and Francis, but they had not discussed Veseul. She had denied selling information or taking any new lovers in his absence, but perhaps Veseul was an old lover. Or perhaps she was simply a liar, beginning to end, and he was a gullible, passion-poisoned fool.

Sitting at his desk, Gervase buried his head in his

hands, achingly aware that he had had only one good night's sleep in weeks, had not slept at all the night before. He was in no condition to judge Diana's truth or falsity. All he could do was face his problems one at a time.

First the trip north to locate his wife and make what provisions seemed necessary; Diana's outrage had shown him that this was a task that must be accomplished for its own sake, as well as to demonstrate his remorse and good faith to Diana. He must assure himself that Mary Hamilton was alive and well-treated, and as comfortable as possible.

He must also talk to the mad vicar. Though he had not mentioned the possibility to Diana, it was conceivable that he could buy off Hamilton and purchase his freedom, though he would not do it at the price of the girl's welfare; not again. While technically the marriage was not eligible for annulment, it would be a simple lie to say that it had not been consummated.

He would continue to support Mary Hamilton, so she would not be injured by an annulment. A lie that hurt no one was a small price to pay to have Diana his wife, always by his side, always in his arms . . . always assuming she was the woman he thought she was, rather than the traitorous bitch that the evidence pointed to. . . .

The viscount rubbed his eyes and sat up, battling his fatigue. The work he did for his country was more significant than his tangled personal affairs. The endless wars with France were entering a new phase now that Britain had troops on the Iberian Peninsula, and if Veseul was the Phoenix, he needed to be stopped once and for all.

Gervase thought for a while, then gave a smile of bleak, humorless satisfaction. There was a way to bring the pieces together. It was time for an Aubynwood house party. Once a year he would invite a number of government ministers and other prominent folk to his estate to relax and discuss politics and make policy without the distractions of London. This year the list would include the Count de Veseul. He would also invite Diana.

He began jotting down names of persons for his secretary to write. If Diana were innocent and loving, he would have her with him, and could begin to introduce her to society. And if she were a traitor, perhaps she would betray herself with Veseul.

At the thought, he halted, a drop of ink poised on the tip of his quill until it fell on the paper in a black, spreading stain. If Diana were not what she seemed, it would be, quite literally, unbearable.

Traveling only with his servant Bonner, who could act as both valet and groom, Gervase headed north early the next morning. The location his lawyer had given him was a surprise, but of course the Hamiltons would not have been staying at an inn if their home had been on Mull. At least the journey would be shorter than he had expected. They traveled fast and long, changing horses at every posting stop, taking turns at the reins. In the silences, there was ample time to think of Diana, to wonder what the future held.

The farther north they went, the more optimistic Gervase became. Quite simply, he could not believe his mistress to be dishonest; he had seen her with her son and her friends as well as himself, and no actress could counterfeit such warmth over so many months. And there was no real proof that she was anything other than what she appeared to be; Veseul had not been observed entering her house; the sly apothecary might have been incorrect in his identification. The stolen information had probably been copied at Whitehall by an underpaid clerk who was looking for extra income. It had been foolish to think otherwise.

He even permitted himself to imagine what life would be like if he bought himself free of his marriage. Though technically a courtesan, Diana had never lived the public and flamboyant life of a Harriette Wilson and she should be accepted in most social circles. For Gervase that was not an important consideration, but he wanted Diana to receive all the respect due his wife.

They could have children together. He was genuinely fond of Geoffrey and would see that the boy was well-established. But he also wondered, with increasing urgency, what it would be like to have children of his own, sons and daughters like Diana, whom he could give the constant love and guidance he had never had.

The bright dreams grew through three days of travel.

His wife's residence was not in the village proper, and Gervase was directed out a narrow, rutted track that wound ever higher, ending at an isolated cottage. Wondering what the devil had led Hamilton to bring his daughter to such a remote spot, he left the reins to Bonner and knocked on the heavy oak door.

As he waited for a response, he listened to the wind whispering through the gorse and heather. It seemed a peaceful place, well-tended, with masses of cheerful flowers planted. Perhaps Mary Hamilton was happy here; if she was, he certainly wouldn't take her away, merely assure himself that she was well-cared-for. He wondered suddenly if she would recognize him. If so, he hoped she wouldn't recoil in terror; this was going to be difficult enough as it was.

The young woman who opened the door was a pretty country lass with dark hair and a face that looked ready to smile, though now she studied the visitor gravely. When he asked for Mary Hamilton, the young woman nodded, then directed him through a door on the left. His first quick glance showed that it was furnished in a simple country style of plain wood and colorful fabrics, cozy and unpretentious. but most of his attention was drawn to the woman standing in front of the window, her back to him. The light was bright outside, obscuring detail, showing only erect posture and a slim figure.

At the sound of his entrance, she slowly turned to face him. It took time for his vision to adjust, for him to see enough to confirm his first, impossible impression.

The woman was Diana.

20

GERVASE stared at her, startled and more than a little angry. "For God's sake, Diana, what are you doing here? Did you wheedle the direction out of my lawyer and come to check that I was doing what I said I would?"

Her face was pale over a soft brown dress whose simplicity emphasized her graceful figure and rich coloring. She shook her head. "No, Gervase. I am here because this is my home. I lived here for eight years, and I still own it."

He tried to make sense of her words. "Then . . . you know Mary Hamilton? Have you been the one taking care of her?"

"No." She moistened dry lips with her tongue, then spoke, her voice almost too low to be heard. "I was christened Mary Elizabeth Diana Lindsay Hamilton. I am your wife, the girl you married against your will."

The silence stretched, then snapped. "Impossible." Gervase felt the numbness of shock even as his voice denied her words. "You are intelligent, normal. You look nothing like her."

"Do you really remember what the girl you married looked like? Think back, then say she couldn't be me." Diana's voice was level, but she was braced against the window frame for support, her fingers white-knuckled on the sill.

As they stood separated by the width of the cheerful room, he tried to connect his memories with the woman before him, the woman he knew so intimately. He had thought the girl in the inn had dark brown hair and brown eyes, but Diana's chestnut hair and lapis

eyes were dark in dim light. Surely he would have
remembered Diana's exquisite features, her heart-
shaped face? But the face of the girl he had married
had been veiled in dark hair, distorted with fear and
weeping. She had not had Diana's lush feminine body,
but she had been scarcely more than a child, her body
just beginning to develop.

A slow chill of horror began deep inside him even
as he spoke the key denial. "Her mind was afflicted.
She could barely speak. Her face was slack, her eyes
strange. You could never have looked like that."

"No?" Diana's voice was bitter. "It isn't difficult
when one has been drugged into unconsciousness. You
were wrong about me, but correct about my father—
he was quite, quite mad. When he traveled, he took
me along for fear I would lie with half the parish in
his absence. When we stayed at an inn, he would force
me to take laudanum, waiting until I swallowed it.
Then he would lock the door from the outside to be
sure I couldn't leave."

She waited for the beginnings of belief on his face
before continuing. "Mind you, I can understand why
you decided there was something wrong with me. I
had difficulty waking up, and when I did, at first I
thought you were one of the horrible nightmares that
come with laudanum. I couldn't understand or believe
what was happening."

Diana halted, unable to continue as she recalled the
night in full, agonizing detail. Waking up to the terror
of a stranger's invasion; her father's indecent delight
at the thought of ridding himself of his loathsome
daughter; the strange, unreal ceremony. Then her husband's fury, his implacable strength as he ripped and
defiled her body in unimaginable ways.

She shuddered, then spoke with rapid sarcasm, trying to bury the memories. "Of course, if one is going
to be raped, there is something to be said for being
drenched in laudanum first."

The memories were horrible, but they came from
the past and were of much less importance than the
present and future. Deliberately she slowed her

breathing, which had quickened in remembered panic. "When our paths crossed in London, I was terrified that you recognized me, the way you stared, then came over and took me out of that group. But you never showed any sign of knowing who I was. I suppose that was because you were so sure you had married a simpleton."

He asked flatly, "Did you recognize me?"

"Oh, yes, my lord husband," she said softly, "I recognized you the moment I saw you." The furious face of the man who had so reluctantly married her had been burned indelibly on her brain—the wide cheekbones, the clear light eyes, the chiseled lips twisted into a thin line. She would have known him anywhere, even if half a century had passed.

There had been times in the past when she thought Gervase remote, but they were nothing compared to the bleak withdrawal in his face now. Speaking more to himself than to her, he said, "And so you devised the perfect revenge. You trained yourself in harlotry and sought me out, knowing that no man could resist you."

He was staring as if he had never seen her before, as if she were some unspeakable creature from the depths of the earth. "How long did it take you to discover the finest, cruelest method of injuring me? Did you know in advance, or did you only realize it when you came to know me better?"

"Neither!" Diana was startled and suddenly frightened. "I didn't seek you out for revenge. When I came to London, I had no thought—no *desire*—to meet you. But then I did, and since you wanted me, it seemed like a God-given opportunity to become acquainted, to learn what kind of a man I was married to. And when I did . . ." Her voice faltered. It was difficult to continue in the face of his revulsion. "And when I did . . . I came to love you."

"You lying, traitorous bitch." The viciousness in his voice was scalding. "You can actually stand there and play the innocent, even after so many lies."

He paced a few steps closer, his lean body explosive

with fury. "And I thought your father mad for saying you had a vile nature. Tell me, Diana, how many men have you lain with, or are there too many to count? How many times have you and your friends laughed and mocked me for my incredible stupidity? Were you working with the Count de Veseul all along? Or did he approach you and you decided that compromising my work as well as my soul would be a delightful and profitable bonus?"

"None of that is true!" she cried. "No one, not even Madeline or Edith, knows that we are married. I have never given my body to Veseul or to any other man. Only to you, my husband. And the first time, I didn't *give* it even to you—you took it, against my will." Even in her fear at how disastrously wrong this confrontation was going, she could not restrain the bitterness of her last sentence.

"Do you honestly think I will believe a word you say when you have been deceiving me since the moment I met you?" he asked incredulously. "Only my blind, mind-warping lust kept me from seeing through you. You always seemed too perfect to be true, but I wanted to believe in you." Pain roughened his voice. "My God, how I wanted to believe."

"Of course I deceived you at first," she said with exasperation. "Don't you remember saying that if I ever came near you or any of your properties, or used your name, that you would revoke the settlement and leave me penniless?"

"Ah, yes, I should have known that money was at the bottom of it," he said scathingly, "even though you did such a fine job of pretending to be less grasping than most of your kind."

"That's exactly why I wouldn't let you settle a regular income on me," Diana said, hoping that he would see this as a proof of integrity. "It seemed wrong to be taking your money twice over when you didn't know who I was."

"So instead of asking more for yourself, you had your friend Madeline do it, preserving your facade of saintly unconcern."

"What are you talking about?"

His mouth curved up cynically. "Stop playing the innocent. It won't work anymore."

Bewildered, Diana said, "Gervase, the only money I have is the thousand pounds a year you settled on me, and I've saved as much of that as possible for Geoffrey's future."

"Ah, yes, Geoffrey," he said, his voice soft and deadly. "Do you know who the little bastard's father is?"

Quicker than thought, she struck him. Her palm hit his cheek with a flat slapping sound, the force of it rocking him back. She recoiled, aghast not just at the rage in Gervase's eyes but in horror at herself, that she could be physically violent to someone she loved. For a moment she feared that he would offer violence in return, but with visible effort he held himself absolutely still.

"Another veil falls away," he said sardonically, the mark of her hand reddening on his cheek. "I thought you honest, kind, intelligent, gentle. There isn't much left of my illusions."

Shaking her head in distress, she whispered, "Gervase, I'm truly sorry. But how could you say that about your own son?"

He raised his brows in disbelief. "You want to pass your bastard off as my son? I suppose you can try—he looks so much like you that anyone could be his father. And I suppose that is literally true—any man *could* be his father."

"Don't you ever look at anyone?" she exclaimed furiously. "If you really *saw* Geoffrey, you would know how much he resembles you. That's one reason I didn't want you to meet him. But you no more recognized him than you did me."

His mind worked, trying to find the resemblance. "He's too young. A child of mine would have to be eight years old now, and what is Geoffrey . . . six? . . . seven at the outside?"

Her hands were clenching and unclenching as she said with careful precision, "He was born on the tenth

of February in the year 1800—nine months after our
farce of a marriage. He's small for his age, but he's
eight and a half years old now. I couldn't bear to name
him for his father, so I chose Geoffrey because it had
the same initial as Gervase. Shall I show you the reg-
istration of his birth?''

He looked unbearably torn. She knew then how
much he wanted a son, in spite of his belief that he
was unworthy of children. ''That would prove nothing. You could have borne a babe who died in infancy,
with Geoffrey the child of a later liaison.''

Defeated, Diana covered her face with her hands.
She had known that her identity would be a shock to
Gervase, but had never imagined this total, tormented
repudiation. If he did not have the desire to believe
her, proof would mean very little.

Ignoring her withdrawal, he asked, ''Tell me, did
you pay the barmaid to disappear so you could take
her place? I've always wondered just how big a fool I
was that night.''

She dropped her hands wearily. ''You still don't
know? It was my room you entered. Since you were
drunk, you must have gotten lost in those rabbity pas-
sages.''

''I should have known it was a waste of time to ask
you for the truth,'' he said caustically. ''It couldn't
have been your room—the door opened with my key.''

There was a chair behind her, and Diana folded into
it, too drained to stand. When Geoffrey was an infant,
she used to sit in this chair to nurse him. ''Those were
old, crude locks. Any one of the keys would probably
open every door in the inn.''

That gave him pause. Then, ''You really are a clever
little liar, knowing how to raise doubts. I shouldn't
fault myself for having believed you for so long.''

She looked up, wondering if there was a way to
break through his anger to the underlying fairness.
Perhaps it was too soon to expect him to be fair. Too
soon, or perhaps too late. ''Didn't you ever wonder
where your luggage was? Not in my room.''

He simply looked at her impassively, then turned to

leave. She jumped up and went after him. "Gervase, wait! What are you going to do?"

His hard stare kept her at a distance. "I shall walk out and get in my carriage and return to London. If I am very lucky, I will never see or hear from you again."

She lifted one hand to touch him, then dropped it again. "How can you just leave? We are married, we have a son."

He laughed bitterly. "You are truly an extraordinary woman. Did you honestly think that after you made your grand announcement, told me how much of a fool you had made of me, how our time together was a lie from beginning to end—did you really think I would welcome you as my wife and install you as Lady St. Aubyn for all the world to see?"

Contemptuous lines showed beside his mouth. "You wouldn't like the change in status. The gentlemen who now pay for your favors would expect them for free if you were of their class."

"Will you stop talking as if I'm the Whore of Babylon?" she cried. "I didn't tell you the whole truth, but I never lied to you, not once."

As silence lengthened, a muscle twitched in his jaw. Finally he said, "Your whole life was a lie."

The desolation in his voice was so profound that she could no longer suppress the tears she had been fighting. As they flowed unchecked down her cheeks, she made a last desperate attempt to remind him of what they had had. "I love you, and you said that you loved me. Doesn't that mean anything?"

"Oh, yes, it meant something," he said softly. "But apparently the woman I loved never existed."

"Gervase, please!" Her cry came from the heart.

He put one hand on the doorknob, but turned back to look with the bleakness that lies beyond hope. "Strange. I was willing to make a whore my wife, but I find it quite unacceptable that my wife is a whore. Good-bye, Diana."

The quiet sound of the door closing was a death knell.

Diana stood very still in the center of the room, knowing that when her numbness wore off, the pain would be overwhelming. Carriage noises sounded outside, the jingle of harness, the clopping of hooves, as Gervase left her for the last time.

She had thought often of how he might react when he found out that she was his wife. Certainly he would be shocked. Possibly he might be a little angry, but it had been equally possible that he would be amused, that the idea that he had taken his wife as a mistress might tickle his dry sense of humor.

Most of all, Diana had thought he would be relieved. When they had married, he had committed an unpardonable assault, but after his fury had died down he had been remorseful and gentle with her. When she came to know him in London, she had learned how honorable he was, and how unworthy he felt himself to be. She had thought he would welcome the news that his wife could forgive him, and that, against all the odds, they had a real marriage.

The one thing she had never expected was that revealing the past would destroy what was between them. How could it, when they loved each other? She had always known him to be logical and fair-minded; she had never dreamed that he would react to the discovery of her identity with such furious condemnation.

When the sound of wheels had faded, she walked out of the sitting room. Madeline's niece Annie waited, her expression concerned. Annie was the eldest child of Isabel Wolfe and she had fallen in love with a young man insufficiently godly for her mother's taste. It had pleased Madeline and Diana to offer the use of High Tor Cottage so the girl could marry her sweetheart.

Annie must be speaking, because her lips moved, but Diana heard nothing. Shaking her head as a sign that she wanted to be alone, she went out the front door, across the marks of carriage wheels and horses' hooves, and down the hill to the stream.

Sitting on the grassy bank, Diana took off her slippers and stockings. Still moving with unnatural calm, she dabbled her feet in the small pool where Geoffrey had almost drowned when he was a toddler. In happier times they had played here, her son exhibiting the normal child's affinity for mud.

Gervase was gone. He was not a man to love lightly, or to leave lightly. Or to change his mind once he came to a decision. She had known they were opposites in temperament, but had not realized all that implied. For her, love was enough, would always be enough. She had thought that if Gervase came to love her, the bond between them would be unbreakable.

She had been wrong. Instead, she had injured him grievously, had destroyed his love and trust, perhaps irrevocably, given him a wound from which he might never recover.

Where had she made her mistake? Numbly she reviewed the past months. Perhaps it had been at Aubynwood, when they had weathered their first crisis. Instinct had urged her to tell Gervase the truth then, but she had not; it had been easier to let matters drift. She had thought it better to wait until he could admit that he was in love with her, thinking he would more easily accept the truth then.

Instead, the reverse was true. Loving her, he was far more vulnerable than he had been at Aubynwood; the result was his conviction that he had been betrayed. The thought of his agony was as devastating as her own; more so, because of her guilt.

Rolling over on her stomach, she buried her head in her arms and let anguish take her.

The return to London was accomplished in dead silence. Except for the barest speech required to change horses and stop for the night, Gervase spoke to Bonner only once, when he asked what the servant had found when he had packed his master's possessions that fatal night on Mull.

Without twitching an eyelid at the question, Bonner replied, "One of the tavern girls was there. She'd been waiting quite some time and was incensed at your neglect. I took the liberty of giving her a small douceur for her inconvenience, from the funds I carried for travel expenses.''

"And my luggage was there?" Gervase pulled in the horses to negotiate heavy ruts. He was doing all of the driving; the concentration helped keep thought at bay.

Bonner nodded. "Aye. Appeared to be untouched, but I didn't check because the island Scots are an honest lot. Was something missing?" The servant acted as if the incident had been the previous night, not over nine years before. But of course, it had not been the sort of night one would forget.

"No, nothing was missing." Except his wife, who had not, apparently, been in Gervase's room, but in her own.

He thought back over months of lovemaking and realized that while Diana had always been sweetly responsive, she had never shown the hardened professionalism of the true courtesan. He had been so besotted that he had never even noticed. She might indeed be as innocent as she claimed—or this might be one more example of her brilliant talent for falsehood.

It was only a slight detour to Aubynwood, and the upcoming house party made a convenient excuse for stopping. The necessary orders required very little time; then the viscount asked his housekeeper where his mother's portrait hung. The painting held pride of place in the servants' hall, where its quality was much esteemed. Sir Joshua Reynolds would have been amused, perhaps, to know where his masterpiece had come to rest.

Gervase ignored the beautiful, amoral face of his mother to study the dark-haired boy who looked up at her so wistfully. After he had scrutinized the profile, the shape of the ears, the line of nose and jaw, the conclusion was unmistakable: the picture could almost have been of Geoffrey. The viscount remembered the tenant farmer whom he and Geoffrey had visited at Aubynwood, who had looked so sharply at the boy, and then at his landlord.

Though he had half-forgotten it, Gervase had been small for his age as a child. Only when he reached twelve had he begun to grow, matching and overtaking the height of other boys his age.

And the seizures. He had had a few; Geoffrey had more. Were such things inherited? Quite possibly.

So Geoffrey, with his intelligence and courage and sunny nature, was his son. Thinking of his wife as abnormal, not quite human, Gervase had literally never considered the possibility that that one brief, violent act of sexual union might produce a child. Gervase set the thought aside, not yet able to face it. The fact that Geoffrey was his son didn't make Diana any less a liar or a whore—but it was another complication in the hell of his marriage.

It was late evening when Diana arrived home, exhausted by the long coach journey. After the scene with Gervase, she had spent more than a week at High Tor Cottage, craving the peace as a balm for her misery. Now it was good to be with her family. Geoffrey was already in bed, but Madeline and Edith took one look at Diana's haggard face and wrapped her in affectionate care. She had not told her friends why she went north and they had not asked, but the time had come to reveal her history.

After she had bathed and eaten, the three women gathered in Maddy's sitting room. Over endless cups of tea laced with brandy, Diana described her past in a long monologue, from her childhood in Scotland to her bizarre forced marriage, including how her father had abandoned her to her husband's nonexistent care, and ending with the disastrous confrontation with Gervase.

When she ran out of words, Madeline exhaled with sympathetic wonder. "I knew you were a woman of mystery, but this is much more than I bargained for. May I ask questions?"

Diana sighed. She was curled up in the corner of a sofa, wrapped in a shaggy Highland blanket as much for emotional comfort as for protection against the cool evening. "Ask whatever you like. I've always had trouble talking about what affects me deeply, but *not* talking has caused worse trouble."

"What happened to your mother?"

The teacup Diana was sipping from clicked sharply against her teeth. Setting it down carefully, she said, "She killed herself when I was eleven."

"Oh, my dear girl," Madeline breathed, then changed the subject. "It's hard to believe your father would just abandon you in the inn the day after your marriage."

"If you knew my father, you would know it was quite in character. He was convinced that all women were evil, especially his daughter." Diana's deep blue eyes looked black. "The sooner he got rid of me, the better for his own immortal soul."

A thought had occurred to Maddy during the younger woman's story. She hesitated, wondering if it was appropriate, before deciding to speak. "Diana, is it possible your father was . . . unnaturally attracted to you? And he loathed himself for such feelings, and you for being the source of them?"

Diana's expressive face was stricken as she replied, "It would explain a great deal. He used to glare as if he hated me. And the way he carried on about how men lusted after me . . . it made no sense. I suppose I was a pretty child, but not so mature as to attract attention from most men. He used to pray over me all night, both of us on our knees as he asked God to purify my evil nature. Other times he tried beating the ungodliness out of me." Shuddering, she pulled her blanket around her shoulders.

"I'm sorry, my dear. Perhaps I shouldn't have spoken."

"No, I'm glad that you did," Diana said wanly. "As revolting as the idea is, at least it is a reason. My father always seemed like . . . like a force of nature, mysterious and implacable. I would rather think there were reasons for the way he despised me, things that weren't my fault."

"Is he still alive?" Edith asked.

Diana shrugged. "I have no idea. There has been not one word of contact between us since he left me at the inn."

Madeline was amazed that a man, a clergyman no less, could have so thoroughly dispossessed his daughter; truly, he must have been mad. Turning to something she had always wondered about, she asked, "How did you and Edith meet? You didn't mention that."

"My sister Jane Hayes and her husband own the inn where the marriage took place," Edith answered in her broad Yorkshire accent. "I had married a drunken bully. Both my boys were grown and gone, one to the army, one to America. Jane thought I should leave my husband before he killed me, but I didn't know how, or where to go." She absently traced the livid scar along her left cheek. "I suppose I could have gone to Jane, but I had no money for the journey. More than that, I had no will left after twenty-five years of bullying."

Madeline glanced at Edith with new insight. She knew about the older woman's sons, who wrote to their mother regularly, but not about the husband. It appeared that Edith had developed her quiet, rock-ribbed strength in a hard school.

Diana took up the story. "Mrs. Hayes decided that if Edith had someone to take care of, it would give her sister an incentive to leave her husband. I had just turned sixteen and was pregnant and terrified, but after I contacted Gervase's lawyer, I had money. So Mrs. Hayes packed me down to Yorkshire. Together Edith and I found High Tor Cottage. We both wanted to be alone, as far from other people, especially men, as possible. And Edith has been taking care of me ever since."

She smiled affectionately at the woman who had helped her survive the most difficult time of her life.

Edith chuckled warmly. "It's worked both ways, lass."

"After all that has happened to you, why did you want to come to London and become a courtesan?"

Madeline asked. "A nunnery would appear more likely."

Diana topped up the tea in their cups. "I know it must seem strange, but it felt so strongly like the right thing to do," she replied. "Despite what my father and . . . my husband had done to me, I knew not all men were like that. In the village where I grew up, there were happy marriages, and men who knew how to be kind. Since I had a husband, I couldn't marry, but . . . I wanted to find a man of my own, someone to love me."

Lost in thought, she sipped her tea, then added with a guilty shrug, "I must admit, I liked what you said about beauty giving a woman power over men. I thought it would be nice to have power for a change, to have the choice to give or withhold."

"I also said that it was dangerous," Madeline reminded her.

"I know," Diana whispered, her eyes closed against sudden tears. "I had no idea what I was doing. I guess I am not the stuff of which sirens are made."

"No, my dear, you are not. You are the stuff of loving wives and mothers and friends."

Madeline had meant the words as comfort, but they nearly fractured Diana's control. Burrowing her head into the blanket, she said brokenly, "What am I going to do? He hates me. He said he doesn't ever want to see me again."

There was silence until Edith said, "You're our expert on men, Maddy—you'd best answer that."

Madeline sat next to Diana and put her arm around the younger woman's shoulders. "St. Aubyn may hate you in some ways, but his feelings are surely far more complicated than that. Love, hate, desire, anger—all those intense emotions must be mixed together in his mind. It would be far harder to win him back if he were indifferent to you."

Her voice muffled in the blanket, Diana asked, "Do you think there is any chance that I can change his mind?"

"Yes, I think so, if you'll come out of that blanket

and fight like a woman." Madeline made her voice teasing and was rewarded by the sight of Diana's tear-stained face emerging.

"What does it mean to fight like a woman?"

"Think what he likes about you and use it on him. Love, desire, laughter—you would know better than I. And also try to understand all the reasons why he is so angry."

The hopelessness of Diana's expression changed to thought. After lifting her cup for a sip of tea, she asked, "Do you think it's because I have injured his pride? That he thinks I deliberately set out to humiliate him?"

Madeline considered, weighing what she knew about St. Aubyn with what she knew about men in general. "Pride would certainly be part of it, but not all," she said slowly. "From what you said, he thinks you be-trayed his trust. That is one of the gravest injuries that can occur between man and woman, and St. Aubyn doesn't seem like one who would trust easily. More than that, he had bent over backward to give you the benefit of the doubt, which would make apparent be-trayal all the more unforgivable."

Diana thought about that. "You're right, as always, Maddy. I don't quite know what to do about it, but it is a beginning."

Then she remembered a remark of Gervase's that she hadn't understood. "He accused me of setting my friend Madeline to ask for money indirectly. Do you know what he was talking about?"

"Yes," her friend replied. "I asked St. Aubyn for regular payments to an account in your name. He was quite willing, so you're the richer by two hundred pounds a month since last September." At the stricken expression on Diana's face, Maddy asked anxiously, "Did it cause a problem?"

"I'm afraid so. He assumed that I was behind it, and was pretending innocence."

"Oh, no! Diana, I'm so sorry," Madeline said with horrified remorse. "Life is uncertain, and since St. Aubyn was prepared to be generous it seemed foolish not to save toward your future. It worried me, how casual you were about financial security. And now he blames you for what I did?''

Maddy had had to earn her own security, so it wasn't surprising that she had been concerned for her less experienced friend. Now her well-intentioned deed became one more reason for Gervase to think his wife was a liar . . . Diana drained the last of the tea. ''It doesn't much matter,'' she said wearily. ''I had ample other sins to be blamed for.''

She swished her teacup, then held it for a moment with her eyes closed before handing it to Edith. ''Please, can you tell me if . . . if everything is over between Gervase and me?''

Edith looked doubtful. ''It's not good to look at matters that are too close to the heart. You care too much about this.''

''Please,'' Diana pleaded, ''I must know if there is any hope.''

After a moment's more hesitation, Edith took the cup and stared into the bottom with unfocused eyes. Her breathing slowed and when she spoke it was in a distant voice. ''It has not ended. There is much between you, both dark and light.'' She frowned and swirled the cup. ''The end has not yet been written. There is danger, and not just to you. Darkness threatens.'' Then, in a low, uncanny voice, she finished, ''Darkness, death, and desire.''

The soft intake of Diana's breath broke Edith's mood and she looked up, her voice brisk again. ''You'll get a deal more use from this cup by putting tea in it, lass,'' she said, pouring the last of the tea from the pot and reaching for the brandy.

''I'm not sure I need it,'' Diana protested. ''I'm almost asleep right here on Maddy's sofa.''

''You're exhausted, and we're keeping you up with our questions,'' Madeline said with compunction. Offering a friendly arm, she guided Diana to her bedroom, leaving her after a hug.

Back in Maddy's room, Edith sat with a thoughtful expression on her scarred face. ''Do you know, it's time I paid a visit to my sister Jane on Mull. It's been too long since I've seen her.''

Knowing the older woman's oblique manner of speaking, Madeline poured a dollop of brandy into both their teacups. ''I suppose it's only a coincidence that the route to Mull would take you near that Lowland Scots village where Diana grew up.''

''Aye, just a coincidence.'' Edith sipped her brandy pensively. ''I should think everyone in the neighborhood knows about the mad vicar.''

''Very likely,'' Maddy agreed, curling her feet up beneath her. ''It probably isn't important, but it would be interesting to know more about him. To know if he's even alive.'' She glanced at her friend sternly. ''If he is still on this mortal coil, I trust you will not aid him to his heavenly reward?''

''Of course not,'' Edith said with dignity. ''I've never raised a hand to anyone since I parted my husband's hair with a poker the night I left.'' She halted, then added the laconic explanation, ''The gaffer didn't want me to go.''

''Did you really?'' Madeline asked in astonishment. Then she broke down into giggles. ''I think I've had more than enough brandy, because that sounds very amusing. Did you kill him?''

''No,'' Edith said with regret. ''Wasn't a heavy poker.''

''Is *he* still alive?''

''No. After I left, he found another woman to take care of him. He beat her to death one night, so they hanged him.''

Maddy gulped, sobered by Edith's dispassionate words. After a long silence she said, ''All three of us had our secrets about men. Strange how they are all surfacing at the same time.''

''Aye. I just hope matters work out as satisfactorily for Diana as they have for you and me.''

Diana's facade crumbled after Madeline left her. She tried to be calm and controlled, but she had wept almost continually while she was in Yorkshire, and humiliating tears kept escaping on the journey home. As she had once told Gervase, she was a crier, not a thrower. It would be easier if she could be angry, but she couldn't. The declaration of love that she had wanted so much had made him utterly vulnerable to what he perceived as betrayal, and the horrible things he had said were products of his pain. In retrospect, she guessed that he could have accepted her confession much better before he had opened himself up to her. It was easy to be wise when it was too late.

Grief threatened to swamp her again. Determined not to cry, she sat at her desk and looked at the letters that had come in her absence. There were bills for fabric and shoes, for Geoffrey's school fees, a note from Francis Brandelin saying that he was going out of town but would call when he returned.

There was also a small package addressed in an unfamiliar hand. Thinking it some item she had ordered and forgotten, Diana unwrapped it absently, then stopped dead, fighting a shock wave of dizziness at the sight of the contents.

Inside the velvet-lined box were the rest of the pearls from the necklace Gervase had been giving to her a pearl at a time. There was no note, no message of any kind, even an insulting one. She wondered if sending the pearls was a gesture of contempt or of indifference.

She didn't want to think about it. Her hand trembling, she closed the box and set it to one side on the desk, then picked up the last letter. The envelope was of heavy cream-colored paper and the flap bore the seal of St. Aubyn. Her heart hammering, she drew a deep breath before opening it, only to be bitterly disappointed that the note was in a stranger's hand, the same writing that had addressed the package of pearls. Gervase's secretary, presumably. In the past, the viscount had always written himself to say when he could come.

It was an invitation to a house party at Aubynwood, sent before Gervase had met her in Yorkshire, before he had said that he never wanted to see her again. It had been waiting here ever since, a bleak reminder of

what might have been. Diana made a move to crumple
the invitation, then stopped. A house party meant a
number of guests, probably government people, since
he sometimes invited political associates to Aubynwood.

Checking the dates, she saw that the gathering would
begin at the end of the next week. She absently
smoothed the heavy paper, thinking hard. By rights,
she was the Viscountess St. Aubyn. Would Gervase
throw her out of Aubynwood if she walked in? He
might if he met her alone, but his sense of propriety
made it unlikely that he would do so in front of other
guests. If she arrived a day late, when others were
already there . . .

She stared unseeing across the room, torn between
temptation and terror. She was willing to fight for Gervase, to do everything possible to persuade him that
her love was genuine, but to do so, she had to see
him. She might never have another chance to get so
close.

No conscious decision was necessary. Diana would
to go Aubynwood.

21

KNOWING that her son needed attention from her to soften the impact of the fact that she was leaving again, Diana breakfasted with Geoffrey the next morning, then rode with him in the park. He reveled in her company, chatting, telling her about the books he had read, and showing how much his riding had improved. On horseback, or rather ponyback, he was clearly his father's son; even though he had been riding for less than a year, he had the natural grace of the born equestrian.

As the groom took charge of their mounts, Diana eyed Geoffrey covertly. She wondered what Gervase's feelings were now that he knew the boy was his son. In spite of her husband's denials, she was sure that he would accept the relationship once he had time to think the matter through. She had watched their growing acquaintance with trepidation and hope, wanting them to get on, fearing they would not.

The viscount had seemed fond of Geoffrey and the boy was his heir. Would he hold Diana's imagined perfidy against his son? Knowing Gervase's basic fairness, she didn't think so, but his bitterness had been so great that she would not let her husband near Geoffrey until she was sure he would do nothing injurious. She was ambitious for her son, wanted him to have the title and wealth and power to which he was entitled, and which she knew he would carry well. But she would not let him become a pawn in a war between his parents; she would take him to the colonies and raise him alone before she would let that happen.

Usually Geoffrey groomed his pony himself, but today Diana told him to let the stableboy do it so they

could talk. Looking at his mother askance, he dutifully accompanied her inside to the morning room.
Stripping off her gloves and laying them aside, Diana
said, "Next week I'm going away for another few days,
Geoffrey. I'm sorry, but it can't be avoided."

He scowled. "Can I go with you?"

She shook her head. "No, I'm afraid not." Not
when anything might happen between his parents.

"Why not?"

How to answer that perennial child's question? While
Diana debated, Geoffrey continued pugnaciously,
"You're going to visit Lord St. Aubyn, aren't you?"

She had guessed that Geoffrey's hero worship of the
viscount existed side by side with jealousy that the
man had so much of his mother's time, and her suspicion was confirmed by her son's expression. Deciding to be casual, Diana took off her hat and jacket and
sat down. "Yes, I am. I'm sorry I have to leave again
so soon, but this trip is necessary."

Her son's carefully instilled manners were clearly at war
with his desire to throw a tantrum. Diana extended a hand,
wanting him to come sit with her so she could talk away
some of his anger, but then his head started tilting back
in the first phase of convulsion. He crashed to the floor,
his body arching and his tongue protruding. Diana
dropped by his side, feeling the terror that always possessed her when he had a seizure.

She was reaching out to brace his body when her
hands froze in midair. She had seen many seizures in
her life and this one looked wrong; the desperate gasping sounds and jerking motions were subtly different
than usual. For a moment suspicion immobilized her.
Then she grabbed his shoulders, half-lifting him from
the floor as she cried, "Geoffrey, are you pretending?"

The deep blue eyes that had been rolled back focused
on her guiltily and his body flexed normally, without
rigidity. More furious with her son than she had ever
been in his life, Diana pulled him over her lap and
administered several swift, hard slaps to his backside.
She had never struck Geoffrey before, and he responded
with a howl of hurt and outrage.

Within seconds they were in each other's arms, both of them sobbing, Diana harder than her son. Rocking him back and forth, she whispered brokenly, "I'm sorry, I shouldn't have hit you, but don't ever do that again. Yell at me, throw things if you must, but don't ever, ever pretend to have a seizure. You don't know what that does to me. It's . . . it's not playing fair."

Digging a handkerchief out of his pocket, Geoffrey blew his nose, then twisted the fabric in his hands. His voice conscience-stricken, he said, "I did know. That's why I did it." He swallowed hard. "I'm sorry, Mama. It was a rotten thing to do."

"It *was* rather rotten." Diana blotted her eyes with her own handkerchief, then tried to smile. "I suppose that if we didn't want to do rotten things sometimes, we'd be angels, flitting around heaven with harps and wings."

Geoffrey's glance held a glint of mischief. "The wings sound rather fun, but there wouldn't be any horses, would there?"

"I don't think so."

"Then I prefer being here."

The moment of levity ended. Diana watched her son mauling the handkerchief and made a decision. Sooner or later Geoffrey must be told Gervase was his father. She had intended to do it later, but perhaps now was the time; knowing the truth might make the situation easier for him. Putting an arm around her son, she drew him back so they sat against the sofa, their legs stretched on the floor. "There's something I must tell you."

In spite of her resolution, it was hard to find the words; the subject was one that had always been avoided. Stalling, she asked, "You like Lord St. Aubyn, don't you?"

Her son nodded, looking away from her. Diana drew her breath, then said baldly, "St. Aubyn is your father."

Geoffrey's head whipped around and he stared at her, shock in his wide blue eyes as he absorbed her words. The silence stretched until he said with stiff lips, "So I'm a bastard?"

"No!" she said, startled. Obviously her son was

learning more than Latin and literature in school. "No, he and I are married, and you are as legitimate as any boy in England."

"How come you never told me before? Why don't you live together? And why doesn't he act like a father?" Shock was quickly translating into a stubborn determination to know.

Diana hugged his shoulders. "It's a long story, love." She thought for a moment, deciding how to edit the truth for an eight-year-old. "We were staying at the same inn in Scotland. Your father wandered into my room by accident. It was most improper, and . . . he decided he must do the gentlemanly thing and marry me. However, he didn't really want to be married, so he left after making sure that I had enough money to be comfortable."

"Why didn't he want to be married to you?" her son asked belligerently.

"It wasn't so much *me* as that he didn't want to be married to anyone," she said cautiously, not wanting Geoffrey to blame Gervase for everything. "Your father was set to leave for India to join the army. He hadn't planned on a wife."

Her son nodded, able to understand that, and Diana almost chuckled at the sight of perfect male agreement.

"So I went to Yorkshire and met Edith, and you know about our life there. It was fine at first, but when you reached school age it seemed like time to move to London, so we could all see something of the world." The need for editing increased. She was ready to admit a great deal, but not that she had chosen the life of a harlot, even though she never actually acted as one. Picking her words carefully, she said, "By chance, I met Lord St. Aubyn one night when we visited a friend of Aunt Maddy's. He'd forgotten what I look like and I wasn't using the name Brandelin, so he didn't recognize me."

"Why didn't you tell him who you were right then?"

Just like his father. "I didn't want to. He hadn't shown any interest in us. He didn't even know that you had been born."

"And you were angry?"

"I'm afraid so," she said ruefully. "I wanted to get to know him better, so I didn't identify myself. But since we had become very good friends, last week I told him who I was."

Geoffrey swiveled around to face her, his arms around his drawn-up knees. "And he got angry because you hadn't already told him you were his wife?"

Diana was startled at the accuracy of his perception. Was there something here that men understood and women didn't? She nodded. "Yes, he's very angry at me." In spite of her best efforts, her voice trembled. "He doesn't ever want to see me again. That's why I'm going to Aubynwood. He's having a house party and I was invited, so I've decided to go and apologize."

"He's making you unhappy," Geoffrey said, belligerent again.

"Yes, but don't blame him too much," she said swiftly. "I made him unhappy as well, even though I didn't intend to."

Her son gazed at her with wise blue eyes. "It's like you are always telling me; good intentions aren't enough."

"Exactly so," she agreed.

Looking very young again, Geoffrey asked, "What . . . what did he say when he realized I was his son?"

Knowing how vital her answer was, Diana thought a moment, combining what she had observed with what she had sensed. "He was surprised, of course, and because he was angry, he wasn't quite sure he believed me."

Catching her son's eye, she said earnestly, "But he wanted—very, very much—to believe that you are his son."

More silence. Then, "If you and Lord St. Aubyn become friends again, does that mean we would be a family?"

Diana was shocked by the naked longing in his voice. "I hope so, darling," she said unsteadily, "I surely hope so."

Geoffrey's brows knit together in calculation. "If you

are visiting my father, why can't I go?'' He was no longer jealous; now he, too, had a stake in Lord St. Aubyn, and a need for him that was as great as Diana's own.

For a moment she wished she had said nothing. ''Lord St. Aubyn is very, *very* angry at me. There will probably be a lot of unpleasantness.''

His jaw set. ''He's my father, and I want to see him.''

''This isn't the best time, Geoffrey. It would be better to wait until he finds his temper again.''

Geoffrey simply sat looking stubborn. Then, craftily, ''Maybe he won't be as angry if I'm there.''

Diana sighed and thought about it. Perhaps she was being overprotective again. Geoffrey was intelligent and levelheaded, and he did have a right to see and know his father. And though it seemed calculating to consider it, having their son with her might soften Gervase's anger. ''Very well, you can come, but you must promise to be polite to Lord St. Aubyn, not get angry with him on my behalf. Things are very complicated between him and me, and both of us have made mistakes.'' Since her son looked unconvinced, she repeated, ''You must promise me, Geoffrey.''

''Very well, Mama. I'll do my best to behave.'' The wording was rather equivocal, but before she could object, he said pensively, ''If he's Lord St. Aubyn, you must be Lady St. Aubyn.''

When she agreed, he asked with interest, ''Do I have a title?''

''Not while your father is alive, but you are the Honorable Geoffrey Lindsay Brandelin,'' she offered.

Disappointed but philosophical, he said, ''No one else in my school is even an Honorable. Jamie Woodlow's father is a knight, but that isn't as good as a viscount.''

''Geoffrey, you must not take this title business seriously,'' Diana said emphatically. ''Are you any different today than you were yesterday, when you didn't know who your father was?''

After a moment's thought, her son's face split into a grin. ''Yesterday I was just an epileptic. Today I'm an *honorable* epileptic.'' The idea tickled his sense of humor and he went off into whoops of laughter. Joining him in his merriment, Diana leaned over to give Geoffrey a hug. With every fiber of her being, she prayed that the breach with her husband would be healed, not just for her and Geoffrey's sake, but because for too many years Gervase had been deprived of the joy of his son.

Since Edith had gone to Scotland to visit her sister, Madeline volunteered to accompany Diana as nurse and maid. Diana had been reluctant to treat her best friend as a servant, but Maddy pointed out that they were always helping each other with their hair and clothes anyway, and didn't Diana want someone at Aubynwood who was on her side? Besides, Madeline was restless since Nicholas wouldn't return to London for several weeks.

In the face of so many good arguments and her own undeniable desire for support, Diana finally agreed. Maddy happily pulled her hair into a knot and dug out her most conservative clothes; in spite of her best efforts, she could not be unattractive, but at least she wouldn't draw many second looks.

Rather than make the trip in one day, they spent the night at an inn two hours south of Aubynwood. Diana calculated that if she arrived at the estate about noon, the chances were good that there would be guests around, making it harder for Gervase to refuse her entrance. The idea of forcing herself on him was a terrifying one, both because he could hurt her so badly and because she must confront again how much she had hurt him. She spoke little on the journey.

The next morning Diana dressed carefully in an elegantly simple muslin gown with blue trim that matched her eyes. Maddy pulled her hair to the back of her head in a soft, thick twist with small curling tendrils around her neck and face to soften the effect. She looked every inch a lady and a viscountess.

Too soon they had passed the Aubynwood gatehouse and pulled to a stop in the horseshoe drive in front of the main entrance. Madeline and Geoffrey would wait in the carriage until it was clear whether Diana had gained entrance for them. Wiping her damp palms on her skirt before donning gloves, she said with nervous resolution, "Wish me luck." Maddy nodded gravely. Less aware of what was at stake, Geoffrey was cheerful and excited.

Then Diana stepped from the carriage and climbed the stairs to her husband's house.

Since Gervase was too grimly unhappy to be a good host, it was fortunate that events on the Peninsula kept his guests in a ferment of excitement. Mere days after landing in Portugal, General Sir Arthur Wellesley had won a major battle against the French at Vimeiro, completely unaided by the two hidebound senior officers who were technically his superiors. Britain had reacted with joy at the victory, then with shock when details of the ensuing treaty were received. The treaty, called the Convention of Cintra, removed the French from Portugal, but also repatriated the captured French army in British ships and allowed the enemy to take all of their loot with them.

Wellesley's brilliant accomplishment was overwhelmed by public furor at the treaty terms, and all three British commanders were being recalled for a military inquiry. Gervase cursed with exasperation as events developed. As the most junior of the commanders, Wellesley had not done the actual negotiating even though he had signed the Convention, and it was bitterly ironic that the general's career might be lost in a political melee not of his making.

At Aubynwood, events were no better. Gervase's guests ate and flirted and rode, enjoying country pleasures while settling affairs of state. The Count de Veseul drifted about with an expression of secret satisfaction. In a fit of perversity, Gervase had invited the decorative and predatory Lady Haycroft, since he was in need of a new mistress; unfortunately, he found that her highly practiced overtures repelled him. He had also invited Francis Brandelin because he felt the need of having a friend near, yet even that was a mixed blessing because he couldn't see his cousin without wondering if the younger man was one of Diana's lovers. He could have asked but did not; he didn't want to hear the answer.

The viscount and George Canning had been in the upstairs gallery and were standing at the head of the main staircase, talking about the possible political repercussions of the Convention of Cintra. Below them, in the two-story-high entrance hall, a dozen guests milled about, talking and waiting for others to arrive for a group walk in the gardens.

Gervase did not notice the sound of the knock or the opening of the door. Then he heard an unforgettable voice say with a soft clarity that carried, "Good day, Hollins. Please inform my husband that Lady St. Aubyn has arrived."

Musical though Diana's voice was, a cannon shot could not have produced a stronger impact. Gervase wondered for a moment if he was hallucinating, if he had been thinking so much of her that his mind had conjured up a phantom, but everyone below was staring at the newcomer, so she must be real. Beside him, Canning said, "Well, well, *well,*" on a note of rising admiration.

Diana stood serenely indifferent to the effect she had produced, a shaft of sunlight gilding her hair, her head high and a slight relaxed smile on her exquisite face. Gervase watched in paralyzed shock, feeling a gut-wrenching mixture of black fury that she had invaded his home, reluctant admiration for her effrontery, and aching desire at the sight of her loveliness.

Hollins recognized her from the Christmas visit, and there was a palpable pause while he evaluated her words. Everyone in the household had known what was going on between the master and the beautiful Mrs. Lindsay, and most had approved. It was well within the realm of possibility that the closemouthed viscount had married his mistress without mentioning the fact to his staff. Deciding to err on the side of caution, the butler bowed. "I shall inform his lordship." He turned and disappeared from view.

Lady Haycroft was in the group below. Strange how vulgar her overgroomed blondness appeared next to Diana's gentle beauty. In a voice harsh with surprise, the widow said, "Impossible! St. Aubyn isn't married."

Diana turned to her with an expression of mild surprise. "Have you ever asked him if he is?"

"Why . . . well . . . of course not." Lady Haycroft stopped, temporarily at a loss. "Have you just married?"

"Not at all," Diana said with undiminished good nature. "We have been husband and wife any time these last nine years. Of course, I've spent much of that time living quietly in the north. Our son's health was delicate when he was younger, but he is so much stronger now that finally I can join my husband."

So there was a son. Her voice acid with malice, Lady Haycroft said, "It's been said that St. Aubyn has a mad wife locked up in Scotland."

Diana gave a sweetly humorous laugh, and Gervase watched the men below respond to it like flowers following the sun.

"Heavens, is that what people say?" She shook her head in quiet amusement. "I never cease to be amazed at how word of mouth can alter even the plainest of facts. I did grow up in Scotland, but I have never been either mad or locked up."

Then, with delicate suggestiveness, she added, "My husband has often said how much he would like to keep me to himself. Perhaps that is where the rumor started."

As Lady Haycroft stared in defeated astonishment, Diana smiled graciously. "It was very bad of me not to be here to greet our guests, but I was delayed in Yorkshire. I do hope you'll forgive me. Surely you are Lady Haycroft? My husband has mentioned you to me, and there could not be another blond guest as lovely."

Game, set, and match. Lady Haycroft inclined her head in acknowledgment, her hostility undiminished, but unable to say anything more without appearing churlish. Gervase might have laughed at Diana's deft handling of the situation if he hadn't been so furious. If he had ever wanted proof of his wife's ability to warp the truth, she was providing it.

Forgetting his companion, he started down the stairs. At the same time, Francis came into view. He must have heard most of the conversation, because he walked up to Diana and gave her a light cousinly kiss. "Diana, how wonderful to see you. Gervase was not sure when you would arrive."

Such a greeting by St. Aubyn's cousin sealed her acceptance. The guests began to coalesce around Diana, eager to make her acquaintance and delighted to have been present at an occasion with such gossip potential. Gervase reached the bottom of the stairs and walked toward the group. People turned to stare at him, wondering if something even more interesting would take place. Well, he would be damned if he would air his dirty linen in public. Inclining his head to his wife, he said coolly, "I trust your journey was a pleasant one, my dear."

Diana's head snapped around at the sound of his voice. Their gazes struck and held, and for an instant he forgot the guests that surrounded them, forgot his wife's treachery. He wanted to take her in his arms, taste her lips and loosen her hair, and make slow intense love to her. She made a movement toward him, then checked it, fearful of her welcome.

Closing the distance between them, Gervase took her arm in a punishing grip and led her away. From the calmness of his face, the onlookers would have assumed that he was giving a quiet, husbandly greeting, but his voice was low and furious as he demanded, "Just what the devil are you trying to accomplish with this? Whatever it is, you will not succeed."

Diana's drowning blue eyes met his, pleading and apologetic, but before she could speak, the door opened again and Geoffrey marched into the tense silence. Everyone in the hall looked from the dark-haired boy to the viscount, then back. It was possible to doubt Diana's identity, but not that of the heir to St. Aubyn.

With a temerity to equal his mother's, he walked through the guests to Gervase and offered his hand. "Good day, sir. It is good to see you again." Not an affectionate greeting, but quite in line for a well-mannered son of the nobility.

Geoffrey's eyes were very like Diana's, both in lapis-blueness and the anxious question in them. Gervase studied the boy's dark hair, the jawline, the wide cheekbones, and wondered how he could have been so blind. There was much that Gervase could have said, but not here, in front of others. "Good day, Geoffrey. I trust you have been working on your Latin." His greeting was prosaic, but his handshake far from casual as he welcomed his son to Aubynwood.

Responding to the expression in his father's eyes rather than the actual words, Geoffrey beamed. "Yes, sir. And my Greek too."

Hollins returned with a footman. Perhaps he had listened at the door and knew in which quarter the wind lay. "Get her ladyship's baggage from the carriage," the butler ordered.

Diana gave her husband a grave look. "Pray excuse me. The journey has been so long and I am a little weary. I shall see you all later." She gave the other guests a charming smile.

As her glance circled the room, Gervase saw Diana tense for a moment. Following the direction of her gaze, he saw that the Count de Veseul had entered the hall and was regarding Diana with ironic amusement. Veseul, almost certainly a spy, likely his wife's lover. One of the reasons Gervase had invited both the Frenchman and Diana was to see if they would give each other away; his original plan might well succeed.

His expression rigidly controlled, Gervase watched his wife climb the stairs after Hollins. It took a moment for him to recognize that the meek maid following her was Madeline Gainford, who had entered unobtrusively. So his wife had arrived with her allies; Edith Brown was probably driving the damned carriage.

For a moment Gervase considered following Diana to her room and having the great blazing row she was asking for, but he refrained, knowing he needed more time to control his emotions before he confronted his wife and forced her to leave.

He turned to the accusing glare of Lady Haycroft, the eager widow who had taken her invitation to Aubynwood as encouragement. "How nice that your sweet little wife could join us, St. Aubyn," she said through gritted teeth. "I hope that she doesn't find society too much a strain after life in the provinces."

"Lady St. Aubyn is remarkably adaptable." He spoke without inflection, then excused himself to his guests and went to the stables. Despite the fact that he was not in riding clothes, he took his fastest horse out for a furious gallop across Aubynwood. The physical activity helped a little, but he still churned with bleak anger and despair. Having Diana among his guests, having to be courteous, knowing that she would be sleeping under the same roof—the prospect was unendurable.

As he allowed his blown and sweating horse to slow its pace, he wondered what the devil his lady wife wanted.

Hollins led her to the mistress's room, the same she had stayed in before, with its hidden passage to the master suite. After he left, she removed her bonnet and sank onto the bed, shaking with reaction. She had carried off the scene downstairs well, until Gervase had appeared, his eyes like shards of angry ice. How many of her airy explanations had he heard? And how much had he resented them?

Massaging her temples, she tried to be happy that she had surmounted the first hurdle and had a precarious foothold at Aubynwood, but much worse lay ahead. As she had guessed, Gervase would try to avoid a public scene, but he might well have his servants bundle her off in secret. Or would he consider that too cowardly, and feel he must deal with her himself?

He had been as angry as she expected, but there had been desire in him as well. She was sure of that, and in private, passion might build bridges that could not be forged in public.

Veseul's presence had shocked her almost to immobility. Now that he knew she was Gervase's wife rather than a courtesan, he would undoubtedly leave her alone, but he still frightened her. Memories of his obscene liberties and his behavior at the Cyprians' Ball were so vivid that she shuddered, then brushed her fingertips across the haft of her knife, where it lay quiet and deadly in its leg sheath. She had worn the knife because they were traveling; ordinarily she would not have gone armed at Aubynwood, but with Veseul on the premises, she would wear a knife all day and sleep with one under her pillow. And she would lock the door whenever she was alone in her chamber.

The thought made her rise. If Gervase walked in now, ready to do battle, she would be unprepared. She went to the nursery wing in unabashed flight and helped Geoffrey and Maddy settle in, taking pleasure in the illusion of normalcy. Her son was delighted to be at Aubynwood, satisfied with the viscount's reception, and in short order he went off to visit the stables. Madeline gave tea and bracing talk to Diana; then, taking her maid's role seriously, she went off to ensure that Diana's clothing was properly unpacked, brushed, and bestowed.

Diana considered sending a footman to find Gervase's cousin, but Francis found her first. She almost hugged him for the kind concern on his face when he intercepted her on the main staircase. She settled for squeezing both of his hands in hers. "Francis, I am so glad you are here!"

"So am I," he said with a warm smile. "Obviously you are in need of allies." Tucking her arm under his elbow, he led her across the hall. "Difficult to find privacy anywhere in the house. Care to walk with me while you explain what is going on?"

Avoiding the formal gardens, they took a winding path down to the ornamental lake. Though they had not known each other for long, what had passed between them had created an unusual degree of intimacy, and it was a profound relief for Diana to talk to someone who knew and cared for both her and Gervase. She gave an expanded version of what she had had told Geoffrey, but Francis was an adult, and he understood what she was not saying.

He listened in grave silence until she was done. "So you really are married to Gervase, in love with him, and he can't forgive you your deception. What a tragic, ironic waste."

There was a rustic wooden bench at the edge of the little lake and he steered her to it so they could sit down, his hand resting on hers with light comfort. She glanced into his blue eyes, then looked away quickly, afraid his sympathy would cause her to break down. "You've known him all your life, Francis. What made him react so strongly? Some anger I can understand, but not this blind, unforgiving fury."

"I don't know, Diana." Francis shook his head. "He has been a good friend and cousin to me, but in some ways he is a mystery. Most English gentlemen keep their emotions hidden far from the sun, but Gervase goes beyond that."

He plucked a sprig of speedwell from the ground and rolled it between his fingers, considering. "In spite of his competence and success, there is a quality of tragedy about Gervase. He has always served others, in both small things and great, but never because he expects gratitude. In fact, he can't even accept thanks. I think he feels unworthy of anyone's good opinion."

"I have felt that too," Diana said slowly. "Do you have an idea what could have made him that way?"

"I could make some guesses." He glanced at her with a wry smile. "Lately I have thought a good deal about the many kinds of love. I think a child who is not loved early and well may later have trouble understanding or accepting any kind of love."

He cast his mind back to all the bits of family gossip he had heard over the years. "Gervase's father was a reticent man who did his duty, but never more than that. Duty required him to beget an heir for St. Aubyn, so he married and produced one. Two, actually—Gervase had an older brother who died at the age of six or seven. That was before my time, but my mother said once that his parents regretted that Gervase would inherit. He was small, too quiet, and he had seizures. They considered him flawed.''

After thought, Diana asked, "What was his mother like?''

"Ah, the glorious Medora." Francis sighed and looked across the lake. "As beautiful and amoral a woman as ever walked the earth. She could charm the birds from the trees when she wished, then forget your existence in the space of a heartbeat. She fascinated and daunted everyone who ever crossed her path.''

"It might not be easy to have such a woman for a mother.''

"No, I don't think it was," he agreed. "It would have been simpler if she were evil-tempered, or deliberately cruel. Instead, she was . . . supremely self-absorbed. So concerned with her own desires that the rest of the human race had no real existence to her. One could no more judge her by the standards of ordinary mortals than one could judge a falcon or a cobra.''

"What happened to her?''

"She died in a fire when Gervase was about seventeen. She was staying with one of her lovers in his hunting box in the Shires. The man died too. It was quite a little scandal, I understand. Lovers are all very well if one is discreet, but it was considered bad form to be caught dead with one.''

So Gervase's mother had been a fickle, selfish creature, by turns charming and heedless, and she had died in a flagrant and scandalous way. No wonder Gervase had a passion for privacy and an inability to believe in a woman's constancy. It began to make sense, a little, though Diana was not sure yet what use she could make of the information. But if she could understand Gervase's tortured emotions, perhaps she could learn how to heal them. "Thank you, Francis, for explaining this. Perhaps it will help.''

He turned to look at her, his handsome face grave. "Gervase needs you, Diana, more than he can begin to understand. You could love and be loved by many different men, but Gervase is not like that. If he cannot bring himself to forgive and love you, I'm afraid he will withdraw so far that no one else will ever be able to find him. For his sake, I hope you persevere.''

She closed her eyes against aching tears. "I'll try," she whispered, "but I don't know how long I can endure.''

It took time to master her grief; her deepest emotions were very near the surface these days. Eventually Diana raised her head and blotted her face with the handkerchief Francis produced. Smiling shakily, she asked, "Are your affairs of the heart prospering any better than mine?''

He smiled, an expression of pure, expansive joy. "They are. After you and I talked, it became easier to talk to . . . my friend. We found that we shared not just thoughts and ideas, but . . . infinitely more. In a few weeks we will be taking ship to the Mediterranean. It will be a very long time before we return.''

She asked hesitantly, "And your family?''

"We have not spoken of it directly, but I think my mother has guessed. And like you, she forgives.''

Diana leaned forward and kissed him on the cheek. "There is nothing to forgive, only to accept. I am so happy for you.''

Francis gave her a hug and she relaxed in the warmth of his embrace as he said, "I thought once it was impossible to find the love I craved, but I was wrong. Even in this imperfect world, sometimes one can find a way to happiness. Things may look black now, but if any woman on earth can reach Gervase and win the passion and loyalty he is capable of, it is you.''

She whispered, "I pray to God that you are right.''

Neither of them realized how visible they were to a horseman on a high hill.

The Count de Veseul escorted a fuming Lady Haycroft toward the folly, avoiding the others who wandered through the gardens. The two were occasional lovers and they had a certain cold selfishness in common; they could be considered friends. After listening to her ladyship rail about St. Aubyn's perfidy in letting people think he was eligible, with vicious side comments on the insipid pret-

tiness of the viscount's wife, Veseul drawled, "The little
trollop may not be his wife. Even if she is, they may not
have been married any nine years."

"What?" Lady Haycroft stared at him. "St. Aubyn
didn't deny her. Besides, the boy certainly looks like
both of them, and he must be six or seven."

"Oh, he may well be their child," Vesoul said lazily,
"but not necessarily a legitimate one. She must have
been his mistress before he went to India. More recently, the alleged viscountess has been living in London as a courtesan, using the name Mrs. Lindsay. I saw
her myself at the most recent Cyprians' Ball. In fact,
you saw her with St. Aubyn, too, one night at Vauxhall.
They were in one of those dark little alcoves, so I'm
not surprised you didn't recognize her today."

As Lady Haycroft went pale with shock at his news,
Veseul stopped to pluck a yellow rose, sniffing it before presenting it to his companion. "Among the Cyprians, she was known as the Fair Luna. I'd heard she
was St. Aubyn's mistress, among others. *Many* others.
Perhaps her bed magic is strong enough that he married her, or perhaps he wanted an heir and decided it
was easier to pretend an existing son was legitimate
than to gamble on getting another in marriage. Who
knows? He's a cold, calculating man; were it not for
his wealth, you'd have no interest in him yourself."

"Very true," she snapped, "but the wealth would
be ample reason to tolerate him. He seemed like a
perfect choice as husband: rich, influential without being fashionable, and likely indifferent to what his wife
would do once he had an heir."

Half to herself, she muttered, "He was showing
signs of warming up before that strumpet arrived. If
they really are married, I'll have to give up my hopes
of him. There's no point in taking him as a lover if
marriage isn't possible."

Her lips pinched together, warping her handsome
features with mean-spiritedness as she shredded the
rose petals in her angry fingers. "But with what you
have just told me, I can ruin her forever and make St.
Aubyn a laughingstock. So Miss Butter-in-the-Mouth

is just a high-priced London whore! When that gets out, she'll have to go back to Yorkshire or Scotland or whatever godforsaken place she came from.''

Veseul watched with pleasure at the sight of the mischief he'd sown. When Lady Haycroft's vicious tongue was done, both St. Aubyn and his woman would be miserable, possibly estranged from each other; the viscount was too proud to forgive his wife the ridicule her past would bring on him. If he repudiated her, Diana Lindsay might be eager to bed one of her husband's enemies for pure spite. There was a myriad of delightful possibilities.

He shrugged mentally. Whether she came willingly or not, she could not escape him if they spent the next week under the same roof. And if she was unwilling, he would do much more than simple rape. An ugly smile curled his lips and he caressed the gold serpent's head on his cane. He hoped she would resist; the mere thought of that was enough to arouse him.

22

EVEN at a great distance, it was easy to identify the
couple embracing by the lake as Diana and Francis.
Had she come here in pursuit of his cousin? If so, she
had made an easy capture. In spite of the sick fury the
sight aroused in him, Gervase could not bring himself
to blame Francis. Diana's sensual beauty and illusion-
ary sweetness were enough to win any man who had
the strength to draw breath.

He stayed out until a dull, aching fatigue had replaced his first uncontrollable rage, and he hoped that
he and his weary horse would be able to slip back into
the stables unobserved by his guests. It was a hope
doomed to disappointment; as Gervase led his horse
into the barn, he saw the figure of his son peering into
a box stall, then turning to look up. As the viscount
dismounted, he felt Geoffrey's steady regard and
guessed that the boy would not approach without some
signal.

In its way, this meeting would be as difficult as the
one with Diana, but at least there would be a positive
side as well as awkwardness. Waving off an oncoming
groom, Gervase unsaddled his mount himself, then led
it into the barn toward Geoffrey. "Care to help me
groom Firefly?"

The boy nodded and followed his father into the
stall. After tying Firefly, Gervase took a handful of
straw and began wiping off loose dirt and sweat while
Geoffrey did the same on the animal's other side. After
a few minutes of silence, Gervase said, "I'm not quite
sure what one says in these circumstances."

His son gave a wisp of a chuckle. "Neither am I." His head didn't reach the top of the horse's back.

Gervase had the inspired thought of asking about his son's pony, and this unleashed a torrent of conversation. By the time they had gotten to vigorously brushing the horse's hide, they were as easy with each other as they had become over the Christmas visit. In spite of Geoffrey's short stature, Gervase should have realized the boy was more than six years old. Knowing that this small, intelligent person with his quirky individuality was his own son gave the viscount a glow of pride, even though he could take none of the credit. Whatever Diana's other sins, she had been a good mother to their child.

Finally Geoffrey touched on how things were between his parents. As he brushed out Firefly's tail, blithely indifferent to the animal's back hooves, he said obliquely, "I used to wonder what my father was like. Mama would never say a word."

"It must have been hard not knowing," was the best comment Gervase could come up with.

"Sometimes. But I could pretend that he was like Lord Nelson or Dr. Johnson or Richard Trevithick or Beethoven."

It was nothing if not a varied list. Bemused, Gervase said, "Reality is never quite as interesting as imagination."

Wide blue eyes glanced up to him. "Reality isn't so bad."

Gervase felt absurdly pleased at the statement. "How do you feel about Aubynwood now that you know you'll own it someday?"

Startled, Geoffrey stopped brushing. "I hadn't thought that far," he said in a small voice. "It's very large, isn't it?"

"Yes, and there are other properties as well," the viscount admitted, "but you should have years to get used to the idea, and to learn your way around." Since his son still looked doubtful, he added, "Just think of all the horses you'll have."

It was the right thing to say. Smiling, Geoffrey went

back to work. They had almost finished the grooming when the boy said tentatively, "Mama said you were very angry with her."

The easy atmosphere vanished. Gervase was cleaning the frog of Firefly's right hoof and his tension affected the horse, which shifted uneasily. "Did your mother ask you to talk to me?"

"No, she said not to. But I want to understand what's wrong. Why you didn't care about us at all."

Gervase drew a deep breath and finished cleaning the hoof, then released the horse's foreleg. "I didn't know that I had a son—your mother never told me. Did she mention that?"

There was a stubborn tilt to Geoffrey's jaw. "Yes, but you knew you had a wife. How could you abandon Mama?"

Gervase knew that Geoffrey would not take kindly to aspersions cast on his mother, but it was impossible to speak calmly of her. Instead he asked, "What did she say about it?"

"That you didn't really want to be married to anybody." Then, his tone accusing, Geoffrey added, "She said everyone makes mistakes, and not to blame you. So why are you blaming *her*?"

Gervase started to reply, then stopped. Of course Geoffrey was loyal to his mother; she had been the center of his life since he was born. Diana had been too clever to poison Geoffrey's mind against his father in an obvious way; her facade of long-suffering generosity was far subtler and harder to combat. Unsteadily he said, "We will not talk about your mother."

When Geoffrey opened his mouth, Gervase performed his first really parental act by saying sharply, "Don't."

In spite of the rebellious gleam in his eye, Geoffrey obeyed. The viscount laid a blanket over Firefly and tied the straps. "I have to go in now. Would you like to go riding tomorrow morning? There's a new pony you might like to try."

"Yes, sir, I'd like that." Geoffrey was polite, even enthusiastic, but as the boy turned and left the stable, it was clear that his allegiance lay firmly with his mother. Not surprising; when Gervase was eight, he had adored his own mother, not knowing or understanding that she was a monster. The viscount prayed that when the time came, his son's disillusion would not be as devastating as his own had been.

Diana dressed for dinner with great care. As Madeline helped her into the gown of dusty-rose silk, Diana felt the unusual sensitivity of her breasts, then resolutely pushed away the implication of what that meant. She had enough things to worry about just now.

They decided on a sophisticated coiffure, piling her glossy chestnut tresses high on her head to reveal the perfection of her features. Rather than feathers or ribbons, Maddy wove tiny dark red rosebuds into Diana's hair. A jeweler had strung Gervase's pearls into the magnificent necklace they were meant to be and Diana wore them tonight. The lustrous sheen of the pearls harmonized with her oyster-white underskirt and drew attention to the smooth curves visible above her deep décolletage.

By the way heads turned and conversations stopped as she entered the salon, Diana knew she looked her best, but even so she paused on the threshold, frightened of so many curious strangers. Then Francis Brandelin came forward, moving calmly through the unnatural hush. Giving her a small private smile of encouragement, he took her arm and began introducing her to the two dozen or so guests that chatted and drank sherry before dinner. There were more men than women, many of them famous names like Castlereagh and Canning, and from their admiring bows, they were happy to have her among them.

The only dark note came from the Count de Veseul, who accepted his introduction with a mocking smile and a long kiss on her hand that made her skin crawl in revulsion. When she tried to pull away, he held on, his powerful grip hurting her fingers as he whispered, "What a magnificent whore you are."

His voice was too low for anyone else to hear and

Diana knew that he was playing with her, hoping she would show discomfort or fear. Instead, she showed no reaction at all, simply meeting his black gaze and letting her hand go limp.

Veseul released her just before the length of time might have aroused comment. Francis, who had caught the latter part of the byplay, spirited her away with a low-voiced warning about Veseul's unsavory reputation. His words were quite unnecessary; Diana already knew far too much about the Frenchman's nature.

The women were another kind of ordeal, ranging from watchful neutrality in the wives to outright venom in Lady Haycroft. Lord St. Aubyn himself ignored her, not acknowledging her presence by so much as the flicker of an eyelid. Since fashionable couples were not supposed to live in each other's pockets, he could avoid her all evening and no one would think anything was amiss.

Gervase's neglect was like an icy wind from the north, and it took every ounce of Diana's control not to flee to some private place where she could cry in peace. It was infinitely difficult to see his familiar face, to watch the controlled power of his movements, yet be so utterly estranged.

At dinner, she was given the hostess's place at one end of the table as was her right; Gervase had probably approved that arrangement because it put the full length of the shining mahogany table between them. The meal seemed endless, a mosaic of countless dishes appearing and disappearing, footmen presenting bottles of wine, the two gentlemen next to her vying for her attention. She spoke little, but then, she had always been better at listening, and her dining companions liked that very well. Throughout, she sensed Gervase's gaze on her, yet when she glanced toward him his eyes were always elsewhere.

Dinner was easy compared to the session with the ladies while the gentlemen sat over their port. Even the most congenial of the women were curious, and less inclined than men to approve of her. Most were too well-bred to ask direct questions about her origins, but Diana felt their curiosity and measuring glances.

Oddly, Lady Haycroft said nothing, simply sitting with watchful malice. Wanting the largest possible audience, she did not bring out her guns until the gentlemen joined the ladies. Then, as people circulated and looked for new conversational partners, she attacked. In a clarion voice she asked, "Tell me, Lady St. Aubyn, is it true that you were a London courtesan?"

Her words cut through the babble of voices, leaving absolute silence. Dismayed but unsurprised, Diana curled her hands around the carved arms of her chair as she gathered her defenses. She had guessed that Veseul might give her away, and that Lady Haycroft would be a willing ally. The other women drew back, and she felt the avid curiosity of everyone in the room. Gervase was part of the nearest group of men and she saw his shoulders tense as speculative glances were sent in his direction. If she did not answer well, her disgrace would reflect on him; he would not easily forgive her for shaming him before his friends.

Humor was the best defense; if she showed fear or guilt, the good ladies would rip her character to shreds. Raising her chin, she laughed with complete unconcern. "Where on earth did you hear such a foolish tale? It is even more absurd than the story that I was mad and locked up in Scotland." Glancing at her husband, she said, "You were right, my dear, I should have joined you sooner. The tales that have sprung up are quite remarkable."

Her eyes narrowing, Lady Haycroft spat out, "Do you deny that you lived in London under the name of Mrs. Lindsay and that you earned the nickname the Fair Luna? Or that you visited Harriette Wilson and danced at the Cyprians' Ball?"

Without hesitating, Diana widened her eyes. "Ah-h-h, I see. You have my sympathies, Lady Haycroft. Some mischievous person told you a few tidbits of truth, just enough to lead you to false conclusions."

She raised her silk fan and casually wafted air across

her heated face. Her eyes limpid with sincerity, she said, "It was very bad of me to go to such places. Growing up in the country, I had always heard ladies had more freedom in London, and I decided to use that freedom to satisfy my curiosity."

She sighed, letting her long lashes flutter for a moment. "When I went to the Cyprians' Ball, I realized I had greatly misjudged and gone far beyond the line of what is pleasing."

Raising her gaze again, she glanced innocently at the other ladies, the ones who would be her true judges. "I must confess that, like every respectable woman, I wondered what our rivals are like. Surely some of you have done the same?"

Lady Castlereagh, a very conservative matron with an unusually devoted husband, chuckled a bit. "What decent woman hasn't? The stories one hears . . ." Shaking her head, she added the indulgent warning, "Still, it is quite unacceptable to actually visit such places, my dear."

Diana smiled at the older woman with real gratitude. "You're quite right. I would never do so again."

Another woman whose name Diana didn't recall leaned forward intently. "Did you recognize many of the gentlemen?"

This time a number of the men tensed; several had been at the ball. Without looking away from her inquisitor, Diana promptly said, "I fear I know very few members of the fashionable world. Most of the men at the ball were young bachelors, I believe." Her words produced a palpable wave of relief.

"How did you gain admittance? Did you go alone?"

"I went with my husband's cousin." Diana looked apologetically at Francis, who was watching with fascinated amusement. "Francis was absolutely against it, but reluctantly agreed to escort me when he saw that I was determined to go."

She cast an anxious glance at her husband. "I quickly realized how foolish I was and we left early. St. Aubyn was away and didn't know, of course. I'm afraid you are bringing my husband's disapproval on me, Lady Haycroft.''

While Gervase watched with the angry stillness of white-hot iron, Lady Haycroft returned to the attack. "What about living as Mrs. Lindsay? One would think that if you were Lady St. Aubyn then, you would have used your title.''

Diana laughed with a touch of shy embarrassment. "I fear you have found us out. It amused my husband and me to . . . play at just what you are suggesting.'' With delicate suggestiveness, she continued, "Surely you know the games lovers play, Lady Haycroft, pretending to be what they are not, for the pure pleasure of it.''

Most of the listeners knew exactly what she meant, their faces reflecting their own fond memories of games they had played when they were in the bright throes of love. When the moment had stretched long enough, Diana moved to the offensive. It was time to wield her strongest weapon in this social battle. "I called myself Lindsay because it was my mother's name, and unlike Brandelin, it is common enough to go unremarked. My mother was the only daughter of General Lord Lindsay, you know.''

The famous name struck the room like thunder. Alisdair Lindsay had been the greatest soldier of his generation, ennobled by the crown, a much-loved warrior who had fallen while winning his greatest victory against the French in the Seven Years' War. The younger son of an ancient family, he and his achievements were legend. Diana shot a quick glance at Gervase, but his impassive face showed no surprise; no one would guess that her ancestry was as much a surprise to him as to the other guests.

One of the older women, Mrs. Oliphant, said with interest, "We must be related, my dear. My second cousin married into that branch of the Lindsays. Who was your father?''

"James Hamilton, a clergyman in Lanarkshire,'' Diana replied.

That stirred more interest among the genealogically

inclined. A man asked, "Any relation to the Duke of Arran?"

Diana shook her head modestly. "A mere connection. My father was from a cadet branch, the Hamiltons of Strathaven."

Mrs. Oliphant smiled with pleasure. "Strathaven! I think I met your father there once when we were all young. A tall, dark man with piercing eyes?"

Diana nodded. "That sounds like him. Unfortunately, I remember little of Strathaven myself, though we visited there when I was very small. My father later became estranged from his family. To my regret, I know none of my cousins."

The moment of crisis had passed; Diana had survived the test and been accepted as a woman worthy of moving in these exalted circles. Visiting the Cyprians' Ball would have utterly ruined an unmarried girl, but a matron had more freedom, and proper remorse had gained Diana forgiveness for her scandalous actions. It helped, perhaps, that none of the women present seemed to like Lady Haycroft; the obvious malice of the widow's attack had worked to Diana's advantage.

As Lady Haycroft stalked away in furious defeat, the guests broke into smaller groups. Women clustered around Diana to ask eager questions about what she had seen, whether Harriette Wilson was as vulgar as rumor said, about what transpired at the infamous ball. Lady St. Aubyn was regarded as very dashing.

Diana was glad when the tea tray had come and gone and she could excuse herself. Some of the guests would be up late playing cards and politics, but she could now retire to her room and recruit her strength. Remembering her resolution, she locked the door behind her, forbidding entry to Veseul or any other straying man who thought that such an adventurous female was worth attempting. After undressing and unpinning her hair, she lay across her bed, her eyes open but unseeing, wondering if Gervase would come to her, or if she must go to him.

It was after midnight when she accepted that he

would not come. He was the fortress, grimly defiant, and she the attacker who must breach his defenses. She must go to him.

Dressed in a simple blue silk robe, neither plain nor provocative, her shining hair brushed long and loose, she took a candle and entered the passage that led to Gervase's room. It was quiet and dusty, haunted by ghosts of happier transits.

It was possible that he would have locked the door against her or that he would not be in his own chamber, but somehow she knew Gervase would be waiting for her, and he was. He lounged in a wing chair near the bed, his feet casually resting on a low footstool, his coat off and his bright white shirt outlining his broad shoulders. Even the candlelight that polished his dark hair could not soften the harshness of his face.

He was unsurprised by her entrance. "Good evening, Diana. I have been expecting you. Let me congratulate you on a magnificent performance this evening. I'm sure the tales of your exalted birth can be confirmed—you're far too clever to lie about what could be easily disproved." His shirt was open at the throat, exposing a triangle of dark hair on his chest. "Another piece falls into place. Your speech and education are now explained and you have been accepted as the lady you are not."

A nearly empty decanter of brandy stood near his elbow and he lifted a goblet to take a deep swallow of the spirits. His words were clear and unblurred as he said, "I haven't been this drunk since the regrettable night that I met you," but she saw a hard, unfamiliar glitter in his eyes.

She tensed at the sight; there had sometimes been discord and conflict between them, but only once had he looked like this: that infamous night on Mull. Drunk then, he had been violent, and now there was risk in staying and confronting him. Nonetheless she must speak; she could not spend another day like the one just past, with Gervase ignoring her very existence.

Choosing another armchair half a dozen feet from him, she sat, placing her candle on a small table as her gown fell in soft blue folds around her. "Good evening, Gervase. Thank you for not exposing me to the condemnation of your guests."

His dark brows rose ironically. "How could I without showing myself as a fool? You are the subtlest witch I ever met, Diana. You have found depths of revenge I could never have imagined."

She must remain as calm as he, no matter how difficult it was. "As I told you before, I do not want revenge."

"And as I said before, I do not believe you." He watched the candlelight refract through the cut-glass goblet, then said without raising his eyes, "What do you want, Diana? Why not just tell me, so that we can end this farce?"

"I want to be your wife."

"You *are* my wife, remember? Therein lies the problem."

There was barely controlled savagery in his tone, and she could hear him struggle to steady his voice before he continued. "I want a legal separation. My assets are not limitless, but I will give you an income sufficient to support any degree of fashionable life except becoming a gamester. I hope that you will not do anything to utterly disgrace the name, but short of murder, there is no way I can constrain you, so I must rely on your nonexistent sense of honor."

Trying to ignore the insult of his last sentence, she took a deep breath before answering. "I don't want your money and I don't want a legal separation." Summoning all her sincerity, she tried to catch his eye. "I would rather be your mistress and have your love than be a legal wife forever separated from you."

He flinched. "Certainly the situation was more satisfactory when you were acting the role of mistress than it has been since you revealed yourself as my wife," he agreed, his level tone belied by a tightening of the skin across his high cheekbones.

"Unfortunately, I cannot go back to that state of halcyon ignorance. If you are wise, you will accept the separation—it's my best offer. If you fight me, I may decide to sue for divorce. Doubtless there is an abundance of evidence to prove your adultery, but I would rather not expose Geoffrey or you or myself to that. Especially not Geoffrey.''

''There is no evidence of infidelity, Gervase. I have never lain with any man but you.'' Diana's fingers locked together in her lap, the nails biting deep.

''This very afternoon I saw you and Francis embracing in the gardens. My own cousin, at my own home. And you expect me to believe your lies?'' He leaned his head against the chair back, as if too weary to support its weight.

''It was the embrace of friends. Why don't you ask Francis what the truth is, my lord husband?'' Her resolution to be calm was shredding away in the face of his relentless distrust.

''I have not wanted to hear him admit you are lovers.'' He drank the last of the brandy in his goblet. ''Fond though I am of Francis, I doubt I would be able to forgive him, and I can't afford to lose any more friends.''

She flung her hands up in exasperation. ''Why are you so sure he will confirm your suspicions?''

His eyes finally met hers, the gray depths bleak with pain. ''If he doesn't, I will know you have corrupted him with your lies, and that would be even worse.''

''So you have already judged and condemned me,'' she said unsteadily, frustration stabbing deep inside her. ''In your eyes I am already damned.''

''Undoubtedly,'' he agreed, pouring more brandy. ''When we first met, I thought you looked like an angel of innocence, but now I know that you came from another direction entirely.''

He drank off half the goblet at one gulp, his throat working against the fiery liquid. ''I knew I was damned from the age of thirteen, but with time the knowledge faded. I began to think there might be some kind of salvation for even the worst of sinners. So you were sent from hell to drag me down again. And I . . .'' His mouth twisted. ''Fool that I am, I desire you so much that even now, in spite of everything, I want you.''

She stared. "God help you," she whispered, chilled and repelled by his words, "you sound like my father."

"I'm not surprised. The esteemed vicar thought that women were the source of evil and suffering, and I am inclined to think he had the right of it."

"Stop it!" Her voice was nearly a scream. "I can't bear it when you talk that way. What have I done that you despise me so? I didn't tell you who I was at first because I was fearful, and wanted to know you better. What is so dreadful about that?

"I never meant to hurt you." Her voice was between pleading and anger. "Why am I asking you for forgiveness when it is you who have wronged me, most horribly?"

"Neither of us seems capable of forgiving the other," he answered with dry precision. "You can't forgive my violence, and I can't forgive your duplicity. And judging by the splendid performance you are putting on, you are no more capable of being honest with yourself than with me."

"I don't know what you are talking about!" she cried.

Gervase banged the goblet on the table so hard that brandy splashed on his hand. His face ablaze with angry pain, he leaned forward and said with harsh precision, "You found a man who had the strongest of reasons to doubt that any woman could be trusted, seduced him with sweet loving lies to the point where he believed that trust was possible. Then when he was utterly vulnerable, you betrayed him."

Breathing hard, he ended with a denunciation the more bitter for its softness. "Only a woman could so thoroughly and ruthlessly betray. No man would know how to be as subtly, treacherously cruel as you."

Diana noted that even now, he could not name himself as the man betrayed, and supposed that was a gauge of his pain. All she could do was repeat numbly, "I never wanted to hurt you. One reason I didn't speak was that the more time that passed, the harder it was to explain why I had not spoken earlier. It was easier to drift, to let events take their own course.''

She stopped to marshal her arguments, trying to find words for what she had done by instinct. ''I thought that if you came to love me, we could put the past behind us, that how our marriage began would be unimportant compared to how we had come to feel about one another.'' She spread her hands helplessly. ''I never imagined that you would think I had trapped and betrayed you from a desire for revenge. Obviously I was wrong, but is that so unforgivable? I never claimed to be perfect.''

He leaned back in the chair, his face lost in shadows, his voice tragic. ''Ah, but you see, I thought you were.''

For a moment she was shocked and unbearably moved by his words. Then anger came. ''I can't help that! It isn't my fault if you thought me more than I am. To love is to accept the whole person, imperfections and all.'' She tried to penetrate the shadows with her gaze. ''Why can't you accept that I love you in spite of my misjudgment? I know you are not perfect, that you can be cold and suspicious, even violent, but I love you anyhow.''

''Then the more fool you are, Diana.'' He downed more brandy. ''I could never understand why you claimed to love me. God knows I don't deserve it, but I wanted to believe you, and you were so convincing.'' His eyes filled with weary resignation, he continued, ''It is far easier to believe that you are a liar than that you ever really loved me.''

His statement filled Diana with despair. If he truly believed himself unworthy of love, how could she persuade him of her sincerity? Words were not enough, would never be enough.

Gervase gave a tired shrug. ''Since you are a creature of emotion, not reason, perhaps you believe your own lies. Perhaps I should take advantage of that and retain you as a mistress.''

She could see the hunger and the longing in his eyes,

could sense his barely controlled passion, but his voice was inhumanly detached. "You are the most beautiful of women, superlatively gifted in bed, able to make a man forget his very soul. It would be a pity to waste such talent, especially since I have already bought and paid for it several times over.

"You were a matchless mistress"—his gaze traveled the length of her body, lingering with insulting deliberation—"and the bed was always the most important thing between us. What say you, Diana, shall I continue to call several nights a week and avail myself of your delightful body?"

"And you say that I know how to be cruel! I never felt like a whore before this moment, when you propose to use me as one." She shrank back in her chair, hating the very idea of what he was suggesting. Bitterly she finished, "Anything I know of cruelty, I have learned from you."

"Much better," he said approvingly. "We have no illusions about each other. Didn't you say something about knowing each other in our imperfections? The truth is that I am a rapist and you are a whore. In its way, a perfect marriage."

His words triggered a degree of fury greater than any she had felt in her life. "Damn you," she cried, "demean yourself if you will, but don't put me on your level, for I am better than that. I have tried to forgive, to give love in the face of evil, but you are not worth it."

Helpless tears poured down her face. "In the beginning I hated you. The only being I hated more was God himself, for permitting such a thing to happen. When I first met you in London I was terrified. If I had not been raised to believe that a wife must submit to her husband, if I had not felt compelled to know you better, I would never have allowed you to touch me.

"Then I learned to love you, in the face of your distrust, even when you tried to dominate and possess me." Her voice caught in anguish. "Now, because you believe yourself unworthy, you have destroyed all

the love I felt for you. Only hatred is left, and you
have only yourself to blame.''

Even as she hurled the words like weapons, she
knew that she still loved him, but that the hatred was
real too. ''The morning after our hell-born marriage,
my father abandoned me in that inn, delighted to be
rid of me, with not a single backward glance. I was
fifteen years old, Gervase, raped, confused, and
frightened, and he left me there penniless, with only
the clothes I stood up in, because he said I was now
my husband's responsibility. If the innkeeper's wife
had not taken pity on me, put me to work in the kitch-
ens, and paid for the letter to your London lawyer,
God only knows what would have become of me.''

The remembered panic of a child's abandonment
lanced through her voice. ''Because I was not full
grown, I almost died when Geoffrey was born. For two
days and nights I was in labor, screaming until I had
no more voice to scream.''

Having started, she could not stop, even though she
knew mere words could not convey the sheer terror
she had known. ''I had never wanted wealth or status
or fame. My greatest dream in life was a simple one:
to marry a husband who loved me, to have children to
love and cherish.''

Then, with infinite bitterness, ''In one casual,
drunken act you tore that dream away from me, along
with my innocence. Then you left me, neither wife
nor maid, forbidding me to see or get in touch with
you. My only choices were to live as a spinster for the
rest of my life or take a man in adultery. Finally, turning my back on everything I was raised to believe in,
I chose to do the latter and went to London, hoping to
find a man who would love me in spite of my past.
And the devil in all his humor sent me to you, my
husband, and I was fool enough to love you.''

There was satisfaction in seeing that her words affected him like physical blows, that he felt some
shadow of her suffering. Contempt in every syllable,
she finished, ''As if your damned fortune could ever
compensate for what you have done to me. There isn't

enough money on earth to buy you a clear conscience.''

"I know that. If there were anything on earth I could do to make amends, I would do it. You are angry and have every right to be.'' Gervase's face contorted with despairing guilt, bruised shadows underlining his light eyes. He drew in a shuddering breath, then finished in a voice raw with pain, "Can you listen to your own words and still deny that you wanted revenge?''

His question was like a splash of ice water in the face of her fury. Hearing the echoes of her words, Diana was appalled by her own bitterness. Shaking her head in vehement denial, she buried her face in her hands, her curtained hair isolating her with her thoughts. She had thought that she had transcended the anger about her marriage, that she had become a loving, forgiving woman, and now she stood condemned by her own words.

Terrified that she was not the person she had believed she was, Diana searched the darkest corners of her heart with harsh, relentless will, to learn if vengeance had truly been her motive. It was one of the most difficult things she had ever done. She found anger, some of it for Gervase and her mother, more directed at her father. She found guilt, the tormented doubts she had known at bringing Geoffrey to London when she embarked on a life of shame. But she found no malice toward anyone, no desire to torment and destroy her husband.

When she was sure, Diana raised her head and said with the stillness that comes after storm, "In the years between our marriage and our meeting in London, I despised you, and had no desire to see you ever again.'' Then, with utter conviction, "But vengeance I left to God.''

He shook his head, able to believe her anger but not her conclusion. "Finally, the ugly truth that lies at the bottom of the well, the rage you had hidden even from yourself. You should thank me for helping you discover it. You hated me and sought revenge. And you achieved it beyond your wildest dreams.''

"You are wrong, Gervase." She brushed her hair back wearily. "Yes, there was anger—only now do I see how much—but that is only part of the truth. Though I hated you in the beginning, that passed. I swear before God that I never truly wished to harm you in any way. I wanted you to be sorry, to regret what had happened, but that is far from the viciousness you think me capable of."

"You can't have it both ways, Diana. How could I fully comprehend the injury I did to you and *not* suffer from the knowledge? You have sown the seeds of your hatred, and I will be reaping the harvest as long as I live." He closed his eyes for a moment, then opened them again, their gray depths transparent in the candlelight. "You wanted your pound of flesh, and you got it. It was just bloodier than you expected."

At first she wanted to disagree, but then the truth of his words hit her. Indeed, she could not have it both ways. A just man like Gervase could not turn aside from the consequences of his actions; because he was strong and honorable, his torment at betraying his fundamental values was all the more acute. And as much as she hated to admit it, she could no longer deny that she *had* wanted to hurt him, just a little. Then, after he had shown proper remorse, she would have graciously forgiven him and they could have lived happily ever after in their love and she would have the added satisfaction of knowing how generous she had been.

Instead, because there were already deep wounds in his soul, she had injured him far more profoundly than she had intended, and that injury had rebounded on her. She wished she had not come here, had not opened this Pandora's box of dark and twisted motives, but too much had been said to retreat; she could only go forward. The past and present were unbearable; only the future held hope, and that meant driving away all the dark shadows.

With sudden insight, she knew what must be done. Quietly she asked, "What is the truth that lies at the bottom of your well, Gervase? Who convinced you that you were unworthy of being loved, who made it easier to believe that I was a liar than that I could love you?''

She stood and stepped toward him, remembering what Francis had told her the day before. "Was it your father, who neglected you and considered you an inferior heir? Or was it your mother? You never speak of her.'' Her voice catching, she continued, "My mother killed herself, and I felt betrayed. What did your mother do that wounded you so deeply you cannot trust another woman?''

She raised one hand tentatively, then dropped it, afraid to touch him. "Why are you so terrified that you will send me away rather than risk love?''

"My God, you *are* a witch." He twisted away from her, his long muscles rigid with anguish as his words came forth reluctantly, one by one, admitting the accuracy of her guess. "Before I met you, my mother was the only woman I had ever loved, and it meant nothing to her. Less than nothing.''

Covering his face with taut hands, he said savagely, "I only wish that she *had* killed herself. It would have been a blessing by comparison.''

"What did she do to you?'' Diana pursued him implacably, stopping so close to his chair that the soft folds of her gown brushed his leg. "As you yourself have just shown me, wounds that are hidden from the light of day turn poisonous.''

As he gasped for breath as if he had been running, his ragged voice came from behind his hands. "You don't want to know. I swear before God, Diana, *you . . . do . . . not . . . want . . . to . . . know.*''

Diana placed her hands on his and gently pulled them from his face. As he flinched from her touch, she was shocked to see tears, his features distorted by unbearable memories. He was a grown man, but his expression was that of a devastated child. Softly she asked, "What did she do to you, Gervase, that you are letting it destroy your whole life?''

"You really want to know, mistress mine?'' He knocked her hands aside, using fury to disguise his agony. "I warned you, but you insist on knowing the darkest secret of my soul, so I will make you a gift of it.''

Hoarsely, painfully, his eyes not meeting hers, he said, ''The first woman I ever lay with was my mother.''

Diana stared at him in horror. Nothing had prepared her for this, and she was shocked to the depths of her being.

He could not stop now, his words pouring out with chaotic power. ''Do you think only women can be raped? You are wrong. My mother raped me, though not with force. She did it casually, because it amused her at that moment. Because she was unhappy about the loss of a lover. Because she had drunk too much wine. Because it never occurred to her to deny her impulses.''

He shook his head violently, as if to dislodge the memories. ''I was thirteen years old. At first I didn't understand, then I didn't believe, and finally I could not stop my body from responding even though I knew how unspeakably wrong it was.''

He stood suddenly and she jerked back, uncertain of what he meant to do. Grasping the brandy decanter, in one smooth, furious motion Gervase hurled it across the room to shatter against the wall. As crystal shards spun across the polished hardwood floor and the sharp tang of brandy filled the room, he cried out, ''Is that ugly enough for you? Is that a powerful enough reason to doubt that women can be trusted?''

He had been avoiding her eyes, but now he turned to face her, all vestige of control vanished. ''It repulses you, doesn't it, knowing that your husband is a man who committed incest with his own mother? Incest is the vilest, the most forbidden of crimes. Oedipus was hurled down from his throne, blinded, and cast out into the wilderness for it.''

Half-wild with devastation, he finished in a hoarse whisper, ''It is more than a crime, it is an abomination, a sin against God. There is nothing, nothing at all, that can absolve that.''

His agony was a fiery, tangible thing, and it struck

Diana to the heart. She didn't want to believe that any
mother could do such a thing to her son, that the man
she loved had lived most of his life with such grief and
shame, but the intolerable truth was written in every
tortured line of his face.

With instinctive desire to offer comfort, she cried
out, "It wasn't your fault! She was a woman grown,
but you were scarcely more than a child. It is horrible
that any woman could abuse her child so, but you are
not horrible for having been a victim of her. Don't let
your guilt destroy you."

Then, with fierce entreaty, she begged, "And don't
punish me for your mother's sin."

His raw gaze met hers. He stood a bare foot away,
the fevered warmth of his lean body palpable. "I may
have been more sinned against than sinning at thirteen, but I can't escape the knowledge that I am far
more her child than my father's."

His mouth twisted. "My father was as dry and unfeeling as dust—it is my mother's passionate, wanton
nature I inherited, and I am no better than she was.
You of all women know what I am capable of. I have
tried to control myself; to spend passion where it will
do no harm, to expiate my sins by working for goals
greater than myself." His shoulders lifted in a gesture
of despair. "I have tried to believe that I am no worse
than other men, but in spite of all I have done, I have
been unable to escape the truth: I am flawed beyond
redemption."

"That's not true! No one is beyond redemption. You
are no more flawed than any other mortal man." In
her fierce desire to defend him from himself, she
grasped his upper arms, trying to break through his
guilt and self-hatred.

She knew instantly that she had made a disastrous
error. Her touch dissolved the fragile control that held
Gervase's violent emotions in check, and his taut muscles spasmed under her hands. Then he pulled her into
a fierce, painful embrace, his mouth devouring, his
arms crushing her against his hard body. She felt noth-

ing of love and tenderness, only anguish and a bitter
desire to strike mindlessly at the darkness within him.

In two steps he had dragged her to the bed and
thrown her onto it, trapping her body beneath him,
bruising her lips as he invaded her mouth. Wrenching
the neckline of her silk robe, he exposed her breasts
to his hungry grasp.

Diana fought him, trying to get enough leverage with
arms and knees to free herself, but he was far too
strong, far too lost in his own private hell, for her to
escape. If he had wanted her in any other way she
would have given herself gladly, but not like this, not
in an act of violence that would sear them both beyond
the possibility of healing.

He half-lifted himself to get a better grip on her
robe, and she used his shift in weight to reach down
to the knife sheath on her leg. Lost in darkness beyond
thought, Gervase didn't even see the bright flash of
blade as she raised her knife and slashed it across his
left forearm.

Pain penetrated his madness as words could not have
done. As blood dripped onto her bare breasts, Gervase
rolled away, his features contorted with horror at what
he had almost done. His rigid body was an eloquent
reflection of his despair as he buried his face, his hands
clenching the heavy quilt. Even though his assault on
his wife had been unsuccessful, the attempt was bitter
confirmation of his own worst beliefs about his nature.

Diana raised herself on one arm and stared at Gervase, too shaken to know what to do or say. Trembling
with shock, she laid the bloodstained knife on the bed
and used one hand to pull her robe together as she
struggled to draw breath into her lungs. The room
seethed with the force of the emotions that had been
unleashed, and she wondered helplessly how a man
and woman who had loved could hurt each other so
profoundly.

After an endless time Gervase spoke, his voice dead,
devoid even of pain. "Don't speak to me of redemption. Some souls are beyond forgiveness. Surely even
you will admit that now."

When language failed in the past she had always used touch to convey what words could not, but when she laid a compassionate hand on his shoulder he twisted violently away from her. "Don't touch me. *In the name of God, don't touch me!*"

Shocked, she jerked back, huddling on the edge of the bed, her arms clenching across her. Trying to be matter-of-fact, to bring this nightmare scene back to normal, she said, "Your arm needs bandaging."

He had rolled onto his back, his good arm screening the upper half of his face. Utterly hopeless, he said, "Not by you. Get out, Diana. Just get out."

She stood, clutching her torn robe around her as she gazed down at him. She had never been more aware of his strength than now, when he was on the verge of breaking. Diana had known more than her share of suffering, but she had also known love, from her mother, even from her father when she was very young. Later, Edith and Geoffrey and Madeline had warmed her life. In spite of receiving so much love, she saw now that she had not fully recovered from her experiences.

Gervase had had no one, ever. A father who wasn't there, a mother who abused him in the most unpredictable and poisonous ways. Yet even so, he had not succumbed to cruelty. He had the wealth and power and intelligence to cause great evil, yet he was fair and honorable to those who depended on him. As a lover, he had been more than fair; he had been generous and kind, even tender. Repeatedly he had risked his life for the greater good, both in the army and in the mysterious, thankless work he did now.

Never having known real warmth and love, no wonder he feared accepting it, feared the power she might gain over him. As starved as he was for intimacy, no wonder he had been desperately jealous and possessive, unable to believe in her constancy. No wonder he had been shattered by her apparent betrayal. It wasn't just that he believed her to be treacherous; her actions had released the dark trauma that lay at the very roots of his soul.

She had never loved him more than now, when she was aware of the full dimensions of his valor. It is not hard to be good when circumstances encourage it; how incredibly more difficult it must have been for Gervase, who had been raised by the examples of selfishness and neglect. Yet he had done it, become a far better man than his upbringing had decreed. If not happy, he had been content, had known his place in the world and was living an honorable life.

And in her heedless self-righteousness, her unacknowledged desire to exact a subtle payment for what he had done, she had brought him to this. She remembered the words Madeline had spoken long ago in a sunlit garden: *Some people . . . can be brought to their knees, with all their pride and honor broken by the ones they love.*

Diana was bitterly ashamed for having played on Gervase's uncertainties. To feed her own desire for power, she had refused to promise fidelity when he had so desperately craved it. Yes, she had been injured by him, but she had been in a position to know better than to injure him in return, and she had failed.

Diana sensed that he was now in some black place beyond light or hope, and feared that nothing she could do or say would make any difference at all. But she could do no less than try. Her voice shaking, she said softly, "No matter what you have done, or how much you hate yourself, I love you, because you are worthy of being loved."

Her mind was numbed by all that had passed, and choosing words was an immense effort. "I think it was fate that drew us together. We have both been wounded, but together, if we try, we can heal each other. You are part of me, and I will love you as long as I live, and beyond."

She could see a quick, convulsive tightening in the part of his face that was visible, but his harsh breathing was his only reply. The abyss between them was too wide to be bridged, and she feared that the damage was beyond repairing. There was nothing more to be said, so she lifted her candle, now burned low and guttering.

She also took her knife. If he wanted to destroy himself rather than live in his pain, she knew he could find a way, but she would not make it easy for him.

Only the knowledge that her presence was hurting him made it possible for her to leave.

23

FOR Gervase it was a night without end. After improvising a crude bandage to stop the flow of blood, he had lain in the shadow-haunted room, unable to face full dark. He had been too profoundly scarred by the fact of his mother's seduction to have forgotten, but for years he had walled off the event in his mind, rigidly suppressing all memory of the details. Now his spinning head was full of her beautiful, corrupt face, her amused murmurings, her mocking incomprehension of his horror. Medora was a form of the name Medea; Medea, the sorceress who had murdered her own children. He had wondered sometimes if she would have been different if she had carried a different name.

He had never seen her again after that afternoon. Instead, he had run away, blindly, heedlessly. When his father's men had found him weeks later, he refused to go back unless it was understood that he would never, ever set foot under any roof that sheltered his mother. His father had raised his brows in mild surprise, but had no desire to know more. It had been a simple matter to leave his son at school or send him to remote properties where Lady St. Aubyn would never go.

Gervase had been seventeen when his mother died, an age when young men are most fascinated and caustic about sexual peccadilloes. In spite of his youth, he had fought two duels before his classmates realized just how unhealthy it was to refer to the late, notorious viscountess within earshot of her son. Gervase had been careful not to kill, since nothing could be said about his mother that was more insulting than the truth, but the duels increased the sick, angry ache deep inside him.

His nightmarish marriage had confirmed his unworthiness to ever live a normal life. It had been fitting to think himself tied to a mental defective, with the punishing guilt of how badly he had used the child. But in spite of his remorse, he had never truly thought of his wife as a person in her own right. Now, in this night of purgatory, he could not escape the face of the girl he had known as Mary Hamilton, with her dazed, drugged, terrified eyes. More and more clearly, he recognized under the terror the soft features and haunted loveliness of Diana.

The harsh realities and savage beauty of India had burned away any remnants of his youth; military service had hardened him, and it had been a blessing to feel less. Since returning to England, he had built a satisfactory life, honoring his obligations and finding the chesslike challenges of intelligence work quirkily gratifying. Until Diana had appeared, weaving sweet illusions of warmth and happiness, then tearing them asunder. His wife, whom he had raped and abandoned, who had returned to become the love of his life, who even now, incredibly, heartbreakingly, claimed to love him.

He had never been more grateful to see a dawn, though it came with glacial slowness, giving the promise of light long before fulfilling it. When Bonner appeared, the valet bandaged his arm with military precision and no comments or questions. Diana had done an excellent job; the slash was long and shallow, messy but causing no real damage. Briefly he wondered where she had learned to use a knife, then shrugged; there was much he would never know or understand about the woman he had married. He bathed, as if hot water could wash away the stains of ancient evil, then wrote a note to Geoffrey, postponing their ride with apologies. He was unable to face innocence this morning.

There were advantages to having a reputation for

silence, for no one seemed to notice that he was any different than he had been the day before. Except perhaps Francis, who looked at him with furrowed brow. Diana, thank heaven, kept herself out of his sight. At the moment, being in the same room with her would have been more than Gervase could bear.

Breakfast in the nursery was a cheerful affair, or would have been if Diana had not looked so drained, her fair, fragile skin shadowed with fatigue. It took no great intelligence for Madeline to guess that there had been a clash, and she wondered how his lordship of St. Aubyn looked this morning.

Maddy and Geoffrey engaged in a tacit conspiracy to cheer Diana, talking back and forth merrily. After breakfast, Geoffrey slipped off to visit some of the estate children whom he had met on his Christmas visit. Madeline wondered how they would regard him now that it was known that the boy was the heir to Aubynwood; it was bound to make a difference. Shrugging, she turned to read two letters that had just been delivered, while Diana gazed blankly into space, her hands clasped around her teacup.

The first letter was from Nicholas, full of the most marvelously improper suggestions, and with the happy news that he would be able to return to London sooner than expected. He was also pressing for a definite wedding date, and Madeline was inclined to let him have his way. A year and a day after the death of his wife, perhaps . . . in a very quiet ceremony. She read the letter three times before setting it aside.

The second letter was from Edith, who had taken the mail coach and made fast work of the trip to Scotland. In a firm, inelegant hand, she laid out her findings:

Dear Maddy,
   I'm sending this to you since you will know the situation & can judge when it is best to tell Diana. Learning about her father has been easy—the local doctor, Abernathy by name, was most forthcoming when I said I was

a friend of Diana's. She was well-regarded here, & he talked fondly of what a bonnie puir wee lassie she was.

First, James Hamilton died last year, of the same disease that made him mad—the French disease. (Also called sifilis?) Abernathy says the vicar was quite the gay society lad in his youth, drinking & wenching & gambling & all the rest. Even after his marriage, he did not entirely reform—he contracted the sifilis after Diana's birth.

Abernathy says Diana's mother killed herself the day after the doctor confirmed that she was pregnant again. The poor woman already knew she had contracted her husband's illness & couldn't face bringing a diseased baby into the world, nor, likely, seeing herself go mad like her husband was beginning to. So she drowned herself. Even among the stern godly Scots, sympathy is on the side of the lady, & her husband was universally condemned.

After his wife's death the vicar went all queer, getting madder & madder. His daughter had always been called Diana but he started calling her Mary, since he said Diana was a pagan name. When he came back from a trip to the Hebrides without Diana & a faradiddle about her marrying, there was some fear he'd done away with her, but everyone was afraid of him & nothing was done about it. At the end of his life, Hamilton was locked up & raving mad, all his clerical work done by a curate.

Abernathy was delighted to hear that Diana was alive & well & urged her to bring her husband & bairn for a visit. Or if not that, to write to him anyhow, because as her father's sole heir she inherits a tidy fortune. The madder Hamilton got, the less money he spent. Apparently her parents were quite wellborn, but you & I had guessed that.

I'm for Mull & my sister Jane now. Give my love to Diana & Geoffrey.

V'truly yours, etc.
Edith.

Madeline read the letter once, then again, before glancing speculatively at Diana. On balance, she thought her friend could do with a distraction, even a melodramatic one. "Here's a letter from Edith. She's been to your village in Lanarkshire. You'll want to read it yourself."

Her words startled Diana out of her abstraction and she accepted the letter. As she read, she turned very pale and was silent so long that Madeline finally asked if she was well.

Diana said, "I'm all right, Maddy." She buried her face in her hands for a time, but there were no tears. Finally she raised her head, her features sad but resigned. "So all of those years my father was suffering from venereal disease. No wonder he cursed lust and considered women a source of contamination."

"He must have been guilt-ridden as well," Madeline ventured. "For contracting the disease through adultery, for giving it to your mother, for being the cause of her suicide."

Diana nodded slowly, her eyes distant. "It would have been enough to drive him mad even if the disease didn't. After my mother's death, he terrorized me with his ravings about sin and corruption and the evils of worldliness. And yet, as the letter says, he'd been very fashionable in his youth. After going into the church he gave up silks and velvets and all the other trappings of wealth, except for a gentleman's pistol that he carried for protection."

She sighed, her face deeply sad. "He was very quick to condemn others, yet he succumbed to temptation himself. For a few moments of carnal pleasure, he destroyed himself and his family. Such a tragic waste."

Her voice broke for a moment before she could continue. "He must have suffered greatly from his guilt. And he must have known that he was going mad."

"It's generous of you to feel compassion after all he did to you," Madeline observed.

Diana smiled wryly. "It's far easier to be compassionate now that he's safely dead. Besides, it was a long time ago. I've lived a whole lifetime since I saw him last, and it has been a much better life." She folded the letter into precise quarters. "When I was little, he wasn't a bad father; stern, but not unkind.

Sometimes he was even affectionate. I'll try to remember him like that. I hope he is at peace now.''

"And your mother?"

Diana closed her eyes in pain at the question. "Now I understand why she was so distraught before . . . the end. She left no note. I think she must have decided on impulse that she just couldn't face the future, and walked into a pond. Wearing heavy winter clothes, it wouldn't have taken long." She shivered, then opened her eyes. "The official verdict was death by misadventure so she could be buried in holy ground, but everyone knew that she couldn't have drowned there unless she wanted to."

"Can you forgive her for leaving you?"

Diana nodded, biting her lip. "Mama knew how to love, generously and wisely. She taught me to read, to love music and books. Most important, she gave me a sense of spirituality quite different from my father's harsh, condemning religion. It was from her that I learned that love is more important than hatred or revenge. It was because of her that I was able to survive my farce of a marriage as well as I did." She smiled wryly. "Not, mind you, that my conduct was all that saintly. I was angrier than I knew. But it wasn't hatred or anger or desire for revenge that dominated my life, in spite of what my husband believes."

Gently she clasped the folded letter between her palms, her eyes distant. "I would never have emerged from my childhood with any health or sanity if it hadn't been for my mother. You remind me of her." While Madeline absorbed the compliment, Diana drew a shuddering breath, then ended unsteadily, "That's why it was so hard to comprehend why Mama would kill herself. With what Edith writes, finally I understand. May God have mercy on both their souls." Then her face crumpled and she began to cry, with the healing tears of release.

The Count de Veseul deciphered his letter with mixed emotions. He had proposed a plan to his superiors that was so brilliant and subtle that he would carry it out whether they approved it or not, just because of the pure, wicked pleasure he would find in the execution. Only the imbeciles at the Horse Guards would have wasted Arthur Wellesley's talents for so long, and only those same imbeciles would actually bring the Victor of Vimeiro up before a court of inquiry for a treaty that the general had not negotiated. The fools did not deserve Wellesley; in France he would have been a marshal by now.

Veseul admired Wellesley; his accomplishments in India had been breathtaking. The general was perhaps the only soldier in Britain who might conceivably threaten the emperor, and that knowledge made it so much more pleasing to bring him down. The details were hazy in the count's mind, but it would be simple to manufacture evidence that would taint the general's name so thoroughly that he would never hold another military command again. Wellesley was very vulnerable now—any scandal would do—and when Veseul was done, the best the general could hope for would be a lifetime rotting in Ireland, mediating potato wars.

It was gratifying that Veseul's superiors were properly impressed with the count's proposal, but their enthusiasm meant that he would have to return to London prematurely—the very next day, in fact. He had only a few hours left to seek out the elusive Lady St. Aubyn and take his pleasure of her.

Veseul knew he should have attempted Diana Lindsay the night before, but Lady Haycroft had come to his room and, what with one thing and another, the night had passed quickly. Her ladyship liked pain as few women did, and there was a special pleasure in that, though her willingness removed the joys of conquest.

This morning, when he was ripe to try an unwilling woman, the blasted viscountess had sent a message down that she was indisposed, though more likely she was avoiding her stone-faced husband. The count knew she was not in her chamber because he had expertly picked the lock, only to find the room empty.

It would take time to locate her. He had planned a

far more elegant campaign, spinning a delicate web
that only she would see, and now he would have to
move in haste. The crudeness would be unaesthetic.
But not, however, without enjoyment.

Gervase looked up wearily when his cousin entered
the estate office. He had been busying himself with
routine matters that would be better handled by his
steward, but it was a convenient excuse to remove
himself from his guests, who were having a fine time
and hardly noticed his absence.

Francis, however, was not so easily avoided. Choosing a chair right in front of the desk, he sat down.
"Good day, Gervase. Do you have time to talk for a
few moments?"

"If I don't, will you leave?" Gervase asked dryly.

"No," was the cheerful reply.

His expression lightening, the viscount settled back
in his chair and prepared to hear what Francis had to
say. He had never considered it before, but his cousin
had a quality of calm acceptance that was like Diana's.
Abruptly he changed the direction of his thoughts; he
could not bear to think of his wife. "I'm glad you
could come to Aubynwood. I haven't been at my most
social, and I appreciate the fact that you've been acting
the host in my absence."

"Quite all right." Francis waved his hand casually.
"I know you've had other things on your mind, such
as having your wife and son here publicly for the first
time."

Gervase stiffened. "I do not wish to discuss my
family."

"Don't give me that look, cousin. I mean to have
my say, and the only way you can avoid hearing it is
to run faster than I." Francis' tone was light but his
blue eyes were intent. "I know and value both you
and Diana. Since you are each looking quite miserable, I wanted to offer my services as a mediator.
Sometimes another person helps. She's very much in
love with you, you know. You seem hardly indifferent

yourself, so whatever the problem is, it should be soluble."

The viscount pushed away from his desk, distancing himself from the words. Venom in his voice, he asked, "Did she tell you that over a pillow?"

"Good God, no! Surely you don't think Diana and I are lovers?" Francis seemed genuinely shocked by the assumption.

Gervase felt his mouth twisting. He had not wanted to begin this conversation, had known instinctively that nothing good could come from it, yet now it could not be stopped. "It's a logical assumption. I know that you visited her when I was away, on the most intimate of terms."

It took a moment for Francis to understand the reference, and then he frowned. "Good Lord, were you having Diana watched? Why on earth would you do that?"

"The woman's a whore by profession, remember? I wanted to know how good her business was." Even as he said the bitter words, Gervase hated himself, but his tongue would not stop.

"Don't speak of your wife that way," Francis snapped. "It does you no credit. In fact, it's utter nonsense. Apart from a couple of visits to the sort of function any man can attend without comment, she has been living in London as quietly and respectably as any woman could. There is no impropriety in having male friends call."

"Before you dig yourself any more holes, I should warn you that yesterday I saw you with her by the lake."

His cousin's narrowed eyes were colder than Gervase had ever seen them. "She was upset—because of you—and I offered her what comfort I could. As a friend. No more, certainly no less."

"Do you expect me to believe that?"

Francis was absolutely still. "I will let no man call me a liar, Gervase, not even you."

"Oh, I don't blame you for being entranced by her," the viscount said wearily. "What man wouldn't be?

She could tempt a monk from his vows simply by walking into a room, and young men are notoriously unmonkish. Just don't lie to me.''

Francis slapped his hand down on the desk so hard that the pens jumped. ''Damnation, Gervase, you are slandering both Diana and me. She is a gentle, loving, beautiful woman, and you don't deserve her.'' Then, his voice breaking, he added, ''If I could love a woman, it would be her. But I swear before God that there has been nothing the least bit improper between us. Or are you too blind with jealousy to believe me?''

Gervase stared at the younger man, feeling pain shifting deep inside him. Francis was his closest friend; he was also notoriously truthful. Would his cousin really lie about this? More than that, did Gervase himself really believe that Diana was a liar, or was his own bleak despair distorting his image of her? There was no evidence that she was disloyal, except for his own belief that any woman he cared about must be.

Setting his elbows on the desk, he massaged his temples, where anguished confusion stabbed deep into his brain. He had tried to avoid all thought of Diana, and in the face of Francis' challenge he understood why. It was easier to believe in her anger than in her love; easier to condemn her than to accept that she was as loving and true as he had believed, and that he was wholly unworthy of her.

Now he could no longer avoid the knowledge that Francis was damnably, undeniably right: Gervase didn't deserve the woman he had married. On some deep level he had always known it, but that didn't make his present recognition any less agonizing.

Because Gervase was lost in bitter self-condemnation, it took time for the full import of Francis' words to penetrate his mind, and then he didn't grasp the implications. If he had, he would never have asked without thinking, ''What do you mean, if you could love a woman?'' There was a long taut silence, and Gervase saw that his cousin's face was ash pale.

''I meant exactly what I said.'' In spite of his pallor,

Francis' gaze was unflinching. "I'll be leaving England soon, with . . . a friend. I believe that in the future, I will be making my home in Italy. Or perhaps Greece. The ancient world is more tolerant of people like me."

Considering how emotionally drained he was, it was surprising how much shock Gervase could still feel. Shock, and revulsion. He knew that men who preferred their own kind existed, but to the extent that he ever thought of them, it had been as depraved creatures slinking about the edges of society; men whose perversion would somehow be visible on their faces. They could not be men like Francis, who were intelligent and honorable. They could not be friends. "No," he said harshly, rejecting belief. "It's not possible."

"It's not only possible—it's undeniable. If I could be different, I would be, but I had no choice." In spite of the calmness of Francis' words, a pulse beat visibly in his throat. "You are the head of the family as well as my friend. I thought you should know that you cannot count on me for any heirs after Geoffrey."

Gervase realized that he was clenching a Venetian-glass paperweight in his hand, and he forced his cramped fingers to loosen and set it down. In the chaos of emotions that jammed his mind, one oblique sentence emerged. "If you lay a hand on my son, I'll kill you."

Francis flushed violently at first. Then the blood drained from his face, leaving it a deathly white. Standing with such sudden fury that his chair tipped over, he said in a voice scathing in its softness, "I knew that you could be blind and insensitive, but I never realized you were a bloody damned fool."

He spun on his heel and stalked out, the echoes of his words hanging heavy in the room.

Gervase rose halfway from his chair, stretching one hand toward his cousin as if to call back his words, then sank down again. He felt such a crushing weight on his chest that for a disoriented moment he wondered if his heart was failing under the strain of all that had happened. But his heart continued to beat, his blood to pulse, his lungs to draw in air and to force it out. His body, in all its rude health, continued to function even though his life lay crashed in ruins.

Once more he buried his face in his hands, trying to come to terms with the unspeakable truth about his cousin. Francis was no different today than he had been yesterday; only Gervase's perception of him had changed. His cousin had trusted him enough to make a devastating confession and Gervase had failed him, offering insult instead of understanding. Desiring men was not the same thing as desiring children; it was Gervase's own experience of being molested by a trusted adult that had made him utter such an unforgivable insult.

As he had failed Francis, so had he failed Diana. She, too, had trusted him to understand, and instead he had overreacted wildly, accusing her of every kind of betrayal and dishonesty. *No matter what you have done, or how much you hate yourself, I love you, because you are worthy of being loved.*

Gervase wished he could believe her words, wished he could go to her and beg her forgiveness, bury his head against her soft breast and absorb her warmth until the anguish went away, but the gulf between them was too vast, too many unpardonable words had been said. Last night, in momentary pity, she had offered him comfort, but her fury and hatred had been real, as had been her appalled reaction to the story of his mother's seduction. She had been unable to disguise her revulsion, and that was something else that would always be between them in the future.

His mind painfully sorted through the options for the future. He had offered her a legal separation, but since their marriage had been the result of coercion it might be possible to obtain an annulment; money and influence would help there. As Diana had said with such contempt, there wasn't enough money in the world to buy him a clear conscience; the only gift he could give her that might make amends would be her freedom. Without the stigma of divorce, she could find the honorable, loving husband she had dreamed of as a child; a man who might be good enough for her.

Utterly alone, Gervase accepted the hopeless knowledge that his loneliness would last a lifetime.

Diana spent a quiet day in the nursery, sewing shirts for Geoffrey and letting the repetitiveness of the task soothe her as Madeline kept her company in undemanding silence. She felt suspended in time, not knowing how to go forward, yet knowing that it was impossible to go back. She ached for Gervase's pain, could feel it even through the barrier he had erected against her, but could do nothing to leaven it. In time, he would bury his ravaging memories at the bottom of the well again and get on with his life. He was a man of incredible strength to have survived what he had, and she didn't doubt that his strength would bring him through this crisis as well.

Unfortunately, she doubted that Gervase would ever be able to see her without reviving the pain of everything that lay between them. He must hate her for forcing him to admit what he could scarcely admit to himself. She wished that she could retract the furious denunciation she had hurled at him. Yes, she had been angry and she had the right to be; nothing could justify his initial rape. But her father was the greater villain; it was he who had forced the marriage, then abandoned her even though he knew that her new husband had left the inn.

Nor were her hands clean; if she had been half as saintly as people thought her, she would not have had that unacknowledged desire to see her husband pay for what he had done. She had not wanted to crucify him, but the difference was only one of degree. And had it not been for her cowardice and secretiveness, she and Gervase would never have come to this.

Her sewing lay neglected in her lap as her thoughts continued in their ceaseless round. It was a relief to have an early dinner in the nursery, and when Geoffrey suggested a walk in the gardens, she accepted in the hopes that her son's liveliness would hold her depression at bay.

The fresh evening air was a pleasure after a day inside. Gervase's houseguests would be gathering in the salon for predinner sherry now, and there was no one outdoors to whom she would have to be charming. At the moment, she was not sure she could manage even the barest civility.

High above her, a pair of avid dark eyes watched from the house. The Count de Veseul didn't see the boy who skipped ahead of his mother; he saw only the woman, with her distinctive grace and slim, alluring body. The vast gardens were empty at this hour, and Diana, Lady St. Aubyn, would not escape him this time. He must be quick about it, since he would have to join the other guests before his absence was remarked.

He would also have to ensure that she was unable to report the rape; St. Aubyn might be estranged from his wife, but he would certainly take a very dim view of someone else damaging his property. Veseul absently stroked the serpent's head. It was a delicious prospect. He would take and destroy St. Aubyn's wife, then go to London and destroy the viscount's hero. And St. Aubyn would be helpless either to prevent or to retaliate.

Geoffrey was like a playful puppy, ranging ahead, then back to point out items of particular interest. The Aubynwood gardens had developed over centuries, and included everything from herb and knot gardens to a maze. It was the maze that Geoffrey led her to now. "Cheslow, the head gardener, says our maze is the best in England," he said proudly. "Even better than the one at Hampton Court."

For a moment his identification of "our" maze stabbed her; it belonged to her husband and would someday be her son's, but there was no place for her at Aubynwood. She had belonged more truly as a mistress than as a wife.

Nor was there a place for self-pity; she put her thought aside. "Did Cheslow say how old the maze is?"

"It was planted in the time of Queen Elizabeth. The outside is a perfect square, but inside is all tangled. There is one route to the center, and another, shorter one leads out. Did you know that you can find your way through a maze by keeping your hand on the left wall, and always taking the left turning? Or you can go to the right," he added conscientiously. "As long as you always turn the same way."

"No, really?" she said with interest. She thought about it for a moment. "I see. One would have to go down all the blind alleys and doublings-back, but there would be no chance of getting lost and eventually one would get through. Rather like the tortoise and the hare."

They were at the maze entrance now and it was undeniably a fine sight. The yew bushes were incredibly dense, clipped with mathematical precision and towering well above a man's head. The entry was flanked by a Greek god and goddess who seemed up to no good; Diana recalled reading somewhere that ancient mazes were associated with fertility, which explained the anticipation on Apollo's face. "Have you been through the maze before?"

"Oh, yes, lots of times." Geoffrey's eyes lit up. "Would you like to try to catch me inside?"

She chuckled. "You want to take advantage of my ignorance."

He smiled mischievously, knowing it was unnecessary to admit the truth of her statement. "Very well," she said with mock resignation. "Make a fool of your mother. But if I can't find my way out, you have to come back and rescue me."

"Don't worry, I'll wait in the center till you find me, so I can guide you out," he offered magnanimously. Then he raced into the maze, giving one squeal of delight before remembering that his cries would give away his location.

Diana decided to give him a one-minute head start

and began counting while she studied the statues more closely. They appeared to be original; just another pair of priceless Aubynwood baubles. Absorbed in her thoughts, she didn't hear the quiet footfalls on the grass, or realize that she was not alone until her bare neck was grasped by a large male hand. As long fingers stroked and caressed with insulting familiarity, she froze, knowing instantly that it was not Gervase who touched her.

Pivoting away from the interloper, she found herself face-to-face with the Count de Veseul. He was dressed all in black and looked so nonchalant, so elegantly evil, that a bolt of panic ran through her. But she was the mistress of Aubynwood now, not a demirep, and he would not dare to coerce her. In her best *grande dame* manner she said, "Good evening, *Monsieur le Comte*. You are not dining with the others?"

"I shall join them soon," he said lazily, "but I saw you walking in this direction and decided to . . . pay my respects. Business calls, and I must leave in the morning."

"What a pity. I trust you have enjoyed your visit here." He stood too close for comfort and she edged away.

"The best part is yet to come." Lifting the cane he always carried, he laid the golden serpent's head against her cheek.

Jerking away, she said, *"Monsieur,* you take unacceptable liberties. Do not do so again."

"I shall do whatever I wish." He laughed with gentle amusement, his dark eyes a fierce contrast to his languid tone. "I shall take what I have desired since the first moment I saw you at the theater. You are a work of art, *ma petite,* and great art should not be kept for the pleasure of only one man."

In the face of his unmistakable meaning, she stepped back again, beginning to be frightened. "My husband would not appreciate your impertinence any more than I do," she said sharply. "If you do not leave immediately, I shall tell him of your insulting behavior. A

wise man would not wish to incur St. Aubyn's dis-
pleasure.''

"You will tell him nothing, *ma petite.*" The civilized mask began slipping. "I will take my pleasure
of you, and when I am done, no one else shall ever
have you again.''

He reached for her, laying one hand on the juncture
of neck and shoulder, his thumb stroking her throat
with threatening pressure as he raised the cane with
his other hand, his physical strength overpowering at
such close quarters. The underlying evil she had always sensed in him was fully visible now, and she had
no doubt that the count was capable of raping and mur-
dering her, then joining the other guests for a blithe
dinner. That thought was instantly followed by the
horrific realization that if Geoffrey returned to find
what delayed his mother, he would have to be murdered too.

Forcing down her panic, she twisted free of Veseul's
hand before he could get a firm grip. Her mind racing
at lightning speed, she knew she could not outrun him
across the grassy lawn, and he was so close that if she
reached for her knife he could easily disarm her. With
no perceptible pause in her actions, Diana gave one
scream, hoping someone might be near, then whirled
and darted into the maze.

Gervase circulated among his guests, using his host's
duties to avoid getting into lengthy conversations. He
noted that Veseul was missing from the crowd; the
count had sent a graceful note apologizing for the fact
that he must leave in the morning. Gervase would have
said good riddance, except that he had made no progress toward exposing the treachery of which he suspected the Frenchman. Over the last few days Veseul's
sociability had had a smug quality, as if he knew that
he was under suspicion, and was thumbing his nose at
the man who wanted to expose him. At times like this
Gervase could see the appeal of the French police
state; it would be pleasant just to throw Veseul into
prison. In Britain, however, that wasn't feasible, es-

pecially not when the suspect was wealthy and well-connected.

He smiled automatically at Mrs. Oliphant, who was saying that she hoped dear Lady St. Aubyn was feeling better; such a lovely young woman. Murmuring something suitable, he made his escape as quickly as possible. Gervase was grateful that his wife was still keeping out of his way; his decision to give Diana an annulment was the wisest course, but if he saw her again it would be very difficult to hold to his resolution.

Since he had decided what to do about his wife, it was time to make amends to Francis. He began working his way through the crowd toward his cousin. When Francis saw him, the younger man's lips tightened and he deliberately turned back to his discussion with a man from the Foreign Office. Impatiently Gervase waited for a break in the conversation, then said in a low voice, "Could you come out in the hall for a moment?"

Francis gave him a stare that could have chipped ice. "Afraid I'll contaminate your guests?"

"No! Please, just come." Apologizing was going to be hard enough without having an audience.

Together they made their way through the milling, good-natured crowd.

The entrance passage to the maze was short; then it turned to the right and split with paths to both right and left. Without stopping to consider, Diana ran to her left over the short-clipped velvety grass, hoping that she could be out of sight before Veseul reached the intersection. Another intersection, another turn to the left. This one led to a dead end, and she raced back the way she had come, hoping that the scream she had given would bring Geoffrey to her without alerting Veseul to the fact that a third person was present.

When she was halfway down the passage, Geoffrey appeared at the far end and dashed toward her. He was about to call out when she put her finger to her lips in a frantic demand for silence. He was surprised but obedient, and in a moment Diana was beside him, dropping to her knees and putting her lips by his ear to speak in a breathless whisper. "Geoffrey, there's a bad man behind me in the maze. Do you know the way well enough to lead us through and out the other side without any wrong turns?"

He considered, then whispered, "No." He was intrigued by her words, not yet fearful.

Diana thought rapidly. If she and Geoffrey stayed together, it was likely they would both run into Veseul and neither would escape alive. Her glance fell to the base of the thick green hedge. The heavy yew branches grew almost down to the ground, but at the very bottom there was a little space between the hedge and the earth. Not enough for an adult to wiggle through, but adequate for a small child. With a swift prayer that Veseul would not appear, she asked urgently, "Could you crawl under the hedges and get out of the maze the shortest, quickest way?"

After a quick look, Geoffrey nodded. "Yes, but I might ruin my clothes."

"That doesn't matter!" Diana caught at the note of hysteria in her voice, wanting her son to be alert but not panicky. "Go as quickly as you can and try not to let Veseul see you. He's a very, very wicked man. If he catches you, shout and I'll come. When you're outside, run as fast as you can to the house and bring back help. Do you understand all that?"

Geoffrey nodded. Grasping some of the danger, he gave her a grave, searching look, then threw his arms around her for a quick hug before burrowing under the hedge nearest the perimeter.

Diana spared a moment to send a fervent blessing with her son, then lifted her skirts to ankle level and ran, her thin kidskin slippers silent on the grass. At the next intersection she turned left again. The sky above was still sunlit, but here in the maze all was cool shadow as dusk approached. There was still no sight of the Frenchman, but she heard a rustling sound on the far side of the right-hand hedge. In his confidence, the count moved at a leisurely pace, scorning both silence and speed.

Wanting to distract him from any chance of hearing Geoffrey, Diana gave a small gasp, just loud enough for him to hear before she plunged down the new path. A thick evil chuckle pursued her. "I am so glad you are trying to escape, *ma petite,* it is more exciting this way." His voice was a confident, threatening hiss, like his golden serpent come to life. "You will not succeed, you know. It is just a matter of time until one of your turns will bring you right into my arms."

The frightened whimper she gave was only partly for effect. Was Geoffrey out yet? Pray God he wouldn't come back to investigate. Another dead end, the dense green hedge a blank barrier in front of her. She turned and ran back.

At the next junction she stopped and listened. She heard heavy breathing and the soft rustle of a body brushing the shrubbery, but within the tangled pathways of the maze it was impossible to tell where the sounds came from. Veseul could be almost anywhere. He could have gotten ahead of her and be lying in wait, or be as close as the other side of the hedge. The uncertainty was almost as terrifying as his actual presence.

She moved down the next aisle. The maze seemed much larger on the inside than it had from the outside, and the fragrance of a late-summer garden was an ironic contrast to this nightmare game of hide-and-seek. How long until she came to the center and found the path out? If she could escape the maze with even a minute's head start, she could win free of the Frenchman.

She paused again at the intersection, listening intently as her lungs struggled for breath. Then, with shocking suddenness, a black-clad arm shot through the dark yew wall and grabbed her upper arm with vicious strength. This time there was nothing calculated about her scream.

* * *

Geoffrey wriggled out from under the outside hedge, leaving his coat tangled in the yew branches. As he sprang to his feet, he heard his mother's terrified cry, and he instinctively moved toward the maze entrance. Then he stopped. He couldn't fight the bad man alone; he must go for help as Mama ordered.

Running as never before, he cut through the formal rose garden toward the main house. The gardens were too large, the house impossibly distant. A stitch stabbed at his side and he was gasping for breath but he refused to slow down. Then, as he came to the edge of the gardens, he felt a tugging on his forehead, the invisible rope that would pull him backward into an epileptic seizure.

The Frenchman's grasp was cruelly tight. His other hand emerged from the hedge and fumbled blindly at Diana's body, squeezing viciously when he found her breast. The clawing hands revolted her, and her only comfort was knowing that the hedge temporarily blocked his passage. But he could disable her, then follow through the maze to her location. At the thought, she struggled harder.

Veseul crooned his threats in a low, sibilant voice. "First I shall cut off your clothes so I may see if the whole of you is as perfect as what is visible. Then I will ravish you, invade every depth of your body while you fight me." He was panting with eagerness now, his perverse visions stimulating him out of his cool *savoir faire*. "So fortunate that no one is around at this hour—I won't have to gag your screams."

His depraved excitement infuriated Diana, and she managed to lean over and sink her teeth into his wrist, biting as hard as she could. He gasped and his fingers loosened, permitting her to tear free. She fled down the aisle, pursued by the hissing threat, "You should not have done that, *ma petite.*" His voice and hoarse breathing filled the whole maze, coming from every direction at once, and she could hear his heavy steps, no longer leisurely as he pursued her.

Another intersection. Another left turn. Terrify-

ingly, another dead end, at the same moment that Veseul appeared behind her, a scant twenty feet away. A
vicious, satisfied smile spread across his face, all
handsomeness eradicated by his emerging madness.
With the desperation of a cornered rabbit, Diana saw
that the gap at the bottom of the hedge was unusually
wide here, and she dropped to the ground and wriggled frantically under.

It was possible to force her body through, just
barely. The thick, ancient yew limb gouged her back
painfully, ripping the light muslin of her dress. She
lost one slipper but won a brief reprieve; a man the
size of Veseul could·not squeeze through the gap,
though his furious curses pursued her.

As she ran once more to the left, her heart thun-
dered, as if it would burst from her body. Her strength
was fading, and with it any faint hope of escaping.
She considered stopping and waiting for her pursuer,
knife in hand, but she didn't know if she could kill a
man, even to save her own life. And she didn't dare
find out.

Geoffrey fought the seizure with every iota of will
and concentration that he had developed in his demanding childhood. "No!" he shrieked, bending forward at the waist, clutching his temples as if to hold
on to consciousness. "No!"

Fueled by desperation, his willpower succeeded.
The tugging at his forehead receded, though not very
far. As he straightened up dizzily and staggered across
the drive toward the house, he could feel the seizure
at the edge of his consciousness, waiting like a predator for his concentration to fail so that it could take
away his mind.

Behind her, Veseul was panting, no longer suave.
His hissing threats had deteriorated into a string of
French obscenities, words that mercifully she did not
understand. Another turn, then ahead of her lay the
circular heart of the maze.

Light-footed, she plunged into the clearing. When·

she was halfway across, she heard the sibilant voice exult, "Now I have you, little whore."

She hurled herself forward with all her remaining strength, but just as she reached the far exit a hard blow between her shoulder blades knocked her to her knees, leaving her gasping for breath. Veseul had hurled his cane at her, and from the corner of her eye she saw the golden serpent's head shining bright and evil against the green grass. For a moment she was too spent to move; then she scrambled to her feet frantically.

Before she could flee again, before she could even reach down for her knife, he had crossed the clearing and seized her.

24

GRIM and uncompromising, Francis waited for Gervase to speak. Though a hum of conversation came from behind the door to the salon, they were alone in the soaring two-story entrance hall, joined by blood and divided by tension.

Not knowing where to begin, Gervase examined the fourteenth-century suit of armor standing by the wall and wondered why the devil it was there. His grandfather must have liked it. Or maybe his great-great-grandfather. He laid one hand on the visor, and without looking at Francis, he said haltingly, "I'm sorry for . . . what I said earlier. It was unpardonable."

"Yes, it was."

Francis would not make this easy for him. Blindly staring at distorted reflections in the polished helmet, Gervase forced out the words: "What I said . . . had nothing to do with you, or with Geoffrey. Only with me."

The time, there was an arrested quality to his cousin's silence, and Gervase turned to face him.

Francis watched him with an uncomfortable amount of perception, and with diminished hostility. His cousin undoubtedly saw more than Gervase would have wished, but said merely, "Very well. Consider it forgotten. The news I gave you would shock anyone out of good sense. But surely you know"—his voice dropped as he glanced around to be absolutely sure of their privacy—"I would no more molest a young boy than you would rape a young girl."

The viscount flinched; he did not doubt that Geof-

frey would be far safer with Francis than the young
Diana had been with Gervase. Trying to conceal his
reaction from those too-watchful blue eyes, he said
after a moment, "I doubt you will ever be able to
match me for disgraceful conduct."

Suddenly Francis chuckled, lightening the atmosphere. "We'll have to get together at my club one
night before I leave, and trade lies about our wickedness."

This part of his life, at least, could be mended.
Gervase offered his hand. "I'm going to miss you."

"And I, you. I will come back to England occasionally. And you can visit me as well, when we have
settled somewhere." Francis clasped Gervase's hand
in both of his and they stood locked together for a
moment, joined not only by blood but also by happy
memories, from the time Francis had shadowed his
large cousin's footsteps, to this moment of poignant
acceptance.

Then Geoffrey hurtled into the hall, pelting across
the polished marble floor before skidding into his father as he tried to stop. The boy was coatless and
dirty, with a bleeding scratch across one cheek and
frantic eyes. "Please, you must help Mama," he
gasped. "She's in the maze and there's a bad man after
her."

Gervase froze for a moment as lingering remnants
of jealousy made him wonder if his wife had met a
lover and the boy had misunderstood. Suspicion dissolved when Geoffrey grabbed his hand, shaking it in
his frenzy. "Veseul, she said. She sent me for help.
Mama screamed. He wants to hurt her."

Then, to the horror of the two men, the boy's eyes
rolled back and he pitched to the hard marble floor in
the first stages of seizure, his breathing a harsh rattle
in the empty hall.

Swearing, Gervase knelt by his son, pulling off his
coat and shoving it under the boy's head for whatever
protection it might give. Frightening as the seizure
was, Geoffrey needed him far less than Diana did.
Cold with terror, the viscount saw fragments of infor-

mation click into a terrifying new pattern. It wasn't
spying that had brought Veseul to loiter near Diana's
house, but her extraordinary beauty and her closeness
to Gervase. The Frenchman had been barred from
London brothels for his violence; he would not dare
attack Diana here unless he intended to leave no witness to his crime.

Springing to his feet, Gervase said in staccato sentences, "The fit will be over in a minute or two—make
sure he doesn't hurt himself. Get his nurse, Madeline—she'll know what to do. Then send someone after me to the maze—Veseul is dangerous."

As the viscount tore across the hall toward the door,
Francis knelt by the convulsing child, his hands gentle
and a glowing warmth in his heart in spite of the circumstances. By the simple act of entrusting his son to
his cousin, Gervase had atoned for his earlier insult in
a manner far more meaningful than any spoken apology.

Veseul grabbed Diana in one powerful hand, looming over her in all his broad muscular strength. He was
panting, the wildness of his eyes showing the beast
that had always lurked beneath his polished surface.
With great deliberation he used his other hand to give
a hard, open-handed blow to the side of her head.
"That should take some of the fire out of you, little
bitch."

Diana's head snapped sideways and she nearly
blacked out. She was helpless as a doll as he lowered
her to the ground and straddled her body, his heavy
weight on her thighs completely immobilizing her. His
violence had subsided again and, ignoring the feeble
brushing motions of her hands, he laid one heavy palm
against her cheek and crooned, "So exquisite, so entirely perfect. If you had only been more accommo-
dating, I could have shown you delights you have never
reached with an Englishman. Cold of heart, cold of
hand, the English."

The fingers of one hand slipped into her hair and
his other palm cupped her breast. "Silk and softness

. . . everything a woman should be. In a way, it is a tragic waste to kill you, but destroying beauty is a high, pure art, and I will draw strength and power from the destruction. No one else will ever know, which will give me all the more power."

His madness was nearly as paralyzing as the weakness of Diana's body. Almost casually Veseul ripped the bodice of her gown, exposing her breasts to his touch. As his hand moved back and forth, he sighed, his lower body beginning a slow, voluptuous pulsing against hers.

"A pity there is so little time, but it will be enough," he said in the same eerie, conversational tone. "I am an artist of destruction, you know. Today I will destroy you, the purest essence of woman I have ever seen. Then I will go to London and weave a web of brilliant lies that will destroy Wellesley, the purest warrior of our age after Bonaparte himself. And the destruction of the first two will destroy your husband, the purest form of cold, hard Englishman."

All her life Diana's beauty had attracted unwanted attention and violence, but never had she felt so helpless and victimized as she did now. As she struggled, Veseul easily caught both her wrists and pinned them to the ground above her head with one of his hands. He wore a faint tangy cologne that turned her stomach with nausea, and the serpent-quick tip of his tongue darted out to lick his lips. Her legs numbed beneath his weight, and his bright, blank eyes bored into her with hypnotic intensity.

"And when I have accomplished all that, perhaps I shall destroy myself," he said reflectively. "For the rest of my life will be anticlimatic, and I abhor anticlimax."

Diana began to scream, hoping that someone, anyone, was within earshot. She had scarcely begun when he bent over and forced his mouth on hers, smothering her gathering voice easily with his thick lips and pointed tongue. She was far too thoroughly caught to fight free, and for all the good her struggling did, she might as well be lying utterly passive.

Hopeless with despair, she felt the demon of violence that had stalked her for a lifetime closing in for the kill.

The maze had been his playground and retreat as a child, and Gervase forced himself to slow enough to remember the route, not to waste precious seconds on dead ends. For the whole of his relationship with Diana, he had gone down blind alleys, running in fear from what was so freely and generously offered. He would not let himself do that again at this moment of greatest crisis.

Even though he knew the path, his progress seemed slow as he raced between the tall hedges, barely slowing as he hurtled around the corners. He was halfway through when he heard Diana's voice raised in a scream that was suddenly, terrifyingly, cut off.

Gervase froze for an endless moment, paralyzed with anguish, convinced beyond doubt that he was too late. Lost in the selfishness of his guilt, he had rejected his salvation, and the one bright light of his life was extinguished. He had failed Diana, himself, and their son, and for his sins he was cursed to spend eternity in darkness.

In the aftermath of catastrophe, there was nothing left except the absolute need to avenge her.

When Gervase burst into the clearing at the heart of the maze, in the gathering dusk he saw the Count de Veseul's broad body pinning Diana to the cold earth. So total was Gervase's certainty that his wife was dead that at first he disbelieved the evidence of his eyes, did not accept that she was alive, still fighting her attacker. When he saw her move, joy lanced through him, an instantaneous awareness that this time he had not failed, that redemption was still attainable.

He did not pause to savor the exultation of his relief. His body moved forward unchecked, possessed by fierce warrior's instinct. In three strides he crossed the clearing, bellowing a wordless challenge to Veseul.

The Frenchman knew who came without even looking up, and with the speed of a wolf he leapt to his feet. With swift calculation he kicked Diana in the ribs to weaken her so she would not interfere. Then he turned to face his attacker, his burly frame crouched in the stance of an experienced fighter.

Gervase recognized that skill and slowed, knowing that a headlong charge could put him at a lethal disadvantage. He had perfected his knowledge of hand-to-hand fighting in the unforgiving school of combat, and he moved lightly toward Veseul, his eyes narrowed in concentration as he circled sideways, watching for a weakness. To test his opponent he threw a single blow with his left hand, watching how easily Veseul blocked it and riposted with a blow of his own.

To Diana, dazed and gasping for breath on the soft turf, there was a nightmare silence as Gervase and Veseul circled each other, each probing the other's defenses before risking an all-out attack. A swift blow smashed Veseul's face, opening up his cheek and rocking him off balance, but before Gervase could follow up his advantage the Frenchman responded with a kick that grazed the Englishman's knee and sent him staggering.

In the advancing darkness they started to close with each other, their blows beginning to do damage. Diana saw how equally matched they were, Gervase lighter and quicker, Veseul with a bearlike power that would be disastrous if the count got a grip on his opponent and could use it fully.

Doubling over after a pulverizing blow in the ribs, Gervase faltered in his defense, his arms dropping. Veseul moved in for the kill, aiming a granite fist at the Englishman's jaw, but Gervase's weakness was a feint. Seizing Veseul's forearm in a wrestling hold, he levered the larger man from his feet and sent him spinning to crash heavily onto the ground.

As the Frenchman lay in stunned silence, Diana managed to regain her feet, her ribs aching with pain. Gervase turned toward her, taut and muscular. Even across the width of the clearing she could see the desperate love and concern in his gray eyes.

As their gazes locked and held, Diana could actually

feel the breach between them close. Like a rainbow of love, the emotional bond that connected them sprang to full shimmering life once again, joining them heart-to-heart.

"You're all right?" he asked urgently, his dark hair in disarray, his chest heaving from exertion.

Unable to speak, she nodded. Then, from the corner of her eye, she saw that Veseul had fallen by his cane. In the brief moment that Gervase's attention was on her, the count unscrewed the serpent's head, revealing a long, wicked blade, dull and deadly in the fading light. Aghast, Diana screamed a warning as Veseul leapt to his feet and lunged at Gervase, his sword aimed directly at the Englishman's heart.

Seeing his danger, Gervase dodged, but he was too close to the thick hedge and it blocked his retreat. Off-balance, he flung himself sideways, Veseul's blade pursuing him. Diana saw with hideous clarity that Gervase would be unable to avoid the fatal thrust of the sword for more than a few instants more.

There was no time for thought, only instinct. With the skill born of hundreds of hours of practice, Diana lifted her hem and drew her knife from its sheath. Then she hurled it across the clearing with all her trained strength. The knife spun in the air, hilt over blade, too swift for the eye to follow but implacable in its murderous accuracy.

The force of her throw drove Diana to her knees. With paralyzed horror she saw the knife intersect Veseul's throat, saw gouts of blood gushing from severed arteries, saw the count's body, dead but not quite aware of it, crash into Gervase, carrying them both to the ground.

As they fell, Veseul's weight knocked all the breath from Gervase, and the edge of the swordstick grazed his ribs as the count's blood sprayed over him. The mad black eyes glared as life flickered out, but no words could escape that ruined throat. Gervase lay stunned for a moment, not quite believing that he was still alive. Then he shoved the Frenchman's body violently aside. Veseul had no more importance; what mattered was Diana.

Gervase staggered to his feet, then darted to where his wife crouched in a numb little ball, shock and horror indelibly clear in her frantic blue eyes. Dropping beside her, he pulled Diana into a crushing embrace. She was trembling violently and he felt the frenzied beat of her heart against his chest as she burrowed into his shoulder, whispering his name over and over.

"It's over, love, it's over," he whispered raggedly. "You're safe now." As Gervase shook with the reaction that follows battle, his mind became a broken jumble of thankful prayers. Even as he held Diana's slim body tight in his arms, he had trouble believing that she was truly there, alive, not seriously injured, and as desperately grateful for his presence as he was for hers.

The dark, deprecating part of his nature jeered that she would have clung to any rescuer the same way, but he rejected the thought instantly. No longer would he allow his life to be ruled by doubt and self-hatred. He had read once that grace was being loved despite one's sins and weaknesses. Gervase had not truly understood then, but he did now; Diana offered him that kind of love, and he would accept it as the miracle of grace that it was.

As he held her, a kaleidoscope of images flickered through his mind: that first heart-stopping sight of Diana at Harriette Wilson's; the first time they had made love, when she had taught him to rediscover innocence; the soul-deep need that grew stronger every time they were together. Even the bitter estrangement of the last days had value, tearing away the lies and secrets until the two of them were fully revealed to one another.

Diana was cold with shock, her lapis-blue eyes dazed as she clung to her husband, her mind rejecting the scene of violence. A few minutes later, that was how Francis found them when he ran into the clearing, followed by two of the larger footmen. Without loosening his embrace, Gervase glanced up at his cousin. "Ve-

seul tried to kill her. Have someone . . . take care of
the body. May I have your coat?''

Wordlessly Francis took off his finely tailored wool
coat and handed it over. Gervase wrapped the garment
around his wife for warmth and for modesty, then
stood. She was light and fragile in his arms, her eyes
closed now as her head rested against his shoulder,
her loosened hair veiling her face.

''I'll take her inside,'' he said to Francis. ''Please
look after the guests, give them my apologies or whatever—anything but the truth. Keep them eating and
drinking. I'll worry about the legal aspects of this
later.''

''Of course.'' As the viscount left with Diana, Francis was issuing crisp orders to the footmen.

Gervase entered a side entrance where there would
be no one to see or ask questions. He had reached the
upstairs corridor when he was intercepted by Madeline, her eyes wide with fright as a dazed Geoffrey
tugged her down the hall. Understanding the boy's
need for reassurance, Gervase knelt, bringing Diana
within Geoffrey's grasp. The boy reached for his
mother, his blue eyes questioning. ''Mama?'' he
asked, touching her hair.

His voice penetrated the mists of Diana's mind and
she gave a crooked smile, reaching up to clasp her
son's hand briefly. ''I'm . . . fine. . . . You did . . .
well.''

Geoffrey's small hands brushed her face before he
glanced up at his father. ''She's not hurt, just
shocked,'' Gervase assured him. ''She'll be all right.
The blood is Veseul's, not hers or mine.'' Shifting
Diana's weight, he stood, adding with grave commen-
dation, ''If it hadn't been for you, she would have been
killed.''

His fears allayed, Geoffrey sagged against Madeline, who swiftly steadied him.

Looking at Diana's friend, Gervase said, ''Don't
worry, Madeline, I'll take care of her.''

The older woman evaluated him with a penetrating
stare. Approving what she saw in his face, she nod-

ded, turning to guide Geoffrey back toward the nursery.

Gervase took Diana, not to his room, scene of their alienation, but to hers, where they had shared so many hours of joyous intimacy. He laid her on the bed and tried to stand, but she said, "No!" with sudden urgency, her arms tight around his neck, unwilling to let go for even a moment.

They were both stained with Veseul's blood, but bathing and fresh clothes were trivial compared to Diana's need for warmth and reassurance. Besides, Gervase shared her primitive desire to stay in close physical contact. Carrying his wife to a deep rocking chair, he cradled her in his arms, gently stroking her back and slender neck, feeling the tension slowly dissolve from her body as the room darkened.

Gervase had been twenty-five when he had first killed a man in battle. His attacker was a wild-eyed stranger intent on slaying an Englishman, and even so Gervase had been sickened and haunted afterward. Difficult though the experience had been for him, he still could not imagine the full dimensions of the shock Diana had suffered. Her whole nature was love and gentleness, for her son, her friends, her husband. He had seen her capture a trapped butterfly so she could release it again to freedom. And this evening she had killed a man.

He began to talk again, surrounding her with sound, telling her that the danger was past, that Geoffrey was well, and how much he loved her. Eventually she stirred, her breath quickening. Her eyes were still dark with shock, but no longer unseeing. "I killed him, didn't I?"

Nothing but the truth would do. "Yes. I'm sorry it had to be this way." He pressed an infinitely tender kiss on her forehead. "You've taught me much about forgiveness, Diana, both by words and by example. Weep, or curse, suffer if you must, but in the end, forgive yourself. To take a life is tragic, but you saved my life and your own. That can't be wrong."

She began to cry then, burying her face against his

bloodstained shirt, her hands knotting in the fabric as her body shook. The paroxysm of grief passed quickly and her sobs faded into silence as her head tucked under his chin, her glossy chestnut hair falling across his chest. Finally she raised her tear-smudged face to Gervase. "I want you to make love to me."

For a moment he hesitated, wondering if Diana really knew what she wanted. She was bruised and bloody and had been the target of far too much violence in the last day, from him as well as from Veseul.

"Please, love," she whispered huskily, "I need you so."

When he looked into the depths of her eyes, Gervase understood, his heart leaping to a perception beyond logic. She needed to forget, and they both needed to be joined in love, to seal their unspoken reconciliation in the most profound and intimate of ways. He stood and carried her to the bed, pulling back the covers before he laid her gently on the smooth, cool sheets, then lit a candle so they could see each other. Holding her gaze with his own, he said, "Nothing heals as swiftly as love, and no one, not the friends of your heart, not even the child of your body, can ever love you as much as I."

Without moving his eyes from hers, he continued, "You are my salvation, and in your love I see the reflection of the loving God whom I never believed in."

He stripped off his clothes, making himself vulnerable in nakedness, careful that part of his body was always touching hers so she would not feel alone, even for a moment. Then he removed her bloodstained clothing, still talking softly, the words less important than the tone. The fair silken skin over her ribs was turning dark and ugly where Veseul had kicked her. There were other bruises and scrapes as well, and he gently kissed each mark as it was revealed, worshiping her with touch.

She was passive at first, watching him trustingly, drinking in the words that flowed over her as a healing balm. They had not made love in nearly three months except for that one joyful night when he had returned from the Continent and his body hungered for her. But strangely, this time there was none of the frightening obsession he had felt before when they had come together after separation. Now that he had accepted her love, his desire was uncontaminated by desperation.

Gervase lay down beside her, admiring how exquisite her slim body was in the soft light, a harmony of curves and shadows. Laying one hand on her heart, he whispered, "You are beautiful, but only now do I see how beautiful. Mere perfection of face and form are only the beginning. You have the beauty of soul that will not fade, but grow greater with the years."

Then he lowered his head to kiss her, his lips gentle and undemanding. Her mouth welcomed him, first with sweetness, then with increasing urgency as her passivity faded.

Diana raised her hands, stroking his arms and back, wanting to feel his warmth and firm strength against her. With delicate sensitivity, Gervase made slow love to her, using all his knowledge of what pleased her. She was aware of how carefully he moved, how he supported his weight, never trapping her beneath him in a way that could remind her of the terror of Veseul.

With unhurried skill he worked his way down the length of her body, tasting her mouth, bringing her nipples to tingling delight, trailing kisses across the soft curve of her belly. With his warm expert lips and tongue he brought her to the edge of ecstasy, but she did not want to make that journey alone; she wanted to feel Gervase buried deep inside her, to know that he was as open and trusting and needful as she.

Understanding her wordless signal, he rolled onto his back and lifted her on top of him. She gave a soft cry as he entered her, wanting to weep at the rightness of their joining, at the exquisite sensation of her breasts pressing against the hard muscles and softly textured hair of his chest, at all the differences of surface and firmness between his body and hers.

For all his practiced control, she knew from his sharp, involuntary gasp and sudden tightening that he was as aroused as she, as close to the edge of explosion. Prolonging their intimacy, for long minutes they lay wrapped almost motionless in each other's arms, on a high plateau of pleasure, so close together that it was impossible to tell one pulsebeat from the other.

When floating was no longer enough, she began moving her hips against his, wanting to feel him deeper and deeper. She was in control, setting the pace of their lovemaking, and it was perfect for this night. In a distant part of her mind she marveled that a man who had so long been severed from his emotions could now understand hers with such uncanny perception.

And then reason and logic were swept away, and there was only the primal rhythm of love, building to an unbearable pitch of intensity before shattering like a shower of stars. Once before she had felt their souls briefly touch, but tonight they soared far beyond that, their spirits as intertwined as their bodies, discovering levels of passion and fulfillment that neither of them had ever reached before.

In her release Diana escaped the horror of the maze, unwinding the fearful tension that had knotted deep inside her. Only this closeness mattered, and she knew beyond doubt that nothing in the future could separate her from Gervase again.

It was marvelously comfortable to lie cradled on top of him, their bodies fitting perfectly together and his arms around her. Eventually she turned her head, propping her chin on her arm to look into his face. His eyes opened at her movement and he smiled up at her.

Diana caught her breath in wonder; she had never seen him look quite like this, the spare, chiseled lines of his face utterly relaxed, his gray eyes as transparent as quartz. "I love you," she whispered, knowing how inadequate the words were, but having no others.

His hands linked securely around her waist, Gervase raised his head to kiss her. "I'll never know why," he said huskily, "but I no more intend to question it than I would question the sun or the sea or the wind for existing."

After the kiss he settled back on the pillow and

chuckled ruefully. "In spite of what I just said, I find that I do want to question. Wanting to understand is my besetting sin. Or at least, one of them."

She laughed and slid down beside him on the mattress, tugging him until they lay face-to-face. "Ask away, love, though I don't promise a rational answer."

His shadowed face was somber. "You said that . . . after our marriage, you hated me, and then you didn't anymore. I can understand the hatred—you had every right to it. What I can't understand is why it ended."

She closed her eyes for a moment, remembering that time. "The answer to that actually *is* logical, at least to a woman. I hated you until I began to feel my child move inside me. It was such a wondrous thing that there was no more room for hatred."

She sighed, then opened her eyes. "And to hold my son in my arms . . . it was a miracle. I decided then that any man who could father so sweet a baby couldn't be all bad. That while you had behaved wickedly, that did not make you a wicked man."

Her eyes distant, she searched for words. "When I came to London, it was with the desire to find a man I could love. Though technically it meant that I would be an adulteress, you were not quite real to me; I did not feel like a wife.

"Then I met and recognized you as my husband. I knew I must learn to know you better, that I could not seek another man until I was absolutely sure that my marriage was meaningless. And when I came to know you"—she smiled with deep joy—"I fell in love."

He pulled the blanket up to tuck it around her shoulders tenderly. "I still can't understand that."

Perhaps if he had some idea of what she loved about him, he could accept it more readily. Diana had never tried to define the reasons, even to herself, but after a moment's reflection she said, "Around you, I feel . . . safe and protected. I knew that if you could ever bring yourself to love me, you would never stop. That you would always be there for me in the future. That I will always be able to rely on you."

A dark expression showed in his eyes, and she knew

he was remembering both Mull and his blind assault of the night before. She raised a hand and laid it along his cheek, feeling the slight roughness of whiskers under her palm.

"To be human is to be capable of violence under extreme circumstances," she said gravely. "I am no more a saint than you. I abhor violence and am a coward. I doubt that I could have killed Veseul to save my own life—yet I could kill for the life of someone I love. Yes, there has been violence between us, but that is past."

Diana inhaled sharply, struck by a sudden insight. "I never thought of it in these terms before, but I would not change what happened on Mull even if I could. If it hadn't happened, I would not have had Geoffrey, and I would not have you. No one voluntarily chooses pain and anger, but by having them forced on me, I have gained the love and the life that I had dreamed of as a child." She gave Gervase a smile of infinite sweetness. "I always knew that if you would let me in behind those walls, you would shelter me forever."

He rubbed his face against her palm. "You were quite right—you knew a great deal more about how my mind works than I did."

"Not your mind," she said gently. "Your heart."

His expression was very still before he answered. "Once more you are right. I didn't realize myself how much I had tangled lust and love together." He toyed with a strand of her hair, twining it around his finger as he thought. "You became an obsession. It frightened me because I felt that I was losing control, that I would be at your mercy. And the fear came out as jealousy and possessiveness."

He stroked back a larger tress of hair, exposing her shapely neck. "You have a dangerous kind of beauty, Diana. It's almost impossible for a man to think clearly near you. For months I persuaded myself that my need for you was only physical desire.

"Instead"—he bent over for another kiss, his breath mingling with hers—"what really drew me was your warmth . . . your endless, blessed warmth, like a life-saving fire in a night of eternal dark and cold. Even now, when desire is temporarily exhausted, I want and need you as much as I ever have. That has nothing to do with lust, and everything to do with love.''

''Your strength and my warmth.'' She lifted her hand and lightly touched the shallow scrape on his ribs where Veseul's sword had grazed him. Oh, yes, Gervase was strong, his strength so much a part of him that he was not even aware of it. But she was aware, and felt safer now than she ever had before. ''Today we saved each other. Now do you believe me about fate? That as unlikely as it seemed when we first met, we were meant to be together?''

With wry humor he said, ''This is all too improbable to be chance, so I think I must believe you.'' Then, more seriously, ''The first time I saw you in London, you touched my heart, but I had to call it by a different name. Chance might have produced the wedding in Mull, but perhaps only some divine plan could have made ours a real marriage after such a disastrous beginning.''

Wrapping one arm around his chest to pull herself even closer, she said what should have been said months earlier, when he had needed to hear it. ''You need never be jealous about me, Gervase. I came to London to find a man, and after we met, I knew that man was you. There had never been anyone else before, and there never will be again.''

''And because I believe that,'' he said, his deep voice thick with emotion, ''the obsession is gone. Jealousy came from fear of losing you—it has vanished in the presence of love and trust.''

Diana raised her face for another kiss, then rolled over, her back fitting against his front in the way that was so particularly comfortable. As she was settling in, she remembered some of what the count had said, and realized that it might be important. ''I'm not sure what he meant, but Veseul was raving about destroying Wellesley.''

As closely as possible she repeated what he had said, adding, "Do you think it means anything?"

There was a lengthy silence as Gervase evaluated her words. "Though I hadn't the evidence to prove it, I've been convinced for a long time that Veseul was the most dangerous French spy in England, a man who called himself the Phoenix. Veseul was clever and he was received everywhere. It's quite conceivable that he was plotting against Wellesley—the general is very vulnerable just now. I think the army inquiry will acquit him and he will be given another command, but Veseul could easily have fabricated some scandal that would discredit Wellesley permanently."

His voice hard, he added, "There will be no more damage from that direction." One of his hands cupped her breast as his mind continued to work. "I suspect that he overheard us talking in Vauxhall that night before I left, and that is how the French knew that I was coming. As for the information that I left overnight in your drawing room being discovered . . . is there any servant in your house who might be an informant for Veseul?"

As pleasurable sensations spread from her breast, it was hard for Diana to think clearly, but she tried to oblige. "We have a French cook. She talked her way into the position and I've never understood why. She is good enough to command the kitchen of a much larger establishment."

"Perhaps that is the answer," Gervase agreed, his hand stroking lower on her body. "Now that Veseul is dead it probably doesn't matter, especially since you will be leaving the house on Charles Street."

She rolled on her back, making it easier for his hand to rove over her, and for hers to rove back. "Does that mean you want me to move in with you?"

"Was there any question?" he asked with surprise. "I assumed you and Geoffrey and Edith would come to St. Aubyn House. It could use some life and laughter." He smiled. "I imagine that Lord Farnsworth has other plans for Madeline."

She laughed. "I just wanted to hear you say it. I

enjoyed being your mistress, but I am looking forward even more to being your wife."

"Not half as much as I'm looking forward to that," he said, his voice rich with happiness. "I don't ever want to spend another night apart from you in my life."

He leaned over to capture her mouth as his hand probed the moist, waiting depths of her. She moaned, wanting to dissolve in the rising tide of pleasure, but knowing one more matter must be mentioned. "There is something I must tell you."

His hand stilled and she opened her eyes to see him regarding her questioningly. Before his imagination could conjure up anything too lurid, she said shyly, "I . . . I think I'm pregnant again. I know that it is too early to be sure"—she unconsciously touched a sensitive breast—"but I felt the same way with Geoffrey."

She had thought he would be pleased, but seeing the expression on his face, she was no longer sure. "I'm sorry," she said uncertainly. "It was the night you returned from the Continent. I wasn't expecting you, and was not prepared. Are you angry?"

"What right do I have to be angry? We are equally responsible." His voice was light, but when he raised his hand to her cheek his fingers were cold and she saw the fear in his eyes. "You said you almost died when Geoffrey was born."

Understanding, she relaxed. "That was because I was young and small for my age, still growing. It won't be like that this time. The midwife said that since I was strong enough to survive that first delivery, I shouldn't have problems in the future."

She saw the shadow of anxiety still in his eyes, and laid her hand over his. "I promise it will be all right."

His answering smile was sheepish. "I have the feeling this pregnancy is going to be much harder on me than on you. But this time I will be there at the end as well as at the beginning."

"I talked to Geoffrey's physician about whether another child of ours might have seizures."

"And . . . ?"

She shrugged. "He said it was possible. Not likely, though there is no way to be sure."

Gervase relaxed. "If another child turns out half as well as Geoffrey, I'll be satisfied, seizures or no seizures. Whatever comes, together we can deal with it." Worries allayed, he became more enthusiastic. "It would be nice to have a girl this time," he said thoughtfully. "With lapis-blue eyes and the ability to enchant any man who comes near her."

Diana linked her arms around his neck and pulled him down for a kiss. "Or with gray eyes and a stubborn streak. Or twins. It doesn't matter." Sliding her hand under the blanket, she gloried in the passionate response that she found. "At the moment I am far more interested in the present than the future. Aren't you?"

In the morning they joined Geoffrey in the nursery for breakfast. Their son beamed, as proud as if he had been the one to invent the idea of "family." He beamed even more when he learned that soon he would no longer be the smallest Brandelin.

With half the government under Gervase's roof, all of them indebted to him in one way or the other, it was easy to put out the story that the distinguished French royalist, the Count de Veseul, had succumbed to an unexpected heart seizure. No one was anxious to let it be known that a spy had been intimate with so many important men. In the secret corridors of power, there was great thankfulness that the Phoenix was no more. When she heard the news, the French cook hastily decamped from the town house at 17 Charles Street.

Francis Brandelin and his friend left England unshadowed by scandal. His letters from Greece were filled with the usual tourist talk of temples and antiquities, but their real subject was happiness.

In late autumn Madeline became Lady Farnsworth in a quiet ceremony, attended by the Viscountess St. Aubyn. Although the new Lady Farnsworth's past was obscure, her disposition was so agreeable that only the most ferociously snobbish refused to receive her. And Maddy and Nicholas didn't give a damn about them.

General Sir Arthur Wellesley was cleared in the military inquiry in November and sent back to the Peninsula. After his tremendous victory at the Battle of Talavera in July 1809, he was created a viscount. The title he chose was Wellington.

Gervase gave Diana a free hand to make St. Aubyn House more welcoming, a task she accomplished to his complete satisfaction. One of her first acts was to install a fitted tub in the master suite.

Several months later, when browsing in the library, Diana came upon a verse written by Jonathan Swift. The lines had been scribbled on the certificate of a marriage Dean Swift had performed, and they were so perfectly, ironically amusing that Diana had them engraved inside the lid of a silver box, which she gave to Gervase for their second Christmas together. The lines read:

> Under an oak, in stormy weather,
> I joined this rogue and whore together;
> And none but he who rules the thunder
> Can put this rogue and whore asunder.

Historical Note

Gervase's mission to Denmark was based on an actual event. However, instead of a tall, dark, and handsome aristocrat, the real hero was a "short, stout, merry little monk," a Scottish Benedictine named James Robertson. Sir Arthur Wellesley, the future Duke of Wellington, himself commended Robertson to Foreign Minister Canning. Later Robertson did diplomatic work for Wellington; later still, he was known for his pioneering work with the deaf and the blind.

A Note on Epilepsy

Even in the late twentieth century, epilepsy is a little understood condition that arouses fear and prejudice. Nonetheless, in the past as well as the present, many people with epilepsy lived reasonably normal lives.

In Great Britain the terms "seizure" and "fit" are both used, and that usage is reflected in this book. However, I would like to note that in the United States, the preferred term is "seizure." I would also like to give a special thanks to the staff of the Epilepsy Association of Maryland for their help.